Barbara Hambly is the author of many highly successful fantasy novels, including *The Darwath Trilogy, Dragonsbane* and her series of tales about the mercenaries Sun Wolf and Star Hawk. She has also written a vampire tale, *Immortal Blood*, two Star Trek novels and the novelization of the television series *Beauty and the Beast*.

As well as a Masters degree in medieval history, she holds a black belt in karate.

By the same author

THE DARWATH TRILOGY
Time of the Dark
Walls of Air
Armies of Daylight

The Ladies of Mandrigyn
The Witches of Wenshar
Dark Hand of Magic
Dragonsbane
The Silent Tower
The Silicon Mage
Immortal Blood
The Rainbow Abyss

BARBARA HAMBLY

Magicians of the Night

Grafton
An Imprint of HarperCollins*Publishers*

Grafton
An Imprint of HarperCollins*Publishers*
77–85 Fulham Palace Road,
Hammersmith, London W6 8JB

Special overseas edition 1992
This edition published by Grafton 1993
9 8 7 6 5 4 3 2 1

First published in Great Britain by
HarperCollins*Publishers* 1992

ISBN 0 586 21697 9

Set in Times

Printed in Great Britain by
HarperCollinsManufacturing Glasgow

Special thanks to Donald Frew, Diana Paxson, Steven Jacobsen, and Adrian Butterfield, for letting me raid their libraries and pick their brains. Thanks also to John Hertz, Allan Rothstein, Aaron Blechman, and Betty Himes for details great and small, and especially to Lester Del Rey.

1

'I think he's coming around.'

The words reached Rhion of Sligo as he hung in darkness, suspended above cold screaming infinities of lightless chaos, slipping back . . . slipping back . . .

He tried to cry out, tried to fight, unconsciousness dragging at his limbs like the darkness that lies between Universes, the darkness of the Void through which he had come. *Jaldis, help me* . . . But his numb lips and mouth would not form the syllables of his master's name. *Don't let me die* . . .

Burnt vinegar kicked his brain like a crystal boot. He gasped as the darkness of unconsciousness stripped away like a rag; strong fingers closed around his flailing wrist. The dagger of amber light that stabbed his eyes faded to the glow of candles, a constellation of six small flames in an iron holder opposite the bed where he lay. The light of them still hurt, and he closed his eyes again. The hideous leaching of the Void's remembered cold eased. A voice asked, 'Are you all right?' in a harsh, guttural alien language, and Rhion thought, with what little strength was left in him, *At least the Spell of Tongues works here*. His master Jaldis had warned him that in this strange universe magic no longer existed – he had been afraid the spell which allowed a wizard to understand speech mind to mind would no longer be effective.

'I – I don't know.'

He opened his eyes. The candle-flame seemed warm now, comforting in its familiarity. Around him the room was dim, and they'd taken away his spectacles. Without them the face of the young man seated beside him on the narrow bed was, even at this distance, blurred, but Rhion's eyesight was good enough to show him a face pale and beautiful, the pitiless beauty of a god carved in ivory, beardless, with short-cropped fair hair and a sword-scar crossing one high cheekbone like the careless slip of a sculptor's chisel. Beyond that he could see only ombrous shapes, glints of silver on close-fitting black garments, and the shadow of exhaustion, strain, and some dreadful grief that informed every line of the face and the set of those wide shoulders.

'Rest easy,' said the beautiful young man. 'You're quite safe.'

A shadow stirred in the darkness; candlelight flashed across spectacle-lenses and a boy of eighteen or so, unhealthily fat, pallid, sweaty, and likewise clothed in close-fitting – in his case ill-fitting – garments of grey and black loomed beyond the young god's shoulder. 'Should I tell the others, P-Paul?'

'In a moment, Baldur.' The kindness in his voice, the infinite control, spoke worlds about the young mage's relationship with this boy, whoever he was, who stared at him with such eager adoration in his eyes.

Paul, thought Rhion, turning the alien name over in his mind. The two wizards whom Jaldis had contacted through the Dark Well, the two wizards who had begged him to cross the Void and help them restore magic to this magicless universe, had been called Eric and Paul.

He whispered, 'Eric . . .' and the wizard Paul's control cracked, infinitesimally, his lips pressing taut and his eyes flinching away.

But a moment later his glance returned to Rhion, and he said, quite steadily, 'Eric is dead. The Dark Well . . .' He hesitated, then went on as if repeating something he had memorized, his grey eyes focussed resolutely on the pillow next to Rhion's head, 'He said, "We are losing him . . ." He cried out . . .' His fingers, which still held Rhion's wrist, began to shake and he released his grasp quickly, pressing his hands together to still them. The boy Baldur lurched forward, reaching towards those square, dark shoulders, but after all he did not quite have the courage to touch.

Like a nightmare ghost of pain, Rhion remembered the terror of feeling his own life slide away. Those eternal seconds in the Void whispered where he had tried to blot them from his consciousness – the howling abysses of all the colours of blackness, the horror of realizing that though the tiny gold emblem of the burning sun-cross flickered somewhere in the darkness to guide them, there was no magic to bring them through.

Remembered Jaldis' soul, his strength that was so much greater than the twisted fragile shell of his body, surrounding the failing core of his own being and holding him up.

Then the marshfire flicker of a sudden spurt of light, the thread of magic that had come through to bring them across at last . . .

'He . . . He stepped into the Dark Well, into the Void.' Paul stared beyond Rhion as if he could still see into the Well that had given them a window to the Void. 'And it collapsed upon him. Fell in on itself around him. He screamed – the sound seemed to come from . . . from very far off. And when we pulled him out he was dead.'

His hands had begun to shake again. Rhion whispered, 'I'm sorry,' but looking up into that set, ravaged face, he doubted the young mage heard.

While Paul had been speaking a door had opened behind him, and a harsh bar of unnaturally steady yellow light fell through. Two forms stood there – Rhion fumbled for his spectacles, resting, he now guessed more than saw, on the small table near the head of the bed where he lay. The forms clarified into a very tall man in his fifties with hollow cheeks and a burning dark glance beneath a handbreadth of greasy black hair, and a smaller, slighter man perhaps twenty years older than that, flowing white mane and beard framing a pale, fanatic stare. The light behind them haloed them with its bizarre, motionless glare, brighter than a hundred torches. Rhion remembered Jaldis had spoken of *electricity*, artificial light that was made without magic, made for the benefit of anyone who cared to use it.

With his spectacles, Rhion was able to see a little more of the room, small and spartan and lined with more books than he'd ever seen in a private residence with the exception of the stone house of Shavus Ciarnin, Archmage of the Morkensik Order, his own Order of wizardry at home.

Paul seemed to pull himself together a little, sitting up in his leather-covered wooden chair. 'These are Auguste Poincelles and Jacobus Gall, my colleagues in the effort to restore wizardry to this world,' he said in his soft voice. The tall man acknowledged the first introduction with a nod, the bearded fanatic the second. 'Baldur Twisselpeck . . .'

'I'm Rhion of Sligo.' He saw the swift glance that passed between Poincelles and Gall behind Paul's back. 'The Dark Well is gone, then?'

In his own world, where magic still existed, simply breaking the Circles of Power which held the shuddering dark of the window into the Void was sufficient to destroy it. In this world, who knew?

'Yes,' said Paul, after long silence. 'Yes.'

'You can see the place where it was,' added the wizard Gall, still standing, arms folded, in the doorway.

'We did everything we knew how to bring it back.' The wizard Poincelles gestured with one long arm, like a spider against the light. 'But it was useless.'

Dizziness caught at Rhion as he stood up. Paul, clearly now the leader of these otherworld mages, put a steel-strong arm around him to keep him on his feet, and Gall and Poincelles fell back before them as they passed through the door and into the hall. Baldur trailed behind like a lumpish black dog at Paul's heel.

The walls of the hallway, Rhion noted automatically,

were of plaster and wood, like the houses in Felsplex, impregnated with stale incense and the smoke of burnt herbs – some form of nicotina, he thought. Their feet rang hollow on the oak planks of the bare floor, and he guessed even before he turned to glimpse a wide stairway leading down that they were on an upper floor of some good-sized building. Voices murmured from below, echoing in the well of the stairs; he saw Poincelles and Gall trade another glance, but their eyes were chiefly on him, wondering at this chubby, bespectacled little man with his scruffy brown beard and his shabby brown-and-black robes, as if they could not actually believe they'd seen him come stumbling out of that column of darkness.

He wondered what they'd made of Jaldis' thick jewelled spectacles whose magic gave his blind eyes sight, of the wooden box of silver whistles and gut which to some degree replaced the voice that the old King's men had cut out of him with their knives, to keep him from witching them all those years ago . . .

As they had said, the Dark Well was gone.

The stars and circles of its weaving still sprawled, smudged with a confusion of hurried foot-scuffs, over the worn plank floor of the upstairs room a few doors down the hall from the one in which he'd come to. The air was heavy with the cloying sweetness of dittany and the copper-sharp stink of dried blood. Baldur put out his hand and touched a switch in the wall, and glaring yellow light sprang to being in the room from a glass globe in the middle of the ceiling. Rhion blinked up at it for a moment, shading his eyes against its blaring strength, then looked at the floor again.

But there was nothing to be seen among the spirals and circles of power – dribbled candle-wax, dried blood, a few dark spots where the Water-Circle had been drawn. Only the great ritual sun-cross they had drawn as a guide, the emblem of magic's eternal renewal, scrawled upon the floor, and the prosaic air of this world dispersing the last veils of smoke.

'Well,' he said shakily, putting a hand on the wall for balance to stand. 'It took Jaldis three days to weave one on our side of the Void – the gods know how long it will take him here. But I don't expect he'll be well enough to for weeks – the Void's magic drained his strength very badly the last time he touched it – and after one crossing I for one am in no hurry to have him start. Is he . . . Is he all right?' It came to him that none of them had mentioned his master; as the cloudiness and exhaustion cleared a little from his mind he cursed himself for not asking earlier. Jaldis might need him – tampering with the Void or working with the Dark Well had always left the old man prostrated, too exhausted to work so much as a simple fire-spell, for days, sometimes weeks . . . Seven years ago, during an earlier vain attempt to contact the wizards whose voices he had heard crying out of magic's death, he had suffered a mild stroke . . .

But the four men surrounding him remained silent.

Cold touched him inside, an echo of cries in darkness, forever unheard.

At length Paul asked quietly, 'You mean . . . Jaldis came with you after all?'

Looking up into that beautiful angel face, Rhion felt as if the floor beneath his feet had given way. 'He . . . He stepped into the Void with me, yes . . .'

No, he thought numbly, greyness beginning to creep into the edges of his sight. *Oh please, gods of magic, don't tell me he's dead . . . Jaldis my friend . . . Don't tell me I'm here on my own . . . Jaldis dead . . . no way back . . . Jaldis my friend . . .*

From what seemed to be a great distance Paul's voice came to him. 'He said he was trying to get another wizard to come in his stead.' His grey eyes were worried as he touched Rhion's elbow with a steadying hand. 'He was blind, he said, and in need of certain magical implements to see and speak . . .'

Dear gods . . . Rhion's mind stalled on the brink of a roaring vortex of panic and despair. *Dear gods, don't do this to me* . . . 'The other mages couldn't come.' He was surprised at how steady his voice sounded, even though barely audible even to his own ears. 'He and I . . . I wasn't going to let him come alone . . .'

'But you are a wizard too, aren't you?' Baldur demanded, sudden anxiety in his watery brown eyes. 'We c-can't have wasted . . .'

'Shut up, pig-dog!' Paul snapped viciously, his own face chalky in the hard yellow glare.

A thousand images swam through Rhion's mind in a single hideously elongated instant of time – Tally, his beloved, the sunlight dappling her hair as they lay together in the grotto at the end of her father the Duke's palace gardens; the laughter of his sons. Jaldis' thin mechanical voice saying *We can afford to think neither of the future, nor of the past which we leave behind* . . .

So this was the end of the dream Jaldis had cherished these seven years – the dream that had sustained him, obsessed him. The dream of restoring magic to a world in which it had vanished. The dream of, perhaps, saving magic, if it came to be threatened in their own.

I'm here alone.

No magic. And no way home.

Jaldis had never showed him how to weave a Dark Well. And though he had studied magic for seventeen of his thirty-five years, he knew that his own power was no more than average, his learning scanty in comparison to what his master's had been, what Shavus the Archmage's was, or any of the great wizards of his own or any other of the major Orders . . .

'Come.' Paul urged him gently back through the door. Blindly Rhion was aware of Baldur touching the button on the wall again, and the light vanishing as instantly as it had appeared, with a hard metallic *click. So that's electricity.*

'Lie down and sleep. We'll speak of this in the morning, find some way to continue the work your friend wanted to help us do.'

Rhion staggered, faintness rising through him with sudden, dizzying heat. He caught himself on the jamb of a door across the hall. Through that door the soft luminescence of candles wavered; his sight cleared again, and he saw within the half-lit darkness a tall man lying dead upon a leather divan, candles burning at his head and feet and an ornamental silver dagger unsheathed upon his breast. Rhion looked back quickly, and saw beside him Paul's drawn grey face. He was not, he realized, the only one to have lost a friend tonight.

'Eric,' said Paul softly. 'Eric Hagen. It was he whose dream this was. The dream of bringing back magic to this world, before the enemies of magic who encircle our realm destroy us all.'

Perhaps ten years older than Paul, like him Eric had been strong-featured and fair, and like him was clad in close-fitting garments of black and grey, with buttons and buckles of gleaming silver. A little emblem of the sun-cross, red and black and white, glistened like a drop of blood on the collar of his shirt. Behind him, illuminated in the hard bar of light that fell through from the hall, hung a banner, the sun-cross wrought huge in black upon a white circle against a ground of bloody red.

The sun-cross, Rhion noticed for the first time, was reversed, so that it turned not towards light, but towards darkness.

'My name, by the way,' said Paul's voice quietly, 'is Captain Paul von Rath, of the Occult Bureau of the Ancestral Heritage Division of the Protection Squad. And though it is a sorry and tragic welcome, I do welcome you nevertheless, in the name of the German Reich.'

Solstice

2

'As far as we can determine,' said Paul von Rath, the light wind generated by their vehicle's speed flicking the fair hair like a raw-silk pennon from his forehead, 'magic has not existed in our world for at least a hundred and seventy years. Whether this was the result of the actions of the men who hated it – and in our world magic has been deeply hated by both society and the church, as Jaldis told me that it is in yours – or whether it was an accident, a natural event like the fall of night, we have not been able to determine.'

He sighed, and turned his head, watching the endless monotony of dark pine-woods flashing past them: the low roll of moraine hills still shawled with cold blue shadows on their western sides, though the sky overhead was bright; the grey loom of granite boulders among soft green bracken or pine-straw the colour of dust, a landscape occasionally broken by abandoned meadows rank with weeds and murky with shallow, silted ponds, and here and there a crumbling barn.

'We only know that accounts of what can be termed actual magic have become more and more sparse, and harder and harder to authenticate, until they ceased entirely. And that when we attempt to work what magicians of old claimed to be spells, we achieve nothing.'

Rhion shivered, wondering what it must have been to be born with the power of wizardry – as he had been born – in a world where magic no longer existed. Where such power, such longing, such dream, could never be consummated, could never be anything but the slow oncoming of madness.

It was something he didn't like to think of at present.

It was difficult enough to tell himself, as he did daily, sometimes hourly, that even the smallest of his own powers and perceptions – his ability to scry through a crystal, to channel energy into divining-cards, to deepen his senses to perceive sounds and scents and vibrations beyond the range of ordinary human awareness – would return. That they had not been permanently stripped away by the passage through the Void.

Three weeks isn't so long . . .

Lying feverish and weak in the great, grey granite hunting-lodge called Schloss Torweg, mourning for Jaldis, sick with terror, disoriented and more alone than he had ever felt in his life, the first two weeks had seemed an eternity.

He had been up and around for some days now, but it was good now to be out in open air.

They came onto the main road through the hills. Gold morning sunlight slanted into their eyes as they drove eastward, palpable as javelins of gold. It splashed with light the tangles of wild ivy crowning the steep banks of the road-cut, turned to liquid gold the buttercups in the roadside ditches, made stars of the frail white spangles of dogwood and may. Somewhere in the woods a robin called, the sweet notes a comforting reminder of the thickets of the Drowned Lands, where for seven years he had served the Ladies of the Moon as scribe. A grey hare flickered momentarily into view at the top of the bank, but bounded away at the roaring approach of the vehicle they called a car.

Rhion had to grin at the thought of the car. It was a conveyance straight out of a fairy-tale, moving without beast to draw it at speeds that covered in an hour the distance it would take to journey in a day – Except, of course, that no talespinner he'd ever encountered in any marketplace in the Forty Civilized Realms had ever thought to describe such a marvel as being so raucously noisy or so comprehensively smelly.

Beside him, von Rath went on, 'Germany is the only realm now whose rulers believe in magic, who will support wizards, and give them aid and help. And now her enemies have declared war on her, and are massing on our borders, ready to attack as soon as the weather dries. It is essential that we recover magic, that we learn what became of it, and how we can bring it back. For if they conquer, even what belief still exists will perish, and there will be nothing left – only those mechanistic bureaucracies, those believers in nothing, who seek to destroy what they cannot understand.'

In the front seat the young blond titan named Horst Eisler who had been assigned as their driver by the Protection Squad – Schutzstaffel, in the harsh German tongue, shortened, as the Germans did with all long words, to SS – gazed straight ahead at the broken black cut of the pavement where it passed through the hills. Baldur, sitting beside the driver, was as usual twisted half-round in his seat so that he could hang onto von Rath's every word. The driver slowed, easing the car around a place where last night's rain had washed a great slide of mud and boulders down from the twelve-foot banks that hemmed in this stretch of road – because of a car's speed and power it required a deal more concentration to drive than a horse, and moreover required a far better surface to drive upon.

To Rhion's right, Auguste Poincelles was arguing with Gall, who sat perched on the little jump-seat that folded down from the door: 'Of course Witches Hill was a place of power, a holy place!' Gall was fulminating in his shrill Viennese accent, his silver mane and beard streaming in the wind. 'It lies upon a crossing of the leys, the energy-tracks that cover all the earth in a net of energy. Moreover, upon the night of the last full moon I slept among the time-runnelled menhirs there, among the Dancing Stones, and a vision was visited unto me of eldritch Druids and olden warriors with the sacred swastika tattooed upon their broad breasts . . .'

Poincelles let out a crack of rude laughter. 'Druids in Germany? You've been reading Bulwer-Lytton's novels again, Jacobus.' He took from his pocket, and lit, a cigar. Most of the people in this world were addicted to the inhaled smoke of cured tobacco-leaves, and everything – cars, houses, furniture, clothing – stank of it.

'Scoff if you like,' replied the old wizard calmly, and his pale, fanatic eyes took on a faraway gleam. 'I saw them, I tell you. Upon those stones they performed sacrifices which raised the power to keep the mighty armies of Rome at bay.'

Poincelles laughed again, shaking back his greasy black forelock. 'Ah, now when Mussolini invades us we'll know just what to do!'

Rhion sighed inwardly, not surprised at the constant bickering of the three wizards under von Rath's command. Wizards in his own world squabbled constantly. He wondered, with a stab of grief and regret, what Jaldis would have made of them.

He wondered too, when they reached the place called of old Witches Hill, whether Jaldis would have been able to detect the ancient magic Gall claimed had been raised upon that spot.

The hill itself was clearly artificial, standing alone at one end of an overgrown meadow to the east of the long pine-cloaked ridge which backed Schloss Torweg. As they waded towards it through the knee-deep grass Rhion studied the low, flattened mound, guessing that there had probably once been an energy-collecting chamber of some kind underneath – it was a good guess that if ley-lines did exist in this world, this was raised on one. According to Gall, Schloss Torweg had been likewise built upon a ley. Certainly the little hill upon which it stood, larger than this one but probably also artificial, had enjoyed a rather queer reputation in centuries past.

Standing among the three lumpish stones which crowned the hill – the Dancing Stones, they were called, one erect, two lying fallen and nearly covered with dew-sodden weeds – Rhion could feel no magic here at all.

And yet, he thought, that didn't mean it didn't exist. While the others moved about among the stones, Poincelles caressing the worn dolomite with half-shut eyes and Gall swinging pebbles on pendulum-threads, their feet leaving dark-green swathes in the flashing diamond carpet of the dew, Rhion sat at one end of a fallen stone, breathing silence into his heart and listening. Though he was unable yet to detect the faint, silvery pulse of ley-energy through the ground, still the sweet calm of the April sunlight that warmed his face eased something within him. For the first time since his coming to this world the hurt of losing Jaldis, the fear that he would never be able to find his way back, lessened. He found himself thinking, *If magic still existed here it might give von Rath and his partners another energy-source, help them in their efforts . . .*

Suddenly curious, he got to his feet, brushed the dirt and twigs from the hand-me-down Wehrmacht fatigue-pants he wore, and turned his steps down the little hill. Pinewoods surrounded the meadow on all sides, rising to the west almost at the hill's foot behind a tangled belt of laurel and blackberry brambles. Though Rhion still sensed no buried energy as he picked his way among nests of fern and bracken, and fallen grey branches, still the cool spice of the pine-scent, the sigh of the moving boughs, the occasional coin-bright warmth of stray beads of sunlight, were balm to him. The land sloped gently towards the main ridge as he walked on. There was some hope, he thought, both for himself and for this world, for magic's return . . .

'Halt!'

Startled, Rhion stopped and raised his head. A Storm Trooper in the black uniform of the Protection Squad – the SS – stood beside a boulder a few yards away. His rifle – another product of the magicless magic of this world – was levelled at Rhion's chest. Like most of the SS, this man's hair was fair, his eyes light and chill and empty, reminding Rhion of something, of someone else . . .

'You will return to the meadow, please.'

Rhion blinked at him in surprise, pushed his spectacles more firmly onto the bridge of his nose. 'I'm just investigating . . .'

'You will return to the meadow.' Dapplings of light strewed one sleeve of his black uniform jacket, made the silver buttons flash. Upon his left sleeve the sun-cross – the swastika – splashed black on a crimson ground, pointing backwards, towards chaos, towards darkness, towards death. 'This was Captain von Rath's order.'

'Look,' said Rhion reasonably, 'I'm sure Captain von Rath didn't mean I needed protection from getting hit on the head by a falling pine-cone . . .'

'It is not my business what Captain von Rath meant,' said the young man, without change of inflection, though his pale arrogant eyes travelled over Rhion's short, stocky form, his curly brown hair and beard, with chill disapproval and suspicion. 'Nor is it yours. He said you were not to be permitted to leave sight of the others. You will return, or I will take you back there myself. I assure you I will shoot you if you attempt to flee.'

'You're making flight sound more and more appealing,' remarked Rhion, turning back towards the meadow, and realized the next second that the guard probably took his jest literally and had his rifle cocked and ready. He was conscious of it behind him, all the way back through the trees down the slope towards the sunlight.

'I am dreadfully sorry,' von Rath apologized, as the car

picked its way along the rutted and potholed black pavement once again. 'The young man was only following orders – he will be reprimanded for his lack of tact. But indeed, it does not do for you to wander too far alone. For one thing, you might have become lost, and having no identity papers . . . We are getting you some, of course, but these things take time.'

And, seeing the expression on Rhion's face, he added gently, 'The government has taken wizardry and all its workings under its protection, has given the Occult Bureau guards to make sure it is not interfered with. We are at war, with forces that do not believe in wizardry, that hate our government and seek to destroy us. Believe me, this protection is needed.'

'If you say so.' Rhion settled back into the leather seat-cushions and watched the landscape whisk by, the occasional silted meadows and crumbling barns among the dark trees speaking of a time when the countryside had been prosperous and well-tended.

'It was the war,' von Rath explained, when Rhion asked about it. 'We were defeated in the war . . .'

'We were betrayed,' put in Baldur, twisting around in the front seat where he sat next to the driver. 'Betrayed by C-Communists and Jews who had wormed their way like maggots into the government while true men were fighting. Everyone lost their money, except the Jews. That's why the Nazi party appeared, with the SS as its adamantine spearhead: to save the German race from the muck into which it had been dragged and to lead it to its d-destiny.'

Poincelles' dark eyes gleamed with malice. 'And I suppose slitting the throats of most of its original members was a part of the Party's destiny?'

'That's a lie!' snapped Baldur, his fat cheeks mottling red. Since leaving the meadow he had been increasingly jittery, the restlessness of his weak brown eyes behind their thick glasses and of his twitchy, curiously shapely hands confirming Rhion's earlier suspicions that the boy was addicted to some kind of drug. 'And anyway they were traitors to the Party and h-h-homosexuals . . .'

'All – what was it? Nearly a thousand? – of them?'

'I think now is not the time for a discussion of the Party's internal politics,' said von Rath, with quiet smoothness. 'I doubt there is a government in the world that did not go through its formative upheavals. I trust, Rhion, that this expedition has not proved too tiring for you?'

Poincelles sneered, but settled back without argument and applied himself to fouling the air with another cigar. His fingernails, Rhion noticed not for the first time, were long and dirty and filed to points, his fingers stained yellow with nicotine. Gall, throughout the discussion, had merely stared ahead of him, perched again upon the little jump-seat. Though as far as Rhion could ascertain neither Gall nor Baldur were actual members of the SS, both wore the close-fitting black trousers and clay-coloured uniform shirts of the Order, a garb which was less than flattering to the lumbering boy. Poincelles retained civilian clothes, in this case a pair of rather loud tweed trousers and a tweed jacket, reeking of cigar-smoke and old sweat.

'I'm tired, yes, but I think that will pass.' Rhion turned to look up at the young Captain beside him. 'The ritual of meditation we've been doing in the mornings helps; all week I've felt my strength coming back.'

The grey eyes changed, losing their coldness. 'Eric – Major Hagen – had used the morning ritual for years, since he was a youth at school.' His soft, steady voice still echoed with the grief of loss, a grief as sharp, Rhion knew, as his own mourning for Jaldis. Was it Gyzan the Archer who had said, *Perhaps the ending of all dreams is death . . .*?

'That was what first brought us together, years ago – the dawn opening of the ways to power. I had the Crowley texts and was looking for those that had been *his* sources – I was only sixteen, and terrified that the masters at the Academy would find out I was interested in such matters. A bookseller in Brandenberg gave me Eric's name. He was living in the most awful garret while he pursued his studies . . .' He shook his head, his mouth quirking a little as he recalled the young student he had known, the haunted, conscientious little cadet he had himself been . . . 'He was the only one who understood. The only one I could talk to, about that which was within me – that which I knew *had* to be true.'

Then he laughed a little, like a sudden flash of sun on frost-hard December earth. 'I remember the winter night in that garret of his, when we first contacted Jaldis. It was a few days before Christmas and freezing cold – I had to be on the train home the next morning, to a true old Prussian Christmas with every aunt and uncle and cousin I possessed. With the drugs we were using to mentally project our minds into the Void I still can't imagine why we didn't kill ourselves . . .'

The car slowed as it swung into the shadows of the road-cut, where earlier they had edged past the washed-down rocks and mud. Now a gang of men was there, chained together and wearing shabby grey shirts and trousers, shovelling the clayey yellow mud into a sort of sledge under the rifles of four or five grey-uniformed guards. One of the guards yelled 'Get that *verfluchter* sledge the hell out of the road!' and others cuffed and shoved the corvee to obey – the men moved with the slow shakiness of borderline starvation as they set down their shovels and stumbled to comply.

The officer in charge hastened to the side of the car as it pulled to a halt. 'Heil Hitler. My apologies, Captain, we'll have it clear in a minute. This road sees so little traffic . . .'

'That's hardly an excuse for blocking it!' flared Baldur, and von Rath waved him quiet.

'Quite understandable, Lieutenant.'

'I – I heard about Major Hagen, sir,' said the officer after a moment, touching the brim of his cap in respect. His uniform was grey instead of black, but Rhion recognized the insignia of the SS on collar and shoulder-tabs, and reflected that the Reich of Germany was probably the most comprehensively-protected realm he had ever seen. 'A great loss to the service of the Reich, but I was afraid something of the kind would happen. The drugs you were using for those experiments . . .' He shook his head. 'He should have taken a little more time. After all the men who died while he was experimenting for the right dosage, he should have been more careful. Hell,' he added, nodding towards the workers, stumbling as they dragged at the sledge. 'The Commandant would have sent him over as many more of these swine as he needed to make sure.'

'We were under a time constraint,' said von Rath politely. 'Thank you, officer . . .'

With a gravelly scraping on the rough asphalt of the road, the sledge was hauled clear. Horst put the car in gear and started to move forward slowly. The officer touched his cap again. 'Ah, well, there it is. If you need any more, just let us know!'

'That troubled you.' With a touch on his sleeve von Rath halted Rhion in the doorway of the library, a long room occupying much of the main lodge's eastern face, and let the others go past them along the upstairs hall to their own rooms to prepare for lunch. Only Baldur stopped, and came back to trail them into the long, gloomy chamber, unwilling, Rhion suspected, to let his hero have a conversation with anyone in which he was not included.

Still shaky with shock, anger, and a vague sense of betrayal, Rhion didn't much care. 'Just a little, yes.'

Neither von Rath nor Baldur seemed to notice the heavy sarcasm in his voice. Baldur snuffled, wiped his nose on his crumpled sleeve, and said matter-of-factly, 'I d-don't see why it should. They were just . . .'

'I did debate about whether to tell you how we arrived at the drugs under whose influence we were able to project our minds into the Void,' von Rath cut the boy off gently, seating himself at the library's long table. 'I did not know what your attitude toward it would be. Further, you were sufficiently grieved over your master's death that I did not wish to burden you with the possibility of fancied guilt.'

'*Fancied* guilt?'

Even at this hour of the late morning the library, facing east into the little courtyard between the wings of the grim, grey lodge, was thick with gloom. The tobacco-coloured velvet curtains, which were never opened, created a dusk thick and palpable as the smells that seemed to have accumulated over the hundred-odd years of the building's life: the odours of dust and the stale, gritty foetor of ancient wool carpets, the faint mouldery atmosphere that clung to the desiccated trophy-head of an antelope over the doorway, the dry breath of old paper and crumbling cloth and glue and the beaten-in reminiscence of tobacco-smoke that would never come out. The walls here were thick with books, more books than Rhion had ever imagined: Lanz and von List, Blavatsky's *Isis Unveiled* and the *Chymische Hochzeit*, Nostradamus' prophecies, the collected works of Charles Fort, and the *Library of Those Who are Blond and Defend the Rights of the Male*. They had overflowed the original mahogany shelves and stacked two-deep the newer pine planks that had been erected over the ornamental panelling. Neat boxes of half-decayed scrolls and chests of parchment codices were arranged upon the floor, and in those few spaces of wall not occupied by books hung fragments of Assyrian carvings and the long, fading columns of Egyptian glyphs. Rhion, used as he was to the libraries of the Duke of Mere and the Ladies of the Moon, had been staggered at the prodigality of books in this world.

Here he spent most of his afternoons, listening to Baldur, or Gall, or von Rath as they read to him from these endless texts. The Spell of Tongues which permitted him to understand German worked, in essence, from mind to mind – thus he could understand what was read aloud, if the reader understood it, though the written languages were a mystery to him. And here Baldur spent most of his nights, taking notes, looking up obscure references, reading his way patiently through collections of ancient letters, centuries-old diaries, crumbling grimoires and yellowing broadsides and scandal-sheets that the SS's Occult Bureau in Berlin had sent them, searching for some scrap of knowledge, some clue that would show them how and why magic had died in this world, and how it might be restored.

Baldur was sitting now hunched over his notes, puffy, untidy, and sullen, snuffling and wiping his nose on his soiled sleeve. In Rhion's world Lord Esrex, son-in-law of the Duke of Mere and an old enemy of his, was addicted to a drug brewed from certain leaves given to him by the priests of the dark cult of Agon. Here a similar substance was – rather disgustingly, in Rhion's opinion – rendered to a powder which was then snorted through the nasal membranes, with the result that Baldur's sinuses always ran.

'Fancied, yes.' Von Rath's well-shaped brows drew down slightly, shadowing his clear grey eyes. 'The men who were used in Eric's experiments were criminals, traitors against the state, men whose crimes in any society would have rendered their lives forfeit. The SS has the management of the labour-camps and the concentration-camps in which they in some measure atone for their deeds by service to the state they have tried to destroy. We had to find some way of speaking through the Void, some way of renewing contact, and drugs – mescaline, psylocybin, and others – were the only things we had found which worked. We were permitted an arrangement with the commandant of the Kegenwald camp to obtain men for experiments with the correct dosage. But the men themselves would have died anyway.'

There was a polite tapping at the door; von Rath looked up as one of the guards assigned to watchroom duty in the old parlour at the foot of the stairs entered. 'Mr Himmler is on the phone for you, Captain.'

'Please excuse me.' Von Rath reached for the telephone on the corner of the library table, and Rhion, rising, left him in such privacy as Baldur's company afforded. Telephones were another thing straight out of tales of wonder, though in marketplace fables the means by which two people without magical powers could communicate instantaneously over distance generally involved sight as well as hearing. Curiously, though the Spell of Tongues held good when the speaker was in his presence, Rhion could not understand an electronically transmitted voice, either over the telephone or on that totally unexpected device, the wireless radio. Last night, when he had gone down to the big drawing-room downstairs for the first time to watch a cinema-film being shown for the benefit of the guards – the simple and unspeakably tragic story of a wise man's love for a whore – Poincelles had had to translate for him.

He turned down the hallway of the south wing, paused before the door of what had been the great master bedroom – pushed it open, and stood looking in.

The room was still empty. Yellow sunlight filled it from the wide south-facing windows; through the uncurtained panes could be seen the rude and hastily-built block of the guards' barracks, and, beyond, the wire fence which enclosed the entire low hill upon which the Schloss had been built. Telephones, automobiles, even the huge quantities of books available in this world, hadn't staggered Rhion so much as the cheap plentifulness of wire. In his own world it was so difficult to manufacture that it was generally only used for decorative jewellery. When the gate was closed at night the wire fence was charged with enough *electricity* to knock a man down, and Rhion had been warned repeatedly against going anywhere near it. *Not,* he reflected wryly, remembering his experiences that morning, *that the perimeter guards would let me.*

And in the chamber itself . . .

Dust-motes sparkled in the mellow sunlight. On the oak planks of the floor every trace of the Circles of Power had been eradicated.

Jaldis, dammit, he thought, grief for his master's loss mingling with exasperation and regret. *Why didn't you trust me with the secret of its making? Even though I worked for the Ladies of the Moon, you know I wouldn't have passed that secret on to them.* But Jaldis had never trusted wizards of any other Order, as far as his secrets were concerned.

'I'm sorry.' Von Rath's soft voice spoke at his elbow. Rhion, leaning in the sunny doorway, glanced back to see the tall black figure in the shadows of the hall. He said nothing in reply, and there was a long moment's silence, the younger wizard looking over his shoulder into the room, empty and filled with light, where the darkness had been.

'I'm sorry,' said von Rath again, and this time he was not simply apologizing for the interruption of their conversation by a telephone call from Berlin. His voice was quieter, gentle with regret. 'You know, I do think that the use of drugs to create the Well probably had something to do with . . . with its collapse. With Eric's death. I am sorry . . .' He shook his head, closing his grey eyes as if doing so would erase the image from his mind.

After a moment he went on, his voice hesitant as if he were carefully choosing his words, 'I swear to you, Rhion, that as soon as it is possible to . . . to risk it . . . we will weave a Dark Well again. We will get in touch with wizards on your own side of the Void, to take you back through. But you understand that it is not possible now.'

'Yes.' Rhion sighed almost inaudibly, leaned once more against the oak door-jamb, weary in every bone. 'Yes, I understand.'

'Spring is the time for war,' Paul said quietly. 'When the weather clears . . . I fear that the English, the French, the Dutch and Belgians and Russians, are only waiting for that. They will launch an attack upon us at any time now, and we cannot risk losing another one of us, should what happened to Eric happen again. Not when we have made this much progress towards returning magic to our world.'

'I understand,' Rhion said again.

The strong, slender hands rested for a moment on his shoulders, tightened encouragingly, as if willing him strength, like a commander willing his men to be brave in coming battle. For a moment something in that touch made Rhion think the younger wizard was about to say something else, but he did not. After brief time he turned away, and Rhion heard the highly polished boots retreat down the hall to his own small study, leaving him alone.

In the silence the faint chatter of the radio in the watchroom downstairs seemed very loud. Outside in the yard, a Storm Trooper cracked a rude soldier's joke – another guard guffawed. Rhion remained where he was, bone-tired and hopeless, leaning in the doorway of that sun-flooded room, remembering . . .

There HAD to have been some magic on this side, he thought, *even the tiniest fragment – there had to be magic on both sides of the Void for a crossing.*

Somehow, just for that instant, at the stroke of midnight on the night of the Spring Equinox, some spark of magic had been kindled in a fashion that von Rath and his colleagues still did not understand. Enough to bring him through.

His mind returned to that fact, again and again. Perhaps

Eric had known . . . But Eric was dead, destroyed in the Well that he had made. If that magic could be duplicated, even for an instant . . .

If he could only find some way to re-make the Dark Well, contact the wizards in his own world . . .

But even if Baldur had found notes of it in the library, he reflected, they'd never reveal that to him. And without someone to read the texts to him he was helpless, illiterate, as utterly dependent upon them as he was for clothing and food and – he grinned wryly at the irony – protection.

He stared down at the bare oak planks of the floor, seeking for some remaining trace of the Circles. He only remembered from seeing the ones Jaldis had made that they were hellishly complicated, blood and earth, silver and light, interwound and woven with smaller rings and curves and crescents of power. And even so he did not know the words that went with their making.

In any case there was nothing to be seen. Only the bare oak planks . . .

. . . bare oak planks . . .

What was it, he wondered suddenly, about the oak planks of the floor that touched a chord of wrongness in his mind? As wrong as the backward-turning swastikas, as wrong as the eyes of the guards in the watchroom, cold and caring nothing except to follow whatever orders they were given . . .

And then he remembered.

Remembered coming to in darkness, sick and freezing and exhausted to the marrow of his being, wondering with what strength was in him that he was alive at all and thinking how the *stones of the floor would have been cold if any warmth had been left in his hands.*

The stones of the floor.

His eyes went back to the oak planks, naked and worn and scuffed with a thousand scrubbings.

Von Rath lied.

His heart jolted with a lurching surge of certainty, knowing that it was true.

Von Rath lied so that I'd think there wasn't a way home. So that I'd be at their mercy. So that I'd do whatever I could to restore magic in this world, because only in restoring magic could I get myself home . . .

Excitement, rage, dread that he was wrong and bone-deep awareness that he was right swept through him in a confused wave, like the stab of needles and pins in a long-numbed limb coming once more to life. He began to shake, his breath coming fast with hope and blazing anger.

They drew up fake Circles here while I was unconscious, to make me believe them. Hell, they could have brought me here from another building, another place entirely, the way cars can travel . . .

They could have drugged me . . . I have only their word on how long I was out.

I have only their word on everything.

For a long time he stood there unmoving: a stout little man with his shabby, greying beard and thick-lensed spectacles, listening to von Rath's quiet voice talking to Baldur in the hall by the library door, listening to the crunch of car-tyres on gravel outside, the distant, indistinguishable murmur of the guards exchanging greetings as they walked the barbed-wire perimeter of the fence. He felt exactly as if he had been crossing a floor which he had thought to be solid, only to feel it buckle suddenly beneath him, and to hear the echoes of bottomless chaos yawning under his feet.

A floor enormously wide, he thought. And no way of knowing which way to run for safety.

And then, *If I have only their word on everything . . . What else are they lying to me about?*

3

'You want me to find a *what?*' Tom Saltwood tossed the slim dossier of photographs, maps, handwritten notes and one or two cheesily-printed magazine-articles back onto the desk, and regarded the man who had been his commander in Spain with mingled bemusement and uncertainty. 'With all due respect, Colonel Hillyard . . .'

'I know.' Hillyard's mouth flicked into its wry, triangular grin. 'I'll admit that's how it sounded to me.'

'And to me.' The third man in the nameless London office, a stooped Englishman with very bright black eyes peering from a heavily lined face, reached across to the dossier with one arthritic finger and flipped free a snapshot which hadn't been very good even before it had been blown up to eight-by-ten. Mayfair, Hillyard had introduced him to Saltwood, though Tom was pretty certain that wasn't his name.

'But some rather strange rumours have come to us from some of the more secret bureaux of the SS, and this one we've had – er – independently confirmed. We think it bears looking into.'

'Not,' added Hillyard, settling his lean form back in the worn brown leather of his chair and reaching briefly, almost automatically, behind him to tweak the tiniest chink out of the bow-window's heavy curtains, 'that it would be easier to believe if we'd had it confirmed by personal telegram from Hitler, but there it is.'

Tom was silent for a moment, wondering what it was that was causing the alarm-bells to go off at the back of his mind. A false note in Hillyard's voice, maybe, or the way he tilted his head when he looked across at the man he called Mayfair – the suspicion and query in his eyes. Maybe it was just time and place. What three weeks ago – when he'd got the enigmatically-worded request to report back to London – would have been normal or at least explicable now bore a staggering load of contextual freight . . .

Or maybe he was just tired. Several hours spent crammed in a corner of a destroyer's gun-deck with 700 filthy and exhausted Brit soldiers wasn't particularly conducive to napping even under the best of circumstances. The steady cannonade of shellfire and strafing hadn't helped, nor had the unencouraging sight of slate-coloured water, littered with hawsers, oil-slicks, fragments of mined ships and floating bodies visible every time he turned his head to glance over the rail.

But on the whole it was better than the hell of exhaustion and death he'd left behind him on the Dunkirk beach.

And there on the docks at Dover, among all those nice British ladies with cups of tea and elderly blue-clothed policemen saying, *Step along this way now* . . . had been Colonel Hillyard, tired and unshaven and grimy as any of the troops, but with that old businesslike glint in his dark eyes as he'd said, 'About time you showed up. I have a car.' Tom had barely had time to change and shave – he'd slept on the way up.

And now they were asking him to do . . . What?

He blinked, rubbed his eyes, and picked up the photograph. The reproduction was grainy. The building in the background might have been one of those big mansions rich folks built up the Hudson from New York a hundred years ago – heavy granite walls, peaked gables, crenellated ornamental turrets on the corners and pseudo-gothic traceries on the windows – except that, judging by the number of men in SS uniforms standing around and the little swastika flags on the hood of the car in the foreground, it was obviously somewhere in Germany. A civilian was standing near the car: a bearded, tired-looking little man of forty or so, curly hair long and unruly, steel-rimmed glasses concealing his eyes.

'His name is Sligo,' said Mayfair in a voice crusty and plummy as eighty-year-old port. 'Professor Rhion Sligo.'

'Sounds Irish,' remarked Hillyard from the depths of his armchair. 'Gaelic form of Ryan, maybe.' He ran a hand over his sun-browned bald scalp. 'Any Irishman working for the SS these days would be using the Gaelic form, of course.'

'Perhaps,' agreed Mayfair. 'We have no record of anyone of that name graduating, teaching, or publishing at any University or college we have checked, but then a false degree is as easy to assume as a false name, and both are rather common in occult circles.' He sipped his tea, which a secretary had brought in a few minutes before.

Tired as he was, Tom had to smile a little at the teacups. In an American office they would have been those thick white mugs reminiscent of every cheap diner from Brooklyn to Bodega Bay. Here they were somebody's second-best Spode that had got too chipped for 'company'. The office, in one of those politely anonymous terraced squares so typical of London, likewise had the air of having been donated by a Duke in reduced circumstances. It had clearly started life as somebody's parlour, with faded pink wallpaper framing a stained plaster mantel and a fireplace prosaically tiled over and occupied by an electric grate. The whole setup was straight out of Thackeray. The faded draperies were firmly shut over the bow-window, the blackout curtain beyond them cutting out any possibility of a view. Now and then a car would go by outside with a soft swishing of tyres, or he would hear the swift clip of hurrying shoe-heels on the pavement. But few, thought Tom, would be abroad tonight.

Somewhere in the building someone had a radio on. Tom couldn't make out the words, but he didn't need to.

So many ships safely returned to Dover with their cargoes of beaten, exhausted, wounded men – so many shelled to pieces, or sunk by mines in the Channel. And still more men trapped on the beaches, between the advancing German army and the sea.

No sign yet of an air attack on London.

No sign yet of landing-barges setting out with German troops.

No sign yet.

Sitting here in this quiet, lamplit office, Tom experienced a sensation of mild surprise that he was alive at all. Twelve hours ago he would have bet money against it.

Mayfair's voice called his attention back. '. . . arrangements made, as you know, three weeks ago to transfer you from your unit in Belgium. What was important then, when the entire question was an academic one of if and when, is doubly important now in the light of an imminent invasion.'

Tom looked from the bent, grizzled old man behind the desk to the lean, browned one in the dull khaki uniform, and rubbed his hand over his face, trying to be sure he was completely awake and alert for all this. 'With all due respect, sir . . . a *wizard?*'

'So he claims.' Mayfair produced a pipe from his jacket pocket, began the meticulous ritual of reaming, cleaning, stuffing, and experimental puffing that Tom had observed pipesmokers to treasure, probably above the actual taste of the tobacco itself. 'And the SS seem to believe him enough to cherish him . . .'

'Yeah, well, they cherish Himmler's slumgullion about a master race, too.'

'Perhaps. But Sligo's claim is not only that he is a wizard himself, but that he can teach wizardry to others.'

Tom chuckled. 'Hell – sir. Professor Marvello the Magnificent taught *me* magic in the carney when I was eighteen, but nobody from the government ever tried to hire me.'

'Well,' smiled Hillyard, brown eyes sparkling against a brick-red tan. 'Now they have.'

Saltwood was startled. 'You mean just because . . .'

'No, no.' Mayfair waved a dismissive hand and set his pipe down on the scarred leather blotter before him. 'Although that is what you Americans call a "dividend" for us – that you may stand a better chance of spotting a hoax. No. The reason I asked Colonel Hillyard to contact you – the reason we've arranged for you to be seconded from your regiment . . .'

What's LEFT of my regiment, thought Tom grimly, remembering the men who had fallen at the crossings of the Leutze and the Scheldt, remembering the men who had crouched in shell-holes in the sand with him, who had not got up again.

'. . . is because you speak German like a native, because you look German, and because you've done a bit of intelligence work during the fighting in Spain. Is this correct?'

There was another folder, closed, at Mayfair's elbow on the battered mahogany of the desk; Tom glanced at it, guessing it was his and wondering exactly how much it contained.

'A whole swarm of Germans and Swedes homesteaded the bottomlands along the Missouri near our ranch when I was a kid,' he explained. 'My grandmother was German – she lived with us – and I spoke it at home, and playing with the German kids. For years I had this real hick Saxon accent – I boarded with a German family when I worked on the New York docks and the wife said I spoke German like a pig, and worked to straighten me out.' He grinned a little at the memory, not adding that his landlord had also been his cell-leader in the Industrial Workers of the World and that most of his practice in the language had been obtained in endless summer-night discussions on the stoop about socialist political argument.

Mayfair studied him awhile longer, taking in, Saltwood

knew, the craggy bones of his face, the ridiculously baby-fine dust-coloured hair, the blue eyes, broad shoulders, fair skin. His 'intelligence work' in Spain had come about because he'd been the only man of their company in the Abraham Lincoln Brigade capable of passing himself off as a German. One night he'd got three of the local Anarchists out of rebel hands with only some very unconvincing forgeries of Gestapo ID. Their Russian military advisor had reprimanded him strongly, for the Anarchists, though officially Republican allies, were considered not worth the risk.

'You understand,' Mayfair went on after a moment, 'that you'll probably be impersonating an SS trooper for part of the time – and the Nazis are not signatories of the Geneva accords.'

'Neither were the nationalists,' said Tom quietly. 'I went through all that in Spain.'

'So I see.' Mayfair sat back and picked up his pipe again, puffing at it in the usual vain effort to get the thing to go. He nodded down at the closed folder. 'A volunteer in the Abraham Lincoln Brigade, later seconded to the Internationalist Front headquarters in '36. You were listed as captured . . .'

'I escaped,' said Tom. 'Nobody seemed to be trying very hard to get us out.'

'Ah.' Mayfair took a few more draws on the pipe, then gave it up as a bad job and opened the folder, turning over the pages with an arthritic's careful deliberation. Presumably, thought Tom, it hadn't been his department. At least he had the good grace not to say, as so many did, 'Well, politically we were in an awkward situation with regard to prisoners . . .'

After a moment he resumed. 'You returned to America, though we don't have any record here of an official repatriation . . .'

'It wasn't under my own name.'

The grizzled eyebrows took a whole ladder of parallel forehead-wrinkles with them on their way up.

Saltwood shrugged. 'They weren't falling over themselves to repatriate those of us who'd been anti-fascist enough to go to Spain and get shot at, so I figured somebody who'd been in trouble over labour unions would stand even less of a chance. So when one of my old chess-playing buddies in the Brigade took a bullet in Madrid I sort of appropriated his papers.'

'I see.' By the shrewd glance in his black eyes Tom wondered exactly what he *did* see. 'And *were* you involved with the labour unions in the United States?'

'I was on the fringes of them, yes,' lied Tom, folding his hands over the buckle of his Sam Browne belt and doing his best to look like a dumb, blue-eyed farmboy, something he had always been good at. 'After Pa died and our ranch went bust I spent a lot of time on the road. Working in the mines and the factories you couldn't hardly help running across them.' From the corner of his eye he saw Hillyard sigh and shake his head, but after all his old commander said nothing. Considering Tom's rowdy and violent career as an organizer in the IWW, that was probably just as well.

'Well,' grunted Mayfair at length, 'least said about that the better, perhaps. And you arrived in this country last September and volunteered . . . again.'

Tom felt himself blush as if Mayfair had unearthed a stint with a ballet troupe in his past. After Spain he really should have known better. 'Hell – begging your pardon, sir. But nobody back in my country seemed to be standing in line to do anything about Hitler . . .'

'You need hardly apologize, Sergeant Saltwood.' The old man closed the folder again, looked across at him from under jutting brows. 'Will you take it?'

Tom hesitated for a long time, all the topics that the old man had *not* brought up – like, *Who is this man REALLY and for that matter who are you?* and *Why don't you get somebody from regular Intelligence* and *What's scared you into sending someone at a time like this?* – combining in his mind into a strong odour of Rat. He'd got Hillyard's telegram asking him to come back to London for 'family business' – a code between them from their days with the Brigade that had meant, 'I've got a job for you . . .' – two days before the Panzers had come rolling out of the Ardennes Forest like a tidal-wave of iron and fire. *At least*, he reflected wryly, *I was already packed.*

'There are, of course, a number of explanations as to what might be going on,' said Hillyard, in the deep, brocaded baritone that wouldn't have disgraced a RADA performance of *King Lear*. 'Sligo may very well be a confidence-trickster, out to take the SS for whatever he can.'

'That's not something *I'd* care to try, unless I had some way of getting out of that country real fast.'

'As you say,' agreed Hillyard. 'But stupider things have been attempted – and have succeeded. And in fact, he may know that Hitler has a blind-spot where the occult is concerned. Then again, Sligo may be mad . . .'

'He's definitely mad,' put in Mayfair. 'According to one of our sources he seems to suffer from a number of rather curious delusions, apparently without affecting his usefulness to the SS.'

'The third explanation,' went on Hillyard, 'is that the occult group – composed of several genuine occultists from Paris and Vienna spiritualist and theosophist circles – is a cover for something else, some new weapon or device that is being developed, and *that* is what we're worried about.'

He folded his hands on one jodhpurred knee – like Tom, he'd had a change of uniform, a wash, and a shave in that rented room in Dover, but then always he'd managed to look neat, even when crouching in a Catalan sheep-pen under Luftwaffe fire. 'We still don't know how the Germans took the fortress of Eban Emael – the key to that whole section of the Maginot Line. We only know that it was impregnable, and that it went without a shot being fired.'

'Conversely,' added Mayfair, 'the occult trappings could just as easily be for Sligo's benefit as for ours or Himmler's. From all we can ascertain the man definitely believes himself to be a wizard. Whatever he has, or may have, invented, he may attribute to magic, just as our system of radio directional-finders grew out of an attempt to invent a death-ray – something the Nazis are still working on. The Nazis may have enlisted his assistance by humouring his belief.

'In any case it makes no odds.' He picked up his pipe again, and appeared to be surprised – as pipe-smokers invariably were – to find that it had gone out. For a moment he sat cradling it, his dark eyes gazing out past Tom, into some middle-distance of thought, and Tom saw weariness descend upon him like a double-load of grain-bags carried too far – the weariness of waiting and wondering, less urgent perhaps than the ground-in ache in his own flesh, but ultimately just as exhausting. At least for the past ten days his own thoughts had been absolutely concentrated on the moment: cover, spare ammo, a place in the retreating trucks. He hadn't had time, as this old man had, to consider the larger implications of that tidal-wave of grey-clad men sweeping across the flat green Belgian landscape – he hadn't spent the past ten days wondering, *What the hell will we do when the Germans land at Dover?* knowing that every gun, every truck, every grenade and clip of ammo the British Army possessed had been left on Dunkirk beach.

Then Mayfair sighed, and straightened his shoulders again, as if reminding himself, *First things first*. 'Are you interested? You'll be put ashore by submarine, probably near Hamburg; we'll give you the names of contacts in Hamburg and in Danzig as well – if you have to flee in that direction – for you to radio for instructions about when and where you'll be taken off again. You'll have a couple of German identities, with uniforms, passbooks, ration-cards, maps . . . photographs of the men involved, if we can get them in time. Colonel Hillyard tells me you're a man to be trusted to do the job and not to panic if things come unstuck. At present Sligo's group is headquartered somewhere in the wilds of Prussia near the Polish border, and you may have to make a judgement about which direction to run. But that can all be worked out later. The question is, Are you willing?'

'To kill Sligo?'

Mayfair nodded, unfazed at the bald statement that the mission was, in fact, being undertaken for the purpose of murder. 'If you can ascertain what they're up to, of course we'd like to know that, too. But I understand you're not a scientist. The main object is to kill Professor Sligo, at whatever cost.'

Tom glanced over at Hillyard. His brain was still ringing with the alarm-bells of unanswered questions, where it wasn't thick with sleepiness and exhaustion, but he guessed if he were to ask now he wouldn't get answers anyway.

But two years of fighting in Spain, of ambushes in dry ravines and blowing up bridges and trains, of firefights in the streets of Madrid and of the thornbush morasses of guerrilla politics, had taught him that Hillyard was a man to be trusted. Hillyard met his eyes, and nodded.

'I'm your man,' said Tom laconically. Then he added, 'God willing and the creek don't rise.'

Mayfair's mouth tightened. 'As you say,' he agreed, and his tone was dry. Elsewhere in the building, the radio announcer's voice chittered frightenedly on.

'So what's the story?' Tom fished in the pocket of his uniform tunic for makings as he and Hillyard emerged on to the high porch and paused to let their eyes adjust. With every window in the city swathed tight in blackout curtains the darkness was startling, darker even than open country would be, for the shadows of the buildings blocked the dim ambient glow from the dusting of stars overhead. The night was fine and warm, the moist, thick smell of new-cut grass drifting to them from the little park in the centre of the square, the colder, damper breath of moss-greened pavement and last year's dead leaves rising from the sunken areaway that dropped, like a dry moat, below the porch to either side of them. The freshness of the air, the sweet calm silence of the night, cleared his head and drove back the exhaustion that seemed to weight his bones.

Tom's match made a startling glare in the blackness. 'You know as well as I do they've got guys in regular Intelligence who know German.'

'So they do. I've booked us rooms over in Torrington Place.' Starlight gleamed on the bald curve of Hillyard's head as he led the way down the narrow porch stairs, his gas-mask swinging awkwardly at his belt. 'My guess is that Alec – Mayfair . . .' he corrected himself '– couldn't get approval from Intelligence to send one of their men. It's not his department, you know.'

'It's not?' They passed the little park, and against the pale scars of cut-up earth Saltwood saw the low, dim bulk of a red-brick air-raid shelter, new and raw and waiting. He remembered Madrid again, and what he'd seen of the village of Guernica. Though the night was warm and peaceful he shivered.

Hillyard shook his head. 'He approached me privately, asked if there were anyone from the Brigade who'd be reliable. Most of the native Brits, I might add, have already vanished into the FO's murky ranks – not that that affected my choice much. If he hadn't arranged to call you back now over this, I'd still have been waiting for you on the docks.'

'I bet you meet all the ships, honey,' grinned Tom, and made a smooching noise in the dark. From behind them came the sudden, full-throated rumble of a car's engine – a big eight-cylinder American job by the sound of it – and a moment later a lightless black shape swept gleaming past them and away into the dark. 'Whoa – somebody was sure thinking when they drew up the blackout regs . . . What's up?'

'Well, there's been a certain amount of discussion about forming guerrilla forces, probably based in Scotland . . .'

'You don't think England's going to surrender, then?'

'Never,' said Hillyard decisively. 'You've been in the fighting, so I don't know how much you've seen of what the Luftwaffe and the German Army did to Rotterdam . . .'

'I've heard.' Saltwood's voice was grim.

'It's going to be bad here,' went on Hillyard, suddenly quiet, as if he sensed all those families, all those children, all those peaceful lives and day-to-day joys that lay like a vast, murmuring hive around them in the lightless city. 'And it may get bad very soon. But Churchill's never going to surrender.'

'And with all this going on,' said Saltwood thoughtfully, dropping his cigarette-butt to the sidewalk and grinding it out under his heel, 'Mayfair still thinks this mad professor of theirs is important enough for me to go over to Germany *now*?'

There was long silence, broken only by the strike of the two men's boots on the pavement and by the occasional surge of traffic – punctuated now and then by the startled screech of brakes – a few blocks away in Gower Street. But there were few passers-by. Everyone in London – everyone in England, thought Tom – would be glued to a radio tonight.

They turned a corner – Hillyard seemed to know where he was going, but then he always did, and could see like a cat in the dark. He steered Tom carefully across the street to avoid an entanglement of sandbags and barbed-wire around some large building, nearly invisible in the pitchy gloom. Once they were stopped by a coveralled civilian, a fat old white-haired man wearing a warden's armband and carrying a gas-mask strapped to his belt, and asked for their papers, but when he saw their uniforms by the quick glow of his flashlight he hastily saluted and waved them on by.

At length Hillyard said, 'We'll probably have a little bit of breathing-space, anyway – the latest reports say the German armoured divisions are already turning south to mop up France.'

'Makes sense if Hitler wants to secure naval bases on the Channel.'

'So it does. But if there is to be an invasion, Mayfair seems to think that whatever Sligo is doing will make the situation worse. He's been scared pretty badly.'

'Yeah, but . . . a *wizard*, Bill?'

And Hillyard laughed. 'Well, I didn't read the reports. That should be the Red Cow opposite.' He gestured towards what appeared to be a solid and anonymous wall of dark buildings on the other side of the narrow lane. 'There isn't a wireless in the hotel-room – Think you can stay awake long enough for a beer?'

'I always knew you could smell beer across a street.'

Together they plunged across the bumpy pavement, dark as the inside of a closet, narrowly missing being run down by something powerful and nearly silent – a Dusenberg or Bentley, Tom guessed by the throb of the engine – which passed close enough to them that the wind of it flapped their trouser-legs against their calves. Having spent twenty-four hours in a shell-crater on the beach listening to machine-gun bullets smacking into the sand on all sides of him Tom didn't bother to jump, just quickened his stride enough to let the whizzing car pass.

'*Here lies the body of Thomas Leander Saltwood*,' he quoted his own epitaph, '*who survived union goons in the West Virginia mines, special deputies in the California orchards, two years of fighting in Spain, nine months in a Spanish prison, the German invasion of Belgium, the shelling of the Dunkirk beaches, Luftwaffe strafing on the Channel, his commander's driving on the way up to London . . .*'

'Watch it, Sergeant!'

'*. . . only to be killed in quest of beer by a careless driver during the blackout in the streets of London.* You remember that case of Chateau Lafitte you found in Madrid?'

'Ah,' said Hillyard reminiscently as he reached into the Stygian pit of a darkened doorway for a handle – even on the step here Tom could now hear the hushed murmur of voices, and smell the inevitable warm fustiness of beer and bodies within. 'A very good year.' More than the champagne, Tom remembered the bombing-raid that had been going on when they'd found it . . . remembered his commander casually pouring out glassfuls for them both in the ruins of the old cellar, listening to the explosions getting nearer and nearer and remarking, *That one's two, three streets away yet . . . plenty of time . . . hmm, sounds like they're dropping mines . . .* 'I remember old Palou insisting on unloading the wine from his cart during that big raid. "They are only Germans, but this . . . this is money . . ."'

'Funny what you get used to. I met Californios when I was working the Long Beach docks who wouldn't get up from the suppertable for an earthquake, but who swore they'd never go east of the Rockies for fear of tornados – *Tornados*, for Chrissake!'

In the broad slit of yellow light as Hillyard opened the pub door Tom saw his commander blench. 'Er – have you seen many tornados?'

And Tom, who'd grown up with them, only laughed.

He took a seat at a table in a corner, under a mouldering trophy-head some aristocrat had shot in Kenya and an enamelled tin ad for Green King Ale. The pub was very quiet, the scattering of workingmen and housewives there speaking softly, if at all, over their pints of ale and bitters, listening to the chatter of the radio announcer's voice.

'. . . general withdrawal of all remaining forces to Dunkirk. On the Channel, the destroyer *Wakeful* was torpedoed and sunk, only a few survivors escaping to be picked up by the motor-drifter *Nautilus* and the damlayer *Comfort*, themselves heavily loaded . . . the *Queen of the Channel*, with 920 men aboard, bombed and sunk, her crew and passengers picked up by the store-ship *Dorrian Rose* . . . *Harvester, Esk, Malcom* . . . the minesweeper *Brighton Belle* sunk in the Channel, her troops rescued by the *Medway Queen* . . . destroyers heavily engaged with shore batteries . . .'

They'll never make it, thought Tom, leaning back against the dark wainscot walls and letting his eyes slip closed. Hillyard had gone to get them drinks – the soft murmur of voices washed over him, men's and women's both . . . It was a neighbourhood pub, a family pub . . . It was good beyond anything to be among normal people, decent people, not in the terror and sweat and dirt of battle, the horrible inferno of waiting under shellfire to maybe have your life saved, and maybe not . . .

The rocking of the old *Codlington* that had taken him off the beach returned to him, seemingly woven into his bones. Like the rhythmic jostle of the freight-cars he'd ridden, he thought, that came back to a man even when he was lying on a stable bed again . . . The memory of the smell of tornado-weather, the dense, waiting stillness, the livid colour of the sky, waiting and watching for spouts . . .

Funny, he hadn't thought about that since he was fourteen, the summer the ranch had finally gone bust and the bank foreclosed on them, sold their hard-held herd and ploughed the whole concern under for a wheat-farm. That was the first time he'd ridden the rails, down to Oklahoma, looking for work in the oil-fields . . .

His head jerked; he realized he'd been slipping over into

sleep. He saw Hillyard still by the bar, bending forward to catch the radio announcer's voice. He tried to remember the last time he'd been this warm, this comfortable – tried to remember the last time he hadn't been expecting to get blown away by the Germans in the next ten seconds . . .

His eyes slid closed again. The smells of tobacco and beer wreathed his thoughts, the gentle patter of voices like falling rain. '. . . expecting an announcement by the King of Belgium . . . *Abukir* destroyed . . . *Shikari* and *Scimitar* at Dover . . . special trains to take the men to rest-camps . . .'

'. . . must use his influence, now more than ever,' a woman's soft voice murmured at the next table. He'd noticed the two women there when he'd sat down, a delicate little white-haired finch of a lady, like a Duchess in plain-clothes, the other a striking red-head with eyes the colour of the sherry in her glass. Like everyone else in the pub they'd had gas-masks with them, incongruous on the floor beside their worn leather handbags and as little regarded. The red-head's voice was low and desperate as she went on, 'I saw it in the crystal. I felt his coming on the night of the Equinox . . . I felt it the first time he used the power of the *leys*. If he isn't found, if he isn't stopped . . .'

'He will be, darling,' came the old lady's comforting tones, motherly and gentle through the drowsy fog of dreaming that padded Saltwood's mind like a goose-down quilt. What they were saying made no sense, but it was good to just listen to women's voices, after all those weeks of men, of gunfire, of the overhead shriek of planes . . .

'Trust my husband to do his part, as we do ours. We have raised the power to keep the skies clear for the planes . . . later we can call down the clouds over the Channel . . . Alec!' she added in surprise, and Tom opened his eyes – or thought he opened his eyes, though he could very well have been dreaming, he thought – Surely it was a dream that Mr Mayfair had come into the pub, gas-mask tucked under his arm, and was stooping, hesitant with arthritis, to kiss the little Duchess on the lips.

'It is all being taken care of,' said Mayfair, and the red-haired woman sighed, her slim shoulders bowing suddenly, as if with exhausted relief. He added, 'As the Americans say, God willing and the creek don't rise . . .'

'No beer for you, Sergeant.'

Tom jerked awake, to see Hillyard standing at his elbow, a glass in either hand.

'I refuse to carry you all the way to Torrington Place.'

Saltwood blinked, and rubbed his eyes. The table beside his was empty.

'Sorry for the delay.' Hillyard settled himself into the chair next to Tom, and gave himself the lie by pushing a pint of Bass across to him. 'They say they've got somewhere near 17,000 men landed at Dover, and more coming over all the time . . . nearly all the army's within the perimeter of Dunkirk. And the German armoured divisions have definitely turned south, towards Paris. That leaves the Luftwaffe to contend with, but we may get a little breathing-space . . . it's my guess, in fact, that with Intelligence in a frenzy there'll be quite a delay in your setting out on your travels. It takes time to assemble papers, arrange transport, get photographs and maps, especially if one is doing it on the sneak . . .'

'Look,' said Tom curiously, as a few cautious sips of the nut-flavoured ale cleared his head a little. 'Just who *is* Mayfair? What department is he in? I mean, how did he find out about Sligo in the first place, if he's not in Intelligence?'

'I didn't ask,' smiled Hillyard. 'Not that he'd have told me if I had. He's in Finance – an auditor. Rumours do get around, especially the weird ones – perhaps he heard it from his wife.'

'His wife?' *Alec*, the little Duchess in his dream – if it had been a dream – had exclaimed . . . In her simple tweed skirt and strand of pearls under the neat home-knitted green cardigan the old lady had certainly been no Mata Hari. 'Is she in Intelligence?'

Hillyard chuckled. 'Intelligence? No – it's just that for years there's been a rumour going about that she's a witch.'

Tom rolled his eyes. '*Wunderbar.*'

4

'Well, Toto,' sighed Rhion, misquoting to an imaginary canine companion a line from the American cinema-film he had watched – with a certain amount of bemusement – last week, 'I'd say just offhand that we are definitely not in Kansas anymore.' Over the din in the tavern The Woodsman's Horn nobody heard, which was probably just as well.

There was a piano in the corner, a relic of the tavern's more respectable days before the SS had been garrisoned at the Kegenwald labour-camp. From Tally Rhion had acquired an interest in all sorts of musical instruments, but the chief virtues of pianos seemed to be that they were capable of far more volume than any similar instrument in his own world, and that it was much easier to play them badly. Both attributes were being lavishly demonstrated at the moment by the Storm Trooper at the keyboard, and a dozen or so troopers around him were bawling out the words to a filthy cabaret song about Jewish girls at the top of their collective lungs. The air was blue and acrid with tobacco smoke, and Rhion, sitting in a dark corner at a table with Auguste Poincelles, pushed up his glasses, rubbed his eyes, and hoped to hell this trip would be worth the headache he was going to take back with him to the Schloss.

'Ten ships, ten of them!' a weedy middle-aged merchant at the bar was whooping triumphantly to the impassive counterman. 'Our boys are blasting the damned English out of the water! We'll be in London by this time next week!'

So much, thought Rhion wearily, *for our enemies attacking us at any moment*. He wondered that he could possibly have been naive enough to have believed von Rath's version of the progress of the war, no matter how it had started. But he had not mentioned the discrepancy to von Rath.

Beside him, Poincelles raised one dirty, pointed fingernail to the nearest barmaid. The girl slithered like a weasel from among a pawing crowd of uniformed admirers and came across the room to them, splendid haunches switching under the thin blue cotton of her dress. It was Poincelles who had proposed tonight's expedition, at a guess, Rhion thought, to discuss matters which could not easily be mentioned in the presence of Baldur, Gall, and von Rath.

He couldn't possibly have come here for the beer.

'A whisky, Sara, if there is such a thing in this place.' Poincelles glanced inquiringly at Rhion. 'Professor?'

Rhion gestured with his three-quarters-full steel mug, smiled and shook his head. The barmaid Sara regarded him with eyes black and bright as anthracite coal in a pointed, triangular face, skin pale to translucence save for the garish redness of her painted mouth.

'So this is your famous professor?' She sized him up with a professional eye, and shifted the tray she held so that her breasts bulged like white silk pillows beneath the half-unbuttoned bodice of her dress. 'Glad you've finally come out of seclusion in that monastery they're running out there. We've heard tell about you. Go on, have another beer, Professor. Old Pauli's good for it.'

'Later,' Rhion smiled gallantly. 'That way I get to watch you walk across the room again.'

She laughed, tossed her frizzed red head, and returned to the bar to fetch Poincelles' whisky, deliberately undulating her hips to the noisy approbation of the group around the piano.

'Nice little piece, that,' remarked Poincelles. He produced a cigar from his pocket, and a lighter – a small gold box containing flint, steel, and a highly combustible liquid fuel, as good as a fire-spell, Rhion thought, at least within arm's length and while the fuel lasted. Rhion coughed in the ensuing cloud of smoke and resigned himself to being ill for the rest of the night. 'The girls here are the only decent thing about the place. That beer has no more relationship to hops than the petrol in the car does. At least the whisky's more or less pure.'

'Pure what?' demanded Rhion, coughing. Poincelles laughed, as at a witticism, and handed another cigar back over his shoulder to Horst, their SS driver-cum-bodyguard. The young man accepted it gratefully and strolled off to join the group around the piano. The other two barmaids were there already, one a honey-fair girl who reminded Rhion heartstoppingly of Tally, the other a little black-haired minx who had only moments ago emerged from the back room with an elderly man in the gold-belted brown uniform of a local Nazi Party leader. The piano thumped tunelessly, the stout barman paused in his steady dispensing of beer to sell condoms to a couple of Storm Troopers, someone turned up the radio to better hear the latest bulletins from the war in the West and someone else shouted, 'Hey, you know what they're going to get Hitler for his birthday? Frontier-posts mounted on wheels!' The noise was deafening, the smoke nauseating as a gas. Rhion sighed, closed his eyes, and wished with everything that was in him that he could simply go home.

May was fading into June. Even at this hour light lingered in the sky, soft as the colour of pigeons' eggs, and the air outside was thick with the smell of apple-blossoms from the nearby farms. Now and then the wind stirred, carrying the scent of pine-woods, whose dark wall enclosed the village, as it enclosed the Schloss, the undulating sandy hills, and, it sometimes seemed to Rhion, the entire world in a whispering monotony of sombre green. In the Drowned Lands the streams would still be high, and broad lakes would hold like quicksilver the shining echo of the light.

He felt a hand touch his wrist, warm and very strong,

and opening his eyes in the choke of cigar-smoke he saw that Poincelles had leaned near him, vulpine face as close to his as a lover's.

He whispered, 'I can help you get home.'

Rhion had been expecting those words, waiting for them – waiting for them, in fact, for several weeks. And he had almost been certain that it would be Poincelles to say them. Still he felt the jolt of adrenalin in his veins, and the pounding of his heart nearly stifled him.

And the words having been said, he must, he knew, go very carefully now. He kept his face impassive, but his fingers were shaking as he moved his arm away from Poincelles' grip and turned his beer-mug a judicious ninety degrees on the grimed and splintery table. Though he neither liked nor trusted the Frenchman, he needed the help of another wizard and needed it desperately.

'You never have trusted them, have you?' went on the French occultist in his deep, beautiful voice. 'Captain von Rath, and Baldur, and Gall.'

'Well,' admitted Rhion, 'I must admit I was a little put off when I found out about the enemies of the Reich who were used for the drug experiments.'

Poincelles blinked, for one second actually looking surprised that this was what had bothered him. Then he quickly moulded his features into an expression of disgust and anger. 'Oh – Oh, yes!' He waved his cigar, trailing a ribbon of blue smoke. 'I was horrified as well, completely shocked – a ghastly business. I was furious when I heard, for of course I wasn't told about any of it until it was too late.' He smiled slyly and added, 'They don't exactly trust me, these Nazis.'

'Now, how could anyone distrust a man of such obvious virtue and probity?' Rhion made his blue eyes wide behind his glasses, and Poincelles grinned like a wolf with his stained teeth.

'Clever,' he smiled, and pinched Rhion's cheek. 'I like

a clever boy.' He cast a quick glance across the room at Horst, presently conversing crotch-to-crotch with the blonde barmaid. Like most Storm Troopers Horst didn't impress Rhion as being terribly bright, but it didn't pay to take chances. Lowering his voice, Poincelles went on, 'They don't trust me, but they needed my help in the rituals that went into the making of the Dark Well. They needed my power. I know von Rath has told you that none of us can be risked just now with the offensive on to create a Dark Well so that you can locate your home again – if he intends to send you home at all, ever. Myself, I doubt it.'

He laid his hand again on Rhion's wrist, the cigar smouldering between two fingers, and his dark eyes gleamed beneath the shelved hollows of his brows. 'My memory for matters of ritual is excellent. I can help you create another Dark Well.'

Rhion looked away, understanding now the nature of the proposition – understanding that with those words, Poincelles had in fact announced that he had no intention of helping him get home. Disappointment settled like a swallow of cold mercury in his chest as he realized the man was not to be trusted, not to be turned to for help.

He said nothing.

'For a price,' Poincelles went on.

Over by the bar there were fresh howls of laughter. A Waffen SS lieutenant in the grey uniform of the Kegenwald labour-camp was pitching pfennigs for an old derelict, a whiskery drunk who made his living selling papers and picking up trash, to crawl for. As the old man groped on hands and knees for the coins the other Troopers would kick them further and further out of his reach, like children tormenting a crippled dog. Horst whooped, 'Here's a drink for free!' and poured his whisky over the old man's head; old Johann sat up, grinning with a terrible combination of terror and fogged pleasure, with hope that this would be the worst that would happen, and lapped at the liquid running down his hair.

The barmaid Sara, who had returned with Poincelles' drink, bumped Rhion's shoulder playfully with her hip. 'No sense of humour, Professor?'

His mouth quirked dryly. 'I guess not.'

She looked down at him and some of the brittle quality eased from her face. 'Kurt will see they don't hurt him, you know,' she said in a quieter voice and nodded at the impassive barman. She shrugged her shoulders, oddly delicate above the jutting splendour of her breasts. In spite of the lines of cynicism and dissipation around her dark eyes Rhion realized she couldn't be more than twenty-two. 'It gives the boys a laugh. They don't mean any harm.'

Neither, supposed Rhion as the girl strolled away, had the guards in the Temple of Agon, the faceless servants of the Veiled God, who had pretended to light his oil-soaked beard on fire when Lord Esrex had had him imprisoned there.

He looked back to meet Poincelles' narrow, speculative eyes behind a haze of putrid smoke. 'What price?'

'I want you to teach me.'

Rhion gave his beer-mug another quarter-turn. 'I am teaching you,' he said quietly. 'I have been teaching you for over six weeks now, and aside from the fact that you now know spells that work in my world, and your technical knowledge is cleaner than it was, none of the four of you is any closer to making magic work than you were before I came. You know that.'

'I know that.' Poincelles leaned forward and the smell of his breath, drowned in whisky and cigar, was like the exhalation of a month-old grave. 'And I know also that you're keeping something back.'

Rhion kept his eyes on the beer-mug but his hands and feet turned perfectly cold.

The Frenchman chuckled throatily. 'My little friend, we

all keep something back.' He drained his whisky with a gulp, stood and shook back the limp swatch of hair from his forehead. Across the room Horst, engaged in buying a condom from the barman to augment the weekly barracks ration of one, hastily departed to fetch the car around. After a long moment Rhion stood up also, and followed the tall occultist shakily from the room.

If the man has to make one true statement in the entire night – which is not a bad average for Poincelles – thought Rhion as he climbed into the rear seat of the open Mercedes that waited for them in the harsh trapezoid of yellow electric light, *why does it have to be that one?*

For Poincelles was quite right. They all did keep something back.

What Poincelles had kept back in the course of the discussion was what von Rath and the others had been keeping back from the start: that the Dark Well had not, in fact, been destroyed.

Rhion had confirmed his suspicions a few weeks after the expedition to the Dancing Stones, as soon as his ability to use his scrying crystal had grown strong enough to get a clear image once more. Those weeks in between, those weeks of suspicion, of not knowing who was lying to him and when, were nothing he would care to go through again. He had known he was entirely at von Rath's mercy, for food and shelter and advice in this strange world – only during those weeks had he realized how much he'd felt comforted by the illusion that he was among friends.

He sighed, and shook his head, glancing sidelong at the tall man beside him as the car shot with its eerie speed along the forty kilometres of woods between Kegenwald village and Schloss Torweg. He still felt keenly the disappointment that had come over him when it had been clear that Poincelles had no intention of telling him that the Well still existed; the fact that the Germans were in the process of invading his erstwhile country evidently did not mean that the Frenchman opposed them in principle. Had that little charade tonight been for Poincelles' own purposes, he wondered, or at von Rath's instigation, to find out if Rhion knew more about magic than he'd taught them in the weeks since his recuperation?

In either case it made no odds. Poincelles was not to be trusted, and it left him in a horrible position, for he desperately needed the help of a wizard he could trust.

For Rhion, too, was keeping something back.

He had found – or thought he had found – the thing for which the wizards of the Occult Bureau had begged Jaldis to come here in the first place: the trick of making magic work in this magicless world.

The problem was that without the help of another wizard, bringing this about in order to get himself home would almost certainly kill him.

'Captain wants to see you,' reported the guard at the gate when the car pulled up and the electricity was turned off long enough for the gate to be opened. When the SS had taken over Schloss Torweg, in addition to erecting the fence and cutting down all the trees that surrounded the lodge itself, it had rigged floodlights to drench the grounds in a harsh white electrical glare. The sentry at the gate furthermore shined the beam of an electric torch – a flashlight, they called such things – into the back of the open car before passing it on through, presumably, Rhion thought, to assure himself that no 'enemies of the Reich' were hidden under the lap-rugs.

Von Rath was waiting for them in the library. The voices of Baldur and Gall were audible – arguing as usual – as Rhion and Poincelles ascended the wide, wood-panelled stairs.

'I still say that electricity must have *something* to do with the disappearance of m-magic! There is no d-documented, authenticated case of magical operancy – of the human will being converted to physical instrumentality – after the middle of the eighteenth century, and that was just when experiments with electricity were becoming p-popular. Benjamin Franklin . . .'

'Nonsense! Magic is a quality of the *vril*, the mystical power inherited by the Aryan Race from the men of Atlantis whom Manu, the last of the Atlantean Supermen, led across Europe to the secret fastnesses of Tibet. It is not electricity, but the slow race-pollution by mutants and Jews after the fall of the third moon that has robbed the race of its power. In Tibet the Hidden Masters and Unknown Supermen still hold this power . . .'

'And it's in Tibet that this c-curse of electricity does not exist!'

'Nor does any way of verifying the reports one hears of magic and Hidden Masters,' added Poincelles maliciously, lounging in the doorway.

Baldur looked up swiftly from a huge mass of notes, his weak, piggy eyes slitted with irritation and cocaine; Gall merely sniffed. 'That is the sort of argument one would expect from a Frenchman,' he remarked.

Von Rath, from the depths of his red leather armchair, raised a finger for quiet. Though the Schloss had been fitted with electricity thirty years ago the wizards – for varying reasons – avoided using it, and the library, like the Temple of Meditations in what had been the ballroom of the north wing and the workshop above it, was illuminated by candles. They made a soft halo of his ivory-pale hair, and caught sparks of molten gold in the silver buttons and collar-flashes of his black uniform as he leaned forward to speak.

'You've been listening to the news, I suppose,' he said, and Poincelles folded his long arms and grinned.

'Yes – it looks like the Luftwaffe's botched the job pretty thoroughly and let the English army get clean away.'

Baldur jerked to his feet furiously. 'The German Air

Forces are mo-more than capable of d-d-destroying those d-d-debased b-b-b . . .' Rhion knew from past outbursts that the youth's stutter was infinitely exacerbated both by anger and by cocaine, and the present combination was deadly. Poincelles' grin widened at the boy's blazing-eyed frustration and he was about to speak again when von Rath's soft, level voice cut him off.

'I've had a call from Himmler. The German Armies will invade England before the summer is out.'

'Of c-course we must,' declared Baldur, sitting clumsily down again and knocking a sheaf of his notes to the floor. 'The destiny of the Reich demands that all of Europe be ours,' he went on, rather thickly as he spoke while bending over to collect them. 'It is obvious that . . .'

'What is obvious,' said von Rath, with a quick sidelong glance at Rhion's impassive face, 'is that the Jews and Communists who run the government of America from behind the scenes aren't going to permit that country to mind its own business. If we don't have England secured for our own defences before they force the government into a declaration of war, the Americans will use it as a base to overrun us.'

When Rhion did not dispute this he turned to him more fully, his grey eyes grave in the deep shadows of his brows. 'Himmler was quite emphatic in his demand that we of the Occult Bureau have something to contribute to this final battle, something to tip the scales in our favour to resolve the conflict in Europe once and for all. And I believe Baldur may have arrived at a way to solve the problem of the raising of magical power.'

Young Twisselpeck sniffled and wiped his nose on his sleeve, then rooted around in his notes again. Rhion settled himself on the red leather hassock beside von Rath's chair, his mind still half preoccupied with the problem of how to gain the magical assistance he needed without giving Poincelles – the only thing resembling a maverick among the group – any information which could be used against him.

'My insight into this n-new line of reasoning,' Baldur began in his reedy tenor, 'goes back, I think, to Major Hagen's d-death . . .'

And for one cold, sickening instant Rhion thought, *They've guessed . . .*

The boy sniffled loudly and pushed his glasses more firmly into place on his nose. 'He d-died stepping into the Dark Well, you see. And it was only after that, as he was dying, that our spells reached out into the Void and got anywhere. It must have been his death which released the magic.'

They haven't guessed . . . thought Rhion, shaken with relief. They hadn't stumbled into the keystone of his own secret . . .

Then he realized what conclusion Baldur *had* stumbled into.

'Now in the Grimoire of Pope Leo, and d'Ehrliffe's *Culte des Goules*, and in any number of letters and diaries, there are reports of power being raised by drawing it out of a human being at d-death. We have partial accounts of the Blue Hummingbird Society of the Aztecs, and these tally closely with what we know of the rites practiced by the Adepts of the Shining C-Crystal in the sixteenth and seventeenth centuries . . .'

'No!' cried Rhion sharply, almost before he was aware he was speaking.

'*DON'T INTERRUPT ME!*' screamed the boy passionately. 'Everybody's always interrupting me . . . ! Here!' He fumbled in the notes, dropping papers all around him like a tree shedding leaves in a high wind. 'There are seven references in the Vatican letters, two in the communications of the Fuger banking-house, one in Nostradamus' third letter to the Viscountess de la Pore and in Bernal D-Diaz's account of . . .'

'I'm not arguing that you can't make magic from the energies released from the human psyche at death,' retorted Rhion, aware from the corner of his eye of the interest on the candlelit faces of Poincelles and Gall. 'But it's a damn dangerous thing to do and in my world there isn't a respectable wizard who'd try it . . . I take it you're not talking about using volunteers.'

'Of course not!' snapped Gall indignantly. 'The ancient Druids raised power from the sacrifice of prisoners of war! The spirits of the noblest of their foes . . .'

'Here!' Baldur straightened up, and thrust out a mass of references with trembling hands. 'Letter from Gustavus Dremmel to the Fugers, November of 1612. *B-By reliable witnesses these Adepts have been seen, by various rites and ceremonies involving the murder of the aforesaid wo-wo-women, to empower talismans which later enabled them to find hidden treasure, to drink poisons unscathed, to draw the love of both wo-wo-women and men* . . .'

'Well, that should interest you, at any rate,' remarked Poincelles *sotto voce*, studying his pointed fingernails.

'If we c-could discover what those rites were . . .'

'Is it truly so dangerous?' Von Rath crossed his knees, his tall boots gleaming like oil in the wavering light. 'You understand that we are willing to take the risk.'

YOU are willing . . . ?!? Rhion almost shouted at him. But there was nothing in those grave eyes that he could shout it to.

There was long silence, von Rath waiting politely for his answer and Rhion, struggling with shock and outrage, trying to come up with an argument against murder that the Nazi *would* credit. At length he said, 'You seem to think dropping dead like Hagen did is the only thing that will happen. You've never seen a magic field go septic. I've talked to people who have. I'm telling you: Don't do it.'

Down at his end of the table Jacobus Gall straightened his thin shoulders militantly and stroked his flowing silver beard. 'That is nonsense. On Witches Hill, in my dreams of ancient days, I saw the ancient priests cut the throats of their tribal enemies, pouring out the sacred blood of sacrifice to bring them victory . . .'

'Like you saw the Roman Legions surrounded and routed by their Teutonic foes in places the maps show to have been permanently underwater since the retreat of the last glacier?' retorted Poincelles, his black eyes glinting wickedly.

'You understand none of these things . . .'

'My friends . . .' The Frenchman raised his hands. 'We've gone to a great deal of trouble to bring in an expert as a consultant, and while I've got no objections on principle to slitting a few throats, I'd say that we listen when he says something is dangerous, because he does know more about this than we do. But it's up to you – do as you please.' And with that he pushed with his flat, bony shoulders against the doorframe and stood up straight, lighting a cigar as he strolled out of the room and down the electric brightness of the hall, the acrid whiff of smoke as disrespectful as the snap of fingers.

With a massive sniffle Baldur started to jerk to his feet to go after him, and von Rath waved him down again. 'I agree,' the young Captain said with a sigh, and rubbed the high bridge of his nose with his fingers, as if his eyes were suddenly weary even of the candlelight.

'That still doesn't give him the right . . .'

'Of course one doesn't need voluntary sacrifice!' declared Gall. 'That was a different matter entirely . . .'

'No.' Von Rath lowered his hand, and looked over at Rhion again. 'You're right. We do not know what might happen. But we must find something, some way out of this impasse, before the Americans decide to interfere in our struggle against England and its allies. We lost Eric . . . we cannot take another risk like that . . .'

'I'll search,' promised Baldur, bending down clumsily to

gather his notes again from where he'd dropped them on the floor. His hands were nervous and fidgety, his eyes flicking restlessly from von Rath's face to the shadows of the bookshelves, thick with ancient knowledge, that crowded the long room. 'The ancient societies performed the rites in safety. The p-proper rites, the correct means of making the sacrifices, have to be there . . . I'll find them for you, P-Paul . . . C-Captain . . .'

'Books.' Gall got contemptuously to his feet and shook back his snowy mane. 'Books are the refuge of those who need such things. It is by the purification of the body and the mind that the True Adept will come to an understanding of the *vril* within him . . .' He was still muttering as he left in Baldur's shuffling wake.

Von Rath expelled his breath in a sound of mingled amusement and exasperation, and got to his feet. 'Children,' he laughed, shaking his head. 'All of them – Jealous and quibbling and fractious. In the past six months I've acquired an enormous respect for my old nanny . . . Would you care for some cognac?' He crossed the room to a cabinet whose brass-grilled doors formed one of the few places in the wall not solidly paved in books. Rhion wondered where the Occult Bureau had collected so many, and according to von Rath, Himmler, the Bureau's head, had a library of his own three times this size.

The young Captain paused with his hand on the cabinet door. 'Or did you have enough of liquor among the camel-drivers?'

'Camel-drivers?' Rhion leaned back against the arm of the red leather chair, looking up at von Rath in the swimming halo of candlelight. Two minutes ago he'd been furious with outrage at this black-uniformed wizard's callous readiness to practice blood-sacrifice; for weeks he had lived with the knowledge that he was his jailor, that he was lying to him about the existence of the Dark Well and had lied from the moment Rhion had regained consciousness.

But the other side of him was genuine as well, the quiet courtesy, the soft-voiced charm, the gentleness with which he handled Baldur's nervous worship, and the homesickness which he had made clear he understood Rhion felt.

'*And some who went into the wilderness*,' quoted von Rath, returning with two fragile glass bubbles of henna-coloured liquor, '*and thirsted with the beasts of prey, merely did not want to sit around the cistern with the filthy camel-drivers*. Nietzsche. A wise man and a brilliant one – I'll have Baldur read him to you sometime, if your German isn't up to it yet, as a break from the *Malleus Maleficarum*. Do you still thirst, my friend?'

'For something that hasn't obviously come out of a cistern, yes.' Lacking a friend, the undeniable pleasure of the man's company was difficult to resist.

A smile of great sweetness momentarily swept the cold angel face. For a time he stood cradling the glass in his hands, his eyes like smoky opals gazing into a candle-lit middle-distance, his face in repose young and very sad.

'You understand what is at stake here?' he asked softly, after a long time in thought. His gaze returned to Rhion's, tiredness and old wounds in his eyes. 'It is not only victory over the English, you know; not only doing what our Leader demands that we do. It is the ability to do it that will be our victory, a victory over magic's true foes: a matter less simple. It is . . . vindication. Do you understand?'

Sitting on the hassock, bespectacled and unprepossessing, Rhion looked down into his glass for a moment, unwilling to admit how much he understood. 'I think so.'

'Since I was a boy,' the young wizard continued slowly, 'I have felt – I have *known* – that there had to be something else, something other than the sterile pragmatism of Freud, of Marx, and now of this man Einstein – Jews all, incidentally, but it goes deeper than that. Something . . . I don't know. And as the years went on and I kept looking, and there was nothing . . . Just the world closing in, and bleeding to death without even being aware of what it was losing, of what it had lost.' He stared for a time into the depths of his glass as if to scry there where the magic had gone. 'But it had died,' he said, very simply, his voice almost too low to hear.

'Eric said he had felt the same thing,' he went on after a time, and his eyes flinched shut for a moment in remembered pain. 'Eric was the first man I ever knew who had felt it. He and I . . .' He shook his head quickly.

'Without magical operancy – without the ability to transform the will into physical being – magic remains only a legend, and the fire that consumes me – that consumed us – is no more regarded by other men than a thousand similar crank curiosities, on par with phrenology and ginseng and that mediocre bureaucratic keyhole-listener Himmler's stupid attempts to locate the ancient races that are said to dwell in the hollow earth. And so it will remain, unless you and I can prove to them that it is . . . real.'

Rhion was silent, remembering again his first meeting with Jaldis on the bridge in the City of Circles. *Are you searching for secrets . . . ?* Remembering the sensation of ice-locked bone breaking open inside him, when he had first called fire from cold wood. Remembering the aching relief of knowing he was not mad.

'How old were you,' asked von Rath quietly, 'when you first understood that you were a wizard?'

'Twelve,' said Rhion slowly. 'I mean, I didn't understand what it was then, but I knew I was different.'

'I was fourteen.' His voice sank almost to a whisper, as if he spoke, not to another man, but to the quiet, gold-haired boy he saw across all that gulf of years. 'Immured in a military academy in Gross-Lichterfelde, learning parade drill and classical Latin while outside a pound of sausage was going for a million marks . . . The fact that you had any choice in the matter makes me so envious that I could kill you.'

Choice. Had there really ever been any? Tally had asked him once why he'd become a wizard, if he had known what it would mean: that he could not marry the woman he loved to desperation, that he could not admit that the children she bore were his for fear that they would be killed. That he and Jaldis had spent most of their ten years together as outcasts, living on the love-spells he concocted for sale to people who despised them. He remembered the growing fear of what he was, pain so awful he had wanted to kill himself, hollowness and fear of what he sensed was growing in his dreams. Then the worse pain of knowing what it would cost him to pursue those dreams.

I tried so damn hard to be good, he had said to her.

And for Paul von Rath there hadn't even been that choice. Only the disreputable shadow-world of cranks and covens and charlatans, of theosophists and hollow-earthers and those who sought Atlantis or Shangri-La, infinitely less thinkable for the only child of Prussian aristocrats than a career as a wizard had been for the son of the wealthiest banker in the City of Circles.

'I'm sorry,' was all he could say.

Von Rath shook his head, and smiled again. 'No, it is I who should apologize to you, for becoming maudlin in my cups. I like you, Rhion, and I truly regret that you are here in my world against your will . . . and I know it is against your will. I know you miss your own world, your loved ones – do not think that I don't know.'

Rhion was silent, remembering Tally – remembering his sons – remembering his home in the Drowned Lands – with a poignance that shook him to his bones.

Von Rath hesitated, struggling briefly with some inner decision, then said, 'I promise you that as soon as the war with England is won we shall . . . we shall open another Dark Well, no matter what the risk to us, and search through it to find the wizards of your home.' His voice was wistful at the thought of a world in which his dream of magic was reality. 'But for the time being we must serve destiny. Yours – mine – the Reich's.' He sighed softly. 'Heil Hitler.' His hand barely sketched the salute.

'Heil Hitler.' Setting his glass down quietly, Rhion returned the gesture, then rose and stepped out into the brassy electric glare of the hall.

5

In the darkness of his attic bedroom Rhion fetched the hard wooden chair from the corner and put it beneath a certain spot in the rafters. Through the wide windows opposite the foot of his iron-framed bed shone a broad rectangle of chalky arclight from the yard below, making eerie runic shadows of the bare ceiling-beams with their trailing curtains of cobweb. Through the open window he could smell the pine-woods, and the drift of smoke from the cigarette of the guard patrolling the fence; the peep of crickets and frogs, the occasional cry of a night-bird, came to him like comforting echoes of a life he'd once known.

Standing on the chair, he stretched to reach the rafter, edging along it with his fingers until his hand encountered a small wash-leather bag. Thrusting this in his pocket, he climbed carefully down, moved the chair to another place, and climbed up again. This time he brought forth a packet wrapped in several sheets of the *Volkische Beobachter*, a packet that weighed heavily in his hand.

He put the chair back in its corner. The room had been searched three times in the seven weeks he'd occupied it, the last occasion less than a week ago.

Rhion had originally asked for the small south attic room – a servant's, in some former era – because the rest of the Schloss was permeated by the smell of cigarettes. But he'd found that from its big window he could see the light that fell from the window of von Rath's study to the bare ground at the side of the lodge, and thus tell when the young Captain went to bed.

The glow was there now, a citreous smudge on the hard-packed earth below him and to his left. Von Rath must have retired there from the library after their cognac together, to meditate and to write up the endless reports demanded by the Occult Bureau of their daily experiments – with magic, with electricity, with talismans, with pendulums, with anything they or any writer before them had ever been able to think of that might possibly hold a key to the return of magic to this thaumaturgically silent world. But even as Rhion watched, the glow dimmed as von Rath snuffed the candles one by one.

He'd be asleep in an hour, thought Rhion. Resting his forehead on the sill, he closed his eyes, and reached down through the ancient lodge with a trained mage's deep, half-meditative senses. He heard Gall's sonorous murmur as he recited Runic mantras before retiring, heard the jittery crackle of parchment and pen from Baldur's room and the youth's endless muttering and sniffling. Farther down he heard the tinny staccato of the radio in the guards' watchroom at the foot of the main stairs, repeating names he did not understand: Leutze, the Scheldt, Dunkirk. A guard spoke. Newspaper rattled.

Too early. Much too early.

Turning, Rhion crossed the room to the rough plank wall behind the head of his bed. In a tin box – for there were mice in the attics – behind a loose board he kept a stash of coffee-beans. He'd had a beer and a healthy jolt of cognac, and had never had much head for liquor. Eating half-a-dozen coffee-beans made him slightly sick to his stomach, but at least he wouldn't fall asleep.

Then sitting on the edge of the bed, he took up the newspaper-wrapped package and unfolded it, and looked at the thing that lay within it in the dark.

And thought about the nature of magic.

The thing in his hands was a metal ring, roughly the diameter of his palm, formed of strips of iron of varying thicknesses: some meteor-iron, some drawn of iron mixed with salt or with certain other impurities, all carefully pilfered over the course of the last few weeks from the supplies requisitioned from the Occult Bureau. Twisted around the iron were an equal number of strips of the purest silver obtainable, silver so pure it was soft, each strip scribbled with a hair-fine line of runes. Between the iron and the silver five crystals were twined, in a specific shape Rhion hoped he'd calculated properly – he'd never made one of these for the purposes he planned for this, and wasn't entirely sure whether his theoretical estimates would stand up in reality. He had been weeks assembling this, laboriously raising what little power he could in this world, whispering spells as he worked in the laboratory in the dead of night – hoping, as he worked, that von Rath wouldn't guess what was going on and wondering fearfully what would happen to him if he did guess. There was still a great deal Rhion did not know about the Nazis, and he didn't want to find out.

And the making of the ring, he reflected with an odd, cold feeling behind his breastbone, was the easy part.

Since he had come to this world, Rhion had given a great deal of thought to magic: what had happened to it here, why it had failed, how it might be brought back. As the Torweg Group had found out very early, power of a sort could still be raised through the rites of their morning meditations. But it cost an enormous amount of energy to raise even the smallest power, and it was never enough to do much with, even had they been able to convert it to physical instrumentality. The power levels of this world had sunk, as water sinks back into the earth in drought, but it was still there, like the slow silvery pulse of the ley-lines which he had felt through the wheels of the car as they'd driven along the ancient road from the village back to the Schloss.

What had vanished utterly from this world was the point of conversion between power and operationality.

And that, Rhion thought, turning the iron circle over in his hand, was why he and Jaldis would have died in the Void but for Eric Hagen stepping to his death in the Dark Well.

Baldur had almost guessed it tonight. But, his mind running on the ancient cults and societies which he so endlessly studied, the efforts of past wizards to solve the problem of waning levels of power and not the conversion-point between power and magic, the youth had seen only Hagen's death, and not the fact that for one second, before the Void had killed him, Hagen had been working his spells *outside the confines of this world.* For those few moments, he had been standing in the Void itself.

And there was magic in the Void.

Every mythological Fire-Bringer Rhion had ever heard of, when faced with the problem of Darkness, of Night, had had to steal fire from a source. And so, Rhion thought, must it be here. He hadn't the faintest idea how to create a Dark Well, for Jaldis, fearing Rhion's connection with the Ladies of the Moon, had never taught his student the mechanics of the multiplicity of Universes. But in his pursuit of information about water-goblins, Rhion had manufactured Spiracles of Air, devices which, charged with the element of air and then bound upon his forehead, had held that element around him while he walked the muddy bottoms of the Drowned Lands' endless ponds and canals, seeking the goblins in their forests of ribbonweed and cattail-root.

He was theoretically acquainted with the spells by which Spiracles of Heat could be charged to keep their wielder surrounded by warmth in bitterest cold, or Spiracles of Daylight which would permit, within their small field of brightness, the use of spells which ordinarily only had power during the hours when the sun was in the sky. Whether a Spiracle could be charged so that it would hold the essence of the Void's magic about itself he didn't know, for it had never to his knowledge been tried.

Theoretically, once he had a localized field of magic from the Spiracle there was no reason why he had to be anywhere near the Dark Well to open a gate through the Void – all that it required was magic. Practically, of course, unless he wanted to perish in the airless cold chaos between Universes, he needed the Dark Well, needed it to establish contact with the Archmage Shavus and the other Morkensik wizards so that they could draw him through the Void, back to his own world.

Not to mention the fact, he thought drily, though his stomach was sinking with terror and dread, that he would have to be standing *in the Void* to charge the Spiracle.

And that meant the Dark Well.

That meant doing the thing which had taken Eric Hagen's life.

And that brought him back to Poincelles, and the conversation in the tavern tonight.

Rhion got to his feet, and prowled restlessly back to the window. In the acid glare he could see the black-uniformed sentry, rifle on shoulder, walking the perimeter of the fence. He needed help, needed another wizard to ground him, hold him anchored to this world, while he charged the Spiracle with the Void's wild magic, but the thought of putting his life in Auguste Poincelles' nicotine-yellowed hands terrified him. For all von Rath's gentle charm, it was perfectly possible that the SS Captain had put Poincelles up to making a pass at Rhion tonight in the tavern to test his intentions – to see whether he really *was* holding something back.

He didn't know, and the uncertainty, the dreadful sensation of never knowing who to trust and whether his instincts were correct or not, was profoundly disorienting and exhausting.

'And anyhow,' he muttered dourly, climbing back on the chair and replacing the Spiracle in its hiding-place in the rafters, 'the whole question is pretty academic until I can *find* the goddam Dark Well.'

He returned to the window, and checked the stars.

Shortly after midnight. By the glow in the east above the spiky black of the tree-clothed hills, the moon would be rising soon, wan and cold in its last quarter. First dawn was some three hours away. From the drawer in the dresser where he kept his old brown robes Rhion fished the wristwatch von Rath had given him, and after a moment's study confirmed the timepiece's accuracy, at least as far as he understood the way time was reckoned here.

He put the watch back in the drawer. Though he recognized the ingeniousness of the mechanism he seldom wore it, chiefly from annoyance at the obsession these people had with the correct time. But every now and then, when he handled the intricate golden lozenge, he sensed upon it a vague psychometric residue of uncleanness which repelled him but which he could not quite place. Other things in the Schloss had it, too, odd things: the plates of a certain pattern in the big, sunny dining-room in the south wing; the radio in the guards' watchroom; some of the books in the library. He wasn't quite sure what was wrong with them – and indeed, it was something he sensed only intermittently. But he didn't like it.

He listened now, and the lodge was quiet.

His stockinged feet made no sound on the bare floorboards as he crossed first the darkness of his own room, then the vast, dusty spaces of the main attic. The descending stair debouched close to von Rath's study and bedroom, and from the main stair to the lower floor he heard the soft crackle of the radio still. By now he knew enough German to follow the broadcast, though not most of Chancellor Hitler's speeches. Now and then a Storm Trooper's voice would speak, desultory and half-asleep. In his long nights of quiet listening Rhion had learned that inside duty generally involved three sentries who made a patrol or two of the ground floor in between long periods of sitting around the watchroom smoking, reading cheap tabloids like *Der Sturmer*, and comparing notes about the barmaids at The

Woodsman's Horn. Sometimes one or another of the barmaids was smuggled in, to be taken by a dozen of the men in turn in the deserted kitchen or laundry in the south wing – occasionally he heard Poincelles' voice on those nights.

But tonight there was only the desultory conversation of men who have said everything they had to say months ago. He waited until he heard all three voices, then, barely daring to breathe, he stole soundlessly down the stairs and slipped like a shadow past the watchroom door. There was, he knew, a backstairs leading down to the kitchen in the south wing, but its upper end was in the little dressing-room attached to the empty chamber where the Dark Well had allegedly been drawn – the false Dark Well, to convince him that it had been destroyed – and that chamber was next to von Rath's. In any case he would still have had to pass the watchroom door to reach his destination on the ground floor, the old ballroom in the north wing which Hagen and von Rath, upon taking possession of the Schloss the previous fall, had converted into a Temple for occult rites.

Its door lay at the end of a wide oak-panelled hallway, and like all the Torweg wizards, Rhion had a key. As he relocked the door behind him Rhion could feel a sort of afterglow of power whispering around him in the utter darkness of the vast, velvet-draped room, the residue of morning after morning of ritual work and occult meditation, of painfully tiny quantities of power raised and dispersed. Beneath that, he dimly sensed the even fainter silvery tide of the ley-line that ran below.

In years past the site of the Schloss had enjoyed a peculiar reputation – it was on this spot, Rhion guessed, crossing the worn parquet floor to the altar, here where the ley-line bisected the mound, that the ancient god had originally been worshipped, and the witches had later held their sabbats. He settled himself cross-legged against the altar-stone, a six-foot slab of black granite draped, like the walls, in black. Upon the altar a second drape hid the ritual implements of cup, sword, dagger and thurifer. Coming here to scry was somewhat riskier than doing it in his room, but far quicker; in his room it sometimes took him as much as an hour of intense concentration before he was able to see anything in the crystal.

He lit the stub of candle he had to force himself to remember to carry in his pocket these days – thanking all the gods of wizardry that von Rath had seen fit to board up all the windows of this room and no light would show to the guards in the compound outside – and, taking the scrying-crystal from its bag, angled its facets to the light.

The Dark Well was still there, wherever 'there' was. It was quiescent, no more than a half-seen shadow in the absolute blackness of that other, windowless room. Studying it with his wizard's sight through the medium of the crystal Rhion estimated the size and proportions of that chamber: thirty feet wide and immensely long, the low ceiling propped with heavy beams, the uneven floor paved with the rough, damp stone he recalled. In fact, he reflected wryly, it was of a size and shape and composition to be directly beneath the ballroom/Temple where he now sat. Ceiling, beams, and floor were as far as he could tell identical to those in the portions of the Schloss's cellars that he had entered.

'I'm probably sitting directly on top of the goddam thing,' he muttered to himself, closing his hand over the crystal, the image dying in the darkness of his palm. The stairs leading down into the cellar were kept double padlocked, and it was a good guess that the only keys were in the hands of von Rath and of the SS lieutenant in charge of the guards. On one of his trips down there – unobtrusively supervised by von Rath – he had gained the impression that the portion of the cellar which should lie under the north wing was blocked off by a wall, the wall piled high with boxes. That meant a concealed door, undoubtedly locked as well.

He cursed himself mildly for never having taken up Shavus on the old Archmage's offer to teach him to pick locks. The only way he could get into that cellar was by magic . . . and of course he would not be able to use magic until he could get into the cellar and charge the Spiracle. If his spells worked. And if the charging didn't kill him.

And unless he had another wizard to help him, it probably would.

Always, like an ox at the millstone, he came around to that again. To the Dark Well, to Poincelles . . . to trust.

And to his instinct that stepping into the Void alone and unassisted would be safer than trusting the French occultist with the smallest information regarding his real intentions and abilities.

He sighed, pushed up his glasses to rub his aching eyes. Twenty days until the Summer Solstice. Twenty days until he could – with luck – raise enough power from the turning-point of the Universe to open a gap in the Void so Shavus and the others could pull him through.

If he could get in touch with them. If he could find another wizard he could trust. If . . .

He shook his head, and opening his hand, looked down into the crystal again.

In it he saw the sea. Black waves ran up onto beaches in darkness, beaches crowded with men whose faces and bodies were outlined in the sudden, terrible glare of yellow-white explosions – beaches littered with wrecked equipment, hideously strewn with tangled corpses in the shell-holed sand. Men standing knee-deep in water, or huddled in shallow holes they'd scooped out in the sand, desperate for even the illusion of shelter. A long quay extended into the sea, longer than Rhion had ever seen, even in the great harbour of Nerriok, and this, too, was jammed with men. They stood quiet, without shoving, while death spat and whistled around them, burning fragments of metal leaving red streams of fire in the dark. Men waiting. And far out over the water to the west, the gold pinprick of a ship's light gleamed suddenly in the black.

Perhaps, Rhion thought wearily, closing his hand over the crystal again, he should be glad. These men would be the spiritual brothers of those who had blinded and mutilated Jaldis, who looked with distrust upon magic and all that it stood for, who could not see beyond their own pockets and their own bellies and who wanted to turn the world into the image of their own greedy, limited minds.

Perhaps he was simply weak. Because between the Reich's obsessive racism, self-righteous closed-mindedness and casual arrogance, and these corrupt and nameless servants of the mechanist English, there didn't seem to be a lot to choose. The best thing he could do, Rhion thought, would be simply to go home.

If he could.

'Useless!' Paul von Rath thrust from him the body of the dead white rat and the pan of poisoned sugar-water in which a seven-carat garnet gleamed mockingly, a talisman of protection inscribed with the coloured sigil of the interlaced runes of Eohl, Boerc, and Ehwis. 'Nothing – it did nothing at all!'

'I d-don't understand,' Baldur stammered, his weak, bulging eyes peering from rat to gem and back again with baffled outrage. 'The rite we used to charge this talisman came from Johan Weyer's own private journal! There was no way he would have recorded a false rite, or – or changed details. I made every allowance, every transposition of the k-key words and phrases according to the best redaction we possess of the Dyzan manuscript . . .'

Rhion, hitching back the sleeves of the long white robe in which the wizards all worked in their meditations and occult experiments, crossed the big laboratory and picked the jewel from its glass petrie-dish. He wiped the poisoned solution off with a lab towel, and turned the gem a few times in his palm. 'It's charged, all right.'

'Of c-course it's charged!' Baldur whirled to paw through the stack of notes on the near-by bench as if for documentation of the fact, nearly knocking over a beaker of the strychnine distillate they'd used to test the poison-spell's effectiveness. 'The formula was impeccable, the source absolutely certain . . . !'

'Give me that.' Gall, in his flowing robe and shoulder-length white hair looking very much like the ancient priests of whom he was always having visions, almost snatched the talisman from Rhion's hand. From a little labelled box on the laboratory table he removed a smooth stone tied to a silken string – this he held over the gem, watching its random movement with pale, intolerant eyes.

'No one is blaming you, Baldur,' said von Rath gently.

'But nothing can have gone wrong! The p-power you raised in this morning's rite was enormous, stupendous . . .'

'It was certainly greater than it has been,' remarked Rhion, retreating to the corner of the lab. Like the Temple immediately below it, the room which they had fitted up as a wizards-kitchen had had all of its windows boarded over – a pointless affectation from a thaumaturgical point of view but one which had allowed Rhion to work on the Spiracle late at night unobserved by the guards in the yard. The reflections of the kerosene lamps which illuminated the room in preference to electricity gilded the young Captain's fair hair almost to the colour of honey, and glinted on the steel swastika he wore on a chain about his neck. On shelves around what had at one time been a drawing-room on the second floor of the north wing an assortment of jars, boxes, and packets contained everything Rhion had ever heard of necessary to the making of talismans: iron, silver, gold and copper of various purities, salts and rare earths, every sort of herb and wood imaginable, gems, crystals both cut and uncut, parchments and strange inks. There was a small forge, crucible, and press, even an icebox containing samples of the blood of various animals and birds. And yes, he thought, smiling to remember the first time Tally had come to the rooms he'd shared with Jaldis, even a mummified baby alligator . . .

And for all the good it had done them so far, the shelves might just as well have been stocked with twigs and pebbles, like children playing 'store'.

Baldur snuffled, and wiped his nose on the sleeve of his robe. 'Maybe the formulae are p-poison-specific? It could explain . . .'

'Nonsense,' retorted Gall coldly, returning his pendulum to its box. 'I have said before, it is a wizard's sublime faith in himself which conquers poison.'

'It c-can't be! Then a talisman of protection wouldn't protect someone who didn't know what it was.'

'Precisely. It is only the illuminatus, the initiate, the pure, who can draw upon the *vril* . . .'

They were bickering acrimoniously as they opened the door, going from the lamplit gloom of the workroom to the sun-drenched morning brilliance of the upstairs hall outside.

Von Rath sighed, and rubbed a hand over his face. 'I didn't truly expect it to work,' he said. 'And Jacobus would tell me that was why it didn't, of course. But Rhion, we have done everything, tried everything . . . You said the ritual of meditation this morning raised more power than ever before, but you know and I know it wasn't enough, wasn't nearly enough. Not even with every allowance you made for the position of the stars, the phase of the moon . . . Nothing. And with our army going into France . . .'

He paused, seeing the flicker of expression that passed across Rhion's eyes. 'Yes,' he said quietly, 'I know what you would be saying. But truly, war as it is fought now – as it is fought in this world – is the province of the first attacker. Had we not taken the initiative this spring – and it was they who first attacked us a year ago – we would have been driven, as we now drive them.'

'Yes,' lied Rhion, turning away to mop the spilled poison where it had slopped from the dish. 'Yes, I understand that.'

Von Rath's voice was low and urgent. 'Please understand also that the war is nothing – it is, for us, only a means to an end. It is our last chance – the last chance of wizardry – to demonstrate our powers, to regain our powers with the backing of the government. That is why we *must* succeed at what we do here.'

He picked up the garnet talisman, returned it to a box of failed experiments, of talismans – properly made, properly charged – which simply did not work. The lamplight flashed across the jewel's central facet, and caught on a scratch on one side, as if the stone had been prised from a setting. A good-quality gem, thought Rhion, far better than most wizards in his own world could afford for talismanic work unless they had an extremely rich patron. He could understand von Rath's concern – without the support of the government, the group would never have been able to work under these ideal conditions.

But it crossed his mind to wonder, suddenly, where the Occult Bureau got the gems it sent them.

'Rhion,' said von Rath, closing the box and turning with one slender hand still on its lid, 'you haven't been – coming down to the laboratory to work at night, have you?'

Rhion felt himself get cold. In anything but the golden kerosene light he knew von Rath could have seen him pale. 'I did once or twice when I first got back on my feet, but not lately.' He could feel sweat start under his hair and beard.

Von Rath frowned. 'No, this would have been the night before last. I thought the laboratory was disturbed a little yesterday morning, as if it had been used.'

While part of Rhion breathed a prayer of gratitude that he'd always been meticulous about returning things to rights after his nights of work – so von Rath *did* notice things like that – another part of him was able to put genuine puzzlement in his voice as he said, 'The night before last?' He'd finished the Spiracle last week, and had been catching up on lost sleep ever since.

'Yes. And Baldur also seems to think that his room has been searched, though he has become . . . a little paranoid.'

'I'm told cocaine does that.' Rhion remembered his own conviction that his room had been searched.

Von Rath's gem-pure lips tightened; then he sighed. 'He takes it to continue his researches, you know,' he said quietly. 'There is a truly formidable amount of material to get through – diaries, letters, court cases dating back to the fifteenth century . . . I keep a close eye on how much he takes.'

If you're his only source, thought Rhion. But, anxious to turn the Captain's thoughts away from who might have been using the laboratory at night, he suggested, 'Do you think the problem of raising power might be with the composition of this group?' He pushed his glasses more firmly up onto the bridge of his nose, followed von Rath as the younger wizard started moving about the laboratory, turning down the kerosene lamps until their wicks snuffed to nothing and the shadows hovered down about them like the fall of night.

'According to Gall, and to what Baldur's read to me, the old covens seem to have been much larger than ours. Five men isn't a lot, even if they are mageborn and more or less trained. Magic can be raised from the emotional or psychic or life-force energies of human beings, as Baldur pointed out last night. But blood-sacrifice, either voluntary or involuntary, isn't the only way of doing that, you know. Perhaps if you worked with twice as many men as this, and an equal number of women, you'd get better results.'

Von Rath chuckled wearily, and turned from replacing a lamp-chimney, shadows of irony flickering in his tired eyes. 'My dear Rhion, have you any concept of the contortions Eric had to undertake to gather even this group? To find men whose loyalty was as reliable as their potential for power, and who were even willing to work as a group?' He shook his head with a half-comic smile, and led the way out into the sunlit upstairs hall. 'And as for women . . .' The gesture of his hand, as dismissive as a shrug, raised the hackles on Rhion's neck. 'Women have no place in magic.'

'*WHAT*?!'

'Not true magic.' *Surely you must know that*, said the flex of his voice, as Rhion stared at him, too dumbfounded even to feel outrage. 'Their emotions are uncontrollable – surely you've tried to have a reasonable argument with a woman? – and their intellects are on the average less than men's. That's been scientifically proven. Oh, there are one or two exceptions . . .'

'I've met enough exceptions to constitute a rule, personally.'

But the little smile and the small, amused shake of his head were impenetrable. It was not, Rhion saw, a matter even for serious argument, as if Rhion had suggested petitioning the help of the kitchen cat.

Von Rath gave him a boyish half-grin, a man-to-man expression of complicity. 'It's hard to explain, but *you* know. It's one of those things that a true man *knows* by intuition. And at bottom, magic *is* a masculine trait. A woman's emotionalism and woolly-mindedness would only delay us, always supposing we could *find* a woman with even a tenth the level of power of a man.'

Given the intolerable pressures a mageborn girl would have faced in Germany, Rhion hadn't been terribly surprised that the Torweg group was entirely masculine. And yet from Poincelles he knew that there were and always had been women occultists. But not, it appeared, in Nazi Germany.

'And in any case,' von Rath went on, turning down the hallway towards his rooms, 'the question at the moment is an academic one. We must find a way to raise power – we must find a way to convert that power to operationality – and we must find them soon. Only through those – only through the victory that such power will bring – can magic be returned to this world.'

'And did little Ratty die?' Cigar in hand, Poincelles looked around from the doorway of the watchroom at the foot of the stairs. Beyond him Rhion – who had changed once more into his usual fatigue-pants and a brown army-shirt – could see that the room had been curtained to dimness, and the portable screen set up on which cinema films were displayed; the black-and-white images of newsreels of the war in the west flickered across it like jiggling ghosts.

'Did you have money on it living?'

The Frenchman grinned broadly. After the dawn ritual of meditation to raise power he hadn't even bothered to attend the experiment with the talisman. He'd changed out of his robe back into the same loud tweed trousers and jacket he'd had on last night – the same shirt and underclothing by the smell of it. 'Boche idiots,' he said.

Past Poincelles' angular shoulder the fluttering images of huge war-machines appeared on the screen in the gloom of the watchroom, monstrous metal beetles rumbling down the cobbled streets of towns with their turret-guns swinging watchfully back and forth; then with dreamlike quickness transformed to images of men – Rhion did not have enough German unassisted by spells of understanding to catch who they were – being herded out of a building somewhere, herded into boxcars with their hands above their heads. The Ministry of Propaganda sent these newsreels, these moving pictures, out regularly to the SS, even as it sent whatever American cinema-films they wanted to see . . . they had taught Rhion more about the German Reich than von Rath had counted on, and most of all that the Reich was proud enough of those fearsome columns of marching men, those lines of resistant 'slave peoples' being shot for intransigence, to have them thus immortalized and displayed.

Baldur, clattering down the steps behind Rhion in his own ill-fitting and dirty trousers and rumpled shirt, paused and snapped spitefully, 'For a man whose country will be the next to fall to the victorious German armies you have no room to talk!' He pointed into the watchroom, where columns of armoured trucks and marching men flickered across the screen. 'You know where they're headed now? France! Your cowardly government is on the run and they'll be in Paris before the week is out!'

Poincelles only raised the back of his fist up under one hairy nostril and snorted in a mime of inhaling cocaine. Baldur's fleshy neck turned bright red and, wheeling, the youth lumbered away to the dining-room, tripping on a corner of the hall rug as he went.

'Does he think I'm going to weep when the krauts march into La Belle Paris?' The Frenchman's skeletal face grimaced with scorn. 'I am a citizen of the world, my friend, born and reborn down through generations. What is this war to me? What is France to me? I was high mage of the court of Kublai Khan, who conjured for him the eldritch secrets of the Aklo and the Hyperborean races. Before that, in the dark years of glory in the seventh century, I conjured for Pope Leo those things which would have caused his name to be stricken from the pages of history, had any known of them but I. In the black abysses of time I was High Priest of the Cult of Thoth for the Pharaoh Ptah-Hotep, who was accursed in the Red Land and the Black Land for the things that he caused to be done . . .'

He took the cigar from his mouth and blew a stinking stream of blue smoke into the sunlit air. In the watchroom Rhion heard the men give a great delighted cheer; on the screen he saw a country road, jammed with people – old men pushing bicycles laden with household goods, women hurrying, stumbling, dragging frightened children by the hand, old cars manoeuvring slowly through the choking throng of people fleeing with whatever they could carry . . .

And from the sky the war-planes descended, lean and deadly with the twisted sun-cross emblazoned on their silver sides, opening fire with their machine-guns on the fleeing civilians below. The guards in the watchroom cheered and whooped at the sight of the women running for shelter, dropping all they carried and catching up their terrified children, men scrambling like scared sheep into the bushes alongside the road, faces twisted in silent cries.

Rhion felt sick and cold. Beside him, Poincelles' voice went on, 'That Baldur, he puts on airs because he wants to be in the SS, to be one of Himmler's darlings. Himmler, huh! A mediocrity, a crank – using the most powerful and dangerous elite the world has ever known to serve tea in white gloves at Hitler's garden parties. Like using a Damascus blade to cut eclairs! Himmler claims he was the Emperor Henry the Fowler in his former life – pah! I knew Henry the Fowler! I served in his court in the great days of the Dark Ages, in the wars against the Magyars and the Slavs, and Himmler is no more his reincarnation than you are. I learn from them, yes . . .' He waved the cigar in the direction of the sun-washed dining-room, where Baldur's voice could be heard querulously demanding more sugar for his coffee, '. . . as I learn from you. But all this is merely a step along the way.'

The black, knowing eyes gleamed and he reached out to pat Rhion's cheek, the pointed fingernails pricking through his beard like dirty claws. 'I am in this for myself, my little friend. You really ought to trust me.'

On the newsreel screen the war-planes made another strafing-run at the crowded road. A man scrambled out of one of the cars and bolted for the roadside; his foot tangled in the wheel-spokes of a fallen bicycle and for a moment he tugged frantically to free it, desperate, horrified, as the double line of bullets ripsawed the road, bursting a crate of chickens ten feet from him in an explosion of blood and feathers, then swept on to cut him in half. The guards catcalled and shouted facetious advice; Horst Eisler half-turned in his wooden chair, called out 'Rhion, you got to come in and see this . . . !'

And the wizard born and reborn, mage to the court of Kublai Khan and High Priest of the grey cult of Thoth in the silent deeps of time, strolled off down the hall towards the dining-room to get his breakfast, trailing a line of bluish stench in his wake.

6

From his window in the darkness, Rhion watched the cadaverous shadow of Poincelles cross the yard to the wire. The sentry had been loitering on the spot, smoking, for some minutes now – it was this which had first caught Rhion's attention. Now he saw the Frenchman hand the Storm Trooper something, and, reaching out with his mageborn senses, heard him say, '. . . maybe all night. Square the next man, will you?'

'*Jawohl*, mate.' The guard saluted. 'Heil Hitler.' And he strolled away lighting a cigarette, his shadow fawning about his feet like a cat as he passed beneath the floodlight.

Fascinating. Rhion scratched his beard and leaned an elbow on the sill. With his room unlit behind him there was little danger of being seen as long as he kept back far enough to prevent the glare from catching on his glasses.

His first thought, that Poincelles was out to do some courting in the woods, was banished by the rather large satchel the French mage carried. Services rendered were usually paid for more neatly than that. Besides, he knew the man generally got his boots waxed, as the saying went, in the village, or had Horst Eisler bring one of the barmaids up to the Schloss itself.

When, that morning, von Rath had mentioned that someone had been working in the laboratory, Rhion had immediately suspected Poincelles. Deeply interested, he continued to watch as the Frenchman unshipped two short lengths of wood from the satchel's carrier-straps and used them to prop up the lowest of the three electrified strands of the fence. That particular stretch, he realized, at the southeast corner of the compound, was not only hidden from the rest of the yard by the corner of the SS barracks, but was the closest the fence came to the surrounding woods. Though the fence followed the contours of the ground closely, at that point, where a little saddle of land connected the Schloss's mound with the rising ground of the hills behind it, there was a shallow dip where, with the aid of props to keep from touching the wire, a man could get under.

Poincelles removed the sticks, picked up his satchel, and, brushing dust and old pine-needles from his tweed jacket, strode quickly into the woods.

The guard had not reappeared around the corner of the barracks.

Rhion tucked his boots beneath his arm and padded in khaki-stockinged feet down the darkness of the attic stairs.

In the upstairs hall he turned softly left along the corridor past von Rath's study door. It was shut, and through it he could hear the murmur of von Rath's voice, and Baldur's eager whine. It was only an hour or so after sunset, barely full-dark, and far earlier than he would have liked to try his maiden excursion outside the wire. Beside the big chamber where the Dark Well had allegedly been drawn there was what had once been a dressing-room, with a bank of closets along one wall and a discreet door leading to the backstairs and so down to the disused kitchen on the ground floor. The backstairs was narrow and smelled powerfully of mildew and mice, and was choked with bales of old newspapers and bundled-up banknotes, several million marks which had been printed in the crazy time fifteen or twenty years ago when, according to von Rath, this world's credit-paper money had lost its value through fiscal policies that Rhion's banker father wouldn't have countenanced on the worst day he ever had. Rhion emerged into the old kitchen, and crossed it to what had been the laundry beyond, also dusty and disused, for both cooking and washing were done for them in the SS barracks. He cautiously unbolted the outside door which looked out onto the deserted corner of the yard facing the hills.

It was still empty. Poincelles had paid the guards well.

Retracing his steps quickly to the kitchen Rhion collected a couple of short logs from the bottom of the old wood-box. Then he pulled on his boots, took a deep breath, and stepped outside.

No one challenged him. There was no guard in sight. Behind him, in the shadow of the ornamental turrets, the russet curtains of von Rath's study were shut.

Rhion crossed to the fence, propped the wire as he had seen Poincelles do, and, taking meticulous care not to touch it, slithered under.

He was free.

Free of money, food, and identity papers, he reminded himself firmly as he removed the logs and carried them to the shadows of the woods, all the while suppressing the impulse to leap in the air, to shout, to dance; without the slightest idea of where he was or any convincing account of his business. *Wonderful – I'll be shot as a British spy before von Rath has time to figure out what's taking me so long to come down to breakfast.*

But free nonetheless. The cool thin smells of pine and fern were headier than von Rath's cognac. He stashed the logs where he could easily find them again, and set off after Poincelles.

Had Poincelles been able to see in the dark, as the wizards of Rhion's world could, or had he been in the slightest bit used to travelling cross-country, Rhion would never have been able to track him. But the Frenchman was a city creature, a denizen of those bizarre places of which Rhion had only heard tales – Paris, Vienna, Berlin – and moved clumsily, leaving a trail of crushed fern, broken saplings, and footprints mashed in the thick scented carpet of fallen needles underfoot that Rhion, after seven years among the island thickets of the Drowned Lands, could have followed, he thought disgustedly, if he *hadn't* been night-sighted. He overtook his quarry easily and moved along, an unobtrusive brown shadow in the denser gloom, while the gawky form ploughed through pockets of waist-deep bracken and wild ivy, scrambled over fallen trunks or the granite boulders that dotted the steeply-rising ground.

At length they reached the road, neglected and overgrown but still passable through the hills. Rhion recognized the road-cutting in which they'd been stopped, that first excursion to Witches Hill, by the work-party of slave-labourers from the Kegenwald camp. Now on level ground Poincelles strode on more swiftly, jacket flapping and the frail starlight gleaming on his greasy hair, trailing an odour of cigar-smoke and sweat. Atop the cut bank in the green-black gloom beneath the trees, Rhion followed. On the other side of the hills – perhaps three miles' swift walk – Poincelles turned off to the right down a weed-choked cart-track, and in time through the straight black of the pine-trunks Rhion glimpsed stars above a cleared meadow, and the dark outlines of a barn. Part of the old estate farm of Schloss Torweg, he guessed, which had fallen to ruin in the crazy-money years, as Baldur had said. The meadow, like that around Witches Hill, was thickly overgrown and mostly turned to a sour and spongy swamp as the ponds and lakelets which dotted the landscape had spread and silted. The path which led to the barn was nearly invisible under saplings of dogwood and elder, and Poincelles, burdened still with his satchel and puffing heavily now, fought his way through them like a man in a jungle, making enough noise to startle the incessant peeping of the marsh-frogs to offended silence.

He was clearly headed for the barn. Arms folded, Rhion waited in the tepid shadows of a thicket of young maples on the other side of the road. In time the crickets recommenced their cries, the frogs taking up the bass-line, and after a time, a nightingale added a comment in a liquid, hesitant alto. Only after several minutes had passed and Rhion was certain he would be unobserved as he crossed the relatively open meadow did he move on.

Not a light showed from the barn, but as he approached it Rhion scented incense, thick and over-sweet, on the warm spring air. A moment later the deep, soaring bass of Poincelles' voice sounded from within, and Rhion glimpsed a sliver of golden light high up one side of the wooden structure that told him it must be curtained within.

They all kept something back, Poincelles had said.

The Frenchman had created a second Temple.

A secret one, for his own use, though it was good odds he'd pilfered the incense – and whatever else had gone into its construction – from Occult Bureau supplies, even as Rhion had stolen the components of the Spiracle. Which could explain, Rhion thought, the disturbance of the lab. Coming closer Rhion heard the Frenchman's words more clearly. He was chanting in Latin, a language in which many of the ancient books at the Schloss were written, and which, like German or any other tongue, he could understand when Baldur read aloud to him from the unknown alphabets. By the rise and fall of his voice the Frenchman was clearly speaking a magical rite of some kind, not unlike the ones the Torweg wizards used to raise power for their experiments and exercises.

'. . . invoke and conjure thee, O Spirit Marbas . . . by Baralamensis, Baldachiensis, Paumachie, Apoloresedes and the most potent princes Genio, Liachide, Ministers of the Tartarean Seat . . . forthwith appear and show thyself unto me, here before this circle . . . manifest that which I desire . . .'

The voice rolled impressively over the nonsense names of the invocation of demons as Rhion pressed himself to the door. Peering through the cracks he saw that heavy sheets or curtains of some dark material swathed the inside of the structure, whose rotting wooden walls were chinked everywhere with split or missing boards. Finding a thin line of light between two of these curtains he reached through a gap in the wall and fingered them gently apart, angling his eye to the opening.

In the centre of huge interior darkness Poincelles stood, naked and hands uplifted, piebald with the upside-down shadows of seven black candles arranged around him in a wide ring. With his wrinkled and sagging buttocks jiggling at every jerk of his upraised arms, his voice booming out the names of imaginary devils to re-echo in the harlequin of rafter-shadows overhead and his head jerking every now and then to flip his hanging forelock out of his eyes, he should have been ridiculous, but he wasn't. 'Asmodeus I conjure thee; Beelzebub I conjure thee, king of the east, a mighty king, come without tarrying, fulfil my desires . . .'

Standing in the cool outer darkness, Rhion sensed a kind of power being raised, dim and inchoate as all power was in this diminished world but present nevertheless. It reminded him strongly of some of the slimier rites of the renegade sects of the Blood-Mages, with its stink of irresponsibility, of greediness, of contempt for everything but self – contempt even for the demons it purported to summon. Before Poincelles a woman lay on the altar beneath an inverted pentacle, naked also, with a chalice between her thighs. Her head lay pointing away from Rhion, her face obscured by the blackness of the altar's shadow, but the candle-light caught a curl of cinnabar hair lying over a breast like a rose-tipped silk pillow. Beneath the cloying incense the muskier pong of hashish lay thick in the air.

'Give me what I ask!' Poincelles switched to French in his excitement, threw his sinewy arms wide. 'Give me and me only the keys which those men are seeking! Give me influence over the wizard Rhion! Place him in my unbreakable power, bind him to me, deliver him into my hand so that he cannot do other than my bidding. Make him teach me and me alone his wisdom! Cause him to trust me, lure him into my power, blind his eyes and soothe his fears . . .'

His voice cracking with self-induced frenzy, the lean shape stepped forward between the girl's knees and lifted the chalice to the pentacle which flickered like molten silver as the vast shadow of his arms passed across it. 'Oh Asmodeus, Lord of the Mortal Flesh! Beelzebub, Lord of this World! We offer this rite to you, this magic raised out of the flesh that You created, this sacred lingam raised in your honour . . .'

So much for Poincelles. Disgusted, Rhion stepped back and let the curtain's tiny chink fall shut. *Strictly speaking that should be a virgin, but that must be another one of those wartime shortages they keep telling us about, like ersatz coffee*. He hoped Poincelles was paying her plenty for her trouble.

But knowing Poincelles, the money was probably coming ultimately out of von Rath's pocket.

As he waded back through the damp weeds towards the road he heard the girl cry out in rapture, but something in the timbre of that outburst of ecstasy told him it was faked. He shook his head. His father had always said you got what you paid for.

But it left him definitely back at square one, facing the prospect of stepping into the Dark Well alone. 'Always supposing I can get at the damn thing,' he added dryly, stepping out of the shadows of the hedges onto the rough surface of the main road.

The moon was rising, edging every pine-tip, every weed-stem, every sunken pond in milky silver. The night breathed with its singing. Curious, thought Rhion, that even the spirits seemed to have deserted this world. The luminous mirrors of pond and marsh should have been alive with nixies and water-goblins, the long grasses aflicker with the half-seen ectoplasmic wings of the faes, the brown, scurrying feet of lobs. He would almost have welcomed the ghost-cold shadow of an errant grim. Had those bodiless life-essences, like the power in the ley-lines, sunk to hibernation in the ground?

He turned back, and studied the sagging black roof-line of Poincelles' barn. Tonight's expedition was far from wasted, he thought. He'd found another place where power of a sort had been raised – enough of it would cling so that the place could serve as a beacon to Shavus, perhaps enough to give him a fighting chance of opening a gate, if coupled with the power of the upcoming solstice midnight, though he would have preferred a place situated on a ley.

But that thought led to another. It was still early, he thought, looking at the stars. Instead of turning left, up the hill towards the Schloss, he moved on down the road, following its curve back up the other side of the hills.

The moon stood clear over the distant eastern ridge when he reached Witches Hill. Soaked in the pallid light, the Dancing Stones seemed to shine with the wan limmerance of forgotten spells as Rhion waded up the hill in the dew-heavy grass. Exhausted as he had been on his first visit there with Gall and Baldur, Rhion had sensed no magic in the place. But now it seemed that for once Gall had been right. The magic that had been there once was not dead, only deeply asleep.

It was obvious to him now which of the two shapeless stones lying on the ground had been the altar of the ancient rites. Sitting on its higher end, Rhion pressed his palms to the agepitted surface, and felt it cold and wet with dew. Rain and sun had almost rinsed away whatever had been there, dimmed it beyond what could be detected when the sun was in the sky. But in the sleeping hours between midnight and dawn an echo of it whispered, like the memory of voices after the singers have gone.

Closing his eyes, he let his mind sink deep.

It had all been a long time ago. Very little was left: the faded impression of a drum tapping, the memory of other moons. There had been blood – a lot of blood, animal and human. Some of it mixed with semen: a virgin's first experience, the psychic charge still glittering faint as pyrite crystals deep in the fabric of the stone; elsewhere the deeper and more terrible charges of power drawn from pain and death. Power had been raised here, again and again, from that ancient triad of sex, death, and sacrifice, sometimes unwilling and at other times freely given, the magic woven of that power now lost in the turning winds of time.

But its residue remained.

Rhion took off his glasses, bent forward until his face touched the stone. Unlike Gall – or unlike what Gall claimed – he had no visions of eldritch priests, no cinema-show re-enactments of the past. But the stone now felt warm to his palms. Like unheard music he felt the power whisper along the leys that crossed beneath the altar, drawing power from the net of silver paths that covered the earth, dispersing it back to the world's four corners again.

After a long time he came back to himself, lying face-down on the altar, all his muscles aching, his hair and the back of his khaki uniform-shirt damp with sweat. He groped around for his glasses and put them on again, to see Orion's belt hanging low in the east. He muttered, '*Verflucht*!' and stumbled to his feet, knees trembling. It was an hour's walk back to the Schloss and after last night's efforts at scrying he was achingly short of sleep.

On his way down the hill he paused, and looked back at the Dancing Stones. They seemed to have sunk back in on themselves, returned to being no more than three massive, almost shapeless slabs of rock, half-hidden by the long grass of the neglected hill.

If any living magic remained in them it was too dim, too deeply-buried, for his own attenuated powers to raise. But at Solstice-tide it would draw on the powers of the leys, and that would help. And it was bright enough to serve as a beacon, provided he could get word to Shavus about what to look for in the dark of the Void.

He turned, and headed back to his prison again.

He reached it an hour before the early summer dawn. Watching from the edge of the woods he saw no sign of a guard. 'At least Poincelles got his money's worth out of *something* tonight,' he muttered, as he set up his props and wriggled under the fence. On the walk back he'd felt sick from the strain of concentration; now that had passed, and he was ravenously hungry. As he slipped through the laundry-room door his mind was chiefly occupied with ways to sneak a few hours of unnoticed sleep during the day.

Then he saw that the door through into the old kitchen was open. He'd closed it behind him – he knew he had. *A guard*? he wondered, and then his eye lighted on two pieces of wood, suspiciously similar to the short logs still tucked beneath his arm, lying against the wall where the shadows were thickest. If he hadn't been night-sighted he wouldn't have seen them at all.

Poincelles would have bolted the outside door when he came in. So would a guard who found it open.

God damn it.

So someone else was poking about the Schloss at night. Undoubtedly the same someone who had searched Baldur's room, perhaps who had searched his own.

He set down one of his props silently, and hefted the longer one club-wise in his left hand. He wondered if he should summon a guard to take care of the intruder, if there was an intruder, but realized in the next instant that it would only lead to questions about what *he* was doing wandering around at two in the morning with dew-soaked trouser-legs and pine-needles sticking to his boots.

Pushing his glasses firmly up onto the bridge of his nose, he tiptoed to the half-open door.

Like the disused laundry-room, the old kitchen was dark and almost empty, containing little but old counters and a big stone sink. The door opened to his left. Taking a deep breath, he sprang forward and slammed it back fast and hard.

Unfortunately the unknown intruder was hiding under a counter to the right of the door, and an arm was around his neck and jerking him backwards before he could react to the swish of trouser-cloth and the stink of ingrained tobacco-smoke behind him.

He twisted against the grip, fighting for balance. Tearing pain sliced his upper arm; he flailed with the club, wrenching and thrashing, and half-felt, half-heard a knife go clattering at the same moment an elbow smashed him full-force across the face, sending his glasses spinning off sideways as he crashed back against the sharp edge of the sink. Before he could get his breath a fist caught him in the solar plexus with an impact like a club.

For an instant as he crumpled over he remembered the knife and thought, *This isn't fair* . . . Then swift footfalls retreated and left him lying at the foot of the sink wondering if his lungs would ever work again. He had just come to the conclusion that they wouldn't when other footfalls, distant but purposeful in the opposite direction, warned him that the SS was on its way.

'Just what I need,' he gasped, lurching painfully to his feet. 'Protection.' For a moment he thought he was going to vomit; the small of his back where he'd slammed into the sink hurt more than he'd thought possible, and he could feel the side of his face beginning to puff up. His right arm hurt, but he could move it, and he felt blood soaking into his shirt-sleeve. It took him a nerve-racking minute to find what was left of his glasses, twisted metal frames and shards of glass scattered broadcast over the flagstone floor. With the heavy footsteps coming nearer he swept the bits into a black corner beneath the sink, and there he found the knife, a folding pocket-blade honed to a deadly edge and still bloody. He shoved it and his bent glasses-frame in his pocket and, holding his bleeding arm, ducked into the nearest closet and pulled the door to.

Through the cracks he could see the beam of an electric flashlight pass to and fro, then fade as the Storm Trooper crossed the room. Cramped in the mildew-smelling darkness, Rhion considered remaining where he was till the man had checked the laundry-room and departed for good, but realized that he'd find the outer door open and, if he was worth his pay – which half the SS weren't, but Rhion didn't feel like betting his liberty on it – would come back and make a thorough search.

With swift silence and an earnest prayer to whatever gods were in charge of magic in this world that he wouldn't encounter an unscheduled wall or chair in his myopic flight, Rhion slipped from the cupboard and ducked through the door into the hall. He made it back to his attic room without further mishap, trembling with nerves, shock, hunger, and exhaustion, just as the wide window was turning dove-grey with the first light of summer dawn.

7

'Fools.' The slant of the morning sunlight, bright and hard as crystal in these high, arid foothills, splashed into the shadows of the Archmage Shavus' cloak-hood and made his blue eyes glint like aquamarine. At one time the great southeastern gate of the city of Bragenmere had overlooked a wide stretch of open ground, between the walls and the broken slopes leading down to the plains and the marshes of the sluggish Kairn; but in the years of peace since Dinar of Prinagos' usurpation of the Dukedom a cattle-market had grown up there, and then a produce-market of those who did not want to cart their wares through the narrow streets to the market-courts within the city, and lately a number of fair new houses had been built by merchants eager for more spacious quarters than were available within the walls. Even at this hour, barely after sunrise, the gate-square was bustling with drovers and butchers and greengrocers, the warm summery air choking with yellow dust and thick with vendors' cries. 'Imbeciles, both of them!'

Tallisett of Mere, every inch the Duke's daughter despite the plain green gown she'd pulled on that morning when driven from her bed by strange, craving dreams, folded her arms and looked across at the cloaked and hooded old man who had been waiting for her on the steps of the fountain by the gate. 'You didn't seriously think Rhion would let poor old Jaldis walk into the Dark Well by himself, did you?'

'I seriously thought Jaldis would have had the sense not to go without my help.'

'Nonsense,' said the Gray Lady, from her seat on the worn sandstone steps at the old man's side. She looked up at him and Tally, shaking back the long braids of her malt-brown hair. 'You spoke to Jaldis – you know how he was about his dream of helping the wizards of the world without magic . . .'

'And *you're* the one who spoke to our little partridge Rhion just before they left,' countered the Archmage. 'You could have forbidden him to go, and without him Jaldis wouldn't have been able to . . .'

'I think you're wrong, my friend,' said the quiet voice of the third hooded form on the steps, a tall, thin man leaning on a long black bow of horn and steel – Gyzan the Archer, greatest of the Blood-Mages. 'Jaldis would have gone with or without his pupil to help, and how would Rhion have stopped him? He wasn't that powerful a mage, you know . . .'

'He still should have done something,' snapped Shavus irritably, and glanced back at Tally. 'And *you* might have done something, missy, to keep them both out of trouble, instead of letting them lose themselves, perhaps for good, at a time when the Order of the Morkensik Wizards needs all its strength.'

'And we others don't?' inquired the Lady tartly. 'As I've heard it the rumours of a conspiracy among wizards speaks now of one Order, now of another. Vyla of Wellhaven says the Earl has banished all the Hand-Prickers from the In Islands, but in Killay it was Filborglas they arrested . . .'

'Oh, Filborglas.' With a scornful wave Shavus dismissed the Archmage of the Black Ebiatics. 'His creditors were behind *that* arrest, most like.'

'I would not be certain of that,' said Gyzan. 'There has been unrest everywhere, like a pervasive malaise. In every city of the Forty Realms one sees posters and broadsides denouncing wizards and workers of magic, depicting us as seducers, liars and thieves. Even those people who have spoken with us, who know the untruth, are uneasy . . .'

Tally was silent, thinking about her own coming out to

the market this morning. Last night at dinner in her father's hall there had been strawberries for the last course, cool and heartbreakingly sweet, and all night, it seemed to her, she had dreamed of them, dreamed of wanting more. Shortly before dawn the unreasonable conviction had grown upon her that she could find more strawberries like those in the market outside the gates – she no longer even recalled the train of reasoning which had led her to this conclusion – but the craving had grown, in the pre-dawn darkness, to obsession. Perhaps had she slept in the same room with her husband, Marc of Erralswan, that lazy young nobleman would have talked her out of it, but they had never shared a bed, having married to scotch the scandal of her affair with Rhion. In any case Marc was God knew where with God knew what woman . . .

At last, unable to stand the desperation any longer, Tally had risen, dressed in her plainest gown, and ridden down to the market by the gates. Only to be met by Shavus, Gyzan, and the Gray Lady of Sligo, and to come to the realization that the strawberries, and the dream-inspired yearning, had been part of a spell to bring her outside the gates to meet them.

And despite all the years she had known Rhion, despite her friendship for his master Jaldis and her understanding of their wizardry, her first emotion had been one of extreme resentment, of violation. They had tinkered with her freedom, tampered with the secret chambers of her dreams.

And she understood suddenly how easy it would be, to fan this kind of distrust to consuming flame.

'That was why we called you here, Tally,' said the Gray Lady gently, almost as if she had read her mind – or at least, Tally thought wryly, her expression. 'To ask you if it is safe to be seen entering Bragenmere – to ask how things stand with your father the Duke. And so that it would not be seen that you had had a message from us, if it so befell that it is not.'

'Of course it's still safe,' said Tally, a little uneasily. 'Father has been under pressure from a number of people – merchants, and the priesthood of Darova, and especially the priests of Agon – to ban wizards from the Realm, but he's never gone back from his stand that they do no more harm than apothecaries or knifesmiths or rope-spinners or anyone else whose wares can cause harm . . . or, he'll add, for that matter, priests and lawyers. The rest of it he says is all silly rumours . . .'

'Silly rumours,' murmured Gyzan, his scarred hands shifting on the smooth shaft of the bow. His hairless, ugly face broke into a grin. 'I like that.'

'Like the silly rumour at the turn of the spring that a Blood-Mage's spells were responsible for the latest seizures suffered by the High Queen's son?' demanded Shavus, his pale eyes glinting under the coarse shelf of his brows. 'That was when the Queen locked Gyzan up, though no complaint was ever made and no trial would have been held . . . nobody even knew where that rumour had started, any more than they know who's been putting up those broadsides and posters.'

'Was that what happened?' Tally remembered vividly the cold of that bitter spring night, standing in the black shadows of the gateway watching the procession of masks bob away into rain and mist, while she huddled in her ash-coloured cloak, waiting for a man who never came. She still remembered the leaden awfulness of hearing the tower clock strike midnight, and knowing that Rhion was gone.

Rhion was gone.

'But why would you have done such a thing?' she asked, turning to Gyzan. 'That's what those rumours never say, is why. You aren't even in the employ of one of the Lords . . .'

'People believe anything of wizards,' returned Shavus dourly. 'The Earl of March believes I can fly – that I just travel horseback, when I can afford it, to confuse people.

Silly bastard. They call the Lady Nessa "Serpentlady" because her patron the Earl of Dun's got it through his thick skull that she has a snake with ruby eyes and couples with it to get her power. Your father's been a good friend to us, missy, but these days with rumour spreading like bindweed, it pays to take precautions, that's all . . .'

From the gates nearby there was a sharp clattering of hooves; Tally turned, startled, to see a small group of riders emerge, bound for a day's hunting. She glimpsed her father, tall and broad-shouldered in his red leather doublet and plumed cap, and his fair, fragile, pretty second wife; saw her husband Marc, like a bright bird of paradise in green, flirting already with one of her stepmother's ladies; and near beside them, her sister Damson, corsetted brutally into yards of plum-coloured brocade and plastered with jewels. With her rode her husband Esrex, pale, cold, and slender, and looking like he detested the whole business – of their son, Dinias, heir to the Dukedom from which her father had ousted Esrex' grandfather, there was no sign. Probably he was having another bout of chest pain and wheezing, thought Tally, trying to summon up sympathy for the boy in spite of his thoroughly unpleasant personality. She noted that her own son – Rhion's son – six years old and rosy and fierce as a lion-cub, had somehow finagled his way onto the saddlebow of one of the huntsmen, and shook her head.

Beside her she was aware of Shavus' gesture, a slight tracing of runes in the air with his fingers; though Damson turned her head their way Tally saw her sister's bulging grey eyes pass over them unseeing.

And for all she had said about her father's support of wizards, about how safe it would be for them to enter Bragenmere, she was glad the old man had surrounded them with the thin scrim of spells that had prevented Esrex and Damson from seeing her in the company of mages.

She sighed, and turned back to them. 'They should be

back a few hours after noon – it's too hot to be hunting after then,' she said. 'Father put Jaldis' rooms under seal when Jaldis went away, and asked me if Rhion had gone with him – I think to make sure Jaldis hadn't gone alone. Esrex has been after him to destroy the contents of those rooms, and to burn the books Jaldis left with him, but Esrex has always hated Rhion and Jaldis and is out to impress the priests of Agon.'

'And as far as you know, the Dark Well's still up in that loft of his?'

'As far as I know.' Tally reached forward, and helped the Lady of the Moon get to her feet. The matter must be serious, she thought, for she had never heard of the Gray Lady leaving the Drowned Lands in all the years Rhion had been Scribe there. 'I know Father will let you up there . . .'

'Good,' grunted the Archmage. His blue eyes grew grave, losing that cynical sharpness as they met hers once more. 'For I'll tell you the truth, missy – there's a smell in the air that I don't like. I tried to talk Jaldis out of going to that other world of his, saying wizardry here would need as much help as he claims it does there, and he wouldn't listen. But now I think things are serious enough – with the spies of Agon everywhere, and strange rumours going about – that it's time I contacted Jaldis and our little Rhion and brought them back, whatever they may feel about their other world. And I've a feeling we're going to need all the help we can get.'

8

'I never liked the idea of you staying in the attics.' Von Rath handed Rhion a chunk of raw beef and frowned down at him severely. 'Now you see what happens?'

'It was my own fault.' The meat was cold on the gruesomely swollen flesh. A glance at the mirror had showed him the whole area had turned purplish-black. 'And I'd rather fall down the stairs once than wake up every morning with a headache from the cigarette smoke in the rest of the house.' Rhion leaned back against the iron spindles of the bedframe and shut his other eye, hoping his explanation had covered all the physical evidence and that the sentry hadn't seen fit to report the unlocked door of the laundry-room.

'I shall speak to the men . . .'

Rhion waved his free hand irritably. 'No! They think I'm a lunatic already, for Christ's sake. The last thing I need is for the guards to have a grudge against me for keeping them from smoking in the lodge.'

Von Rath frowned. Rhion guessed the concern in his eyes was genuine, but mixed with it was a Prussian officer's almost disbelieving indignation that his orders might not be obeyed. 'They would not dare . . .'

'They would.' He cocked one nearsighted blue eye up at the tall black figure standing over him. 'Ordinary troopers have ways of getting back at people who cause them trouble. It's something I don't want to deal with. Besides, you'd have to tear out the panelling and burn every rug and curtain in the house to get rid of the smell. Don't worry about it. I'll be fine.'

'You are not "fine".' Von Rath folded his arms and

looked down at the little wizard with an expression of exasperated affection. 'I have not noticed any smell of tobacco, though I am not a smoker myself, but I will take your word for it. I have sent for Dr Weineke from the labour-camp at Kegenwald. She should be here this afternoon to do something about getting you new eyeglasses. All right?'

'All right.' The knife-cut on the back of his right arm hurt damnably under a clumsily improvised dressing. Though shallow, it would take twice as long to heal unstitched and leave an appalling scar, but Rhion could think of no way to work that into an explanation of a fall down the stairs. Fortunately he was left-handed, and the arm's stiffness could, with luck, pass unnoticed. 'Thank you.'

Curious, he thought, as von Rath's footfalls retreated across the attic and creaked, with a slight vibration, down the narrow stairs, how the young SS wizard was equally capable of such consideration and charm, and of that calm arrogance, that close-minded assumption of his own rights at the expense of everyone whom he considered less than himself. It was, Rhion had found, one of the things that lay at the heart of Nazism, along with a paranoid sense of persecution by imperfectly identified forces – and one of the things that reminded him most of the masked followers of the cult of Agon, the Eclipsed Sun.

Only here the mask that hid the follower from himself was subtler, not concealing the face, but changing it as it was perceived by others and by the face's owner. An illusion, if you would – an illusion of altered perception.

Yet another of those things, he thought wryly – like horseless vehicles and flying machines, like artificial light and the ability to talk across great distances – that was magic without magic: magic without the disciplines and limitations that all mages learned.

He shut his eyes against the thin white afternoon light, and wondered just how much of what he had said von Rath believed, and whether he should dig his boots from their hiding-place beneath the bed and clean the pine-needles off them – wondered for all of five seconds before he dropped into a heavy and exhausted sleep.

He woke, late and suddenly in the afternoon, from a confused dream about the Dancing Stones. Tallisett had been there, sitting on the altar-stone in the old green gown she sometimes wore, her unbraided hair a wheaten cloak stirred by the faint night winds. Though he'd been far away in the deep grass of the meadow he could somehow see her face, calm and serene and a little sad, and past her shoulder saw the looming darkness of a shape, and the glint of cold starlight on a blade. The Gray Lady, he thought dimly, remembering the sacrifice of the Equinox . . . the blood black upon stone in starlight, the calling-down of power. Frightened, he'd started to run, weeds pulling at his knees and his boots sucking in the heavy mud, stumbling, calling out her name, knowing he must reach the place by midnight and that midnight was near.

But when he'd got there she was gone. Only the stones remained, and on the altar-stone, like a long puddle of ink in the darkness, lay a pool of blood. His chest hurt from running and he stood over the stone, fighting for breath, while all around him the whisper of crickets and tree-toads murmured in the meadow below.

A terrible sense of *déjà vu* overwhelmed him, as if he had been here before – as if he knew what must happen here. He could feel magic rising up through the hill, radiating from the stones, the earth, the turning wheel of the universe, fragmenting out along the ley-lines to the farthest corners of this magicless earth and back again to the place where he stood at the crossing of the leys. Then faint and very close, as if the unseen musician stood at his elbow, a flute began to play. He looked around and saw no one. But in the chancy glimmer of the summer starlight, slow and ponderous and infinitely graceful, the Stones began to dance.

He woke staring at the ceiling-rafters, the music of that ancient dance fading from his mind. He tried to hold it, to call back the shape of the tune, but it slipped away – in the yard below his window a sentry called out a joke to some crony about why Hitler held his hat in front of him while reviewing military parades, and the music slipped away and was gone.

Stiff and aching, Rhion rolled from the bed. Though it hurt to move he fished out his boots and laboriously cleaned them, using rags torn from the bloodied shirt. Fortunately it was one of four or five identical Wehrmacht hand-me-downs and unlikely to be missed. He'd already torn off part of it to fashion a bandage and swabs for the alcohol he'd pilfered from the workroom downstairs; he started to rip off another piece, and, as the effort pulled agonizingly at his injured arm, he fished from his pocket the knife he'd picked up in the kitchen last night.

It was a folding clasp-knife of the kind many people in his own world carried, but contained in its handle of old yellow ivory several blades instead of just one, blades of varying sizes and types. The longest had been recently sharpened to a deadly edge; the second was smaller, of a convenient size to carve feathers into pens, had these people done such a thing. Pens here were metal tubes which either held ink or more usually sputtered it broadcast over documents, hands, and shirt-pockets. The third blade seemed to be a punch, the fourth a corkscrew, the fifth a short, flat-tipped slip of metal Rhion could guess no use for but which was bent and scratched as if it had, in fact, been used. He cut the shirt apart, folded it carefully, and hid it behind the loose board with his coffee-beans. Then he returned to sit cross-legged on the end of the bed, back propped against the iron-barred footboard, the knife gripped lightly in his hands.

He closed his eyes and sank into meditation, feeling the smoothness and age of the ivory, the coldness of the tiny silver pins that held it to the body of the clasp, the curious, hard lightness of the steel, while his mind probed into the fabric of the tool itself, as it had probed into the stone last night.

Dimly he became aware of the smoke-stench and racket of The Woodsman's Horn, the dirty songs and the stinks of tobacco, men's bodies, spilled beer. Overlying it he felt the charge of the perceptions of the one who had held the knife, bitter red rage, disgust, hatred – a poisoned hatred of men, of self, of Germany. *A woman*, he realized, a little surprised – one of the barmaids almost certainly. The pungence of sex clouded all surface impressions, messy, dirty, and dangerous, a thing to be got through quickly, a tool to be used as men were all tools to be used . . .

For what? He probed deeper, feeling the texture of that rage. Violent, despairing, contemptuous . . . but not hopeless. A moving anger. Moving towards a goal.

Searching. Searching this house.

Searching for what?

He slowed his breathing still more, deepening his trance. He sank past the images of greedy, fumbling hands and obscene laughter, of smutty songs and the smell of incense – *incense*? – seeking what lay in the deeper shadows beyond.

A man. Age and wisdom, or at least what were perceived as such . . . And beyond those perceptions, overlain by all else, he became aware of the man himself. Long ago this had been his knife. Then sharply, distantly, Rhion saw a grey-bearded man using this knife – yes, to carve feathers into pens like a civilized human being. To write . . . To write . . .

(*magic*.)

??!?!!

'Rhion?'

The touch of a hand on his shoulder broke him out of his trance with a gasp and he nearly cried out as his startled jerk wrenched every bruise and ache and cut. Von Rath caught his arm – fortunately the left one – to steady him, and Rhion stared up at him, sweat springing out on his face, for a moment not recognizing who or where he was.

'Are you all right?'

'Uh – yeah,' he managed to say, breathless with the shocked disorientation of being brought cold out of a deep trance. His hands were shaking as he fumbled the knife back into his pocket. 'Fine. Just – just give me a minute.'

Von Rath stepped back, clearly puzzled. Shutting his eyes Rhion tried to gather what remained of the trance back into his mind to close it off, but fragments of his consciousness seemed to be floating everywhere around him in a cloud, and his head throbbed painfully. 'I did knock.' Von Rath's voice was apologetic and concerned, grinding disorientingly into his consciousness. 'It is not the time for meditations . . .'

'Oops,' grinned Rhion shakily. 'I've been looking all over for the piece of paper with the meditation schedule on it . . . Never mind,' he added, seeing von Rath's baffled expression. 'Joke. Very small joke.' And one that would be lost on a German anyway. He inhaled deeply a few more times, then gave it up as a bad job. In time his head would clear, certainly after he slept again, which didn't sound like such a bad idea. He finger-combed back the thick curls of his hair. 'What is it?'

'Dr Weineke is here. For your eyeglasses.'

Dr Weineke was a cold-faced woman of forty or so whom Rhion hated on sight. Having been startled from deep meditation he was far more conscious than usual of the auras that clung to things and people, and in her voice, and her hands when she touched his face, he felt an evil terrifying in its impersonality. The place she had come from had left a smell upon her soul, like the ubiquitous stench of cigarettes that permeated the ugly female version of the SS uniform she wore.

She examined his eyes in the dining-room, a long and rather rustic hall with heavy beams and what was obviously intended to be a Gothic fireplace at one end. Wide windows looked out onto the south end of the compound yard, facing the garages. Beyond the wire, molten patches of late sunlight lay halfway up the rusty coarseness of the pine-trunks, and gleamed far-off on a pond away among the trees. Poincelles, Horst, and an older SS Trooper named Deiter were drinking coffee at the far end of one of the several long tables that occupied the room, Poincelles in his booming voice listing every rival magician, former in-law, and disapproving scholastic colleague he knew in Paris and just what he hoped the Gestapo – the Secret Political Police – would do to them.

'It will take at least ten days for the dispensary to fill this prescription,' Dr Weineke said as she put away the last of her small glass sample lenses and jotted a note on a piece of paper. 'Perhaps much longer, with the demands of the troops in the field.' She gave a cursory glance to the bruise on Rhion's face, and made a small disapproving noise with her tongue. Then she turned to von Rath, who sat on the table nearby like a schoolboy with his feet on the seat of a chair. 'Knowing the importance of the Professor's work I took the liberty of bringing an assortment of eyeglasses which might serve him in the interim.'

'How very clever of you!' Von Rath's smile, like his words, were something he'd obviously learned in a manners class, gracious and warm for all they weren't genuine. Weineke coloured up like a girl as she reached under the table and brought up a cardboard carton, which she set on the table beside Rhion. It was half-full of pairs of eyeglasses.

'Try them on,' she invited in what she evidently considered a genial voice. 'One will surely be close enough to allow you to continue your so-valuable labours.'

Rhion put his hand into the box, and nearly threw up with shock.

The psychic impact was as if he'd unsuspectingly plunged

his arm into acid. Yet at the same time what was in the box – the dim miasma floating over those neat, insectile frames and dust-covered lenses – was ephemeral, gone even as he jerked his hand out, sweating and grey-lipped and sick. He glanced quickly to see if von Rath and Weineke had noticed, but they were talking together, the SS doctor dimpling under the young mage's adroit courtesy as if his words were a glass of cognac. If she'd known how she would have smiled.

Hands shaking, sweat standing cold on his face, Rhion looked back at the box. For a moment it seemed to him that those flat, folded shapes of metal and glass were the skeletons of men, stacked like cordwood for burning, sunken eyes sealed shut and mouths opened in a congealed scream of uncomprehending despair.

He blinked. The vision disappeared.

'Where did you get these?'

Weineke glanced over at him with a clinical little frown; von Rath, too, looked worried at the sudden whiteness around his mouth. The doctor said, 'They were confiscated from political prisoners, criminals, enemies of the Reich. Is there something wrong?'

'Just . . . I – my head aches.' He turned away quickly, and aware of their eyes upon him put his hand into the box again.

Now that he was braced for it the sensation was almost gone. The gold-rimmed spectacles he picked up were only spectacles. The concentration of evil, of horror, of a depth of despair unimaginable to him – of the truest touch of hell he had ever encountered – had slipped beneath the surface of reality again like a bloated corpse momentarily submerging in a pool. He could have probed into the metal and crystal to look for it, but didn't dare.

He hated the thought of putting them against his face. They were an old man's glasses, meant to adjust far-sightedness rather than myopia. He blinked, and took them off. One of the most evil men he'd ever encountered, the old Earl of Belshya, had been ninety-four, and he supposed the Reich could have enemies that ancient who were dangerous enough to be locked up in the hell whose aura hurt his fingers as he reached into the carton again. He didn't believe it.

The next pair, silver-rimmed, he couldn't even touch. The boy who had worn them was dead. Through the silver, the most psychically conductive of metals, he could still feel how it had happened.

Beside him, von Rath and Weineke were engaged in soft-voiced conversation. '. . . victory slipping through our hands. Those prisoners I asked you to hold in readiness for us . . .' The primrose air smelled of cigar-smoke and coffee, and across the room Horst was roaring with laughter over one of Poincelles' witticisms. Rhion barely heard. He doubted he'd have been so aware of the auras clinging to the glasses if they hadn't been all together in a box, if he hadn't just been shocked from a psychometric trance, but he realized, now, where he'd felt that aura before. It was the same sense that clung to the yellow-patterned dishes on which they were sometimes served lunch, to one particular chair in the library he hated, to the watch they'd given him and the books in strange tongues he found it hard to touch.

Things that had been confiscated when their owners – those mysterious and ubiquitous 'enemies of the Reich' – had been taken away to be tortured and to die for crimes, it was clear from the aura of the glasses, they for the most part did not even comprehend.

He picked a tortoiseshell pair – tortoiseshell being almost completely non-conductive – but the man who had worn them had been far more short-sighted than he, almost blind. Horst and Poincelles sauntered over, still carrying their coffee-cups, the Frenchman's cigar polluting the air all around them. 'Oh, not those,' objected Poincelles, taking the tortoiseshells from Rhion's hand, 'they make you look like a mole.'

'How about these?' Horst took a pair from the box and tried them on, making faces through them; Poincelles laughed.

'Trudi will go for those. You know she loves intellectual types.'

The young Storm Trooper crowed with laughter – Trudi, if Rhion recalled correctly, was the little black-haired minx at the Horn who had yet to give any evidence of literacy. Of course, in a country whose ideal woman was a devout and pregnant cook this would scarcely be held against her.

'These are close.' Rhion put on a pair of rimless glasses with fragile silver temple-pieces. They weren't as close as another pair he'd tried, but the horror that clung to these was less suffocating, less terrifying, than some.

Poincelles grunted. 'They make you look like a damn rabbi.'

The word – not in German – came to his mind with the meaning of 'teacher', but was overlain with a complex of connotations Rhion could not easily identify. Von Rath laughed gaily. 'You're right! All he needs is side-curls,' but Dr Weineke gave him a long, thoughtful scrutiny that turned his blood cold for reasons he couldn't guess.

'How about these?' Horst balanced a pair of gold-framed lenses without temple-pieces on the high, slightly skewed bridge of his nose, and assumed an exaggeratedly pedagogical air. 'If the class will now come to order!' He rapped with his knuckles on the table, and pinched up his lips.

'You're right,' Poincelles grinned. 'I had a Greek teacher at Cambridge who wore some like that, the straight-laced old quean. You've captured the look of him . . .'

'Ah!' Von Rath laughed again, plucked them off the Storm Trooper's face, and adjusted them on Rhion's. 'Now *that's* the thing for you. Distinguished and scholarly.'

The old man. The thought came to him instantly and whole,

and was as swiftly gone, a half-familiar face glimpsed while crossing a crowded street. He touched the delicate frame hesitantly – the lenses balanced by pressure alone – and, though afraid of what he might find, closed his eyes and dipped within.

It was the same old man whose personality he had felt buried in the depths of the knife. But he sensed clearly here a grey old city, a basement room of stove, table, thick-crowding shelves of worn books, a bed behind a faded curtain of flowered calico – grimy windows affording only the view of passing boots. He saw bony hands using the ivory clasp-knife to sharpen old-fashioned quills. The smells of cabbage soup, the sound of contented laughter, constant learned argument, droning chants – a little dark-haired girl with coal-black eyes . . .

And beneath the patina of pain and shock and dread, of hunger and the ever-present stinks of filth and degradation and death, he tasted again the elusive wisp of magic.

Beside him Horst was laughing, 'No, a monocle! Hey, doc, any of those dung-eating communist Jews wear a monocle?'

'You don't look well.' Von Rath's voice slipped softly under the younger man's coarse guffaws. He leaned one flank on the table next to Rhion, stood looking down at him, head tipped a little to one side, level brows drawn in a frown of concern.

Rhion removed the pince-nez and inconspicuously slipped it into his shirt-pocket, and eased the rimless glasses carefully on over the swollen left side of his face. Though he felt as guilty as if he'd erased a plea for help written in a dying man's blood he knew he'd have to ritually cleanse them if he were going to wear them regularly.

Did he know? he wondered, looking up at that beautiful face, delicate even with its sword-scar – dreamer, wizard, as much an exile in this world as he was himself.

He'd been talking to Dr Weineke with the casual intimacy of long-time partners.

He knew.

Rhion closed his eyes, fighting the tide of inchoate realization about what the Nazis did and were. 'My head aches,' he said truthfully. 'You have no idea how stupid I feel falling down the stairs like a two-year-old, but if you don't mind, I'm going to go back up and lie down again. I'll come back in a couple of hours. Maybe you and I can work through the Dee and the Vatican letters tonight, so the day won't be a total loss.'

Von Rath shook his head. 'It does not matter if it is. Baldur and I will finish them. Rest if you need to rest.'

Horst and Poincelles were still playing with Weineke's collection of eyeglasses as Rhion mounted the stairs to his own room.

9

'Who's the old man?'

Taken unawares by the question the barmaid Sara turned sharply, slopping beer on the tray she had been about to lift from the bar, and for a split-second uncertainty and fear gleamed in those spitcat eyes before they melted into warmth as ersatz as the average cup of German coffee. Then she smiled, and brushed her hip lightly against Rhion's crotch. 'Don't worry about my old man, Angeldrawers. Old Pauli does the settling-up with him.' But he knew she was sparring for time.

'I don't mean your pimp,' said Rhion quietly, and took from the breast-pocket of his shabby brown shirt the gold pince-nez. 'I mean the old man who wore these – the old man who used to cut quills with the knife you tried to stab me with . . .'

Her hand shut around his wrist with the same startling strength he'd felt dragging him off-balance in the laundry-room, and her eyes changed from a courtesan's to an assassin's. 'Where did you get those?'

They were jammed shoulder-to-shoulder in a mob of black-uniformed men and locals in shabby serge around the bar; with the cessation of the newscaster's staccato voice a few moments ago The Woodsman's Horn had returned to a chaos more characteristic of Saturday nights than of the normally quiet Thursdays. But with the triumphs in the West the locals had all crowded in to listen to the broadcasts. Now men slapped each other on the shoulder and laughed, congratulating and triumphant – the French falling back in utter confusion, the British ousted, helpless, waiting for the Reich's conquering armies, Belgium and

Holland on their knees . . . An extremely drunken man in the golden belts and brown uniform of a local party leader was explaining at the top of his voice to a bored-looking Trudi how England's work force would be organized for the good of the Reich, and over at the piano a group of the guards from the Kegenwald labour-camp were singing '*When Jewish blood spurts from the knife, things go twice as well.*'

Rhion transferred the glasses to his free hand, and thence to his shirt-pocket again. He didn't raise his voice. 'Can we go somewhere and talk?'

She drew breath to speak, not sure, he guessed, whether to try out another lie. The next instant someone grabbed Rhion roughly from behind, twisting his arm painfully as a boozy gust of breath from over his shoulder demanded, 'This Jewish squirt bothering you, sweetheart?' Twisting to look back Rhion saw two Storm Troopers, camp guards, blonde clean-shaven men with iron eyes. 'You want us to give him a lesson in manners?'

Since you're so highly qualified in that field . . . Rhion, panicked, had the sense not to say; his gaze cut frantically to the smoky room, but Horst, who'd driven him into town, was nowhere in sight. *Christ, I'll report the bastard* . . .

For a moment Sara considered the matter. Then she dimpled coquettishly, and shook her head. 'Oh, let him go.' She made bedroom eyes at the men and insinuated herself between them, and they released Rhion to make room for her. Her little hands fluttered, caressing collar-flashes and sleeve-bands as if in childlike admiration of the insignia. 'But it's good to know German maidenhood is being so well protected . . .'

Obviously the qualifications for maidens have been lowered for the war, thought Rhion, edging out of the crowd as quickly and inconspicuously as possible and heading for one of the vacant tables in a shadowy corner of the room. *I wonder if Poincelles made that clear beforehand to the lords of the Tartarean Seat?* As he sat down he found he was shaking. He hadn't counted on Sara having allies, nor considered the possibility of being beaten bloody in an alley in mistake for a Jew.

He studied her as she teased and flirted with the growing circle of Storm Troopers, always in motion, touching the wrist of one man as he lighted a cigarette for her, the arm of another as she looked up into his face with those huge black eyes. Her garish hair was sticky with the sweat that sheened her face in the frowsty heat; in her cheap green flowered dress her body seemed to crackle with nervy energy and the promise of sensual outrageousness.

Though there was always one barmaid on active duty it was never the same one – the girls appeared and disappeared regularly through the inconspicuous door near the bar. Old Johann was slumped unconscious in a corner, no more regarded tonight than a half-dead dog. Music blared forth from the radio again, soaring, passionate, incongruously beautiful – the music of this world was some of the loveliest Rhion had ever heard, totally unlike anything he had known in his former life. He wished he could write some of it down for Tally, who would be fascinated by its complexities . . .

'Who are you?'

Rhion looked up. Sara set two tankards of beer on the table before him. He had seen nightshade sweeter than her eyes.

'Professor Rhion Sligo.' He took a sip of one of the beers. 'But Auguste told you that last week.' He produced the pince-nez again and held it out to her. 'I found these in a box of about two hundred pairs that the doctor from Kegenwald brought for me to choose from after you broke mine the other night.' Up at the bar he'd seen her take in the black eye and the bruise on the side of his face.

Her hand, which had started towards the glasses, flinched back and clenched on itself, and the red mouth, wide and generous under its paint, hardened. She blew a cloud of cigarette-smoke at him and laughed. 'I was pretty drunk here the other night but I think I'd remember breaking your glasses for you, Professor. Maybe it was Trudi – she's pretty much like me when the lights are out.' She plucked the glasses from his hand and tucked them in the soft chasm between her breasts, and gave him a mocking smile, daring him to lay a hand on her with the men within call.

'I'm talking about three o'clock in the morning the day before yesterday,' said Rhion quietly. 'At Schloss Torweg, after you got done helping Poincelles raise his – ah – ritual energies. As the closest thing this country has to a professional wizard when someone tries to kill me I can usually figure out who it is.' He pulled the knife from his pocket and slid it across the table towards her.

She laughed again, shaking back her hair. 'Christ Jesus, a wizard! What'd you do, cut the cards and get a number that added up to the Gematria of my name? Going to turn in your ouija-board notes as evidence to the local Gauleiter? You'd better find your keeper and head on back to the Schloss, or you *will* get a lesson in manners . . .' With a cocky flip of her skirt she turned to go.

'Wait a minute! Don't call the Etiquette Squad . . . !'

She turned back, irresolute, and he talked fast.

'If I'm Gestapo all I have to do is pull an ID and it's you they'll be taking out of here, not me. If I'm not . . .' She came back like a feral cat, ready to scratch or flee. He lowered his voice again. 'If I'm not you don't have anything to lose listening to me, do you? What have you been looking for up at the Schloss?'

Her dark eyes shifted. The soft mouth flexed a little, and she brushed aside a sticky tendril of hair from her cheek. 'Drugs,' she said quietly. 'Cocaine – Baldur keeps a stash of it under a floorboard in the corner of the workroom upstairs . . .'

'Don't be ridiculous. Why risk being shot for spying over

something you can get out of Poincelles in trade for a couple of trips up to his Temple? And you know as well as I do that in this country they make arrests on a lot thinner evidence than party-tricks and numerology.'

Slowly, still tense and unwilling, she pulled out a chair and sat across from him, dropping her cigarette and crushing it out beneath one high red heel.

'Are you working for the old man? You've been searching the place – what are you looking for?' He leaned across to her. 'I have to know.' And when she didn't answer, only studied him with those wary black eyes, he added, 'I haven't told von Rath. I can't – I couldn't let him know I'd been out of the compound that night. I'm more or less a prisoner there myself. The old man is a wizard, isn't he?'

She picked up the knife where he had left it on the table, turning its blunt brownish length over in her hands. The red paint on her nails was chipped and chewed, the nails themselves bitten off short. 'Yes,' she said, after a long time. 'He's my father.'

'Can you take me to him?'

Her voice was vicious. 'It's word of him I'm looking for.' She fumbled another cigarette from her dress pocket, flicked the wheel on a brass lighter made from a rifle-bullet, but her fingers were trembling. Rhion, though he hated cigarette-smoke, reached to steady the flame for her but she jerked her hands away with a vitriol glare that made him remember how the knife had reeked with her loathing of men.

The mild narcotic of the nicotine seemed to steady her. 'I've seen people do psychometry,' she said after a moment. 'One of the girls in my dorm at college used to do it at parties, but she had to be two drinks drunk . . .'

'College?'

Under the sweaty points of her red hair her glance was scornful. 'You think I could get into every SS barracks between here and the Swiss border by waving my degree in Chemistry, pal?'

'Ahh – no.'

She smoked in silence, her lipstick leaving lurid stains on the white paper of the cigarette, her eyes avoiding his. As she smoked she swallowed back her rage, a little at a time, like a bile of nausea. 'I heard the SS had an Occult Bureau that was holding people like him in special custody. Then I found out about your place . . .' She raised her eyes to his, and in them he saw how she hated him for having the power to tell her what he knew. 'You say those came from Kegenwald. Could you tell me if he . . . if he's still alive?'

In spite of his black eye and the wound on his arm that smarted every time he moved, Rhion's heart went out to her. For all her hardness she was very young. She would, he knew, far rather have been hurt herself stealing the information, would rather have traded her favours for it, than simply ask it of a man. 'He wasn't dead, or in immediate fear of dying, when they took his glasses off him,' he said slowly. 'But I have no way of telling how long ago that was, or what might have happened to him since. Do you know why the Occult Bureau is imprisoning wizards?'

'God knows.' She shook her head wearily.

'And the magic that he uses . . .' The name of it, half-glimpsed in the deepest fabric of the pen-knife, returned to him. 'The – the Kabbala . . .'

Her eyes, closed in momentary frustration, flicked open again, and in them he saw the bitter look of a cornered animal. 'So you know,' she said, and suddenly all the tautness seemed to go out of her, all the catlike readiness to scratch and flee. She sighed, her eyelids creasing with an exhausted irony. 'The damned thing is that if he wasn't a Kabbalist I think he'd be dead now. Most of the people they arrested in Warsaw that first week ended up dead – not just Jews, but gypsies, teachers, priests, Communists, newspaper editors . . .' She pushed wearily at her hair. 'Papa's brothers are all rabbis, they thought what he studied was crazy. But I think it's the only reason he was separated out, locked up instead of shot. I've been searching the Schloss for information, something that might tell me if he's still alive, and where, and what they want with him . . .'

'You're a Jew, then?' said Rhion, enlightened but keeping his voice as quiet as possible.

Sara rolled her eyes ceilingwards. 'So what are you, the flower of Aryan manhood?'

He blinked at her, startled. 'I'm from another universe,' he explained. 'I don't even know what a Jew looks like . . .'

'Holy Mother of . . . The boys in the barracks said you were crazy. Are you circumcised?'

'Yes,' said Rhion, nonplussed by the apparent switch in topic. 'What does that have to do with anything?'

She regarded him, baffled, through the bluish haze of smoke, then shook her head. 'I'm beginning to *believe* you're from another universe,' she said in a tone which indicated she believed no such thing. 'Just don't get yourself picked up by the SS, pal. And you might remember that if you breathe one word about my own ancestry they won't even take me outside to spare the furniture before they shoot me. All right?'

'All right,' agreed Rhion, still puzzled. 'How powerful a wizard is your father? I've heard von Rath mention the Kabbala, but he seemed to think it was worthless by definition, being Jewish. *Is* there power in it?'

'Is there . . .' Sara stared at him, mouth open. 'It's all hooey, you poor deluded shnook! The whole goddam business is about as real as the tooth-fairy! If there was anything in it do you think they'd be *able* to round up Kabbalists and their families like sheep for the . . .'

'Sara!' bawled a voice behind her, and two Storm Troopers came swaggering up. One of them, a guard from the

Schloss, saw him and muttered, 'Oh, Professor . . .' but the other eyed him with utter contempt.

'C'mon, Sara, the beer don't taste as good without you to serve it . . .'

'What you want with this little kike, anyway?' added the other, pulling her to her feet and into his arms.

Sara smiled, kittenish, her body suddenly supple again, all hips and breasts and teasing little hands. 'Well, what's a poor girl to do if *real* men don't give her a cigarette now and then?' She took one from the camp-guard's breast pocket, and put it between soft pouty lips. The man's arm was around her, his hand cupping her buttock, as the three of them vanished into the crowd around the bar.

Rhion sipped his beer, deep in thought.

So much, he thought, for the last country in the world to believe in and support wizardry. Evidently the Reich only supported such wizards as would give it what it asked for, and somehow it made him feel better to know that other wizards had had the good taste to be 'enemies of the Reich'. There was a wizard as close as the Kegenwald camp, five miles at most from where he sat.

Adrenalin scalded his veins. There was, in fact, a possibility of getting out of here alive.

He thought back on what von Rath had told him of the Kabbala. It hadn't been clear because it was a field of studies rather than any specific book or rite, a tangled labyrinth of meditation and spells rooted in a central symbol called the Tree of Life and spreading in endless thickets of numerological calculation, esoteric scriptural exegesis, and six thousand years' worth of learned quibbling. Sara had taken the knife – her father's folding pen-knife – from the table, but he recalled vividly the sense of magic deep within it, like the lingering brightness that lay deep within the Dancing Stones.

Horst appeared at his side, adjusting his tie by touch and clearly unaware of the immense smear of fuchsia lipstick under his left ear. The blonde girl Ulrica was walking with that leggy stride back to the bar, already smiling a mechanical smile for the next man or men, and Rhion saw Sara heading towards the recently-vacated back room with the two troopers who'd taken her from him.

He glanced up at Horst. 'Would you talk to whoever you have to talk to about having that Sara girl come back to the Schloss with me tonight?'

Horst's face split into a grin of complicity and delight. 'Sure thing!' he said, and then added hastily, 'Sir. I mean – I knew you'd like her.'

He turned at once towards the bar and Rhion said quickly, 'When she's not busy.' No sense adding a couple of sexually frustrated drunk Nazis to his other problems.

He settled back in his chair, nursing his beer and wondering how difficult it was going to be to break Sara's father out of Kegenwald.

'And don't get any ideas, cupcake,' murmured Sara, snuggling against him in the dark back seat of the open car and running a hand along his thigh. 'Your chauffeur eavesdrops – he can see us in the driving mirror, too. Unless that's part of your price?' She turned her head against his shoulder, and he felt the tension in her muscles as he put his arm around that slim hard waist and drew her close.

'I have a wife and two kids at home and I never sleep with women who've tried to knife me.'

'I bet there's lots of those.'

The men were leaving the tavern. As Horst turned the big blue Mercedes in the yard the yellow headlight-beams splashed across the Schloss's three-ton Benz flatbed, catching a firefly glister of silver buttons and gleaming eyes beneath the rolled-up canvas cover. The grey-uniformed Kegenwald guards were mostly walking back to the camp, and as the open Mercedes passed them, striding along in threes and fours down the single narrow street of the village, one or another would wave and call out to Horst, or to Sara.

The street ran past the new church, and the old church, and so out into the dark of the endless pines.

It was thirty minutes' drive to Schloss Torweg, a walk of nearly forty kilometres. Railway trains – the primary means of long-distance transportation in this world – went faster than that, flying machines faster yet. Rhion smiled, hearing the Gray Lady's voice in his mind: *To go so far at such speed, and yet you will still arrive there with what you are inside.*

He leaned back in the soft leather of the seat, watching the stars flick in and out of the black frieze of branches. The constellations were the same ones he knew, though their names here were different.

This potential for perfection, for comfort, he thought as the wind riffled his hair, *and what are they doing? Using their airplanes to strafe fleeing civilians, and their radios to incite men to hate.* He remembered what he had seen in the scrying-crystal, and in the Ministry of Propaganda's newsreels.

Had the world gone insane when magic had disappeared?

Not a pleasant thought.

Then they turned a corner where the road returned to its ancient, sunken track, picking up once more the line of the Kegenwald ley, and his blood turned cold.

Power was running along the ley. He could sense it like a sound, a texture in the air, and even stronger, there came to him the chill psychic stench of evil. But as he reached to touch it, to see what it was and where, it was gone. Sara felt the flinch of his body and raised her tousled head sharply from his shoulder, and he realized that quiet as she had been, she'd been waiting tensely for his slightest move.

'What is it?'

'I don't know.'

But a hundred yards' distance from the Schloss he felt it again, as the harshness of the yard lights glowed between the black trees, and this time he knew.

They had raised power.

The whole lodge – even the air around it – were lambent with energy, darkly glowing with a horrible, unfocussed strength. Sara asked him again softly, 'What is it?' as she felt his breath catch in horror; she sat up and pushed back her ruffled curls, but by her voice he could tell she felt nothing. A guard came whistling casually to open the gates. Horst cracked a joke with him about Goering's wedding-night, that he'd heard at the Horn.

In the luminous square of the lodge's open door von Rath stood waiting. He still wore his white ceremonial robes, and the electric glare in the hall behind him showed his body through. It was only when Rhion got close that he saw blood-spots on the hem and sleeves.

'We've done it!' Von Rath sprang down the steps to seize his arms, and staggered. Even allowing for the lesser light of the floodlit yard the younger wizard's eyes were dilated to black, and he swayed on his feet like a drunken man. His hands, gripping Rhion's shoulders, were convulsively strong. 'We've done it!' The smell of his robes was horrible: fresh blood, burned flesh, incense. Past him Rhion could see the air in the hall pulsing with power, power that flowed uncontrolled down the panelling and moved like snakes of cold light on the stairs. Instinctively he balked when von Rath tried to draw him over the threshold.

'Horst,' he ordered shakily, 'take the girl up to my room. Sara, wait for me . . .'

Von Rath waved impatiently. 'Let the guards have her, you don't want a woman at a time like this. Come.' His hand like iron on the nape of Rhion's neck, he dragged him up the steps and into the accursed house.

'Baldur was right, you see,' he whispered exultantly as he pulled Rhion past the watchroom and down the wide, panelled hall. His drugged eyes had a hard, terrible shine, like opals in which some evil spirit had been bound. 'Gall was right. The Adepts of the Shining Crystal – they knew! They had the secret of how life-force can be woven into magic! Baldur found the Rites – they were coded, concealed in the Lucalli Diaries . . . How to draw forth power, all the power we need . . .'

As von Rath pulled him through that hideously vibrant house Rhion held out his hand, summoning witchlight to his palm. Nothing happened. He fumbled a match from his pocket and held it out, half afraid to call fire to the dried red sulphur-paste at its tip. He felt almost afraid to speak, for fear of waking some terrible force by the softest of words.

No fire burst onto the match, but out of an obscure fear that things were on the verge of uncontrolled chaos Rhion put the match-tip into his mouth and wet it thoroughly before dropping it onto a table in the hall. 'Were you able to convert it?'

'Not yet.' Von Rath halted with him before the Temple's doors.

There were no guards in this part of the house, no lights. The Temple doors stood open, and Rhion recoiled before the dark power he saw moving within, shifting and quivering in the blur of candlelight and smoke. Within the long, black-painted room he could see horribly half-familiar marks scrawled everywhere on the parquet, save around the altar, where Gall, stripped to his underwear, was engaged in washing the floor.

The smell told Rhion what had gone on that night, and the hair lifted on his neck.

'But don't you see?' giggled von Rath, shivering all over with triumph and glee. '*We won't need to*. I made Baldur see the things I wanted him to see. The three of us here in the Temple, performing the blood-rites of power, and him on the other side of the house . . . I made illusions in his mind and *he saw them!*'

Rhion pulled away from the clutching hands, disgusted and horrified. 'If he was as crocked as you are I'm surprised he didn't see Venus on the half-shell rising out of the sink!'

'No.' He caught Rhion's face between his palms, staring down into his eyes and seeing in them nothing but his own triumph, his own vindication, his own joy. 'He saw nothing, no hallucination, but those which I projected into his mind. He wrote them down, with the exact times of their appearances – they were the same, Rhion!

'Don't you see? Maybe we can't convert power to physical operancy, not yet, though that will come. But once we can control illusion, *we can take out the British air cover*. And that will be enough to ensure the success of the invasion of England. And after that . . .' His voice sank to a whisper. '. . . They'll give me anything I want.'

10

Sara was waiting for him when he got to his attic room. The door was barricaded; he tapped at it softly and spoke her name, and after a moment heard a chair being moved. Her hair was rumpled, half the buttons torn off her dress to show a sailor's paradise of bosom, her smile sardonic. 'Big hotshot wizard and you can't levitate a little chair?' The electric bulb over the bed was on; Rhion automatically switched it off and took a match from his pocket to light the candles. In the diffuse glow of the yard-lights outside Sara put her hands on her hips. 'Now, look, *boychik*, I've had enough . . .'

'I hate that light,' he said wearily, pushing up his glasses to rub his eyes. From his trouser pocket he took the notes he had been given – notes von Rath had insisted on going over with him, while Gall cleaned up something in the corner of the Temple that clattered with soft metallic noises – and put them in the drawer with the wristwatch he never wore these days. 'Horst brought you up here?'

She sniffed, sitting back on a corner of the bed but watching him warily. 'After a couple of the boys in the watchroom who'd heard old Pauli declare open season got done pawing me, yeah.'

He winced. 'I'm sorry.'

'The hell you are. You got a cigarette?'

He shook his head. 'I don't smoke.'

'You and Hitler.' In the candlelight her eyes were dark and very angry. 'You're all bastards.'

'Do you want to go home?'

'Home?' She laughed bitterly. 'I haven't *got* a home. You think after all this I'm gonna be able to go back to Aunt

Tayta and Uncle Mel in New York and be their little girl again?' She turned her face from him, the wide mouth clenched taut under its smeared lipstick. He wanted to go to her, to comfort her as he would have comforted anyone in that much pain, but he knew if he touched her she'd break his jaw.

Then she drew a deep breath, forcing some of the tension to ease. 'Oh, hell,' she said in time. 'I get pinched and kissed all the time at the tavern – it wasn't anything I don't do every day.' Rhion thought about the two Storm Troopers and wisely said nothing. '"Invest in good faith", Uncle Mel is always saying – he's a tailor. "Make them smile when they remember you." Auntie would kill him if she knew how I was applying that particular sample of avuncular wisdom.'

And still she watched him, like a cornered animal, waiting for him to make a move towards her, to prove to her that he was, in fact, like every other man. After a long minute, when he didn't, she said in a much quieter voice, 'I want to see my Papa. You say you're a wizard. You show me him in that damn crystal of yours.' She jerked her head towards the scrying-crystal's hiding-place in the rafters and he realized she must have taken some opportunity, either now or during her earlier searches of the place, to go through his room. 'Then I'll go back to town.'

Rhion took a deep breath, brought over a chair, and fetched the crystal down. 'I can't show you him . . .'

Her mouth twisted. 'What a surprise!' she said sarcastically. 'How come it's always the wizard who gets to squint into the crystal ball? It's only his word to the marks what this person or that person is doing . . .'

'Well it's the goddam best I can do!' flared Rhion. 'Now do you want it, or do you want to just get the hell out of here and let me go to bed? Jesus, why do I always end up dealing with you at three in the morning . . . ?'

'I want to see him,' said Sara, her voice suddenly small and tight, and looked away.

She had, as she'd said, slept her way through every SS barracks between here and the Swiss border to find him. Rhion felt the anger go out of him, remembering that. Of course she expected him to cheat her. Sitting on the bed with her dishevelled hair and rumpled dress, she looked very young and alone. Rhion moved the chair out of the way, wincing as the cut on the back of his arm pulled, and said, 'All right, give me the glasses. But I can guarantee you right now if your father's as wise as you think he is what he's doing is sleeping.'

He took a piece of chalk from his pocket, and sketched around himself a Circle of Power. As he settled his mind, deepening it into preliminary meditation, he noted that Sara, chatty as she was with the men in the tavern, seemed to realize the need for silence. *Of course*, he thought. *She's a wizard's daughter*. Whether she thought it was hooey or not, her father had taught her the rules.

The moon stood low, a sickly scrap of itself tangled in the black of the eastern trees. Even the crickets' endless screeking in the warm spring night had fallen silent. With the moon's waning the dark field of power enveloping the house felt stronger yet. Rhion guessed he could have tapped into that field to make the scrying easier, but instead blocked it from the Circle as best he could, and as a result it took him the usual endless forty minutes to raise the strength. His head began to ache, but nothing would have induced him to partake of what had been done tonight. The pince-nez lay like an insect's cast chitin in his right hand, the crystalline lattices of the glass holding the psychic energies that had surrounded them; in his left the scrying-crystal flashed sharply in the reflected candlelight. He pursued those flame reflections down into the stone's structure, sinking through the gem's familiar pathways until colours came, then darkness, then the clear grey mist which rolled aside so suddenly to reveal a tiny image, like something reflected over his shoulder or in another room.

'It's a cell about eight feet square,' he murmured, and somewhere behind him the bedsprings creaked as Sara leaned forward. 'Cement walls, cement floor, iron cot, bucket in one corner.' A part of him whispered in relief. He had been afraid to look into the place where the glasses had come from, afraid of what he might see. 'There's a window high up, floodlight outside . . . A man sitting on the edge of the cot. Tall and skinny . . .' Rhion frowned, concentrating on details. 'His head's been shaved, the stubble's grey and white . . . Long eyebrows, curling – grey. There's a scar on his lip, not very old . . .'

The glasses still between his fingers he touched the place, and heard Sara's hissing intake of breath. 'Bastards. *Bastards*!' Poisoned tears shook in her voice. 'He had a mole there, under his beard. They shave them when they put them in the camps . . .'

If he thought about it – if he let anger or outrage or anything else intrude on the effort of concentration – he would lose the image altogether, and be unable to get it back. His training had given him discipline to exclude even the worst of horrors from his mind. But it was a near thing.

After a moment he went on, 'He's wearing dark pants of some kind, patches . . . grey shirt in rags. His knees are skinny, bones sticking out through the cloth – long thin hands, brown age-spots – He looks too old to be your father . . .'

Dimly he heard her voice say, 'He was forty-one when he met Mama.'

'He's standing up, walking to the window, trying to look out but it's over his head. He's worried, fidgety, pacing around.'

'Can you tell where the place is?' She leaned forward, her hands with their bitten red nails clasped on her knees. 'Is he still at Kegenwald?'

'I don't know.' He spoke dreamily, detached, struggling to keep his concentration focused on the old man's face. A curious face, beaky and strong in spite of its egg-like nakedness, the dark eyes as they gazed up at the narrow window filled with horror and concern that held no trace of personal fear. Rhion felt a kind of awe, for having tasted the aura of the place, through the box of glasses and through Dr Weineke's cold smile, he knew he himself would have been huddled in a corner puking with terror. And he knew there were still things about this that he didn't know.

'Have you seen the camp?' he asked softly. 'I can go up and look through the window myself, describe what I see . . .'

Within the crystal he saw the old man look up swiftly, at some unheard sound outside. Then he pressed to the wall beneath the window, straining to hear, and Rhion concentrated on moving past him, up the wall until he was level with the opening, which, he saw now, was barred, wire laced into the glass. Through it he could see a vast, bare yard under the glare of yellow floodlights, row upon row of bleak wooden barracks beyond, and, past them, a wire fence closing off the compound from the dreary, endless darkness of the pine-woods. Wooden towers stood along the fence, manned by dark shapes with glinting machine-guns. Between two such towers was a wire gate, which grey-clothed sentries opened to admit the smaller of Schloss Torweg's two flatbed transport-trucks.

The truck turned in the yard, pulled to a stop before a building opposite the barracks; more guards emerged from the building's lighted door into the floodlit glare. With them was Dr Weineke, her greying fair hair pulled back tight and every button buttoned, though it must be nearing four in the morning, and another man in a more ornate black SS uniform whom Rhion guessed was the commandant of the camp. Auguste Poincelles climbed down from the truck cab, rumpled and unshaven but moving with that gawky, skeletal lightness characteristic of him. He said something to Weineke, and gestured; she nodded, and the camp commandant craned his head a little to see as guards untied the canvas flaps of the truck's cover.

They brought out three stretchers, one of which they hadn't had a spare blanket to cover.

'Jesus!' Rhion shut his eyes, but not fast enough – for an instant he thought he was going to be sick. The facets of the crystal bit his palm as he clenched his hand over it, as if that could let him unsee what he had seen. 'Oh, God . . .'

'What?'

He pressed his hands to his face, unable for a moment to speak. By the face – or what was left of the face – of the woman on the stretcher, she'd been conscious for most of it.

Then anger hit him, terror laced with rage. Though violence had never been part of his nature he'd have horsewhipped a man who'd perform such acts upon so much as a rat. Baldur had read him second-hand accounts of the accursed Shining Crystal group, but the thought of such things actually being done, no matter in what cause – the thought of the kind of power that would result, and what it would do to those who summoned it – turned his stomach and brought sweat cold to his face.

'Are you all right?' Hard little hands touched his shoulders, soft breasts pressed into his back. 'What did you see? What is it?'

He shook his head, and managed to whisper, 'Your father's all right,' knowing that would be her first concern. 'It's just – I looked out through the window . . . He's at Kegenwald, all right, Weineke was there, and Poincelles – Poincelles drove the truck . . .'

'What truck?'

He shook his head again, trying to rid it of what he knew would always be there now, as if burned into his forebrain.

'What did you see?' She pulled him around to face her where she knelt on the floor. When he wouldn't answer she snagged her purse from where it lay at the foot of the bed, took out a tin flask and pressed it into his hands. He wasn't sure whether the stuff inside was intended to be gin or vodka, but it didn't succeed at either one. Nevertheless, it helped.

After a long moment he whispered hoarsely, 'Back in my world those in the Dark Traffic – the necromancers, the demon-callers – usually have trouble getting victims. I see now they just don't have the right connections.'

'You mean von Rath's doing human sacrifice.'

Though he knew she was only thinking in terms of throat-cutting he nodded.

'Papa . . .'

'It's all right,' he said quickly, seeing the fear in her eyes. 'I'll help you get him out.'

For the length of an intaken breath she was just a girl, wonder and gratitude flooding her wide dark eyes. But the next moment all that she'd done to get this far came back on her, and her body settled again, her parted lips close and wry. 'And what do you get out of it?'

'I need his help. I need the help of a wizard to get me back to my own world.'

He almost laughed at the speed with which she adjusted the cynical exasperation on her face to an expression of grave belief.

'All right. What do I have to do?'

'You don't believe me, do you?'

'Of course I . . .' She paused, regarding him for a steady moment, then shook her head. 'No. But I know I can't spring him alone.' For a moment they sat in silence, their knees almost touching in the smudged ruin of the chalked circle, candlelight warming the translucent pallor of her face and throwing wavery thread-lace shadows from every tangled red strand of her hair. Then she looked down at the tin flask still in her hands, and twisted and untwisted its metal top as she spoke. 'That's the other reason I'd put up with Poincelles and those grunts in the barracks to get a chance to search the house. It wasn't only word of him – records and files – I was looking for, but documents, seals, signatures to fake – anything. I've been out to look at the camp – I know all the roads around here – I've got faked IDs, ration-cards, clothes, pick-locks . . . But I know that's not gonna get me spit, walking in there alone. A woman . . .' She shrugged. 'I thought maybe Poincelles . . .'

Her mouth flinched with distaste at the memory of the darkness in the barn temple, and Rhion saw again the point of the downturned pentacle like a silver dagger aimed at her nude body, heard Poincelles' evil chant.

'You tell him anything?'

She shook her head. 'I was always afraid to, when it came down to it. He really believes that crap . . .' She paused, her eye darting up to meet Rhion's, and then grinned apologetically. 'Present company excepted. But he's . . . Some of the stuff Trudi told me about what he did with her . . . some of the stuff he asked me to do. And there was some rumour about him and one of the local League of German Maidens, a kid about twelve . . . Jesus! There was a stink about that – it was before your time. So I never had the nerve. And besides, I don't trust the momzer to keep his word.'

'Don't,' he said. 'But you're going to have to trust me.'

After Sara had left, Rhion looked over the scrawled pages of notes.

He had mastered sufficient spoken German to understand radio broadcasts, and enough of the spiky, oddly curliqued alphabet to read simple notes, though the thick tomes of histories, records, accounts of magic over the centuries still defeated him. But though Baldur's handwriting had been made no easier to decipher by the vast amount of mescaline the boy had taken, the meaning was clear.

22.17 – Buzzing. Large bee in corner of ceiling near door.

22.38 – Three red lights about seven inches apart on the wall behind me, four feet above floor.

23.10 – Something in corner of room? fur?

23.50 – Hole in floor, three feet in front of door. Twelve inches across. Can see edges of floorboards cut cleanly as with saw. No light down inside.

Below, in von Rath's neat handwriting, was appended the note, 'Illusions projected for sixty seconds at a time, perceived for between five and thirty seconds.'

It was dawn. The sky had been lightening when he'd walked Sara down to the waiting car, which had passed Poincelles' covered flatbed in the sunken roadway before the gates. Birds were calling their territories in the dew-soaked pockets of bracken among the pine-trees, the thin warbling of the robins answering the chaffinch's sharp 'pink-pink', reminding Rhion hurtfully of mornings when he'd sit in meditation on the crumbling stone terrace of the library in the Drowned Lands, listening to the marsh-fowl waking in the peaceful silence.

Around him, the forces which had been raised by the blood-rite were slowly dispersing with the turn of the earth. He could feel them clinging to the fabric of the house like some kind of sticky mould – called up, incompetently tampered with, but unable to be used or converted to operancy, they lingered in shadowy corners, ugly, dirty-smelling, dark. Did the rites of the Shining Crystal even include dispersal spells? he wondered wearily. It was lunacy to suppose a group capable of raising this kind of power wouldn't have the sense to use them, but any group fool enough to raise power out of an unwilling human sacrifice, a pain-sacrifice, a torture-sacrifice, was probably too stupid to realize what they were tampering with in the first place.

In any case that part of the ritual might have been taken for granted and not written down – they frequently weren't – or written down elsewhere and lost. He should, he thought, have gone down to the Temple himself and worked what he could to neutralize the energies raised.

But there wasn't enough money in Germany to make him go into that Temple tonight.

Rhion flipped to the next sheet. That was in von Rath's handwriting, neat and precise, having been written out before he'd taken the potent cocktail of mescaline, peyote, and psylocibin himself.

Bee – 22.17

Triangle of red lights – 22.38

Fox – 23.09

Glass of beer – 23.25 (That one evidently hadn't gone through at all.)

Hole in floor – 23.50

In a room at most a hundred feet away, which von Rath had been in scores of times, into the mind of someone who knew him and hero-worshipped him and concentrated on his every word and expression and who was, moreover, magically trained himself and out of his skull on drugs.

But he'd done it.

Rhion folded the papers and sighed. He took off his glasses, lowered his head to his hands.

Shouldn't you do something? a part of him asked.

For instance? Every time he closed his eyes he saw the mutilated body of the woman, like some twisted shape of driftwood in the bitter electric glare, the two other forms beneath dripping blankets. Saw the camp, the guards, Weineke, the commandant – all the structure of power that made it so easy for von Rath to order up victims as he ordered up silver or mandrake roots or anything else he wanted from the Occult Bureau; saw, too, the fleeing women and children scattering before the diving planes, and the boxful of spectacles that turned before his eyes into neat little corpses, folded up like frozen insects awaiting disposal.

And the implications were more appalling still.

He had the sensation of being trapped in a nightmare, of teetering perilously on the edge of a dragging spiral of horror incomprehensibly worse in its dark depths than it was up here at its crown.

The grey beach he'd seen in the scrying-crystal came back to him, too, men standing in the sea while boats bobbed towards them – brightly-painted pleasure-boats, some of them, or big strange-looking craft with unwieldy mechanical paddles on their sides and rumps, crewed by men and women too old, too soft-looking – too kind-looking – to be soldiers. English civilians, Horst Eisler had said. A stupid and decadent race, von Rath had called them, but nevertheless willing to brave the choppy sea in whatever craft they could find to take those men off the beaches, out from under the flaming death of the German guns. In the crystal he'd seen the British war-planes, too, searing soundlessly overhead and fighting heartstopping mid-air battles with the German fliers.

We can take out the British air cover, von Rath had said. With illusion at his command, he could.

And then . . . *they'll give me anything I want.*

The thought of what that might be made him shudder.

How much command von Rath would ever gain over illusion was problematical, of course. No matter how much power he raised, unless the hallucinations could be directed consistently and accurately into the minds of large numbers of strangers it wouldn't do much good, and Rhion knew that without magical operancy such control simply wasn't possible.

But having seen the demon unleashed in von Rath's eyes he knew also that von Rath would not hear him when he said that. From his own experience of having the long-denied magic within him released, vindicated, broken forth into the air, he knew just how strong were the forces driving the young mage – how strong they would have been even were it not for the centuries of denial and disbelief being thrown off as well. He would continue trying, continue the hideous blood-rites, continue raising the ghastly energies and releasing them unused and without any sort of control, until . . .

Until what?

Rhion didn't know. He was wizard enough to be academically curious about the results, but every instinct he possessed told him to get out and get out fast.

For a few moments he toyed with the notion of aiding Sara and her father to escape to England, wherever the hell England was, and offering his services to the English King. But aside from the fact that once away from the Dark Well he would lose forever his chance of contacting Shavus and establishing a pick-up point for his jump across the Void – in effect, exiling himself here permanently – there was no guarantee that the English King wouldn't have him imprisoned. Like the Solarists, he seemed to believe that magic not only didn't, but couldn't, exist. Moreover there was always the chance that the English King was as evil as the Chancellor of Germany, though the thought of another realm as comprehensively soulless as the German Reich was something Rhion didn't want to contemplate.

No, he thought. The best thing to do was to contact Shavus, establish a point where their power could reach out to guide him across the Void, and get the hell out of this world of luxurious insanity. And for the first time since he'd come here, that didn't look completely impossible.

11

The Duke of Mere greeted Shavus the Archmage with great cordiality when the old man appeared at the gates of Bragenmere, four nights before the last new moon of Spring. For all his bluff, warrior heartiness, the Duke was a man of learning, and welcomed scholars – mageborn or otherwise – to his court. Even the most disapproving of the cult priests, the chill-eyed Archimandrite of Darova and the silent Mijac, High Priest of Agon behind his funereal veils, dared not remark. Sitting at supper the first night, Tallisett couldn't hear what the Duke and the Archmage had to say to one another, but looking along the glitter of the high table at the two big, middle-aged men, the dark crimson velvet of the one in no way belittling the shabby brown-and-black homespun of the other, she rather thought they were comparing the finer points of shortsword technique with the salt-spoons.

But on the second night, as she was hurrying down the corridor towards the vestibule where the Duke's guests assembled before walking in procession, two by two, into the state dining-hall, she was stopped at the head of the stair by a pale, precise figure which materialized from between the malachite columns, and a cool voice inquiring, 'Whither away, little cousin?'

It was Lord Esrex.

She curtsied politely, but her eyes were wary. She had never trusted her brother-in-law, even before his attempt seven years ago to have Rhion executed and herself disgraced – his friendliness now put her all the more on her guard. 'I'm late. They'll be going in soon . . .'

'Not until I'm there.' He leaned a narrow shoulder

against a column-drum, and drew the white silk of his glove through his slender hand. 'Surely you know the reason they're having a state dinner? I'm the guest of honour – your father's chosen to make me governor of the lands for which he married that brainless little slut at the turn of the spring.'

Tally felt her cheeks heat with anger, for she liked her new young stepmother, but she only said calmly, 'If you've received the impression she's a slut I'm afraid the spy-network of the cult of Agon isn't as accurate as it's made out to be. Even the most careless gossip in the court could tell you Mirane of Varle is devoted to my father.'

She was rewarded by the colour that flamed to the tight-skinned, delicate face. He would, she knew, have been delighted to be able to prove the Duke's new wife unfaithful, even as he had sought for years to prove that Rhion of Sligo, and not her husband Marc of Erralswan, was the father of Tally's children, and for the same reason – to discredit any heirs to rival his own son's claim to the Dukedom from which his grandfather had so rudely been thrust.

But with icy and bitter precision the scion of the White Bragenmeres waved her words away. 'He thinks he can make it up to me, giving me that pittance for the wrong he has done my family. And if he's deluding himself that he's still man enough to father a child on that strawheaded little lightskirt – Is that why he welcomed the Archmage to court? To get him a tincture of potency, now that his own tame conjurer has disappeared?'

She realized he was baiting her, seeking information, and shook her head, reaching to straighten the pendant pearl that hung at her throat with a hand cluttered by unaccustomed rings. For the full ceremonial of a state dinner she wore her husband's colours, emerald green ribboned and tasselled in silver, the bronze-blue eyes of a peacock's tail hanging around her half-bared shoulders in a delicate collar. 'I'm not in his confidence, cousin.'

'They tell me other wizards are arriving in the city now,' went on Esrex softly, his pale eyes studying her face. 'The Serpentlady of Dun came in last night, they say – carrying her lover in a basket, I should expect – and Harospix Harsprodin from Fell. So the ears of Agon are not as inaccurate as you might think.'

'Since everyone who enters the gates, mageborn or not, are under Father's protection,' replied Tally steadily, meeting his gaze, 'there's no particular reason why wizards should conceal their movements. I suppose Agon's spies simply like to feel important, telling their masters at the Temple what they could have learned simply by the asking.' She tilted her head at the sound of a muted fanfare of music echoing in the deep arches of the stairwell, so close above their heads. 'Shall we go down?'

The ceremony of investiture, in which Esrex was given temporary governorship of the dower-territories which Mirane had brought to her middle-aged husband, took place between the Great Course and the sweets, and Tally took her leave as soon as Esrex, Mirane, and the Duke had resumed their seats and the musicians had begun the light, flirty tunes which traditionally heralded the entry of dessert. She did not like the way Esrex's pale, heavy-lidded eyes sought out her own two sons – Kir rosy and vigorous and just turned seven, four-year-old Brenat already asleep with a chicken-bone clutched in one plump hand – or the way he glanced sidelong at the Duke's fair-haired bride of ten weeks, as if trying to guess the reasons for the blooming sparkle that seemed to radiate from the core of her body.

In the deserted vestibule the glow of the oil-lamps showed Tally a piece of paper lying on one of the spindly-legged couches – she picked it up, and saw it was a rough drawing of her father and a wizard. The wizard, a grotesque figure in a long robe with no effort made to distinguish which Order of wizardry or who the wizard was, had removed her father's head and was replacing it with that of a sheep.

Cold went through her, cold followed at once by a hot flood of furious anger. She ripped the paper in half, turned to thrust the pieces into the bowl of the nearest lamp, when a deep voice from the shadows said softly, 'Don't burn it.'

Looking up swiftly, she saw Gyzan the Archer standing with arms folded in the darkness between the vestibule's many columns.

'Give it to your father. He may be able to identify who printed it, and where.'

'Would it do any good?' Her hands shook, her whole body swept with shivers of anger and a curious, helpless dread. From the great hall behind her the clashing of cymbals filtered, a bright glitter of sound – dancers in red with the long noses of goons were bounding and whirling among the tables, to the ripple of laughter and applause. 'They just keep appearing, just like the rumours keep spreading. You can't stop them any more than you can stop rumours.'

'Perhaps not.' The tall Blood-Wizard came over to her and took the paper, held the pieces together to study the drawing. 'But one can do what one can to find the reason behind it. Hmn. One of the milder ones, I see . . .' His hands on the cheap yellow handbill were brown and deft, and in the lamplight Tally noted how both his little fingers had been cut off just above the first knuckle in the strange rites his Order practiced, and how the rest of the fingers were scarred with ritual cuts.

'The reason is because people hate the mageborn, isn't it?' Tally followed him quietly across the vestibule, past the silent guards outside the bronze doors, and over the wavery harlequin of torchlight and darkness that fell like a silken quilt across the flagstones of the great court outside. 'Because they fear them? Only now the fears aren't just of a single wizard using spells to cheat honest men, or seduce chaste women – they're fears that wizards will organize and take over the Forty Realms. Which is funny,' she added, with a sudden, shaky laugh, 'when you think of it. I mean, the idea that any group of wizards *could* get together long enough to conspire in *anything* is something that could only be believed by someone who doesn't know wizards.'

The sounds of argument in Jaldis' rooms at the top of the octagonal library tower were clearly audible as Tally and Gyzan climbed the final flight of stairs from the uppermost of the book-rooms below. 'Why not?' she heard the Gray Lady's soft tones, now clipped and very angry. 'Because you don't want other wizards to learn how to communicate with other worlds than our own?'

'My dear lady,' rumbled Shavus' gravelly bass. 'It's a matter of principle. Were the case different you'd be arguing for me, not against. The magic of the Dark Wells – the knowledge of how the Cosmos is put together and what things can affect its very fabric – is a powerful and terrible lore. It cost Jaldis years of seeking and study . . . it almost cost him his life seven years ago . . .'

Gyzan opened the door and let Tally pass before him into the room, the peacock-feathers of her collar and headpiece flashing strangely in the soft, blue-white witchlight that flooded the neat little chamber. The Archmage paused to note their entry, in the act of leaning forward from Jaldis' carved chair, then turned back to the Gray Lady who stood, arms folded tight about her, in the curtained window embrasure. Near the small hearth sat Nessa of Dun – the Serpentlady, tall and heavy and beautiful in the brown and black robes of the Morkensik Order – and with her the boyish, white-haired Astrologer of Fell, and another brown-robed Morkensik mage whom Tally could not identify, though she knew him by sight as she knew so many of the wizards who over the past seven years had come visiting Jaldis.

'Any magic, any body of knowledge that powerful, must be kept to the smallest number of folk,' the Archmage went on, his ugly face anxious and conciliating. 'You know how quickly such things can be perverted to the worst uses. Remember what happened when the Blood-Mages learned the lore to summon demons . . .'

'That was the Dark Sect, the wizard Canturban's students,' protested the Gray Lady.

'That's true,' added Gyzan. 'Even the other Blood-Mages shun them.'

'Be that as it may.' The Archmage waved a heavy-muscled hand. 'It could as easily have been any of those splinter sects. You know no Blood-Mage has the training in balance and restraint that wizards must have – Your pardon, Gyzan, but you know that's true . . .'

'I know nothing of the kind. All Blood-Mages aren't like . . .'

'The wider the knowledge,' Shavus went on as if his friend had not spoken, 'the more chance there is for . . . accidents. Or spying . . .'

'You're saying you don't trust us.'

'I'm saying I don't trust some of the people who have access to the library on your islands. Suppose one of your Ladies takes it into her head to go over to the Earth-Witches next year, and takes with her whatever she may have found out? Can you guarantee *they* won't . . .'

'The Earth-Witches are perfectly harmless . . .'

'They say,' remarked Harospix of Fell.

The Lady's sharp hazel gaze flicked to the Morkensiks sitting grouped by the hearth. 'I am only saying that this concentration of knowledge can be taken too far.' She looked back at Shavus. 'From what I understand he didn't even teach Rhion how to open a Dark Well, for fear I'd get that information out of him . . .'

'Well, you *did* seduce him in an effort to get Jaldis' books away from him.'

'That was *not* . . .' began the Gray Lady, then glanced sidelong at Tally, and fell silent.

'Oh, Shavus,' chided Nessa, and caught Tally's eye mischievously. 'As if she'd need a reason to try to seduce Rhion!'

Both Tally and the Gray Lady laughed, and Shavus, relieved, rose to his feet and went to clasp Tally's hands in his own. 'I think you know Nessa, the Court Mage of the Earl of Dun,' he said. 'Harospix Harsprodin, and his student Gelpick of Wendt. They've come – and Erigalt of Pelter and Frayle the White should be here by tomorrow – to help in seeking through the Dark Well for some sign of Rhion and Jaldis, and to assist in bringing them back. As you know it needs magic on both sides of the Void in order to make the jump, and since, as Jaldis says, there is no magic in that world, or if any, only a very little which can be raised at the solstices and the equinoxes, it's going to need a great deal on this side to bring them through. We're going to be watching by the Well in turns . . .'

'And the other Morkensiks were kind enough to come and make it unnecessary to share the Well's secrets with myself or Gyzan,' added the Gray Lady, turning back from the window, for all her soft stockiness moving with powerful grace. Her hands, rubbing on the plain meal-coloured homespun of her sleeve, was thick with muscle from the bread-bowl, the shears, the spindle – alone among them she did not wear the robe of a wizard, only a simple dress such as the peasant women of the Drowned Lands wore, with irises embroidered on its breast.

'Nay, I never said that!' protested Shavus.

'Did you think it?'

Shavus hesitated. Harospix inclined his snowy head with a courtier's grace. 'There are different forms of magic, Lady,' he said gently. 'Different frames of reference. At the moment it is not the time to deal with the inevitable misunderstandings of trying to mesh an intellectual system like the Morkensiks' with an organic one such as your own.'

The Gray Lady's lips pressed thin; Gyzan folded his arms, and within his tattooed eyelids his brown eyes were grave and sad.

'Then if you have no more need of our presence here,' the Gray Lady said, 'Gyzan and I will return to Sligo. No . . .' She raised a hand as Shavus got quickly to his feet. 'I'm not angry with you. Just please let me know if you hear anything.'

'Of course,' promised the Archmage, glad to make whatever concessions would let him out of a fight with the Ladies of the Moon.

'The Archer may remain with us as long as he pleases,' she went on, picking up her grey wool cloak from the table and swinging it over her broad, square shoulders. 'Inar the Solarist has taken refuge there with us also, and we've had word that Vyla of Wellhaven is on her way, with two of the other exiled Hand-Prickers . . .'

Shavus' intolerant blue eyes widened in alarm; Tally could easily read in them his relief that the Gray Lady was carrying away no secrets to spread among that motley gang.

'You will, of course, be welcome among us at any time,' added the Lady mildly, 'since Rhion has taught even the most prejudiced among us that there are *some* decent Morkensiks.'

'Well, thank you, my lady,' smiled the old man.

She paused in the doorway. 'Don't smile,' she said gravely. 'The day may come when you need that sanctuary. Good-night.

'Damned arrogant intellectual jackanapes,' she went on viciously, as soon as she and Tally had descended out of earshot – quite a distance, for wizards. They crossed through the scriptorium, their footfalls echoing sharply in the warm, dreamy darkness where the smells of ink and parchment lingered. Gyzan had remained for a few moments to show the pieces of the scurrilous handbill to Shavus; the Lady and Tally walked down the stairs in silence, not speaking until they reached the lowest floor, the many-pillared entry-hall where the coloured glow of cressets in the courtyard cast dancing reflections on the marble walls. The Duke's guests were spilling out of the main hall now and into the court, where the warm summer evening breathed with the smell of jasmine and wistaria, with the lemon-grass of the torches and the thin pungence of the dust that always seemed to hang in the dry upland air.

'Listen, Tally,' said the Lady, halting in the darkness and touching the younger woman's beribboned sleeve. 'What Shavus is refusing to understand is that knowledge is not simply for use. It is for saving, for passing along, maybe to people we don't know in the distant future. Yes, I tried, by means of spells and coercion, to get Rhion to show me where Jaldis hid his books when they stayed among us, though it is a lie to say that I used my body to try to coax that knowledge out of him . . . I tried because I feared that the knowledge would be lost.'

Tally frowned. 'But if you don't know who will be using it in the future, ill could come of it . . .'

'Ill can come of any knowledge,' said the Gray Lady softly. 'There is only so much that we can control. Rhion tells me that seventeen years ago nearly all Jaldis' books were torched out of existence by the old King's soldiers when they arrested him – when they put out his eyes, and tore out his tongue, and crippled him. There was knowledge in those volumes that was lost forever, Rhion says. Now something about these rumours of conspiracy troubles me, something about the fact that they seem to be centred here, and in Dun, and in Fell, and wherever any of the Great Lords has a wizard in his employ. Though I've never liked the thought of a mage selling his powers to a lord – it is not for such that these powers were given us by the Goddess – I will say that it does keep the lords themselves in balance, and prevents any one of them, or any Cult, from aggrandizing too greatly. Without them . . .'

She frowned, rubbing her hands again uneasily over the coarse wool of her cloak. 'Without them it would become a contest of strongmen.' She glanced up at Tally in the woven shadows, studying her face.

'We need Jaldis' books, Tally,' she said softly. 'Rhion told me before he left that Jaldis turned them over into your father's keeping.'

Tally was silent for a long time. She was remembering the handbill she had found, remembering others that had appeared, pasted to the walls of taverns and public baths; remembering the way Esrex had looked at her sons, and the black-robed priests of the Hidden God who seemed always to be about the court these days.

But they were Jaldis' books, Jaldis' secrets. He had trusted her with them, as he trusted her father, trusted Rhion. 'I – I can't,' she said softly, and wondered if the Gray Lady would put a geas of some sort upon her, as she had put a geas upon the strawberries, to draw her out of the city that morning. She turned away, crossing the vestibule to the doors, and the Lady walked with her, her soft-booted feet making little sound on the speckled red terrazzo of the floor.

'He is my friend,' Tally finished simply, turning within the shadow of the great bronze doors. 'And Rhion . . .'

'I understand.' And in the darkness she could hear the sadness in the Lady's voice.

'If what Shavus says is true,' went on Tally hopefully, 'they'll . . . they'll be bringing Rhion and Jaldis back through the Void at the Summer Solstice, when they can raise enough power on the other side – Nessa, and Harospix, and Erigalt, and the others.' She shivered with the thought, the desperate hope, of seeing Rhion alive and safe and with her again. *Please, Goddess*, she prayed to Mhorvianne, the bright-haired lady of illicit loves, *please bring him back safe* . . . 'That's only a few weeks.'

But somehow she heard in her own voice the note of false heartiness she would have pitied in another, and cringed from it.

'So it is,' said the Lady quietly. She drew her cloak about her, though the darkness outside, alive with torches like jewelled gold lace, was balmy with the summer's lazy warmth. 'And perhaps all will be well. If it is not . . .' She reached out, and touched the younger woman's hand.

Her voice sank almost to a whisper, sweet and strangely audible beneath the voices of servants and grooms, the jingling of horse-gear and the laughter of guests, in the court beyond the arcade where they stood. 'If it is not, remember that you and your children will always find sanctuary in the Drowned Lands.'

Another shadow seemed to thicken from the general gloom behind them; Tally got a brief glimpse of Gyzan the Archer. Then the two wizards stepped back, and seemed to melt into the darkness again, becoming one with the shifting reflections of torchlight beneath the arcade.

Tally straightened the collar of pearls and feathers about her neck, and tucked with her fingers at the stray tendrils of her hair, preparing to return to the lights and music of the feast. Beneath the green silk of her husband's colours and the thick bullion and pearls her heart was beating fast. Shavus had brought the others of their Order, to watch beside the Well until the turn of Summer – and at the turn of Summer, they would bring Rhion and Jaldis back.

If something hadn't happened in that other world.

If they could even *find* that other world in the darkness of the Void.

Mhorvianne, guide them . . . Goddess of the Moon, help them . . .

Resolutely stifling the fear that had walked with her every

day since the equinox of spring, she started back along the arcade towards the main palace. As she did so a moving shadow caught her eye, slipping from pillar to pillar. At first she thought it was Gyzan and the Lady, but a moment later, as the shadow stepped into the court and vanished into the crowd, she saw that it was only a servant, hastening on some errand from the empty library to the colour and life of the feast.

12

'Why wasn't I told you were going to do a major ceremonial last night?'

Von Rath looked quickly up from his breakfast porridge, and then away. In the buttercup brilliance of the sunlight pouring through the wide dining-room windows he looked ghastly, drawn and grey and sleepless. As if, Rhion thought, even after he had gone to bed, staggering from the drugs he had taken, he had not slept, but had only lain awake in the whispering darkness, wanting more.

'Baldur only came to me after you had left for the village.' Von Rath set his spoon meticulously across the top of the bowl of barely-touched oatmeal. On the other side of the room Poincelles was consuming a hearty plate of bacon and eggs in blithe disregard of Himmler's recommendation that SS Troopers breakfast upon porridge and mineral water – Himmler owned the largest mineral water concession in Germany. On top of Rhion's memories of last night the greasy smell of the bacon was nauseating. Neither Baldur nor Gall were anywhere to be seen.

A little too airily von Rath went on, 'Oh, perhaps we should have waited for you to return, but when he showed me the rite he had discovered – decoded from the Venetian Lucalli's diaries – somehow I knew we did not need to wait.'

'Like hell.' Rhion dropped into a chair. 'It takes more than an hour and a half to push through the paperwork to get three prisoners sent over here from Kegenwald for you to disembowel. They're efficient, but they're not that efficient.'

The grey eyes met his, the cold opal gaze a stranger's,

and Rhion saw again the demon move in their depths. 'Do you object to that?'

'I object,' said Rhion slowly, picking his words with the utmost care, 'to you doing a rite involving human sacrifice, especially an unwilling human sacrifice, without consulting me. The field of power raised from such a sacrifice is septic and unpredictable. Without stronger guards than you can raise in this world you could end up killing everyone in the house. You don't know how to direct the power you raised last night – you sure as hell didn't know how to disperse it.'

Von Rath frowned, genuinely puzzled. With a chill stab of shock Rhion understood then that the man had not even been aware of the horrors that had gibbered in the corners of the darkness last night.

'It was dispersed,' said von Rath. 'We used the usual formulae . . .'

'The usual formulae are about as effective as a traffic citation against a division of Panzers! The whole house was glowing when I got here. What you did – human sacrifice, especially a torture-sacrifice – is the most dangerous way there is of raising power . . .'

'Nonsense.' There wasn't even defensiveness in his voice – only a kind of brisk relief. 'Human sacrifice has been practised since the dawn of time, and the Adepts of the Shining Crystal never spoke of danger, though they regularly used this method of raising power.' He spoke with the same matter-of-fact calm with which he had quoted his 'scientific' statistics on the intelligence of women or the cultural superiority of the Aryan race. 'And in any case,' he went on, 'they were not true human beings. The women were gypsies, the boy a Jew.'

Rhion looked away from him, his fist clenching involuntarily with rage, fighting back words that wouldn't change the calm conviction in those opaque eyes but would only put paid to what little freedom of action he himself might still have. Von Rath had once said to him *Surely you've tried to have a reasonable argument with a woman . . .* Rhion had had plenty of those, but what he'd never had – though he'd occasionally been foolish enough to try – had been a reasonable argument with a member of either sex in the grip of an obsession which amounted to lust.

After a few moments he said quietly, 'I don't care if they were Hitler's charladies and the King of Belgium: unless the victim is willing, a blood-rite with a sentient intelligence runs the risk of releasing forces that can completely distort the powers raised. You raised a hell of a lot of power last night, but without physical operancy – without technique *you can't control it.*'

Von Rath leaned forward, and with slender white fingers still stained faintly brown under the nails moved his porridge bowl just slightly, so that the edge of the saucer lined up perfectly with the waxed oak grain of the table's wood. 'And whose fault is it,' he asked gently, 'that we do not have physical operancy?'

Rhion experienced a sensation exactly similar to that of a man hanging by a rope above an abyss, when he feels the first strand part.

Oh, Christ.

Von Rath went on in that soft, level voice, 'You were the one who told us that the Rites of the Shining Crystal, should we decode them, would be of no use to us. Fortunately Baldur saw in them more promise than you apparently did . . .'

'What Baldur saw in them was the possibility of power.' Rhion had known that this would come, but still he felt the blood leaving his extremities. He was aware as he never had been before of his absolute isolation in this place, of von Rath's absolute power over him . . . of the beating of his own heart. 'What he didn't see – what my guess is he didn't want to see – is their danger to the magician who uses them.'

'And why was there no mention of this danger made by the Adepts of the Shining Crystal themselves?'

'Maybe because they were so goddam vain they wouldn't admit there might be anything wrong with what they were doing?'

'Or because their own souls were strong enough to shed the petty hates of the weak?' Von Rath broke off suddenly, brows flinching as if at the bite of unexpected pain. He put his hand to his smudged and sunken eyes, and shook his head.

'I – I'm sorry,' he said softly. When he looked up the metallic hardness had faded momentarily from his eyes, leaving them again the eyes of the young man who had dreamed of wizardry, who had asked only to be taught. 'I don't know what . . . Rhion, I respect your learning. You still have a great deal of technique to teach me, and I admit I am still a novice.' He frowned, trying to collect his thoughts. 'But it is plain to me that you do not understand the nature of – of heroism, for want of a better word. There comes a time when a student must realize his own truth, not his teacher's; when a man must see with his own heart and his own eyes, not through books written by other men. It is intuition and courage which lie behind great deeds, not hairsplitting pedantry for its own sake.'

'In other words experience isn't valid if it isn't *your* experience?' retorted Rhion dourly, recognizing the image of the intuitive Aryan hero from the cheaper sort of pulp fiction and the more fatuous articles in *Der Sturmer* available in the watchroom. He knew that at this point he should have got up and left, but he was angry as well as scared, angry at that arrogance, angry for the old man he had seen with the wounded lip, angry for last night's dead.

'I'm saying it is valid only up to a point. Then a man must learn, and know for himself. It isn't the first time human sacrifice has been performed in the cause of the Black Order, you know . . .'

'No,' agreed Rhion slowly. 'But as I understood it, the sacrifices performed by the SS at Welwelsburg were of volunteers, SS men themselves. A willing sacrifice is an entirely different matter, a completely different way of raising power.'

'Is it?' Von Rath tilted his head a little, that opaqueness, that curious opalescent quality, slowly filtering back into his fatigue-shadowed eyes. 'I wonder. But in any case our needs now are different. We must obtain the wherewithal to defeat Britain and defeat her quickly. And in so doing, we will give the SS power to become the Holy Order it should be, so that it can take its rightful place in the defence of the Reich and its destiny.' His cool gaze seemed distant, fixed upon some unknown point, some ancient dream. 'And that power now lies in my hands.'

'It doesn't,' said Rhion, his voice steady but his heart beating hard. 'And it won't.'

The grey gaze didn't even shift, didn't acknowledge that anything could stand in its way. 'It will. Given time – and correct teaching.' He turned back to Rhion, studying him with glacial, objective calm. 'Tell me . . . Do you object to the blood-rites on so-called humanitarian grounds, or because of the danger?'

Rhion closed his eyes, seeing again the brown gypsy-woman's body, the inked blue symbols of the Rites barely visible under the blood that glistened everywhere on the shredded skin. He understood then the black self-loathing he'd read on everything Sara had touched. 'What you do with your criminals here is no concern of mine,' he made himself say. 'But for preference I'd rather not be in the Schloss at all while you're performing a blood-rite.' Everything within him was screaming, *Coward. Coward and whore.* And looking up, he saw the words re-echoed in the contemptuous thinning of von Rath's colourless lips.

'Of course I respect your wishes,' the SS wizard said. 'But you will give us the benefit of your wisdom and your teaching between-times? Because we will master this, Rhion.' His tone glinted like the blued edge of a knife. 'And let us have no more – ah – judgments on your part as to what is and is not safe for us to know. Understand?'

And with a gesture infinitely graceful he drained his glass of mineral water, and rising, walked from the room.

'*In other days,*' Baldur read, his thin voice freed for once of its nervous stammer as it framed the sonorous Latin of the ancient text, '*a mage alone could call forth power by simple acts, or by words spoken either aloud or within the mind, as in ancient times men spoke face to face with gods.*'

He paused to turn a page: a narrow book, bound in brown leather mottled and crumbling with mildew, its parchment pages hand-copied, so Baldur claimed, by a scholar in the old city of Venice three centuries ago from documents far older, documents copied in Byzantium from sources more ancient still. This was a usual claim made by occult societies, in Rhion's world as in this one. Baldur, no novice at dating manuscripts, had affirmed that this copy had indeed originated in the seventeenth century – a designation which puzzled Rhion, for, though records went back over forty centuries in places, this world seemed to count their years in both directions from the middle. The seventeenth century (counting forward) had been a time of intensive occult activity just before the rise of mechanistic industrialism. Through a sentence in a Papal letter and a reference in the Dee correspondence, Baldur claimed to have identified the Venetian scholar Lucalli as a possible member of the infernal Shining Crystal group, though no direct mention was made of it either in Lucalli's diary or in this *Praecepta*, which, though catalogued in his library in the 1908 (counting forward) inventory, might or might not have been his. But from what he had heard of the text, Rhion thought it was a good guess.

'Now men must have resort to the wills of a great congregation of folk, joined together with one accord and stirred up by dancing and the beating of drums and by the act of generation promiscuously performed [all these methods being anciently employed to rouse up the vital flames]. More and more the Adept must rely upon the turning of the stars and the taking of the Universe at its flow-tide, and upon the use of potions and salves which free the spirit and stir forth the vital flame of life from their flesh. For mark this: there is an energy, a fire, in the human flesh and the human soul, from which magic can be woven.'

Lounging in his corner near the window of the dimly-curtained library, Poincelles glanced up from his own book and smiled.

'All possess this flame in some measure, but to greater or less extent, as fire burns the more or less brightly from oil depending on the degree to which it is pure. Most brightly it burns in the True Adepts, who by means of drugs and potions can call it forth from themselves at will; but lesser men of wisdom still have great measure of this flame. Even the dross of humanity, the human cattle which eat grass and breed and exist only for the purposes of the True Adepts, possess it in some degree, and thus can be used, as the flesh of cattle is used to sustain the life of a true man. This the Indian wizards of the New World knew, when they made their sacrifices; this the devotees of the black cults of Atys and Magna Mater understood, when they performed deeds for which the Emperor Trajan had their names stricken from the records of history. And this knowledge has been handed down unto those who Understand.

'And it's true, it worked,' Baldur added, looking up.

In the filtered afternoon light coming through the library windows the boy looked absolutely awful, his face like putty behind the thick spectacles, his hands trembling where they lay on the stained parchment page. His repeated sniffling informed Rhion also that Baldur had fortified himself with a quick sniff of his favourite poison before leaving his room, where he'd lain in a stupor since concluding his part of last night's experiment. *No fear from this group,* thought Rhion with dour irony, settling deeper into the tapestry embrace of a worn wing-chair. *They'll dope themselves to death before they can destroy the world.*

But it was what they would do in the meantime that had him worried.

'What?' he asked cautiously.

'Don't you see? Of c-course you have to see!' Baldur almost shouted at him, twitching impatiently in his chair and dragging a damp and crumpled sleeve under his raw nostrils. 'Those gypsy b-b-bitches last night, and the Jew . . . Pau – er – the Captain sent for them specially. The wo-women were fortune-tellers, the brat a psychic of some kind, I forget what. The Captain was wise enough – it was his idea to have anyone with p-power picked up. "Sp-Specially Designated". He knew we'd need them . . .'

'You mean, whether they'd done anything wrong or not?'

Baldur stared at him, flaccid lips agape. 'They were *Jews,*' he pointed out. 'And anyway the experiment worked! We were right! Thursday night – at the dark of the moon – we'll work the Rite using someone of greater power, greater magic, and we'll make a talisman of p-power that'll blow the roof off the building . . . !'

'That's exactly what I'm afraid of.'

Baldur heaved a sigh and slumped back in his chair, his weak brown eyes dreamy. 'What a pity they destroyed it. The Shining Crystal . . . Do you think it might have been one and the same with the Holy Grail? Wolfram von Eschenbach describes the Grail as a stone, you know. Just like the Jewish-Christian Church to have pulverized such a talisman, and slaughtered its guardians!'

'Jewish-Christian Church?' Rhion was startled. 'I thought the Christians spent the last ten centuries killing the Jews!'

Baldur waved an airy hand. 'They all come from the same source,' he declared, as if that made them a single organization. 'They hate and suppress m-magic, the same way they've tried to suppress the pure Aryan race, whose birthright true magic is.'

'And whose most sterling representative and spokesman you are?' purred Poincelles maliciously.

Baldur's pasty face blotched with red. 'My family can trace its German heritage back past 1640!'

'Ah, I see – that should get you into the SS with no problem, then, shouldn't it?'

The boy jerked furiously to his feet, his pudgy hands bunching with rage, and Rhion caught his arm and pulled him back as he started towards the Frenchman. To Poincelles Rhion snapped, 'Look, if you're going to waste your time pulling the wings off flies, why don't you do it someplace where it won't waste my time, too. Christ, it's like being in a girls' school – except if Baldur were a schoolgirl you'd be doing more to him than calling him names.'

Poincelles' grin widened appreciatively. '*Touché*,' he murmured, rising, and, book under his arm, strolled out onto the veranda just beyond the long windows, where Gall, stripped to a loincloth, was engaged in boneless runic yoga in the pale afternoon sun.

'French-Jewish pig,' gritted Baldur, bending down to scrabble for the notes he'd knocked off the table in his hysterical haste. He puffed a little as he moved; the thin bar of sunlight penetrating from the curtain Poincelles had left open picked out a mist of sweat on his pimpled forehead.

'Is he Jewish?' Sara hadn't mentioned it.

Baldur shrugged. 'All the French are,' a statement Rhion knew to be untrue. 'They're a degenerate race – ape-men, beast-men, whose only desire is to genetically pollute the Aryans, the true descendants of the Atlantean root-race, through the s-sexual corruption of their wo-wo-women.' He straightened up, barely missing the edge of the table with his head, his hands shaking badly as he shuffled his papers into order once again.

His pouchy eyes gazed past Rhion, after the older occultist with sudden, jealous hate. In a low, furious mutter he went on, 'It's against him, and men like him, that the SS was formed. The real SS, the inner core of the SS – the shining swordblade of the Aryan race that will turn the tide of genetic slopwork that threatens to engulf us from the east! We're more than just an Imperial guard, you know,' he went on, turning to meet Rhion's eyes. 'We're a religious order, like the ancient Teutonic Knights: a sacred band of all that's best of the Aryan race. It's only fitting that we, with our birthright of magic, of *vril*, should be doing what we're doing now – forming a point of adamant for the spear of our destiny. Paul – P-Paul understands.'

He gestured angrily towards the windows, beyond which, by Gall's furious gesticulations, it was obvious Poincelles had succeeded in baiting the Austrian mage. 'And Himmler uses men like *that* for his purposes! When P-Paul comes into his own, when they make him head of the SS – as they'll have to, when by magic we encompass the British defeat! – the Order will be as it should be, as it has always been destined to be, a sacred band of blood and fire and m-m-magic . . .'

'Baldur . . .'

The boy almost leaped out of his chair at the sound of von Rath's quiet voice. Without so much as an *Excuse me* he abandoned Rhion and hurried into the hall – from his seat in the wing-chair, Rhion could see the two of them standing together, the boy clutching his notes to his sagging breasts and nodding, the man speaking softly, his head tilted a little to one side, sunlight from the hall window dappling his black shoulders, his pale hair, the scarred left profile visible through the door with pallid gold. Von Rath said something and gestured towards the library door – Rhion thought he heard his name, but the Nazi mage made no move to greet him or to enter the room.

He understood – he had understood at breakfast – that he had placed himself outside the circle of those whom von Rath considered his own kind, placed himself, in effect, with the women and children being used for strafing practice on the road. He was now merely useful, for as long as that would last.

13

'You're crazy!'

'I thought your degree was in Chemistry, not Psychiatry,' retorted Rhion, pulling up his feet to sit cross-legged on the lumpy bed. 'You have a better suggestion?'

'Yeah,' said Sara hotly. 'I smuggle my father a gun instead of those silly pills and have him shoot *himself* instead of letting the guards do it.'

'If you could figure out a way to smuggle your father a gun instead of the pills we wouldn't be having these problems.'

'No.' She sighed and shook her head, frizzy red hair catching the light of the candles in gold threads all around her square, slender shoulders as she leaned back in the room's rump-sprung stuffed chair. 'If Papa tried to blast his way out he'd just hurt himself. Or get into an argument about time travel or the internal combustion engine with the guards . . . Not that he knows anything about the internal combustion engine. When Mama would go visit her sisters in Pozen my heart was in my throat every time Papa tried to light the stove or cut up a chicken to cook. He once nearly killed himself taking the chess-board down from a shelf.' She nudged the two pills – clumsy wads of gritty tallow on a twist of paper – on her knee with a fingertip, not meeting Rhion's eyes. 'Maybe we'd better just forget it. Thank you for wanting to help, but . . .'

'You don't think I'm really a wizard, do you?'

She raised black-coffee eyes to his. 'Oh, come on,' she said gently. 'You're sweet – you really are – but I was *raised* around people who thought they were wizards, you know? And about half of them claimed to be from another dimensional plane, or from the future or the past, or reincarnated from being Albertus Magnus or the Dalai Lama or some kind of Inca sachem. They'd talk with Papa for *hours* about magic and spiritual forces, and they'd swap spells like a couple of grannies trading recipes, and for what? I never saw Papa so much as keep the mice away, let alone make himself invisible so the Nazis wouldn't see him . . .'

'I'm not going to make him invisible,' explained Rhion patiently. 'I'm just going to make the guards look the other way while he crosses from the infirmary to the fence.'

'If you can do that how come you're sneaking in and out of here under the wire like the rest of us poor mortals?'

'Because it takes about an hour and a half of intense meditation and mental exercises to do it and it wipes me out for the rest of the night.'

'Yeah,' said Sara wisely, getting to her feet and taking a cigarette from the pocket of her scarlet frock, 'they always had some reason why they couldn't do it, either.'

Down below the voices of the guards drifted faintly up through the open window, the ubiquitous stink of tobacco-smoke vying with the sharp sweetness of the pines. The last of the lingering northern twilight had faded less than an hour ago. As he'd listened to Sara's high heels and Horst's escorting jackboots ascend the attic stairs, Rhion had thought about how badly he'd missed the sound of a woman's voice, surrounded as he had been for months by men.

'Sara,' he said, 'I know you don't believe in this. But believe that if your father doesn't escape from Kegenwald, he's going to die on the night of the twenty-first of this month in a way you don't want to know about. I need his help, and we've got damn little time. You say you can get into the camp on Sunday?'

She nodded. She'd risen from the chair and walked to the window, to let her cigarette-smoke drift out into the luminous dark. Candlelight softened the sharpness of her features, sparkled on the little gold chain she wore around the slender softness of her throat.

It was Saturday night. Von Rath must have paid the owner of the tavern a hefty wad of marks to make up for her absence – beyond a doubt Sara would have to surrender some of what was given her as well. The dress she wore, bias-cut cotton crepe that clung to the curves of breast and hip, was better than her usual work-clothes. It had taken Rhion awhile to get used to seeing a woman's calves and ankles so casually displayed, though Dr Weineke's SS uniform had effectively killed whatever erotic interest he'd felt in the principle.

'They let families in, if the commandant's not being a putz that day,' Sara went on. 'Sometimes women wait for eight, ten hours outside to see their husbands and then he decides there's no visiting till next week. They come from all over Germany, you know – it's a work-camp, mostly for political prisoners. A lot of the town mayors and priests and union leaders from Poland are there, as well as Germans who said something Hitler or the local party leaders didn't like – or *were* something they didn't like, like Jews or gypsies or Poles. The women bring food and clothing . . .' Her red-painted mouth twisted. 'The commandants budget for it in the rations. They count on the men being fed at least half by their families, whether they are or not.'

'Have you gone before?'

She shook her head. 'Even in different clothes with my hair dyed and those fake glasses I got, I didn't want to risk anyone recognizing me. God knows enough of the guards could.' She smoked awhile in silence, dark gaze fixed on some middle-distance beyond the window, lost in her own thoughts.

'It's funny,' she said softly, her face half turned aside and the cold glare of the floodlights from below picking out the fragile wrinkles, the lines of dissipation around the mouth and eyes. 'When I heard they'd picked up Papa – when I'd heard the SS had him in "special custody" – I thought, Hell, I know how to find him . . . or at least how to make money and get information while I looked. I had God knows how many boyfriends in New York. I worked as an artist's model while I was in school – not that Aunt Tayta ever knew where I was always going in the evenings – and the first year I was in New York, in '34, I worked as a waitress to make money to start at NYU. I used to go out to dinner with one guy, have him bring me home at eight because I said I had to study, have another guy pick me up to go to the movies, have *him* bring me home in time to go out with guy number three for the midnight set at the Cotton Club. So I thought doing what I do now wouldn't be so very different. Christ, was I naive.'

Her lips flinched suddenly, and she looked down, crushing out her cigarette on the windowsill with fingers that shook.

'You must love him a lot,' said Rhion quietly. She nodded, not looking, not willing to give him even the words of a reply. The pride in her, the anger at men and the hatred of having to depend on one, however crazy, for help, was like a wall of thorns. He drew up his knees, wrapped his sweatshirt-clad arms around them. The half-healed knife-cut still hurt like hell. 'How did you get into Germany?'

'Through Basle.' The request for information, for the story, steadied her as he'd hoped it would. 'I used to go out with a guy named Blackie Wein – he ran protection for Lepke Buchalter down in the garment district. A mobster,' she added, seeing Rhion's puzzled expression. 'He was tied up with Murder, Incorporated – the Ice Pick League, they were called – but Blackie was all right. He was a Yankees fan like me. When I heard Papa had been picked up – that he was in "designated internment" – I didn't know what else to do. I went to Lepke . . . He put the word out and got me identity papers for $200 from the daughter of a newspaper editor from Dresden who'd just got out with his family by the skin of his teeth. There was a guy named Fish who did me up a couple more sets to use in emergencies, plus some for Papa – Fish made his living passing bad cheques – and another one of Lepke's boys taught me how to pick locks. That was the biggest help when I got to searching this place.' She shrugged. 'So here I am.'

She straightened up, and walked to the chair again, to pick up the little screw of paper with the two waxy, lumpy pills which lay upon its padded arm. For a long moment she stood looking down at them. Then her eyes moved to Rhion, still sitting curled up on the bed. 'This is crazy-stupid.' The break in her voice was infinitesimal. In spite of everything, Rhion thought, she was young enough to grab at even crazy-stupid hope. She put the pills in her purse.

Rhion took a deep breath. 'You say you can pick locks. Will you help me with something else?'

With an almost instinctive gesture she moved a step or two away, putting the iron-spindled footboard of the bed between them and folding her hands around its upper bar. 'Like what?'

As Rhion had suspected, there were rooms in the cellar under the north wing, directly beneath the Temple, on the ley-line itself, the door hidden behind the piled boxes.

'Yeah, I saw that door,' said Sara, as they climbed down the shaft of the disused kitchen dumbwaiter – an invention Rhion made a mental note to mention to the Duke's Kitchen Steward when he got back, if he got back – clinging to the old rope while their feet sought the tiny slots let into the brick of its sides. 'By the scratches on the floor they didn't get moved back and forth a lot, so obviously they weren't keeping anybody down there.' Her voice sank from a whisper to barely a breath as they crawled out into the damp, pitch-black cavern of the southern part of the cellar. As they ghosted through the huge main chamber, where the furnace slept like some somnolent monster in its aura of oily dust, the tinny echo of the wireless could be heard from the guards' watchroom opposite the door to the cellar stairs. 'How the hell can you tell where you're going?' Her hand pressed his shoulder from behind; without her high-heeled shoes she was an inch shorter than his own barefoot height.

'I told you. I'm a wizard.'

'Sorry I asked.'

She fished the flashlight she usually carried with her from her purse, put her fingers over the bulb and flicked it quickly on to scan the far wall. 'There.'

'Just as I thought.' He glanced at the ceiling-beams in the blackness.

Even through several feet of floor-joists, he could feel the cold evil of the Temple as they came beneath its bounds. True to his word, he had got Horst to take him down to The Woodsman's Horn the night before last – the night of the moon's dark – and had remained there drinking bad beer and listening to a Beethoven concert over the wireless until the place had closed. It hadn't helped. Even at a distance of twenty miles he'd fancied all evening that he felt what was happening at the Schloss, and had dreaded returning there, fearing what he would find in spite of the doubled and trebled spells of protection and dispersal he had taught von Rath. He didn't know what he'd have done if one of the chosen victims had been Sara's father, but it wasn't. They had been another gypsy woman and a noted German runeologist – Aryan to the core – whose runic system had contradicted the one favoured by the Bureau. After one attempt at sleep from which he'd been jerked, sweating in horror, by his dreams, he'd spent the rest of the night staring at the rafters. It seemed to him that the screams of the victims had permeated the very fabric of the house.

That afternoon von Rath had shown to him the talismans they'd made, discs of bone and crystal and stretched skin written over with the dark sigils devised by the accursed adepts; had talked for hours, lovingly, eagerly, obsessively, fingering them with wonderment and not seeming to remember that they had been made of the bodies of men like himself. He had spoken of the power within them, and how it could be utilized, and what he would do when that power was his . . . only that. Rhion did not have to touch the things to know that the power was there, glowing in them against the workroom's lamplit dark as phosphorous glows in the heart of a rotten tree. But neither he nor von Rath could utilize that power for even the simplest of spells they'd tried.

And that, he supposed, was just as well.

The boxes in the cellar were filled with mouldy books, smelling of silverfish and mice; it took him and Sara a few minutes to move them aside. Behind them, as Sara had said, was a door, new, stout, and padlocked shut. 'Probably used to be a wine-room,' he remarked in an undervoice, holding the flashlight as the girl knelt and began probing the lock with the various wire tools she'd taken from her purse. 'There's marks of an older lock here above the new hasp.' Shielding the light with his body, he strained his ears to hear any creak of footfalls in the hall overhead, any sign of approaching guards on the stair, any clue that their activities were suspected. At this point they could never hope to get the boxes replaced in time.

'This door isn't more than a year or so old,' breathed Sara. 'What the hell you think old Pauli has in here, anyway? All the booze is in the cupboard in the library – all the booze he knows about, anyway, Poincelles has a stash of his own. I don't think he knows about the coke Baldur gets from Kurt at the Horn, or those little odds and ends Gall steals from the workroom . . .'

'Gall?'

'Yeah. He's got these little sacks of seeds and herbs and crystals hidden all around his room, a couple of amulets tucked under a loose floorboard, a mortar and pestle, a set of runestones and a crystal ball cached in the bedsprings. It was a whole education, going through this place. Bingo,' she added, an expression not translatable even with the Spell of Tongues. The padlock fell open.

His heart beating fast, Rhion pushed the door inwards.

The Dark Well was there. The smell of the room was the same as he remembered from those first instants of consciousness: moist earth, wet stone, power . . . the strange, ozoneous air of the Void. It was here they had gathered, not in that boarded-up chamber upstairs; it was here they had taken their drugs, reached out over the Void's darkness to guide him and Jaldis. It was here Eric Hagen had died.

The pang of remembering Jaldis again twisted in him like a turned knife. Even now in this nightmare world, he still caught himself thinking that when he returned home the old man would be there. His too-active imagination wondered for a gruesome second whether his master had actually been killed by the Void or was drifting there somewhere, still alive but unable to either escape or die . . . He pushed the thought quickly away. It was something he would never know.

Drawing a deep breath, he stepped back through the door to where Sara waited, staring behind her into the cellar's dark.

'I'm not sure how long this'll take,' he murmured. 'Get back up to the room; if they catch you down here you might be in real trouble.'

'Not as much trouble as you're gonna be if they flash a light down the stairs and find all those boxes moved and the door open,' she replied, peering hard in the direction of his voice. 'I'll stick around.'

'Thank you.' Not that a warning would do him much

good, he reflected. Even if he and Sara managed to reach the dumbwaiter shaft and get out of the cellar and up the backstairs to the dressing-room on the second floor, the boxes being displaced would tell von Rath everything he needed to know. At this point he was certain von Rath would dismantle the Dark Well to keep him here – and that would only be the start of his worries.

Sara closed the door, leaving him alone in darkness.

In darkness he could see the traced lines of chalk and long-dried blood that marked where the original rites of opening had been done. The ritually-charged swastika which had been his beacon across the Void's darkness was still there beside the triple circle of the Well itself, the symbol of the sun-cross at which he could now barely bring himself to look. Beyond it hung the shimmering brown column of shadow which even mageborn eyes could not pierce.

His pulse thudded loud in his ears as he approached it. The Well was quiescent – he could, he supposed, have passed his hand through it with no ill effects, but nothing would have induced him to try it. And it was so tenuous, he thought – the power that held it here so ephemeral that merely the breaking of the Circles, the erasure of any of the marks upon the floor, would destroy the Well, and his chances of contacting the help he needed, forever.

For a long time he only stood looking at the place, trying to steady his breathing and his thoughts.

A window into the Void.

A way to get home.

The thing that had killed Eric Hagen.

He could dimly sense the ley running deep beneath his feet, like ground-water in the earth, but he could no more have used its power to open the Void than he could have washed a tent in a thimble. On the night of the Solstice, he thought, the power would be there, maybe. But there had better be one hell of a lot of power concentrated at the other end.

He took a deep breath, pushed up the sleeves of his sweatshirt, and, kneeling, took chalk and Sara's clasp-knife from his pocket. In the darkness he drew a Circle close to the charged sun-cross on the floor, its edge touching that of the Well itself, and cut open the vein near his right elbow, where it wouldn't show, to mark the signs of Power in his own blood. He had no sense of power in doing this – he never had, in this universe – but he followed the rites meticulously, making himself believe that the faint strength of the ley-path seeped up into the chalked lines, drawing the figures of air as precisely as if they were actually visible, glowing as they would be in his own world. Trying not to think about whether anyone over there was listening.

It had been almost three months. Of course someone would be listening. Jaldis' loft was the only place they could hear, unless Shavus had used the old man's notes to open another Well elsewhere. This close to the Solstice, knowing it was the only time when enough power would be available to them here, of course he'd be listening for them . . .

But Shavus had disappeared the day before his and Jaldis' crossing – arrested, murdered, banished . . . he did not know.

Maybe no one knew.

We can think of neither the future that we go to, nor the past that we leave behind . . .

Don't do this to yourself, he commanded, feeling his resolve drain like the faint weakness and shock of opening his vein. *They may not hear you if you shout for help, but they CERTAINLY won't hear you if you don't.*

Only the long disciplines of his training made him turn his mind from the sweet quicksand of despair – of not having to try because it would do no good – and calm his thoughts, quiet his breathing, even out his heart-rate again. He sank into meditation, not knowing how long it would take to raise the energies, gathering all his strength into his hands. Though the room was cold, sweat stood out on his face. Clear and hard, he focused his mind on the Dark Well, willing it to open, willing the glowing channel across the endless abyss of colour without colour to whisper into life.

Nothing happened. The Well did not seem to change.

Deepening his concentration, he started again from the beginning. Marking the floor, the walls; weaving signs in the air cleanly and precisely, willing himself to know that he was making them correctly – willing himself not to doubt. Willing himself not to think about Jaldis; about Tally; about his own world on the other side of the Void; about that naive young man who'd come stumbling out of the livid darkness ten weeks ago and into the arms of the SS. Willing himself to believe that it worked.

There was still no change in the appearance of the Dark Well, but he sensed – or imagined – a minute drop in the temperature of the room, a resurgence of the queer ozoneous smell. Rising, legs weak, he stepped to the three lines of chalk, blood, and ash that circled the inner core of darkness – a darkness barely distinguishable from the darkness surrounding it – and stood, his stockinged toes just touching the outermost ring, his arms outspread.

'Shavus,' he whispered desperately, clinging to the image of the big old scar-faced archmage, 'Shavus help me. Shavus, I'm in trouble, help me, please. Get me out of here. I'm alone here, Jaldis is dead.'

He was tired now, queasy from loss of blood, and his head was beginning to throb, but he conjured in his mind the images of the stones on Witches Hill. Between the ancient magic of sacrifice glowing deep in the dolomite's fabric and the dim silvery limmerance of the ley, enough power clung to the Stones to serve as a beacon, if Shavus knew what to look for. At that point, provided the Spiracle would hold the Void's magic – provided he didn't kill himself charging it – he could probably collect enough energy at the turn of the Solstice-tide to open the Void and jump.

'I'll be there,' he whispered, perhaps aloud, perhaps only in the dark at the bottom of his mind. 'At Sunstead I'll be there, waiting. Get other wizards, get as many as you can. I can open the gate, but you'll have to get me through. Help me, Shavus, please. Get me out of here. Please get me out.'

He opened his eyes, staring into the heart of the Dark Well, emptying his mind and focusing it with all the strength within him, all the strength he could raise.

He saw nothing.

He closed his eyes, gathering his strength again, patiently willing himself not to think, not to feel. Then he slowly repeated all he had said, conjuring in his mind the image of himself standing on the altar of the Dancing Stones at midnight, surrounded by the Void-magic of the Spiracle, the power of the Solstice and the leys, arms outstretched, waiting . . .

And repeated it again, the strain of it hurting him now, grinding at his bones. And again saw nothing to tell him that he wasn't just a frightened little man standing with obsessive exactness in a scribbled network of chalked lines on the floor, praying to an empty room.

In other words, he thought, mad.

As if he'd stood chin-deep in the ocean and had the rock upon which he was balanced tip suddenly beneath his feet, he felt despair close over him, cold and fathoms deep. A headache clamped like a steel band around his temples, and he lowered his outstretched arms, cramped and trembling, to his sides.

He has to have heard me, he thought, sinking, exhausted, to his knees. *Shavus has to have heard.* Sitting on his heels, he carefully removed his glasses, pressed his throbbing forehead with his hands.

Tally came to his mind, lying by the fire in the green jewelled gown of the Sea-King's daughter; the animal warmth and delight of his sons' small hands pulling at his robe as they cornered him in play. For a moment he saw the matte blue silences of the Drowned Lands under the phosphorous of the rising moon. For ten weeks he had worked very hard at not feeling pain. Now, his defences spent, the pain came, wave after wave of it, breaking him like a child's driftwood fortress under advancing tide.

He bowed down over his hands, hurting with a deep, gouged ache that was worse than any physical pain he had ever undergone. Hugging himself as if the pain were in fact physical, and could be eased by physical means, he doubled over, fighting to stay silent, fighting to hold it in, a chubby, shabby little man in his worn sweatshirt and faded trousers, alone in the dark on the edge of the abyss.

After a long time the pain eased a little, and he knew then that it was close to dawn. The thought of slipping back to his room, of going on with another day, was physically repugnant to him. Easier just to roll down onto his side on the stone floor and sleep. But after a few minutes he got to his feet, and staggered, knees jellied, to push open the door.

Sara had made her way across the cellar to the stairs that led up to the hall above, where she stood listening, the two-foot iron rod of an old mop-bucket wringer-lever in one hand. Above them the Schloss was absolutely silent now, save for the metallic whisper of a wireless turned down dim. The guards would be catching a little shut-eye in the watchroom. A dangerous time, since they'd be guilty enough to wake at a whisper. He breathed, 'Sara . . .' and saw her turn sharply, straining her eyes to pierce the inky dark.

As softly as he could – warily, because of the club she held – he glided towards her over the damp stone floor. 'Let's get the boxes put back,' he whispered, still staying well out of range until he saw her positively identify his voice and relax. Then he took her arm, and led her back to where the flashlight beam couldn't possibly be seen from above.

'You want this locked up again?' she asked softly, touching the padlock. 'I can put it like this but not snib it closed. That way you can get in here again if you need to.'

'I will need to,' he said. 'But von Rath's getting more suspicious of me every day. If he finds it open, he'll know it's me tampering and will probably destroy the Well. I'll need your help getting in here again, two, maybe three more times . . .'

She muttered something really terrible in Polish, and helped him lift each box to avoid scratching the floor and put them back in the order they had been, as precisely as they could recall. As she picked up the flashlight to turn it off she looked briefly at his face in the finger-hooded glow.

'You okay?'

He nodded, turning his face from her and taking her elbow; she switched off the light, and let him guide her across the cellar, through the archway, to the old dumb-waiter with its rope and its tiny set-in steps.

The candles in his room had guttered out. He reached with his mind to relight them, then fumbled tiredly in his pocket for a match, the ache of thaumaturgical impotence bringing back the hurt of all that other pain. While Sara put on her high-heeled shoes he sank down onto the bed, head pounding, struggling to keep his grief at bay until she was gone.

'First time I ever left an evening here wearing the same lipstick I came in with,' she remarked, though she renewed it for good measure, the glossy red giving her thin, triangular face a pulchritudinous lushness in the candle-glow. 'Come down to the tavern Monday and I'll let you know how things went. I'll tell Papa not to take the pills till Monday, so we can go through with the rest of this *mishegoss* Wednesday when the shop's closed . . . Hey? You okay?'

He nodded, not looking at her. Worried, she came around the end of the bed to stand looking down at him with her arms folded beneath the soft shelf of her breasts.

'What happened in there?'

'Nothing,' he whispered.

She leaned down, and gently removed his glasses from his face, putting them on the shelf beside the candle. He ached to touch her – to touch someone, only for the comfort of knowing he wasn't absolutely alone. But to her a man's touch meant only one thing, and she had enough of that, so he didn't.

After a moment she pulled the thin coverlet up over him, turned and blew out the candle. He heard her high heels click away into darkness as she descended the attic stairs, and a few minutes later heard the car engine start outside, and fade as it drove off into the night.

In the iron hour before dawn his dreams were evil. Perhaps it was what he had read of the Rites of the Shining Crystal; perhaps the souls of the gypsy women, of the young Jewish clairvoyant and the elderly runemaster, still lingered to vent their bitter rage on one who had acquiesced in their murders. Perhaps it was only fear. In the dream Rhion found himself bound to one of the pillars in the black-draped Temple, forced to watch the Rite again and again: saw von Rath, gaunt and yellow as a man with fever in his long white robe, and Poincelles in bloodstained red. Over and over he heard the screaming, as if the sound itself were being drawn and twisted as a spinner twists wool into yarn; drawing strands of power from death and pain. He saw the power itself collecting, like dirty ectoplasmic slime, in pools on the altar, pools that moved a little when no one watched.

And in the morning, at the rites of meditation which they still performed though to Rhion's mind they had become a travesty of the calm opening to ritual work for which they had been designed, he observed their faces, wondering if they, too, had dreamed.

Gall, it was hard to tell. There was always a weird serenity about the old man, a calm that had nothing to do with right or wrong but depended entirely on his rigid apportioning of bodily and psychic energies, as if, for him, ultimately nothing really existed beyond the bounds of his own skin. Baldur, standing under the blood-red rune of Tiwaz at the northern 'watchtower', was twitchy and nervous, eyes glittering behind his thick glasses as if between his endless quest for knowledge in the ancient books and the psychoactive drugs he was taking, cocaine was the only thing keeping him together.

Poincelles . . . If Poincelles dreamed, Rhion thought, regarding the gangling, dirty man with sudden revulsion, it was with a smile on his lips. That smile lingered now, as he made his responses with an air of amused tolerance for the peccadilloes of others. If von Rath sought the wine of power in the bloody Rites of the Shining Crystal, Rhion now understood, what Poincelles enjoyed was the pressing of the grapes.

But it was von Rath who frightened Rhion most. Standing by the dark-draped altar, his hands outspread over the ritual implements there – sword and cup, book and thurifer – he was visibly thinner than he had been a week ago, as if the obsession with power – with converting power to operancy – were slowly consuming both flesh and mind.

Nietzsche, philosophical guru of the Nazi party, had spoken of the triumph of the will, but as things were in this world it was physically impossible for von Rath's will to triumph.

And as the warm spring days crept past and the moon

waxed to its first quarter and then to a bulbous distorted baroque, Rhion saw more and more frequently that icy flatness in the young wizard's eyes, and felt them on his back as he came and went.

It made things no easier that on Monday evening, in between her desultory flirting with the local Party official and a couple of guards from the Kegenwald camp – Monday was a quiet night in the tavern – Sara slipped him a note under his beer-mug which simply read, *No soap*. In German the phrase indicated only that bathing would be an unsatisfactory experience, but in the parlance of American cinema-films it meant a miscarriage of plans.

'Scum-sucking momzer didn't even let us in,' muttered Sara savagely two nights later, when she was once again up in his room. The tavern was closed Tuesdays and Wednesdays, and she and the leggy blonde Ulrica had been brought out to the Schloss at Rhion's request and Poincelles'. Her hair, dyed brown on Sunday for her visit to the camp, was now stiffer, frizzier, and redder than ever in the dim glow of the candles and the reflection of the primus stove they'd pilfered from the workroom, a scalding frame for her alabaster pallor that clashed loudly with the pink of the worn and pilled angora sweater she wore.

'We waited from seven in the morning until nine at night – some of those poor broads had been on the train since nine the night before, coming in from Berlin and Warsaw and God knows where – just sitting outside the gates of the camp on the ground, without water, without nothing.' Her small, quick hands squeezed out a rag in the water she was heating; it steamed in the balmy warmth as she crossed to the bed and dabbed at the half-healed knife-cut on the back of Rhion's arm.

As she worked she continued bitterly, 'We were scared to walk across the road to take a squat behind a bush in the woods, for fear they'd say *okay, come on in* while we were gone, with the guards all coming around and hassling whoever they thought was worth it. And there was I, feeling like I was sitting naked in the middle of Ebbetts Field, praying the ones I'd screwed wouldn't recognize me because I sure as hell wouldn't recognize them, hiding behind a pair of fake glasses and trying to look frumpy and middle-aged . . . Christ!'

Her hand where it steadied his bared arm squeezed tight with rage so that even the chewed-short nails bit into his flesh. 'And at the end of it some tight-assed kapo comes out and says "No visitors today. The prisoners are being punished."'

'For what?'

'Who knows? Who cares?' She dropped the cloth on the floor, and the smell of cheap gin filled the room as she soaked a second rag – the last scrap of Rhion's old shirt. The alcohol stung his skin. 'Still looks clean, but you're gonna have a bitch of a scar,' she added, binding the wound up again.

'Whose fault is that?' He pulled on his sweatshirt again, though the night was warm enough to have given him no discomfort; Sara gathered the discarded rags and draped them over the edge of the table to dry, then bent to light a cigarette in the flame of the primus stove. 'That pushes it till next Sunday.' His eyes went involuntarily to the spot in the rafters that was the Spiracle's latest hiding-place. 'And that's the last Sunday before the Solstice.'

'You don't think I know that?' She dropped angrily back onto the bed, back propped on the iron-spindled headboard, and reached across to the tableful of bedside candles to take an angry swig from the flask of medicinal gin. 'Crazy goddam witch-doctors . . .' She blew a stream of smoke.

Rhion decided not to mention that von Rath had spoken of doing another experiment – not merely the making of talismans, but an attempt to convert the power of the sacrifice into workable illusion – on the night of the full moon, six nights hence and a few days before the greater rite and talisman-making on the Solstice itself. If they were lucky Sara's father would be out of danger by that time anyway. The thought of what he'd have to do if they *didn't* succeed in freeing the old man brought the sweat cold to his face.

'What is that thing, anyway?'

He glanced across at her with a start. Sara, her knees crossed in a soft waterfall of skirt-gores, was looking up at the Spiracle's hiding-place. 'That iron and silver gismo with the crystals in it. Do all wizards hide little *tchotchkes* around where they live? Papa did.'

Rhion grinned, remembering Jaldis' propensity for secret devices. 'Pretty much,' he said. 'It's the thing I need your father's help – and yours, since you'll have to get us into that room in the cellar again – to finish.' He pushed the delicate wire frame of his spectacles more firmly up onto his nose. 'The rite of charging it has to be done by the Solstice,' he added, more quietly. 'If we can't get your father out by then . . .' He shivered at the thought of taking the thing down to the cellar, stepping into the Dark Well without another wizard present to keep him from being drawn in and destroyed.

'Then we'll get him out afterwards.' Sara's gaze, holding his, was flint. 'Won't we?'

Rhion said nothing. If they didn't get the old man out before Solstice-tide the odds were horribly good he himself would be dead afterwards. If he weren't, it would be because he'd lost his nerve at the last moment – in which case it was one *hell* of a long time to the Equinox, too long to count on – or because he'd succeeded, impossibly, in charging the Spiracle himself.

And in that case, he thought, could he leave Sara to her own devices? He remembered the brief vision in the scrying-crystal, the old man with the scarred lip raising his eyes to the window far above his head. He owed neither of them a thing – his arm still hurt every time he moved it and he was damn lucky, given his inability to either work healing spells or get proper attention to the wound, that it hadn't festered.

But he knew the man was a wizard. He'd seen it in his eyes.

And yet it was the Solstice or nothing. He hoped he wouldn't have to make that choice.

Walking to the window, he felt Sara's dark eyes follow. Out in the yard one of the floodlights had gone out, and upon the ground below him he could see the ochre smear of reflected candlelight that marked von Rath's study window. A shadow passed across it: the SS wizard pacing, restless, fevered, an animal driven by invisible goads, far into the night.

14

Sara whispered, 'This had better work.' Her hands, as she shoved her crazy hair up under a man's cloth cap, were steady and her white face calm, stark without its habitual disguise of lipstick and paint. But the brazen glare of the camp floodlights at the bottom of the hill caught the fine glitter of sweat on her short upper lip.

Rhion only nodded. He wanted to reassure her, but was too deep in his trance of concentration to speak. In any case they had been through it all on the drive from the crossroads near the Schloss where Sara had picked him up.

In the surrounding dark of the pine-woods a nightingale warbled – six miles away, the Kegenwald village church-clock spoke its two notes, the sound carrying clearly in the moonless hush of the night. These sounds, like Sara's voice, seemed to come to Rhion from a very great distance, clear but tiny, like images in the scrying-crystal. Far more real to him were the two watchtowers of the Kegenwald camp perimeter visible from this hillside, open wooden turrets mounted on long legs like sinister spiders, each ringed in floodlights and dark within.

He stood in each of those watchtowers, a shadowy consciousness more real to him now than the body kneeling in its scratched protective circle just within the gloom of the woods' edge. He spoke to each man separately – a flaxen-haired boy in the left-hand turret, an older man, tough and scarred with a broken nose, in the right. They did not precisely hear his voice, as he whispered to them the dreamy, buzzing songs of nothingness which the Ladies of the Drowned Lands had taught him. But they listened nevertheless, gazing idly in opposite directions, outward into the night.

It was not an easy illusion to maintain. His own awareness split into dim ectoplasmic twins, he had to keep within his mind from instant to instant the separate realities of the two watchtowers – the hollow clunk of wooden floors underfoot, the dark webwork of the struts that supported the roof and the pattern the wires stapled to them made, leading up to the lights above; the moving sharpness of the air from the bristled darkness of the woods; the murky nastiness of the men's dreams. To the older sentry Rhion breathed songs dipped from the man's cramped and limited mind, the taste of liquor and blue tobacco smoke woven into fantasies of endless, repetitive, impossible intercourse with woman after woman, and all of them alike, all gasping with delight or sobbing with grateful ecstasy. To the younger, after searching the narrow hate-stained thoughts, he wove a different dream, of assembling, disassembling, assembling again some kind of automatic weapon, polishing, cleaning, making all perfect. Oddly enough he sensed the same pleasure in the precise click and snap of metal, the neat, controlled movements, as the first trooper had in his reveries of bulling endless willing blondes.

What facets of human nature these dreams revealed he couldn't allow himself to speculate, nor upon how close this magicless magic of dream and illusion was to the very devices von Rath hoped to use against the British pilots when the invasion began. It was difficult enough to maintain them, to renew again and again the sharp sweetness of their pleasure, as if every time were the first – to inject the tiniest twinge of regret and hurt if either man turned his eyes even slightly towards the hillside between the woods and the barbed wire fence, or thought about looking back at the stretch of open ground behind them which separated the fence, with its electrified inner pale, from the long grey building of the camp infirmary.

Fence and camp lay starkly naked beneath the floodlights' acrid glare, exactly as Sara had described them, exactly as he had glimpsed them in his crystal: the hillside bare of cover, clothed only with a thin scrim of grass against which, now, Sara's grey trousers and pullover stood out dark and unmistakable as she crept towards the fence. She moved as he had instructed her, crouched close to the earth. A few slow steps and stillness, count ten, two more slow steps and stillness again, an even, gentle progression that would not catch the guards' dreaming attention. In a long, lumpy muslin flour-sack at her belt she carried wire-cutters, wire, and wooden props to get her under the inner electric fence. Edging forward under the barrels of the turret guns, there was nothing else she could possibly have been.

Yet neither guard moved. The slight relaxation induced by the nicotine they smoked Rhion subtly deepened, increasing with his songs the influence of the drug. To them it had never tasted so good, to them their dreams had never been so fulfilling, so hurtfully satisfying . . .

Just as Sara finished cutting a slit in the wire of the fence the back door of the infirmary opened. Through a haze of oiled machinery and shuddering bosoms Rhion was aware of the tall, rawboned form standing in the shadowy opening, the floodlight throwing a coarse glitter of silver on scalp and jaw as he turned his head, looking doubtfully from one tower to the other. Then he looked across the open ground.

It was nearly seventy feet from the shelter of the shadowed door to the wire. The infirmary stood a little apart from the ugly ranks of green-painted barracks, ground commanded by the wooden towers and the dark muzzles of the guns. Between the towers Sara was a sitting target, propping up the electrified wire of the inner fence with two lengths of wood. The old man shrugged, and walked forward – slowly, as Rhion had hoped Sara remembered to specify in her whispered instructions of last Sunday.

. . . red lips parted in a gasp of ecstasy, a white throat exposed by a thrown-back head . . . Oh, thank you, thank you . . . Just so much solvent on the patch . . . ram home . . .

One of the guards shifted his weight to scratch his crotch, started to turn towards the yard behind him. But sudden cold, sudden sorrow, overwhelmed him, an aching loneliness – and there was, after all, no need. Everything was quiet. His daydream smiled and beckoned, a warm cocoon of virile joy. He gave a sort of sigh and settled back as he had been before, his chin on his fist.

The old man squirmed awkwardly under the wire, sat up, looked with a start at what he must have assumed until then to be a young man, in her trousers and pullover, with her hat pulled down to hide her flaming hair. Rhion saw him grasp her arm, saw her shake free, and signal for silence.

She pulled the props loose, shoved them into her bag and took out a bundle of short pieces of wire. The old man slipped through the hole in the fence and waited while Sara pulled the slit shut again, secured it with a dozen twists of wire so it wouldn't be obvious from a distance that it had been cut. Then they moved forward gingerly, slowly, under the dreaming eyes of the guns.

. . . touch of gun-oil in the lock, a touch in the pin-housing . . . not too much, too much is as bad as too little . . . they can never say I was less than perfect . . . soft white hands with red nails digging into the muscles of the back . . . The sweaty softness of those massive breasts, of thighs clutching at his hips . . . Again, oh please, again . . .

Sweat ran down Rhion's face, his muscles aching as if the intensity of his concentration were a physical labour. *Dammit, come on, I can't keep on with this . . .*

A few steps and pause. Wait. Creep-creep-pause. The floodlights glared behind them like harsh yellow moons, throwing feeble shadows on the bare ground, like two bugs paralysed on a kitchen floor. The night-breeze turned, and Rhion smelled a vast stench of human filth, overcrowded quarters, and deeper and more hideous, the stink of death and narrow-minded evil.

They reached the trees. The old man flung his arms around Sara, bending his tall height to clasp her close, and even in his tranced state Rhion reflected that it was the first time he'd seen Sara respond with uncalculated warmth to any man's touch. She reached joyfully up to fling her arms around his neck, for that one second her father's little girl again, happy, and clean, and filled with love. His mind still on the guards Rhion didn't hear clearly the old man's first half-sobbing words, or what Sara replied, but he saw her place a hand on her father's arm when he turned towards where Rhion knelt, and shake her head. As Rhion had instructed her beforehand, she led her father away through the bracken and impenetrable shadows, towards the road where the Mayor of Kegenwald's car was hidden.

Letting his mental voice die into a gentle soughing Rhion's two dim psychic twins stepped in unison to the wide openings in the turret walls, swung themselves over the wooden rails and out into the dark air. Between the towers they met and melded into one. For a moment from that high vantage-point Rhion looked down on the camp itself, long wooden buildings already beginning to warp and split, heavier cement constructions beyond them – barracks, offices, workrooms, cells of solitary confinement or special purpose, raw-new or the older structures of the old pulpmill the place had originally been – and the pale barren rectangle of the exercise-yard, all lying stark and moveless within the steel-thorned boundary of towers and fence. And because he was not within his body, he saw clearly the glow of horror that hung over the place, a sickly greenish mist, as if the very air were rotting from what was done within that place.

Turning, sickened, Rhion looked out over the woods and road in the luminous chill of the starlight. The sombre pines were still and utterly dark. No cars, no track of trampled bracken, no sign that they had been pursued, observed, detected. So far, so good.

He walked down over the air above the defoliated hillside, and in the darkness at the woods' rim saw a pudgy little form in old army trousers and a snagged white sweater, kneeling with head bowed in the dim scratchwork of a magic circle, the starlight glinting in his silver-rimmed glasses and on the sweat upon his face. He passed through the invisible door that lay between them, settling himself around the armature of those sturdy bones; then closed and sealed the door behind him.

Sickness hit him like a blow with a club. He doubled over, swearing in German as he felt the blood leave his face and extremities; though it was a mild night he shivered with desperate chill, hair and clothing sticking to him with sweat. Knees trembling with cramp he got somehow to his feet, and staggered off through the dark woods to the disused woodsman's track where they'd hidden the car.

Sara was busy hotwiring the little Ford's engine when he arrived. 'Christ, I don't believe it!' she breathed, as he slumped down onto the running-board. 'I don't effing believe it! We must have been out in the open for thirty minutes! What the hell did you do?'

'I told you I'm a wizard,' he managed to grin.

'Are you all right, my son?' A long, bony hand closed around his arm, gently raising him. He looked up, and met the dark eyes of the man he'd seen in the scrying-crystal, the thin old man with the shaven head and the raw, new scar on his lip.

'Yeah,' he whispered, but when the old man opened the door for him Rhion almost fell into the car's back seat. 'I'll be fine in a minute.'

The car moved off, Sara guiding it carefully down

a farmtrack which had mostly gone back to ruts and potholes where it twisted through bracken, wild ivy, and trees. She dug in the glove-box and produced a bar of American chocolate candy wrapped in paper, which she passed to them over the back of the front seat. 'Give him this, Papa.'

Rhion gulped down half of the bar's oily sweetness without even tasting it, then remembered Sara's father probably hadn't had anything resembling decent food for nine months, and held out the rest of it to him.

The old man turned it over in long, blue-veined fingers, sniffed it interestedly, and said, 'Well, according to Sylvester Graham sugar is a pollution of the temple of the body, and I'm not sure whether chocolate is kosher or not because who knows what they put into the stuff, but as Rabbi Hillel said, it isn't what goes into a man's body which defiles it, but the words that come out of a man's mouth . . . So I think an exception is in order. Thanks be to God . . . and to you, my son.' He popped the chocolate into his mouth, and clasped Rhion's hand while he chewed and swallowed. 'And you are? My daughter only said she had a friend who would get me out . . .'

'Professor Rhion Sligo.' The Germanized form of the name was second nature to him now.

'Isaac Leibnitz. I don't always smell like this, but I don't suppose Jonah was any bundle of roses when he came out of spending three days in the belly of a fish, either. So they teach driving cars as well as stealing them in this New York University you went to, Saraleh?'

'You'd rather I stayed in Germany and learned to cook and clean and have babies for Our Fuhrer?' She tossed back over her shoulder. In point of fact the old man smelled like an animal, his patched clothing half-rotted with old sweat and crawling with fleas, his mouth, when he spoke, showing the dark gaps of missing teeth. He was pallid, emaciated, and still shaky from two days of being sick from the pills Rhion had sent to guarantee that he'd be in the poorly-guarded infirmary instead of the concrete cell in which 'specially designated' prisoners were kept. But for all of that, there was about him a daft and gentle charm, such as Rhion had encountered in other wizards in his own world, infinitely comforting in its familiarity after the greed, fanaticism, and inhuman obsessions of the Schloss Torweg mages.

'What *did* you do?' he asked gently after a moment. 'Except deliver me from out of Gehinnom, for which I will always be more in your debt than you can ever conceive. What's your birthdate, by the way?'

'Don't thank me yet.' Rhion sat up and produced a handkerchief from his pocket to polish his glasses. 'I'm afraid I'm going to ask you to stick around for a few days and return the favour. As for what I did, I guess it's called astral planing here. I'd meant to cast a spell of distraction on both guards, but I couldn't do it from that distance.'

'No wonder you're tired,' commented Leibnitz, stroking his stubbled lip in a kind of subconscious mourning for his vanished beard, while Sara made an undervoiced comment of her own in the front seat.

Rhion sighed, and put his glasses back on. 'It all takes so goddam much time and energy. I don't know how much Sara told you . . .'

'What could she say, with all those chaperons standing around with rifles? She said you'd get me out if I took the pills, was sick two days, and then got up at two in the morning and walked out across the back exercise yard slow enough to let the guards take real good aim at me. She said I had to have faith.'

'It must have sounded pretty crazy.'

He shrugged. 'They say the Red Sea didn't part for the Children of Israel until the first man got his feet wet. But to get my daughter to believe you – now that's magic.'

Rhion's grin was wry. 'Believing crazy things seems to be

what's done in this country. I'm working for the SS Occult Bureau. They're keeping me prisoner at Schloss Torweg, an old hunting-lodge about forty kilometres from here. Are you familiar with the theory of Multiplicity of Universes, or am I going to have to go through this explanation from scratch?'

'No, no.' Rebbe Leibnitz shook his head decisively. 'Are you from another world on the same cosmic plane as ours – that is Malkut, the plane of material reality – or from one of the spiritually higher planes?'

'Same plane,' said Rhion, since as far as he knew multiplanar cosmic reality was as unprovable in his own world as it was in this. 'I'm a wizard there – operative magic works there as it no longer works here. That was originally the reason my master wanted us to come here – to find out why it no longer works.' He bit his lip, remembering Jaldis again with a sudden stab of unhealed loss.

'Well, my personal theory is that the roads from the spiritual Sephiroth of Tepheret to the Sephiroths of Yesod and Malkut have become blocked due to the increased influences of the elements of sulphur and fire, though that wouldn't take into account why it still works in other universes than this. Numerologically this century lies under the influence of Mars, always a bad time for those under the protection of the Beni-Elohim, the Angels of the Sephiroth of Hod. But I've heard other theories. I've met wizards from other universes before, you understand, both of the dense physical plane and those who were of a higher spiritual order, merely disguising themselves in the form of matter. There was an Englishman named Galworthy possessed by a spirit named Angarb-Koleg – and that young fellow Inglorion who stayed with me in 'thirty-eight – and that Theosophist woman Zelzah the Red who was travelling from dimension to dimension preaching the true path to rightness. She used to hold seances at our apartment on Gestia Ulica to contact spirits in other universes – she said the vibrations there were sympathetic – and in fact it was there she met Antonio Murillo, who it turned out had known her in a previous existence when he was a priest of the ancient Egyptian cult of Ptah and she was a temple prostitute . . .'

Rhion had heard all about ancient Egyptian cults and their reincarnated priests from Poincelles. No wonder Sara looked at him strangely. 'And you?'

Leibnitz made a dismissive gesture. 'Oh, I'm just a student, a scholar,' he said. 'All I can do is keep an open mind. All my life I've studied the Talmud and the Kabbala, searching for order in the universe, but it's a dangerous thing to translate the power one channels down from Higher Aether through the Tree of Life into magic here . . .'

'Aside from the fact that it can't be done, you mean?' chipped in Sara sarcastically, braking gently to ease the car into yet another rutted track.

Rhion opened his mouth to reply, but Leibnitz shook his head with a gentle smile. 'Always she was like this,' he said. 'Well, she's a Taurus. And since she was born in the second degree of her sign, by multiplying the letters of her name by their position and adding the digits, it gives her a Tarotic key of twenty-seven, which is really nine – the Hermit, the sign of Science, but also the sign of scepticism. And added to the year of her birth this gives her a Natal Sum of 1,944, which adds together to eighteen, the Moon, the sign of doubt . . . She has talked to wizards travelling in other bodies through the universe down from fifty thousand years in the future, and she'd say, "It can't be done because it can't be done." Now what kind of attitude is that?'

'The usual one, unfortunately,' said Rhion, remembering with a grin his own attitude about three-quarters of the mystical gobbledygook in the Schloss library and most of what Leibnitz had just said. 'You're right. Magic and those who can work it are distrusted in my own world, hated, legislated against . . .'

'It is because magic is arbitrary,' concluded Leibnitz. 'And so it is. And unfair, and in many cases against the Will of the Creator. It is cheating. What business is it of mine to use the powers of the Universe to make myself richer, when for whatever reasons the Lord thinks that in this lifetime I could learn more as a poor man?'

'He used to give Mama that argument when there wasn't money to buy milk.'

They had reached the edge of the old meadow where Poincelles' secret Temple stood. Though woods crowded thickly on its higher end near the barn, down here the ground was boggy, standing water glinting between patches of rank, waist-high grass. The crying of a thousand frogs prickled the night.

'Can you walk, Papa?' asked Sara worriedly, turning in the driver's seat. 'I don't dare try to take the car through this. Even if we didn't get stuck we'd leave a track they could follow from hell to Detroit. Besides, I have to get the car back to the Mayor's . . .'

'She not only steals cars, she steals the Mayor's car,' Leibnitz informed – presumably – God, looking skyward as he clambered out.

'He was the only one who had a petrol ration . . .'

'I'll take him up to the barn.' Rhion slid along the seat and scrambled out the same door Leibnitz had, for the lane was narrow, and tangled ditches filled with stagnant water and blackberry brambles flanked it on either side. As he put his hands on the doorpost to pull himself out Sara caught his wrist, dragging him back. Her whisper was carbon steel in the darkness.

'You tell him anything about how I'm living now and so help me God I'll kill you.'

Shocked that she'd even think of it, Rhion started to demand *What the hell do you think I am?* But by the vicious glitter in her eyes he knew what she thought he was: a man, coarse, careless, and stupid. He shook his head, an infinitesimally small gesture that her father, standing by the corner of the car staring raptly around him at the milky darkness, would not see. 'I promise.'

She threw his hand from her grip, despising his touch, and turned her face away to put the car in gear. Its rear wheel nearly ran over Rhion's foot as she popped the clutch and drove off without a word.

'Poincelles, feh.' Leibnitz picked his way through the long weeds that surrounded the barn and its three crumbling sheds, disregarding, as Rhion did, the black and terrible Seals of the demons Andras, Flauros, and Orobas written in secret places to defend against intrusion. 'A *paskudnyak* out for what he can get. I knew him when he was still with the Order of the Golden Dawn, and even then I didn't trust him. What can you expect of a man whose numerological Key works out to be sixteen? And if you trace out his name on the number-grid of the geometric square of Saturn . . .'

'In here.' Rhion pushed aside a plank on the back of the barn, slipped through the crack and edged along between the splintery boards of the wall and the tarpaulin which hung inside until he found the opening between two tarps. Behind him, he heard Leibnitz's breath hiss sharply, though it was pitch-dark in the barn until he drew from his pocket a match and the stub of a candle. The tiny light spread gradually outwards, but did no more than hint at the dark shapes of the draped altar, the black candlesticks, the shadowy gleam of the inverted pentagram beneath which Sara had lain. The smell of old tar and dust was almost drowned by an ugly medley of dried blood, snuffed incense, the thick choke of burned wood.

'*Chas vesholem*,' the old man whispered, looking around him in the dark.

Hating the place himself, Rhion moved swiftly to the far wall, where behind another join in the tarps he found the tin box of food and the bundle of clothes and blankets Sara had left there the day before. Rebbe Leibnitz did not move from where he stood, and when Rhion returned to him, the box and bundles under his arm, he turned firmly and, slipping through the tarps again, went out the way they had come.

'Poincelles has already bribed the troopers at the Schloss to stay away from this place,' said Rhion, as they settled down in the darkness of one of the sheds and, after a muttered prayer, the old Kabbalist set to the bread and cheese and apples in the box like a starving wolf. 'When he hears about the hue and cry for you it's a good bet he'll take steps to keep the camp guards away as well. My guess is von Rath knows about the place already but I suspect Poincelles doesn't think so – and anyhow he's stolen too much of the Occult Bureau's property to furnish it to want anyone looking too closely.'

'The *tzadik* Akiba ben Joseph, the greatest of the rabbis, says that it is no sin to eat food which is unclean to save one's life, for your life is the Lord's property, which it is incumbent upon you to preserve . . . and by extension I suppose that it is also permissible to hide behind the demon Lilith's skirts in there.' The old man jerked one greasy thumb at the dark bulk of the barn against the star-powdered sky. 'But that place makes me want to wash more than nine months in the pig-sty of their camp.'

'Amen,' muttered Rhion, drawing his knees up and wrapping his arms around them. Poincelles' spells and curses and protective demon-seals might have no power in them, but the dirty magics done in the barn clung to the place like a stench. 'It's only for a couple of nights.'

The old man grunted, and wrapped what was left of the food again in its papers, and replaced it in the box. 'There. If I eat more I'll be sick. Now – what are they doing in that place? That Schloss, that lodge of theirs . . . I saw the truck go out last week, and twice the week before, taking people they've been keeping, like me, apart from the others, people they don't put onto the lumber-gangs or send to the mills to work. And the ones who work in the crematoria whisper about how they came back . . .'

'Have you ever heard of a group called the Adepts of the Shining Crystal?'

Cocking his head he thought about it for a moment, then frowned. 'No. And I've heard of most, at least in Europe, though in America . . .' He shrugged resignedly, leading Rhion to wonder what this America, whose participation in the war von Rath seemed to fear, was really like. 'They're crazy over there.'

Sitting in the blackness of the shed, his back to one of its splintery doorposts, Rhion spoke of all that had befallen him since he had received, in the rainy solitudes of the Drowned Lands, word that Jaldis had wanted to see him in Bragenmere. He had meant to give a swift and concise encapsulation, but it didn't turn out that way: 'We have the night before us,' said the old man gently, and for the first time in three months Rhion found himself able to talk – about the Nazis, about his unhealed grief for his old master, about his loneliness and his growing fears. Sometimes he touched back on his original topics – the Spiracle, the Dark Well, the need to be at the stones on Witches Hill at the maximum pull of the sun-tides – but more frequently, as the Dog-Star rose burning above the eastern trees and the birds woke and cried their territories, each to each, in the hushed dark of early summer pre-dawn, he found himself talking about Tallisett and his sons, about the Ladies of the Moon and about wizardry, about magic.

'As far as I can tell magic just – just *isn't* in this world anymore,' he said, turning his head a little to look down the slope at the meadow, spread out in a shimmering of water and weeds and a thin white ground-mist. In the stillness and utter peace it seemed impossible that such a place as Kegenwald existed. 'From what I can tell nobody did anything to cause this, anymore than human malice causes the fall of night. It happened. Even the faes are gone, the faerie-folk – water-goblins, pookas, lobs, grims. It might change some day, but there's nothing I or anyone can do to change it.'

He sighed. 'I'm not even sure if the damn Spiracle will work, you know? They work on little things, but something like this . . . It's never been tried. I thought of rigging up a talismanic resonator, which would draw on the Void itself . . .' He shook his head. 'But aside from the fact that it would create a field anyone could use, including von Rath, it just needs too much power. So it has to be a Spiracle.'

He looked back, aware that the old scholar was regarding him quietly in the darkness.

'What you are doing,' said Leibnitz slowly. 'It is irresponsible, you know.'

Rhion closed his eyes. From the first that knowledge had murmured in his heart, try as he would to turn his mind away from it – he knew that the old man was right. 'It's my only chance.'

'That does not matter. If for whatever reasons the Lord saw fit to withdraw operant magic from this world – if that is what happened – it says much for your opinion of your own judgment that you want to bring it back for your own convenience.'

'I'm not talking about my convenience, dammit!' said Rhion passionately. 'I'm talking about my life! I wasn't the first one who circumvented the rules, I shouldn't even *be* here!' But he knew that any of the mages of his own world – Shavus, Jaldis, the Lady – would have told him that it didn't matter. And in his heart he knew it didn't.

But in his heart he could not bear the knowledge that he would never see Tally again, never see his sons. That he would be trapped in this hellish place, a prisoner of the Reich, for what remained of his life.

'*Tzadik*, please,' he whispered. 'There's only one place they know where to look for me now, and only one time when I'll be able to raise enough power to open the Void. Part of it's that I think I really would rather die trying to escape than stay here, but as things are I think it's only a matter of time before von Rath kills me anyway. With or without your help, I'm going to have to try.'

'There.' The old man's hand was warm and strong on his wrist. The first nacreous greyness of dawn showed him the hooked nose, the long brows curling down over shadowed eyes, the strong lips with the shameful stubble of a convict and the red, raw circle of the scar. 'You deliver me from Hell and three hours later I'm coming on you like the *balabos* . . . You have given me my life, and you have found and taken care of my Sara. For that I owe you. And I can't let you remain in this world long enough for these evildoers to figure out some way of bending your knowledge to their wills. So I will do what I can, and let the Lord of Hosts – Who knows more about the whole thing anyway – handle the rest.'

15

'He's sending me away!' Tallisett paced angrily to the long windows of her sister's room, the dark-green wool of her skirt sweeping across the tufted green-and-purple rugs, her hair catching a wheaten gleam as she passed through the windows' latticed light. Her sister Damson, seated beside the cold fireplace in the long brocade gown she favoured in her rooms because it hid her partridge plumpness, didn't look up.

'He wouldn't even see me!' Tally continued passionately. 'He said he was ill, but he was out hunting yesterday . . . He sent his *chamberlain* to tell me . . . !'

'Father is ill,' replied Damson, her voice low. Her short, stubby fingers continued to move over the lace ruffle she was making, crossing and re-crossing the glass bobbins over one another on the pillow with a faint, musical clinking as she worked, the sunlight sparkling on the jewelled galaxy of her rings. 'It's the summer heat, you know. It brings on the flux unexpectedly. He was taken ill last night. So were Esrex and Elucia, a little . . .'

'But *why*?'

Damson was silent for a few moments more, her hands like stout little overdecorated spiders spinning a web. In this room the strong summer sunlight was broken into harlequin shards by the window-grilles and softened by the moire shadows of the trees in the water-garden outside; beyond Damson's shoulder, Tally could see into the small room that had been fitted up as a private chapel to Agon, the Hidden One, Lord of the Eclipsed Sun. The smell of incense lay thick upon the air.

'Father thought it would be best.' She sounded maddeningly like Esrex. Tally sometimes tried to remember whether

her older sister had been that secretive, that calculating, that singleminded, before she'd married their cousin. But it had been twelve years, and her recollections of that time were little more than a child's, passionately worshipful of everything her sister said and did. In those days she had also had nothing to hide herself.

'We've heard that the Serpentlady of Dun is in the town,' went on Damson, her owlish, protuberant eyes still fixed upon the twinkling bobbins. 'And Erigalt of Pelter. With the Archmage still here there are those who say it's scandalous for the Duke's daughter to be spending her time . . .'

'Who says?' demanded Tally, and this time Damson looked up at her, mildly blinking, her face a careful blank.

'It is nearly the Summer Solstice,' she said. 'With what the mages do at that time, Father thinks it would be better if you were somewhere else.'

'*What* do they do?' Tally strode back, to stand over the shorter woman, hands on her hips. 'Don't tell me *you* believe the mages hold orgies at midnight . . .'

'You know they do.'

'Some sects do. Not the Morkensiks, or the Selarnists, or . . .'

'You're arguing semantics now,' said her sister placidly, and went back to her lacemaking. 'I know what Father told me, about why he thinks it better that you leave. Is Jaldis returning then, too?' And without appearing to, she watched her sister's face from beneath straight little bronze lashes.

Tally bit her lip and looked away. A week's custom hadn't dulled the hurt of what Shavus Ciarnin had told her he had heard, in the dark of a dream, sleeping beside the Well.

In a gentler voice, Damson asked, 'You've heard something, then?'

Tally shook her head and turned away. Damson, with remarkable quickness for one of her soft bulk, set aside the pillow and got to her feet, catching her sister's slim brown wrist in her hand. 'Please,' she said, her voice low now as they stood in the chapel door. 'This is for your own good, Tally. You may not think they commit abominations at the turning of the year's tides, but . . .'

'Who told you they were coming here?' countered Tally softly. 'The priests of Agon?'

Damson's round grey eyes shifted. 'Don't mock at Agon's cult.' She glanced into the close, tiny room beside them, as if behind the stone doors of the shrine, smooth and featureless like everything about that Cult, the Veiled God listened to all they said. 'Yes, his devotees are everywhere. Since Esrex has become one of the inner circle of initiates he has learned a great deal; many things are now possible for our House. The influence of the High Priest Mijac may very well end in Elucia marrying the Heir.'

'The Heir?' For a moment Tally thought she meant Dinias. 'You mean the *Queen's* Heir? He's only a toddler . . . !'

'He's turned four,' pointed out Damson reasonably. 'And the Queen has miscarried twice, it isn't likely now she'll give him a rival. What's six years, when he's fourteen and she twenty? It isn't as if she has a – a romantic disposition, as you did.'

She was watching Tally closely now. Rhion's name hung unspoken between them, fraught with a shaky tangle of joy to know he was alive, and terror of the unknown dangers in which he stood. *I'm in trouble, help me, please,* Shavus had reported he had said. *Get me out of here . . . Get me out . . .* Tally said nothing.

'Tally,' said Damson slowly. 'I don't know whether you've done – anything foolish – since you married Marc. Esrex . . .' There was long silence, the old scandal and blackmail and coercion conjured for a moment, like the heart-twisting smell of a remembered perfume. Since the night it had happened – Rhion's arrest, Tally's imprisonment, the terror of not knowing what would meet her when she was finally sent for – neither sister had spoken of it. Of it, or of anything else they thought or felt. They had become strangers, except for the knowledges that bound them at their roots.

After a moment Damson went on, with a certain amount of difficulty, 'I'm telling you now, that kind of thing isn't possible, if Elucia does in fact marry the Queen's son. There must be no breath of scandal. Stop being naive. If Father found out he would never permit it . . .'

'You mean Esrex would never permit it,' replied Tally, her voice low and perfectly level now. 'For whom do you think your husband is doing this, Damson? Uniting the realm of Varle with the Bragenmere lands by becoming governor, making advantageous alliances that will put the lord of those joint realms on any royal Council, putting out of commission *anyone who might be able to use other than military power against him?* You think your husband is doing that to help Father? To help the man who ousted Esrex' family from the Ducal Seat? Who's being naive? Or is that something you'd just rather not know about?'

She pulled her hand away from her sister's moist grasp and stood for a moment considering her, the cold weariness in her heart that comes with the final realization that the one you have loved has not existed for a good many years. It was a woman of thirty-five she saw, finally, and no longer the unconscious image of a plump, witty, brilliant girl of eighteen. She felt tired, and just a little sick – not like a child who has lost a cherished toy, but who has discovered in that toy a breeding-place of maggots and grubs. 'I suppose the real question,' she finished quietly, 'is whether you're a fool or Esrex's whore.'

And turning, she left the vestibule and strode down the corridor, her long green skirts billowing in her wake. For a long time Damson stood without moving, round face irresolute, upon the threshold of the Shadowed God.

16

The girl didn't look to be more than sixteen. She'd probably been pretty once, in a haunting wildcat way, before they'd shaved her head, and even now, after months of starvation and ill-usage in the Kegenwald camp, some of that beauty remained. In bistred pits her eyes seemed huge, the bones of her wrists and hands grotesque as she rubbed her bare arms for warmth. The unfurnished chamber in the south wing – the great master-bedchamber in which the Dark Well had supposedly been drawn – never really got warm. From his post behind a one-way mirror in the adjacent dressing-room Rhion could see the girl's pelvic bones outlined under the worn fabric of her ragged and dirty grey dress as she paced back and forth, barefoot on the uncarpeted oak planks.

When they had first brought her into the room she had huddled unmoving in a corner, like a partridge freezing into stillness in a hopeless hope that the hawk will pass it by. Having talked to Rebbe Leibnitz and the guards in the watchroom, having seen the Kegenwald camp, Rhion understood this. Only an hour ago had she begun, cautiously, to move about, first doggedly examining every corner of the room, trying its three locked doors, its boarded-up windows, peering curiously into the the dark sheet of the one-way mirror on the wall. These explorations had taken her rather less than two minutes, for the room was empty save for a latrine-bucket in one corner. After that she had simply paced, hugging herself for warmth and staring nervously all around her with huge obsidian eyes.

Rhion wondered whether her fear stemmed wholly from being in the power of the Nazis – a condition which scared him sick – or whether, animal-like, she sensed what was going on in the house tonight.

He glanced down at the watch which lay on the padded leather arm of his comfortable chair. Eight-thirty. The sun would have set by this time, though twilight would linger till after nine. He found himself listening intently, though he knew that both these rooms and the Temple downstairs on the other side of the house were quite soundproof.

Nevertheless, he felt it when they started, as he had felt it when the sun had dipped behind the sombre black pickets of the hills. His scalp prickled and he felt the sweat start on his face; if he closed his eyes he could see von Rath lying upon the naked black stone of the altar, like a sleeping god in the thin white robe – '*vestis albus pristinissimus et lanae virginis*' – save for the febrile tension of his muscles, the tautness of eyelids bruised with stress and lack of sleep. He knew the horrors of the opening rites, for he had seen them, again and again in tormented dreams: Poincelles pacing out the bounds of the Temple, a white puppy held aloft by its hind legs in one massive hand, its dying struggles splattering his crimson robe with blood; Gall and Baldur like strange angels in black, merged with the greater shadows which followed their movements back and forth across the velvet-draped wall; the reflection of candlelight in the eyes of the victims. Bound at the foot of the altar, they would know, as occultists themselves, what would come next.

'I told you I didn't want to have anything to do with it,' he'd said to von Rath that morning. They had finished the early ritual work – for which Rhion had barely made it back from bidding farewell to Rebbe Leibnitz – and had been on their way out of the Temple's small robing-room: Rhion, exhausted and ravenous, to a breakfast he felt he had heartily earned, von Rath upstairs to his study. 'I don't even want to be in the Schloss when it's going on.'

'You disapprove of what I do?' The German tilted his

head a little on one side, eyes cold and flat, like frozen quicksilver, voice gentle but perilous.

'If I wrote it on ancient parchment in Latin with illuminated capitals would you believe it?' retorted Rhion, covering his outrage, his anger, his panic with sarcasm. '*What you are doing is dangerous*. It's *always* dangerous to do a blood-rite – it's *always* dangerous to do *any* rite drugged . . .' And within him another voice, made furious by everything he had learned from Leibnitz, everything he had seen and sensed of the camp – by the scenes in the crystal and the laughter of the guards – screamed *How dare you – How DARE you – murder human beings, men and women, for ANY reason* . . . while fear of von Rath and guilt at his own cowardice nearly stifled his breath. Sara would have spat in von Rath's face and died.

He took a deep breath. 'You don't have the control over the forces you're releasing. Without a conversion to physical operancy, you can't.'

'So.' Von Rath's bloodless mouth tightened. 'I find it curious,' he went on, after long silence, 'that of the two reasons you gave which deny me my power, one has already been proven a lie. Is the other a lie as well?' He placed a hand on the nape of Rhion's neck, slim fingers cold as steel and terrifyingly strong, and looked down into his eyes. Against a feverish flush the old duelling-scar on his cheek stood out cold and white. 'Are you lying to me, Rhion? Is this world truly bereft of the point of conversion, the crossover between will and matter?' His thumb moved around, to press like a rod of steel into the soft flesh under Rhion's jaw. 'Or is that merely your final secret, the thing which in your opinion should not be shared with those whose destiny it is?'

Backed to the wall at the foot of the dim stairs, Rhion felt the tension of that powerful hand that could, he guessed, snap his spine with a madman's strength; in von Rath's eyes he saw nothing human at all.

'It's my final secret,' he said. 'I just thought I'd hang around until you got tired of waiting and started sticking hot wires under my fingernails before I disappeared in a puff of smoke.' He pulled away from the thoroughly nonplussed wizard's grip. 'You brought me here as an advisor, all right? And I'm stuck in this world – for the duration of the war, considering the risk of someone else dying to open another Dark Well. That might be years. I'm not happy about that, but do you think I'm going to trade decent food and a comfortable place to live for a permanent berth in an English insane asylum? If I understood how to convert to physical operancy, you think I wouldn't better my own position here by telling you?'

Von Rath flinched, as if from the blow that breaks the self-perpetuating cycle of hysterics, and shook his head like a man waking from a dream. 'No – I don't know.' He passed his hand across his face, and for a moment his eyes were the eyes of the man Rhion had first known, the young man whose dreams had not yet become obsessions. There was even something like pain there, the pain of puzzlement, of knowing he was becoming something else and not quite knowing if he wanted it or not. 'And yet for one second – Eric did. I know he did.'

He frowned, shook his head. 'That's odd, you know, it's been weeks since I've even thought of him . . . He was my friend . . .' He rubbed his sunken, discoloured eyes. From the half-open door of the watchroom across the hall came a guard's laughter, and the nauseating gust of cigarette fumes. 'But without operant magic we could never have brought you here . . .'

'You don't think I've been living on that knowledge, that hope, for the past three months?' Rhion put his hand on the sinewy arm in its clay-coloured shirtsleeve, led the way down the shadowy blueness of the hall. 'I'm still trying to figure that one out. As I keep telling you, I was only brought along to wash out the bottles. Jaldis was the one who knew what the Void is, and how the Dark Wells work. Look,' he added more gently, 'when did you last get any sleep? Or have anything decent to eat? And I'm not talking about that lousy porridge – If Poincelles can get eggs and sausage out of the cook you sure as hell should be able to . . .'

The younger man pulled his arm away impatiently, stepped back towards the stair. 'Later, maybe,' he said in his quiet voice. 'There is too much for me to do now. Perhaps other rites of the Shining Crystal have survived, either in code as something else, or in fragments in letters – I haven't yet found their correspondence with St Germain or Jean Bodin, and I know there must have been some – which can be pieced together. With our position in France solidified we must be able to deal with Britain. Time is of the essence now.'

He passed his hand over his face again, and when he looked up his eyes had changed, as the hard edge of his desires crept slowly back into command. In the golden bar of light that streamed down the hall from the open door of the dining-room he looked, with his immaculate uniform and electrum hair, like a daemon roused, blinking, from the dark of its cave.

'We aren't asking you to be part of the ceremony, you know.' The voice was gentle, but inflexible as steel again. 'Only to observe the subject, and to take notes. We will be working on a naive subject tonight, one whose mind I have never encountered. It will take all the energy the four of us can raise, but it is something in which no outsider should be allowed to meddle. Will you do that much?'

And reluctantly, Rhion had agreed.

Wearied with her pacing the girl – a gypsy, von Rath had said, a race traditionally reputed to number a large percentage of psychics – sat again on the floor in the corner, and lowered her head to her folded hands, rocking her body like a whipped child. Rhion glanced automatically at his watch. Six minutes after ten. He could feel the power growing in the house, a whispering behind him that seemed to be lodged within the walls, a terrible vibration in his bones. The bank of closed cupboard doors at his back made him nervous, as did the small, shut door of the backstairs to the kitchen, which led down from this little room. Part of him wanted to slip down that way and out of this accursed house before something happened, but terror of what might be waiting in that dark and cluttered stair stopped him. He wanted to open the main door into the hall, but feared what he might hear – or see – in its empty shadows.

A chill shook him, as if the air in the room had grown colder, and he had the uneasy sense of things taking place beyond the boundaries of human perceptions. He glanced at the watch again, and wrote down the time. 10:23. The girl seemed to notice nothing.

At ten minutes after eleven she got to her feet again, and began to pace once more, endlessly rubbing her skinny brown arms. There was nothing in the room, no food, no water, no blanket or source of heat. Rhion wondered whether that was a condition of the experiment, or whether they had simply not thought about it.

Power was everywhere around him now, creeping like thin lines of phosphorous along the panelling, dripping down the grain of the cupboard doors at his back, crawling along doorsills and floorboards. A kind of mottling had appeared on the wall to his left, near the backstairs door, as if light were buried deep within it, and he had the sensation of something moving behind him, near or perhaps in the cupboards, almost – but not quite – visible from the tail of his eye. He was too experienced to turn and look. He knew he'd see nothing. One never did. Sweat stood out on his face, crawled slowly down his beard. Sometimes he thought he heard voices speaking, not shouting in agony, but simply muttering with angry, formless rage. It was the third blood-rite, the third sacrifice, of men and women chosen for psychic power or occult knowledge. Their curses would linger.

I'm sorry, he wanted to cry to the cold, beating air. *Nothing I could have said would have saved you!* But the rage of the dead is not selective. It does not hear.

They're fools . . . God, get me out of here! But he knew he was as much a prisoner as the girl in the other room.

At 11:24 she stopped in her pacing, her shaved head jerking up suddenly, as if seeing or hearing something that startled her. Rhion noted it, and the time. But she shook her head and paced on, back and forth, endlessly, tirelessly, not seeing the yellowish ooze of cold light that had begun to drip down the walls, not sensing the freezing iron tightness of the air, not hearing the formless whisper, in Yiddish and German and Romany, that seemed always to growl on the other side of the air. Agony, horror, despair, and a gloating sexual delight filled the air, poisoned ectoplasmic wool from which von Rath's mescaline-saturated mind was endeavouring to spin its magic strands. Sick and wretched, hands shaking and breath coming shallow and fast, Rhion tried vainly to stop his ears, to wall his mind, against it, wanting nothing but to get out, to escape this place and never come back . . .

At thirty-five minutes after midnight the girl wedged herself into a corner of the room again, wrapped her thin arms around her bony knees, and stared into the room dully, her fear at last blunted by exhaustion. She moved as if startled once more, at five of one, but by the way she looked around the room she saw nothing.

At quarter to three, just when Rhion could smell the beginnings of dawn in the lapis infinity of the world outside,

Gall knocked on the door to tell him that the experiment was over.

11:00 – cat

11:24 – face on wall

11:24 – Stopped pacing as if startled, resumed immediately

12:10 – glass of water

12:45 – spider

12:55 – Raised head and looked around room as if checking for something, settled down almost at once.

'Promising.' Von Rath laid the two sets of notes on the library table before him, aligned their edges with his habitual neatness, and surveyed his fellow mages with eyes like glacier ice. 'Your impressions?'

'It was – astounding,' whispered Baldur reverently, black-rimmed nails picking at the edge of a nearby book. 'I c-could feel the power flowing into you, you blazed like a torch with it . . .'

'You were losing twenty-nine thirtieths of it.' Rhion leaned back in his chair. His whole body ached from lack of sleep, the few hours of dream-tortured slumber he'd fallen into that morning doing nothing to make up for two nights without and his exertions on the astral plane on top of that. The splinters of sunlight forcing their way between the library's snuff-coloured curtains were agonizingly bright in the room's brownish twilight; Poincelles and Baldur both squinted and winced whenever they turned that way. Gall, as usual, sat stoically in a corner. From his window during one bout of sleeplessness Rhion had seen him at dawn, walking calmly nude down the path beyond the wire to Round Pond for his morning swim.

'There was power in the room,' insisted von Rath doggedly. 'I know it. I felt it.'

'Some of the Shining Crystal texts mention a talismanic resonator,' put in Baldur diffidently. 'They do not say what it is, but they speak of it as establishing a field of power . . .'

'As the Holy Grail did,' said Gall, shifting his slender form in his chair, the harsh afternoon sunlight making of his long white hair a glowing halo. 'And as certain other sacred relics could. The crystal tip of the golden pyramidion atop the ancient Pyramid of Khufu . . .'

'Which you were privileged to buy from a trusted antiquities-dealer in Cairo?' inquired Poincelles sarcastically, glancing up from filing a broken fingernail back into a neat point.

'A talismanic resonator will only work if there's something for it to resonate with,' said Rhion, firmly cutting off Gall's indignant rejoinder. 'And in this universe you'd kill yourself raising a field as little as a mile across.'

'Perhaps a stronger drug? Or another type of drug?'

'Be my guest,' retorted Rhion sourly. 'Only don't ask me to take any – or to be in the building when you start screwing around with power while under the influence.' He took off his glasses to rub his red and aching eyes. Von Rath looked far worse than he had yesterday morning when they had spoken outside the Temple, as if he had not slept at all. Good, thought Rhion. It meant he'd sleep soundly tonight.

Hurting for sleep himself, Rhion considered putting off breaking into the Dark Well and activating the Spiracle for another twenty-four hours. He needed rest desperately – Rebbe Leibnitz probably did, too – and there seemed little chance of getting any during the remainder of the day. He didn't relish the thought of trying to manipulate the power of the Void even at his most alert.

But some obscure instinct prickled at him, like a damp wind ruffling at his hair; an awareness that tonight would, for a dozen half-sensed reasons, be better than waiting for tomorrow. Tonight was Wednesday. If they put things off until tomorrow night Sara would have to find an excuse not to be at the tavern, and too many of those would begin to make someone suspicious. Tonight the moon would be at its full – a slender source of power, but one the Lady had taught him to use. Tonight von Rath was likelier to be asleep, and tomorrow might see some kind of preparation for the Solstice sacrifice itself afoot. He groaned inwardly, and wondered if he could manage to steal a nap during the afternoon.

The others were still arguing. He should have been keeping his mind on them but couldn't . . .

'There are other d-drugs listed in the Anacopic Texts . . .'

'That are pharmacologically absurd.'

'Not to mention that the body ought to be purified, rather than polluted, before the working of magic . . .'

'Nonsense.' Baldur pushed back his lifeless dark hair with one twitching hand and sniffled. 'The potion Major Hagen used in the D-Dark Well ceremony . . .'

'Which killed him.'

'We don't know what killed him. It was the same potion P-P- Paul – Captain von Rath – used last night, and at the Rites before, and it elevated him, exalted him . . .'

'He could have been flying in circles around the chandelier,' spoke up Rhion wearily, 'and it wouldn't have done him any good. Without the ability to convert power to physical operancy you can disembowel every Jew in Germany and it's not going to buy you one damn thing.'

'Then I will disembowel them.' Von Rath looked up, his face a skull's face in the gloom. 'Every occultist, every medium, every psychic – every child whose house was visited by the *poltergeisten* – every source of personal *manna*, of the inner power, the *vril*, of magic, that we can lay our hands on, will be sacrificed. If we can raise enough power it *must* convert, it *must* answer to my bidding. And for that we will sacrifice every one.'

He was looking at Rhion as he spoke, and Rhion felt the blood drain from his face as he understood.

The soft voice sank still further, like the murmur of the angry ghosts whose power whispered still in the colder corners of the house. 'Every one. You say there is no physical operancy in this world. So. Yet one of the so-called Jew wizards incarcerated at the Kegenwald labour-camp escaped only the night before last, escaped across an open yard under plain sight of the guard-towers without being seen.'

Dear God, no, not when I'm so close . . . 'That's possible with illusion . . .'

'And illusion is what we are trying to raise against the RAF. The thing that you say cannot be done.'

Poincelles laughed. 'Escaping from a prison doesn't need illusion. Just a little . . .' And he rubbed his fingers together suggestively.

'In France, perhaps,' replied Gall coldly.

'This is the real world, my dear Jacobus . . .'

To von Rath, Rhion said quietly, 'It isn't the same.' His lips felt numb.

'So you say.' Von Rath stood up, for an instant in the shadows seeming to be a skeleton in his black uniform, with his wasted face and frostburn eyes. His voice was the dry stir of daemon-wings. 'We have trusted you, Rhion. We have believed your assurances that you have made with us – with the holy order of the SS – with the destiny of the German Reich – a common cause.'

He tipped his head to one side and regarded Rhion, not even as a friend once trusted and trusted no longer, but as a stranger as unknown to him as the men he had killed last night.

'The Summer Solstice is coming – a time of power. The Universe is moving to its balance-point, when its powers can be turned by a single hand. On that day we will make a talisman of power, a battery, against the day later in summer when we can give our abilities to the assistance of our Fatherland in the breaking of our enemies' stronghold. We depend upon the aid you have professed yourself willing to offer us. And if we find that you have lied to us in your assurances, betrayed our trust, I tell you now that it would be better for you if you had never been born.'

Sara and her father were waiting for him in the redolent darkness of the trees beyond the Schloss's yard-lights. The full moon rode high, limpid and regal; a whispered catch of the hymn the Ladies sang to her floated through Rhion's head as he stood motionless in the shadows of the old kitchen door, watching Poincelles stride like a lean and feral tomcat from the direction of the guards' barracks, a couple of props under his arm.

I left the house of the Sun,
I left the houses of light,
To walk in the lands of the stars,
in the lands of the rain.
Children living in darkness,
I give you what I can.
Children of the earth,
I give you what I can.
Children of magic,
I give you what I can . . .

By the drenched quicksilver light the Frenchman set them up – Rhion thought wryly that the ground in that little gully must be getting pretty well grooved – shoved his little bundle of implements under the wire, and then followed with that curious, gawky agility that seemed almost spider-like in the dark.

Rhion hated him. Early in their friendship Sara had shown him the place where Poincelles had taken up the threshold-board at the entrance to the attic to put a talisman of badly-cured lambskin where Rhion would cross it a dozen times a day, a talisman, she informed him, consecrated to bringing him under Poincelles' influence – 'Bastard paid me twenty marks to help him raise "sex magick" to charge it,' she'd remarked, screwing the board down again above the rotting, mouse-eaten thing. 'I should have charged him fifty.' Having no power it didn't trouble him. But in dreams, again and again, he had unwillingly witnessed the torture-rituals of the Shining Adepts, and had seen how they were accomplished – he knew who had laughed when the knife went in.

As Poincelles approached the shadowy verge of the trees a figure appeared. For an instant Rhion's heart stood still – then he saw that the waiting girl was smaller than Sara, and pale blonde of the most Teutonic type. Long braids hung down over the white uniform blouse of the League of German Maidens, framing a face at once pretty and sensual, with a lush mouth and discontented eyes. When Poincelles put a hand upon her waist she raised her arms to circle his neck, and scarcely louder than the rustle of the pines Rhion heard his throaty chuckle.

Then they were gone.

'If he thinks he's gonna deceive Asmodeus with that little *tchotchke* he's out of luck,' remarked Rebbe Leibnitz dryly, when Rhion had reached the lichen-blotched granite boulder behind which the old man and his daughter waited. The old scholar had traded his camp rags for an ill-fitting utility suit of the kind a workman might wear on his day off; his hands were shoved deep in the shabby jacket's pockets, and under the bill of the cap which hid his shorn head his dark eyes gleamed with amusement. Beside him, Sara was dressed as she had been two nights ago, in a man's trousers and pullover, with only a frizzed red tangle sticking stiffly out from beneath a cap of her own. Close to, her clothes smelled of smoke, but she hadn't lit a cigarette for fear of the smell or the pinpoint of its light alerting the guard. Her pockets bulged with her housebreaking tools.

'He doesn't seem to have much luck getting virgins, that's for damn sure,' sighed Sara, with a shake of her head. 'But you'd think he'd have more sense than to go looking for them in the League of German Mattresses.' She glanced over at Rhion, her dark eyes, like her father's, a gleam in the shadow of her capbill. 'Even money he's going to ask those demons of his to bring you under his power again.'

'Doesn't matter.' Rhion put aside the brief memory of Sara's nude body stretched on the altar beneath the down-turned point of the inverted pentacle, candle-flame like honeyed gold on the spread legs and perfect breasts. 'What matters is he's paid the guards to look the other way between here and the house.'

Rhion crossed the open ground first, setting up his props, slipping under the wire, and returning to the darkness of the old laundry-room which he had so recently left. He sank his mind down through the stillness of the black house, picking out the dim chatter of the wireless in the watchroom, the creak of a lazy body shifting in a chair. Mice scratched behind the dining-room wainscot and in the stuffy backstairs, beetles ticked like watches, timing the coming of the Summer-tide. The very air of the house felt uneasy, filled with angry dark things that waited behind some sightless angle invisible to human eyes, hunting for a way out into the world of men. When his fingers brushed the wood of the wall it felt warmer than it should have, charged with unholy power. The whole house was turning into a giant battery, a hideous talisman of the forces released there.

He turned his mind quickly from it, sought in the thick dark air of those turning corridors, those closed-in rooms, for other sounds. He heard the slow untroubled draw of breath from Gall's room – a panting, adenoidal snuffle from Baldur's. Then soft, shallow, and even, the breathing of von Rath in a closed and seemly sleep.

At his low whistle Leibnitz and Sara left the shelter of

the woods, crossed to the fence, set props, slithered under, took the props and moved across the yard to join him with surprising agility and speed. Rhion pulled the door shut; his pulse was hammering and a cold tightness in his chest had driven out all tiredness or thought of sleep. There was no turning back now. The only way out was through.

'Here.' By the reflected glow of the yard-lights beyond the windows Sara led the way to the old dumbwaiter shaft. 'Can you manage, Papa?'

'Fifty years I am learning the wisdom of great men, the Torah and the Talmud and the names of the angels of each sphere of the world and the numbers by which the Lord rules the universe, and now at my age I find I should have studied to be Tarzan instead.' He glanced at the neat footholds recessed into the shaft wall, and the rope hanging down into darkness. 'How many steps are those?'

Sara shrugged. 'I don't know. Twelve or thirteen, I think.'

He waved his hands and addressed the ceiling. 'She doesn't know. If it's twelve it computes to three, which is fulfilment and the realization of goals, but if it is thirteen it computes to four, an astronomic squaring which implies legally constituted authority which around here is not something we want to be dealing with . . .' His voice faded into a mutter as he climbed gingerly down the shaft. 'I should have known that when the sum of my birth's gematria computed with this year's date to give me 3,255, I should have known then to watch out . . .'

Sara rolled her eyes ceilingward, and followed.

The cellar was pitch black. Sara fumbled her flashlight from the deep pocket of her trousers, but Rhion caught her hand, and shook his head, then, remembering she couldn't see the gesture, breathed, 'No.'

'A light's not gonna call more attention than the sound of us tripping over boxes . . .'

'I'll guide you.' Their voices were barely a flicker of

sound in the stillness, but nonetheless made him uneasy. They were close, so close – It seemed to him now that in the silence von Rath must hear, even in sleep, the thudding of his heart.

A rat skittered through the dusty coal-bin as they passed it; ghostly sheets of spider-floss lifted from the old drying-racks with the breeze stirred by their passing. Rhion led them down the long abyss of the cellar, past the crouching, crusted iron monster of the sleeping furnace, his ears straining for the faintest sound from above.

But there was nothing. Only the faint under-whisper that had begun to grow in the house itself, the angry, buzzing murmur of its restless ghosts.

This has to work, he thought desperately, his hands cold in the warm strong grip of Leibnitz' fingers, the hard little clutch of Sara's. *This is our last chance. Please, God, let it work . . .*

But the gods of his own universe and of this one hated wizards. *It figures*.

They shifted the boxes as quietly as they could, and while Rhion and Leibnitz stood between the flashlight-glare and the stairs which led up into the main part of the house, Sara went to work on the lock.

'This also you learn in America?'

Sara opened her mouth to retort and Rhion cut her off hastily with a whispered, 'Will you stand guard?'

'What, you're not going to give her a tommy-gun?'

'Papa, I'm telling you I'd trade Mama's silver candlesticks for one right now.'

Rhion pulled the scandalized scholar through the door before he could reply, and closed it behind him. For a moment they stood, sealed into the darkness; then Rhion took a stub of candle from his pocket, and with a guard's steel lighter with its death's-head engraving, called flame to its wick.

Beside him, Leibnitz breathed, '*Kayn ayhoreh . . .*'

The dim patterns of protective circles drawn upon the floor, the marks of old blood and ashes, lay undisturbed in the darkness. In their centre was nothing to be seen, even with a wizard's sight, yet somehow, though its light touched the dirt-crusted stone of the opposite wall, the candle-flame did not penetrate that inner dark. The air here seemed colder than in the cellar outside; the silence had the anechoic quality of unseen infinity.

'What . . . is it?'

'Can you see it?' Rhion nodded towards the circles.

The old man's grizzled eyebrows knotted, and the dark eyes beneath them were suddenly the eyes of a mage. 'Not *see*.'

Rhion took from his pocket the other candle-stubs he had brought. Doubled and trebled, the soft glow filled the room with a wavering underwater light. Around him he sensed the heavy calm of the earth that grounded away the horrors that had been raised in the house; for a second he seemed to hear the stirring of the night-breeze through the long grass of the meadow beneath Witches Hill, and see the glimmer of the full moon in the round pond near the ruins of the old Kegenwald Church. Far-off he sensed other things, long lines of stones in the molten glow of the moon, earthen mounds shaped like serpents among summer trees at dawn, stone crosses, many-roofed shrines gleaming like gold on distant hills in dry afternoon sun. Beneath his feet he was aware of the slow pulse of the ley that joined that dim net of power overlying all the earth.

He set the candles down. His shaking fingers fumbled at the buttons of his shirt, and drew from under it, on its string around his neck, the Spiracle of iron and silver and salt, each of its five crystals seeming to speak one glinting, unknown word as the lights touched them. The candle-glow slid along the silver in a running flow of amber runes.

'This is not a good thing that you do,' whispered the old man. 'But you must be got away from this – this abomination of a place, and let these men here destroy themselves as they will.' He stood stroking the round, ragged scar on his stubbled lip, gazing with a kind of reverie into the dark colours of the circle's heart. The wistfulness Rhion remembered in von Rath's eyes from the early days, the yearning to know only that it was true, shined briefly in his face. 'I am glad that the Lord let me see this,' he added simply. 'Tell me what you need me to do.'

As when he had worked with the Dark Well just after the New Moon, once Rhion entered the trance-state necessary to raise power he had only the vaguest idea of time. For a while he and Leibnitz worked together, drawing out signs of Protection and Concentration, he in his own blood, the Kabbalist in the ochre chalk he'd instructed Rhion to procure from the wizards'-kitchen above. In the candles they burned a tiny pinch of the dittany the old man had insisted was proper for such spells; as a background to his own meditations Rhion heard the murmur of that deep old voice framing one by one the names of the angels of the Sephiroth of Malkut, the protectors of the material world, but oddly enough the sound was soothing rather than distracting, a familiar mantra of magic, no matter what form it took. From the circle of power they drew a corridor to the edge of the Dark Well, and for a long time Rhion stood on the brink of the abyss, staring into a cold darkness of colours he could not consciously see.

But it was there. Endless, lightless, it yawned just – and only just – beyond the perception of his mind, a column of nothing into which it would be perilously easy to step. An angle of perception . . . a degree of difference from the sane and material earth . . . The twisted metal of the Spiracle seemed cold and dense in his hand, and through the concentration of his spells he wondered if he shouldn't have taken the safer route and set up a simple resonator after all.

But it was far too late. The spells of charging coiled like

smoke through his exhausted brain, spells he had learned in the Drowned Lands, in the octagonal library tower in Bragenmere, in Shavus' strange stone house – spells he had no notion of whether they would work or not.

He twisted his fingers through the string that had held the Spiracle around his neck – the crystals bit deep in the soft flesh of his left palm as he grasped it tight. Leibnitz' bony grip closed firm around his right. This had killed Eric Hagen, they had said . . . Taking a deep breath, he stepped into the Well.

Though the Well itself was only half-awakened he could feel its pull on him immediately through his trance-state, the cold pressure on his solar plexus, at the base of his skull, in his eyes. His mind held hard to the spells of protection Jaldis had taught him the night before they'd entered the Void together, and felt the strength of the Void overwhelming him.

But there was magic there. The taste of it, the touch, was unmistakable; he raised the Spiracle in his left hand, and saw the blue light that ran round the iron ring, springing in tiny serpents from crystal to crystal, flickering down his fingers like electrical bug-feet, to lift the hair on the back of his arm. The Void was drawing at him – drawing him in and drowning him – but he held the ensorcelled circle high and whispered the words he had learned and used when it had only been a question of making devices that would let him breathe under water, or keep him warm in places of lightless cold. He could see the dark of the Void now, a coloured abyss without light in which burned not one distant gleam to show him the way through.

And that dark he wove to the Spiracle, like a man tying floating strands of silver spider-thread one by one into a basket's rim, binding the wild magic to follow him like a banner into the magicless world outside. The Void pressed on him, dragged at him. It was becoming difficult to breathe and he had to call on all his strength merely to remain conscious, but he barely noticed. When he moved the Spiracle in the throbbing darkness, he saw how each separate crystal of the ring left a track of shuddering silver light.

Magic was his again.

Eric Hagen must have felt it, bursting on him like argent lightning in the dark – joy like the shattering of a star.

Blackness rushed through the split defences of his mind, sweeping him away. His sight went dark, and he fell.

A hand clutched his, the jerk of its strength nearly dislocating his shoulder. A voice cried his name. Drowning in freezing blackness Rhion could see nothing – darkness, ghost-shapes that tore at him in swirling wind – bitter cold. Then tight and hard a beam of what looked like brilliant yellow light stabbed through the murk, and he thought he heard names being called upon, syllables of power, like falling sparks of fire, a resonant vibration in his bones. Fighting back a wave of faintness, lungs hurting as they sucked vainly at airless void, he tried to make his way along that light, tried to see its end.

Numb with cold and nearly unconscious, still he could feel the hand holding his. He grabbed at the sinewy wrist with both his hands, fumbling desperately, and for an instant blacked out completely . . .

Then he was on his knees on the cold stone floor, gasping at the mouldy air with its faint whiff of ozone, shaking desperately and clutching the tall skeletal body that held him close against it. Though the room was cold and damp it felt warm by comparison – for a moment the lenses of his glasses misted. Groggily he was aware of a name being called.

'Rhion . . . Rhion . . .'

His hands tightened over the smelly wool of Leibnitz's shirt. Both hands . . . He gasped, 'Oh, Christ, no . . .' and then saw the Spiracle hanging by its string, where the string was tangled tight around his nerveless fingers.

'Rhion . . .'

'Rhion, goddammit!' A blast of air struck his face as the door was opened suddenly; he got his feet under him and stood as Leibnitz turned. The new voice was Sara's.

'Get the hell out of there, both of you! All the guards in the goddam world are coming down the stairs!'

17

'This way . . . !'

'The door . . .' whispered Rhion, his mind still cloudy, his numb hands fumbling with the Spiracle as Sara and her father dragged him away into the dark of the cellar. 'Cover it back . . .'

'Screw that! Come *on*!'

A second's thought told him she was right. The jackboots of Storm Troopers thundered in the hall above, the locks rattled open . . . He was a fool not to have realized that von Rath, even in his dreams, would know that magic had entered this world.

They were beyond the shadowy tower of the furnace before the yellow blast of flashlight beams stabbed down into the room, focusing on the open door, the scattered boxes. Leaning heavily on Leibnitz – though he was six inches shorter than the old Kabbalist Rhion outweighed him by a good forty pounds – he cast a quick glance behind them, and saw von Rath himself, naked beneath a red silk bedgown among his black-clothed guards, standing in the black door that led to the Well. Then Sara was shoving him ahead of her into the dumbwaiter shaft.

By the time he'd climbed to the old kitchen Rhion knew there was no hope of escape across the yard. A chaos of shouts and drumming boots was rising like a storm outside, where dark forms raced back and forth in the chilly arclight. As she swung herself across the dumbwaiter counter Sara whispered hoarsely, 'Up the backstairs . . . fast . . .'

Neither Rhion nor her father questioned that she had a plan. She had been over the house enough times to know its every trapdoor and closet. Rhion could hear the guards from the watchroom searching the cellar in groups of three and four while those in the barracks combed the yard outside. They had a few moments . . . Flashlight shielded by her palm, Sara led the way up the old servant's stair, cursing as she banged her shins on the mould-furred bales of worthless currency. They emerged into the old dressing-room with its one-way mirror, where Rhion had watched the gypsy-girl last night.

'There's a trapdoor in the ceiling of the cupboard,' Sara panted, pointing to the dark line of doors which had made him so nervous last night. 'It leads up to the crawlspace above this wing. You have to go first, Papa . . . you're tall, you can pull me up. Rhion, you get your *tochis* back to your attic and get in your 'jammies. There's still time to come down rubbing your eyes and asking what the fuss is about . . .'

'No,' said Rhion softly. He did not look at her – he stood, instead, with his hand on the wing of the leather armchair, gazing transfixed into the gleaming black rectangle of the one-way glass.

'God damn it, we've got no time . . .' Her hard little hand jerked at his sleeve, and he shook it off. He felt chilled all over, as if out of nowhere he'd felt the whistling descent of a swordblade pass within centimetres of his face, as the implications of what he saw beyond the dark glass sank in.

'Help me up there.' He turned abruptly and dove into the closet, where Leibnitz' kicking feet were just vanishing through an inconspicuous square hole in the ceiling. Below, he could hear the voices of the guards as they emerged from the cellar to search the house.

'For Chrissakes . . .' began Sara, and he caught her waist, lifted her towards her father's reaching hands.

'*Get me up there!*' He shut the closet door behind him and reached up. Leibnitz caught one of his wrists in both big bony hands, and after a second, Sara caught the other. In the low, cramped space between the ceiling and the rafters of this wing a dead lift wasn't easy, but they managed to get his shoulders up to the level of the rafters on which they crouched, and after a certain amount of puffing and kicking he pulled himself through the hole and fitted the neat plank trap over it behind him.

'Well, you sure put your foot in it now.' Sara switched off her flashlight, leaving them in pitchy dark. 'Old Pauli has no proof who was potchkeying around in there . . .'

'No.' Bent nearly double he edged around behind Sara where she sat balanced on one rafter, and stretched himself out on the one beyond. The crawlspace rose to a peak of about four and a half feet above either of the lodge's two wings – only in the centre block was there a half-storey for attic rooms. Away in the darkness he could see – and smell – the nests of the rodents which lived there, and catch a glimpse of their angry eyes. *Sorry about violating your Lebensraum*, he thought wryly. *Into every life a little Anschluss must fall.*

'There's no reason for him to guess it was you,' Sara went on. 'Personally, I'd love to see that momzer Poincelles sashay in here an hour from now and try to explain where he'd been . . .'

Rhion shook his head, though Sara saw nothing of the gesture in the dark. 'No,' he said again. 'They changed that room, the one where they put the people on the receiving end of their experiments . . . the room on the other side of the glass.'

'Hunh?'

'It's a one-way mirror.' He felt carefully in his trouser pocket where he'd shoved the Spiracle in his haste. 'I could see into that room . . .'

'Oh, come on, it's pitch dark in there . . .'

'I saw,' he insisted quietly. 'They've put furniture in there in the last twenty-four hours – a bed, a chair, a desk – and they've unbolted the door into the washroom on the other side . . .'

Footsteps thudded in the hall below, and though they had been barely whispering before, all three fugitives fell silent. A thready line of diffused light briefly outlined the square of the trapdoor in the dark, but by its angle the guards didn't even aim their beams at the ceiling. In a guttural murmur of curses they were gone. Rhion laid his head down on his folded arms, and breathed again.

For nearly an hour none of them spoke. Closing his eyes, stretching out his hyperacute wizard-senses in the dense and stuffy blackness, Rhion found he could track the men back and forth, not only on this floor, but on the one below and in the central block and north wing of the house. He heard their voices, and the thick uneasy drag of their breath as they moved from room to silent, haunted room; felt the zapping tingle of electricity as they switched on light after light, unwilling – ignorant though they were of the inchoate powers lurking there – to be moving through the place in the dark. He heard a sergeant curse, and the opening and shutting of closet doors. Then far off, dim and deep, a voice came to him, chanting spells of breaking, of dissolution, and he heard the distant scrape of metal and soap and brickbats on stone.

Von Rath was dismembering the Dark Well.

Rhion shut his eyes, a shudder going through him at this last severing of any means of communicating through the Void. He fumbled in his trouser pocket again for the Spiracle. *This has to have worked*, he thought despairingly. *Don't tell me I'm really stranded . . .*

His fingers touched the twisted iron, and he knew.

Magic was in it. The cold of the Void whispered in his mind as he drew out the braided circlet. It seemed to him a faint spark glinted deep in the heart of each of the five stones. Holding it up, he could see through it down the length of the crawlspace – rafters, dust-clotted cobwebs, the accumulated nastiness of a century of mice – to the narrow black louvres at the end. Yet as if he looked through a smoked mirror, he knew.

Down below he heard the moist pat of von Rath's bare feet, ascending the chipped stone steps to the downstairs hall. Baldur's anxious, stammering voice demanded if he was all right and what he had done. Then he heard Poincelles' deep tones, and caught the sound of his own name. Rhion wondered fleetingly just what account the French wizard was giving of his evening, but satisfied that von Rath's mind was temporarily distracted, he risked one of the lowest level spells he knew, and summoned a tiny ball of blue light to his cupped palm.

It lay there glowing, the size of his little fingernail, a luminous edge of cerulean along his fingers, a chill spark in the scratched glass of his spectacle-lenses and the deep blue of his eyes.

'Jesus H. Christ,' muttered Sara, sitting up and stretching the kinks from her back. 'All right, Merlin, what do we do now? Poincelles has got to be back by this time, so you've blown your chance of pretending it wasn't you . . .'

Pallid dawnlight had begun to thin the gloom under the roof, and in the yard the muffled gunning of engines sounded, the clatter of metal, belt-leather, boots. A man cursed.

'He is.' Rhion closed his hand, killing the light which Sara had not seen. 'And it wouldn't be safe for me to go back even if they didn't think it was me. The bed they've put in the other room . . .'

'Yeah, what was the deal with that?' Beyond her, on the other side of the trapdoor, her father continued to lie full-length on the beam, only turning slightly to prop himself upon one bony elbow to watch them with dark eyes under the brim of his grubby cap. 'The room's got locks on the doors and no windows, it's the logical place if they're gonna hold a prisoner. If you say they're going to be making a big sacrifice on the Solstice . . .'

'If they unbolted the washroom that connects to that room,' said Rhion quietly, 'it argues for longer than a day. And that bed not only had blankets, it had pillows. There's only one prisoner in this joint I can think of who rates a pillow and an easy-chair. That room was fixed up for me. They planned to lock me up the day before the Solstice, just in case.'

'So, you think they don't trust you?' inquired Leibnitz, and Rhion grinned.

'As for what we do now . . . We lie low.' He replaced the Spiracle on its string in the open neck of his shirt, the jewels gleaming softly in the dark tangle of chest-hair. 'Here, for twenty-four hours, while they're out searching the woods. Tomorrow morning, just before dawn, we slip out and hide in the woods . . .'

'Great,' muttered Sara savagely. She pulled off her cap and shook out her hair with an impatient gesture, the grimy light catching metallic splinters of brass in the red. 'You get the whole countryside up in arms – it's gonna be a real trick for me to get back to town long enough to collect the food and clothes and money I've got stashed in my room, let alone getting the three of us to the Swiss border.' Her voice was soft – they were all whispering barely louder than breath – but dripped with sarcasm. 'Not to mention the fact that we don't even *have* identity cards for you, and on the run we sure as hell won't have a chance to get them . . .'

'Don't worry about me,' said Rhion softly. 'I'm not coming with you. And once the Solstice is over – after midnight Friday – von Rath won't be searching nearly as intently for me. He knows he has to catch me before the Solstice, before the pull of the sun-tide gives me the power I need to open the gate in the Void and make the crossing to my own Universe. That's why he's turning out his entire force now.'

'Fair enough,' agreed Rebbe Leibnitz, and, rolling over onto both elbows, pulled a stub of pencil and his pince-nez from his pocket, and began making a numerological calculation of the most auspicious hour and minute to leave the attic on the dusty plaster beneath the beam where he lay.

'I hate to break this to you, cupcake,' whispered Sara dourly, 'but there ain't no Santa Claus. Von Rath has mobilized the goon-squad because he's afraid you're going to high-tail it to England and spill your guts to Winnie Churchill. Within a week this search is going to be nationwide.' She sat up tailor-fashion, slim and straight with her red hair hanging down over her square, thin shoulders and jutting breasts beneath the grimy shirt. Some of the acid left her voice, and there was concern in her dark eyes. 'You poor deluded boob, what do you think's going to happen to you tomorrow night? You'll just go "poof" and disappear?'

'Yes,' said Rhion simply. 'I hope so.'

'*Oy gevalt* . . . We *all* hope so, but it doesn't work that way.' She started to pull up her shirt to get at the money-belt Rhion knew she habitually wore underneath, then paused, cast a quick glance at her father – obliviously working out some kind of calculation from a *vesica piscis* drawn over the Square of Mercury – and turned her back on both men. Rhion looked away from the girl's slender ribcage visible beneath a bizarre strapwork of lace and elastic underpinnings, and tried with indifferent success to think of other things.

She turned back, shirt-tail hanging out and a creased wad of papers and marks in her hand. 'These might do us in an emergency, if I can't get to the rest of my stuff,' she said. 'And I might not. They know I'm your – ah – friend . . .' She cast another quick glance at her father, as though she feared that he had somehow, within the camp, heard rumours about the red-headed bar-girl at The Woodsman's Horn and intuitively connected them with his only child. 'Once we get on the road it's gonna be a trick to hide Papa's head till his hair grows out a little.'

She transferred the papers to her pocket, withdrew from the same pocket a pack of filthy cards, and shuffled them deftly, quietly, in the half-light. In the yard below the sounds of departure had died. The smell of dust was fading. A woodpecker's hammering clattered unwontedly loud in the silence. Deep in his marrow, like a whispering of the leys that netted the earth, Rhion felt the stirring of the sun-tide begin.

'Rhion . . .' Sara looked up from the hand of gin she'd automatically laid out for the two of them between the rafters. 'Why don't you come with us? Forget the goddam Summer Solstice. We'll get you out of this *vershluggene* country somehow.'

He smiled, and shook his head, touched by her concern. 'I know you don't believe me,' he said, 'but tomorrow midnight really is my only chance to get home. It's the only time the wizards of my world will know where to look for me, and the only time I'll have enough power.'

For a long moment she studied him, worry softening the brittle cynicism out of her eyes. Without her customary coating of lip-rouge and make-up she looked far younger than usual, exhaustion and stress darkening the lids of her eyes and sharpening cruelly the tiny lines of dissipation already printed in the tender flesh. Then she shook her head. 'I wish to hell I knew where they got you,' she said softly. 'Or where your home really is.'

'I've told you and you don't believe me,' he smiled.

'I know,' she sighed. 'Munchkinland.'

'So what's not to believe?' Rebbe Leibnitz raised his head and adjusted his pince-nez reading-glasses with long, bony fingers. 'You remember Horus the Invincible, Saraleh, who stayed with us back in '28 when *he* was an exile from his own dimension . . .'

'I remember he never returned the money he borrowed from you.'

Leibnitz shrugged. 'So if he had, would we be hiding in a better class of attic today? He needed the money to continue his search for the Lost Jewels of Power that would open the Dimensional Gates . . .'

Sara rolled her eyes. 'I give up. Give my regards to the Witch of the West.'

The day passed, oppressive and stifling. In the cramped, dark space beneath the roof-tiles the heat grew quickly intolerable; the inability to move about became torment in itself. In spite of it all Rhion slept for hours, a breathless uncomfortable sleep on the eight-inch beam, tormented by cloudy dreams, while unable to smoke, unable to pace, Sara fidgeted her way through endless games of solitaire and her father covered all the plaster within his considerable arm-reach in a scrawled carpet of numerological abracadabra. Now and then Rhion opened his eyes to see the three hard splinters of brazen light that crawled along the slant of the struts overhead, or Sara's face, sweat-beaded and intent with her dark lashes turned to ginger by the sun. Then he would slide back into a gluey abyss of dreams.

He dreamed of Tallisett, riding in a swaying litter up the coiled road that led away from Bragenmere's yellow sandstone walls and into the dry hills of the Lady Range . . . dreamed of the Duke, white-faced and ill, raising his head from the pillows of his sickbed to accept the cup Lord Esrex handed him with an encouraging smile, while in the background a dark, veiled shape stirred a little in the shadows . . . dreamed of the octagonal library tower against a robin's-egg evening sky, its windows rosy with lights that gleamed on the steel helmets of armed men slowly gathering in the court below.

The dreams faded, turned cloudy and strange. Dimly, through his sleep, he felt the turning of the Universe as the sun-tide strengthened and the year approached its pivot-point, where its forces could be seized and swung by a man who knew its laws. Even those who knew nothing of magic felt it somehow, that at those two points – Midsummer and Midwinter – the doors that separated the mortal from the uncanny stood open, to admit sometimes fairies, sometimes the ghosts of the dead, and sometimes God. And even in his sleep his hand, which lay curled around his glasses upon his chest, moved to touch the Spiracle, to feel there the whispered magic of the Void.

Then he dreamed, much more clearly, of Paul von Rath, sitting in his own study, that dark, vast room choked with stolen books, unkempt, unshaven for the first time since Rhion had known him, gaunt cheeks spotted with the dry fever of his obsession and grey eyes chilled and narrowed to cold silver white as he bent over his books, reading . . . He wore no uniform, only the dressing-gown of thick dark silk he'd had on in the cellar, his naked chest visible beneath it and the steel swastika on its chain at his throat catching the light in a flat, hard flash. Like something scried at a distance Rhion saw him raise his head as the study door opened, and saw Poincelles there, dark face flushed with spite . . .

Then he woke, gasping, the heat pressing upon him like a slow ruthless vampire and sweat running down his face, matting clothes and beard and hair. The sun was sinking. The three splinters of light from the louvred vent had stretched to arrows, then to attenuated javelins, and now were fading altogether; in the yard were the sounds of truck-engines and the dulled, angry grate of men foul-mouthed with disappointment and fatigue.

'They sound beat,' whispered Sara, her lips twisting in a grin as she flipped over a card. 'Good – by two in the morning we'd be able to take a steam calliope and horses out of here without them noticing.'

The sentries around the perimeter of the house had been doubled, but the men were, as Sara had said, exhausted from a day of combing the woods, and it was a simple matter to create an illusion near the fence in a spot just out of view of the gully under the wire. It was a fairly ordinary illusion – two dogs copulating – but of sufficient interest to the type of men who made up the SS to hold their attention. Rhion, Sara, and Rebbe Leibnitz crossed the yard together and slipped under the fence and so into the woods.

Rhion and Leibnitz spent the following day hiding in the woods on the slopes behind Witches Hill. The guards from the Schloss, fortified with Waffen divisions from Kegenwald and even from Gross Rosen, were still searching, though not, Rhion thought, scrying for them in a pool of standing water, very energetically. Still the danger from them was real enough to prevent him from sleeping much, or from sinking for long at a time into the meditation he knew he'd need, to gather his strength for tonight.

He attempted to scry for the SS wizards, both in water and in his spell-crystal, and, not much to his surprise, could not. At another time of year, perhaps, with greater concentration . . . But for them, too, the sun-tide held some little power; their seal after all was the sun-wheel, turning in reverse. He did manage to see the Schloss from far off, a tiny image in the pond, and as the afternoon lengthened and the shadows began to cool he saw the grey truck with its black swastikas creeping like a poisonous beetle on the straight track that ran from the Schloss's gates away towards Round Pond and thence to the Kegenwald road. *I will disembowel them*, von Rath had said, leaning forward in the stifling gloom of the Schloss library. *Every one . . . Every one . . .*

They would be saving the most powerful wizard they had for tonight's sacrifice, thought Rhion, and shivered. More than one, probably; to draw out their souls, the essences of their lives, their torment and their pain, focusing them by those ancient rituals through von Rath's drugged mind to make talismans of power in the vain hope that quantity might somehow make a qualitative difference.

If they caught him between now and midnight, Rhion had a horrible certainty about what his own fate as well as Leibnitz's would be.

At sunset Sara returned. Rhion had scried for her half a dozen times during the day, at intervals in a thoroughly enjoyable argument with Leibnitz about the multiplicity of God, not because he thought he could help her at this distance but because he could not do otherwise. But her errand had been uneventful, and she came up the path to the clearing where they were to meet, pushing a stolen bicycle before her with a cardboard suitcase of clothes strapped to its handlebars. 'I got train tickets,' she said briefly, opening her handbag – a considerably older and more conservative one than she usually carried – to hand Rhion a bar of black-market chocolate and extract a cigarette for herself. She wore a sternly-tailored brown dress and low-heeled walking shoes, in keeping with the persona on her identity papers, an assistant bookseller's clerk travelling with her boss on a buying tour. To her father she tossed, from the suitcase, a shabby tweed jacket and a clean shirt, and a better-looking cap. 'I also got you a razor, Papa – you don't have enough beard yet to look like anything but an escapee from a camp, and if you shave it'll look like you've got more hair than you do.'

Leibnitz put a defensive hand over the half-inch of grizzled stubble which covered his jaw. 'The Rabbi Isaac ben Solomon Luria says . . .'

'Well, Isaac ben Solomon Luria didn't ever have to pass himself off as a *goyische* bookseller on the way to Switzerland, so shave! Papa, please . . .'

'The child is a staff for the hand, the Yebamoth says,' muttered the old man, turning back towards the pool which still reflected the sweet silver-green of the sky, 'and a hoe for the grave. "Even a child is known by his doings . . ."'

Sara turned back to Rhion, and for the first time, reached out and took his hand. 'Please come with us.'

He smiled and shook his head. Hate himself though he might for the selfish cowardice of it, with the dipping of the sun behind the black hackles of the hills he had felt himself relax. Von Rath and the others would be beginning their ceremony. He knew where they were, knew that the SS mage's attention would be fully occupied until after midnight. And in spite of his horror at what he knew would be going on, in spite of his loathing for what they did and were trying to do, what he felt was relief. He was safe. It wouldn't be he who lay on the black granite of the altar under Poincelles' knives; it wouldn't be his pain, his magic, his death, which they wove into their unholy power.

It occurred to him that he perhaps owed it to this world to return to the Schloss and burn the place and its books to the ground. But even the ability to convert what energy he could raise to physical operancy wouldn't help him against several dozen Death's-Head troopers. He could not risk even the chance of delay, and his own reserves of strength were perilously low. With the power of the Solstice behind him it was still going to take everything he had, and everything he could summon from the lambent magic of the stones, even to open the Void; Shavus, back at the Duke's palace in Bragenmere, had better be on the other side with one hell of a lot of magic to get him through.

'I'll be all right.'

'You don't even have a goddam identity card!' Her hands, small and delicate and hard, tightened over his and she shook him, as if this would somehow make him understand.

'I keep telling you I won't need one.'

She stared into his eyes for a long minute, then shook her head, and turned away. 'Okay,' she sighed. 'You win. Papa, you stay here. Rhion, I'll go with you to these rocks of yours. If you go poof and disappear, I'll admit I was wrong. If you don't . . . You come out of the country with us, because you're gonna need all the help you can get. Deal?'

It might have been the turning of the earth towards the darkness, the lengthening of the shadows of the black ridge of hills, but it seemed that cold came over him, the leaden taste of defeat and death. He shivered. 'It might be better if you got away while you can,' he said quietly. 'Von Rath's – busy – tonight, I don't think the search will be heavy between now and midnight . . .'

'The hell with that, we can take the seven A.M. train as easy as the eleven P.M. Papa, if I don't come back . . .'

'Then I won't come back,' he said placidly, returning from the pool with a nicked and dripping face, tying his tie. 'I'm coming with you. This,' he added, with wistful eagerness, 'I want to see.'

Light lingered in the midsummer sky as they made their way down the mountain. During the long afternoon Rhion had cut an elder sapling with Leibnitz' clasp-knife, the only weapon or tool either of them possessed, to make a staff, on which he mounted the Spiracle as a headpiece. Now as they walked the last glow of the day flickered along the rune-scribbled silver, and it seemed to him that the five crystals knotted within it whispered to one another in some unknown speech. On the western side of the hills power was rising, power called from pain and savagery and the black crevices of the human soul, but here in the hill's long shadow the night was untouched. Among the dark pines and bracken the cool air whispered of old enchantments. Rhion could feel a second ley when they crossed it, wan and attenuated but living with the life buried deep in the ground, pointing straight and glowing to the crossing at the Dancing Stones. Sunk in a half-trance as he walked, Rhion sensed the lift and swell of the Solstice power, as sun, stars, moon, time drifted to their balance-point, and it was as if every leaf, every fern, every mushroom and needle and fallen fir-cone gave forth a faint silvery shine.

The stones, when he reached them, seemed to glow with it in the dark.

All gates stood open tonight. As he walked towards those two lumpish guardians and the broken altar between them he felt as if he had been here on other Solstice-eves. His fear of pursuit, the sick terror he felt at what he guessed would happen to him if they were caught, eased and fell away. He sensed the whisper everywhere of freely given death and ecstatic mating, as if hundreds of bare feet all around him even yet swished the deep grass that washed the stones' sides.

He had reached the stones by midnight. He could escape. Jaldis . . .

He wasn't sure why he thought of the old man just then. Perhaps out of sorrow that for him, there would be no returning. Perhaps only some echo of a dream that he couldn't recall.

Sara and her father stopped just beyond the edge of the trees that ringed the meadow. Rhion, his mind already settled into the rhythm of the triumphant sun, walked on alone.

The power of the ancient stone rose to meet him as he touched it. Every breath he drew drank light from the murmuring air. Overhead the moon stood, a day past full and half-risen to its zenith, like the sweet swell of summer music drowning the stars. As he invoked the four corners of the earth Rhion touched, like a ghastly shudder in the air, a fragment of the power that was being raised to the west, a stench of burned flesh and agony, and felt along the network of the leys that elsewhere it was the same, rites of hate being performed in ancient places of power whose names were only names to him: Nuremburg, Welwelsburg, Munich. The dread of pursuit touched him again, and with it the strange sense of *déjà vu*, but with the drawing of the circle around the stones he cut out both the thin psychic clamour, and the evil power raised.

By the stars it was after eleven, though he did not need to see the sky's great clock to know that midnight was near. Through a deepening trance he called the last remnants of his own power from his exhausted flesh, linking it with the altar-stone and the turning firmament above, and he knew that no matter how many wizards Shavus had called in to help him on the other side, the jump was going to be bad.

A bluish haze of light trailed from his fingers as they brushed the altar-stone, and everything that had been written there over the course of millennia seemed to swim to the surface: ancient runes, spells of light, hand-prints with fingers cut away in sacrifice. The names of gods that went back to the name of the single power, the oldest names of the Mother and the Sky.

He stepped up onto the altar-stone, barely aware of the world outside the circle he had drawn, of the two dark forms of the only people he had cared for in this world watching from the edge of the trees. Raising the Spiracle on its staff he summoned, and seemed to see, far off and mere inches from his feet, a column of smoky darkness, stirring nameless colours, an abyss without light. All that was within him called forth the power of the Void, of the stone of sacrifice on which he stood, of the turning stars.

And waited.

He knew when midnight came. The whole universe whispered a single word – somewhere, dimly, there were shrieks, but the circle he had drawn around the place held them out. The dark field of the Void's magic enveloped him, and he reached out into it, seeking . . .

And found nothing.

No light, no sign, no answering call.

He deepened his concentration, forced his aching mind

to focus more sharply, more clearly, searching that darkness, waiting, reaching, not thinking about what it meant that they were late.

If late was all they were.

He thought, *No. Please, no.*

In his trance-state time was not the same, but he knew when a half-hour passed, and then an hour. The wheel of the stars moved slightly overhead; the moon climbed, unconcerned, towards her shining zenith.

Please?

The power of the ancient stone, pouring up through him towards the balanced stars, began to fade at three. He clung to it for as long as he could, but felt it go, as the swinging momentum of the Universe slid away and its vast, lazy turning resumed its wonted course. Still Rhion remained, standing upright on the stone, the staff upraised in his hands, until his knees shook with the exhaustion of forty-eight hours of fatigue and dread, and the world lapsed back from its waking dream of magic into its accustomed sleep.

They hadn't heard.

Or couldn't come.

Or had decided, for reasons best known to them, to leave him where he was.

Or it might just be that Sara was right. He had only dreamed of Tally, and Jaldis, of his sons and his parents and the world in which he had grown up, dreamed while incarcerated in a madhouse somewhere. Perhaps the truth – the real truth – was merely something he had forgotten.

He closed his eyes, fighting to believe this was not the case. For a moment it seemed that everything within him ripped and gave, and inner darkness poured into the hollow that was left. Opening them, he called the last fragments of strength, or hallucination, to stare into the darkness – if it was darkness – seeking some tiny splinter of light, a mark, a rune, a thread of magic to guide him through . . .

But there was nothing. Only the slow growing of a pallid dawnlight and the death, each by each, of the stars before the prosaic white of day.

He lowered his arms, letting the field of Void-magic around him die. His back and shoulders ached, his knees and hands were trembling, pains scarcely noticed and nothing beside the hurt that consumed him and left only hollowness behind. Tears tracked down his face, salty on his lips and wet in his beard. He bowed his head.

Then a quiet voice broke the dawn stillness. 'Give me what you have in your hand.'

He turned on the worn stone altar.

Twenty Storm Troopers were ranged in a semi-circle behind him, rifles and submachine guns trained. At the centre of the arc stood Paul von Rath, seared and haggard face somehow shocking in the nacreous morning light. 'I see Poincelles was quite right about where he guessed you would be – he had been watching you for weeks, you know – and what you would attempt. A worthy wizard, if spiteful as a woman. Worthy indeed to have been the sacrifice for our Solstice power. I think when we came for him he was surprised. Now give me what you have in your hand.'

He did not raise his voice. It was soft and balanced, like the way he stood, tense in his black uniform and polished boots, eyes grey and cold as glacier ice. Sara stood beside him, his arm locked around her neck, the silver blade of his SS dagger pressed to her throat.

Equinox

18

The house identified by Intelligence as von Rath's Berlin headquarters stood isolated in the grey autumn wasteland of empty fields, scrubby birch- and pine-woods, and nodding weedstems that stretched along the Spandau canal north and west of the city, a wasteland Berliners called the Jungfern Heide. Limping awkwardly down the long drive which connected it to the tramline of the Alt-Moabitstrasse, Thomas Saltwood studied what could be seen of the building above its grey stone wall. The steep roof had shingles cut out in coy Victorian half-circles like a fish's scales, a bit of rusted iron gingerbread along its ridgecrest, and two rounded dormers that spoke of attics above the second floor. *Or first floor, as the Brits would have it,* thought Tom with a wry grin. In Barcelona he'd nearly got himself killed by climbing one flight of stairs too few to meet a local Communist leader in what ultimately turned out to be the wrong flat. He still remembered the disgusted lecture Hillyard had given him on the King's English, once the shooting was done.

As the long-delayed Intelligence reports had indicated, the nearest house – another middle-class Victorian villa – was boarded up and deserted, over a half-mile away, and the isolation of the SS house was further emphasized by the wire fence enclosing nearly an acre of ground outside its already-forbidding stone wall. 'But it beats hell out of that lodge in the forest they were in all summer,' murmured Tom to himself, as he let himself through the unlocked, unguarded chain-link gate where the drive entered this outer perimeter. But he said it in German. He had been speaking in German, even to himself, since he'd paddled ashore the night before last in Hamburg.

The villa wall was eight feet high, blocks of the same dreary granite from which most of Berlin's overpoweringly heavy public buildings were made. The wrought-iron gate had recently been backed by sheet-steel; on either side of it, cut stumps and a litter of twigs, chips, and rotting berries marked where two beautiful old rowan-trees had flourished. *Blocked the field of fire from the gate,* thought Tom, looking regretfully down at the raw, foot-wide stumps. *Damn Nazis.*

In a way he was a little surprised to actually be here. The confusion of an impending invasion which had followed Dunkirk had put off his errand; the chaos of German bombs hammering London – invariably pulping those East End neighbourhoods whose inhabitants were only trying to make ends meet on two pounds a week, he added to himself – had put it off again. Hillyard had departed for a commando-base in Scotland, taking Tom with him, and though Tom had ultimately spent an energetic summer, he hadn't really expected to get any closer to the SS's tame magicians than Boulogne.

He scratched his unshaven jaw, checked his watch, and turned back to survey the line of telephone-poles which ran from the villa back to the drive's junction with the main road. Acid-drip devices were accurate to within ten minutes or so. Burdened with a heavy toolkit and a massive orthopaedic boot which not only made him limp whether he remembered to or not but which provided – along with the patch over his left eye – a visible reason why a man of good health and military age was wearing no uniform more formidable than that of the telephone company, it had taken him at least that long to walk this far.

He rang the bell by the gate. 'Telephone company,' he said to the young Storm Trooper who appeared, speaking in the slangy Berlin dialect he'd picked up from old Stegler in the Wobblies. 'We had half a dozen complaints this morning; we're tryin' to trace a fault in the line. You having trouble?'

'No,' said the young man, regarding the orthopaedic boot with unconcealed distaste and starting to shut the gate again.

Tom pulled out two cigarettes and offered one to the sentry, who hesitated, then pushed the heavy gate back. ''Preciate it if you'd check,' Tom said, ignoring as best he could the derision in the young man's eye. 'We're short on petrol this month and it's a bitch of a hike.'

'Do you good,' said the guard coolly, taking a lungful of smoke. 'It is better to strengthen feeble muscles than to pamper them.'

Saltwood made himself laugh heartily. 'I keep tellin' myself that,' he grinned, thinking, *I hope you draw guard-duty tonight, creep.*

But the guard, clearly mollified by this gesture of submissiveness, stepped back and opened the gate. Mentally thanking the encyclopaedia salesman he'd once ridden the rails with who'd taught him the value of agreeing with insults, Saltwood limped in, gazing around him incuriously at the house and outbuildings while the young man went into a small wooden gate-lodge and picked up the telephone. By the way he slammed it down again Tom knew the acid-drip he'd rigged in the main junction-box had worked.

The Storm Trooper emerged from the lodge looking at Saltwood as if the crippled telephone repairman had been personally responsible for the nuisance – which was, in fact, the case – and said, 'I'll take you in.'

Saltwood shook his head sympathetically, and stubbed his cigarette out against the granite of the gatepost, carefully stowing the butt behind one ear. 'Bitched-up Jew wiring, that's what it is.' He followed the young man across the yard.

From atop the telephone pole while installing the drip Tom had got a fair look at the house already. In a way he was glad of the summer's delays – it would be a hell of a lot easier to disappear into Berlin once the job was done than to escape the hue and cry in the wilds of the Prussian woods. He guessed this house at ten rooms exclusive of attics, completely surrounded by the wall. The old coach-house and a servants' cottage had been converted to quarters for half a dozen guards, Death's-Head SS, not Wehrmacht. Not an army project, then. The shrubbery all around the inside of the wall was badly overgrown, an easy sneak-up. While the sentry knocked diffidently on the door of the downstairs study Saltwood observed the catches on the windows, easy enough to trip with a knife blade . . .

'I hope for your sake the matter is critical, Trooper Weber,' said a voice as soft as a Thug's silk scarf, and turning, Saltwood saw in the study doorway the man who must be Captain von Rath.

Saltwood shifted his eyes away immediately, knowing he must not stare. But the man who stood framed in the umber gloom was only superficially recognizable as the one whose picture he had seen in London. The man in the picture he'd been shown in London – a picture taken in Prussia in the spring – had had the look of a man dying, burning up inside. This man . . .

For some reason Saltwood, schooling his features into casual respect that had no trace of recognition as he looked back, was reminded more than anything else of a wealthy and well-cared-for woman in the fourth month of a pregnancy which pleases her. Von Rath had that same glow, that same sense of beauty fulfilled and radiant . . . that same very slight air of smugness. The gauntness had filled out without losing the shape of those splendid cheekbones, and even the man's hair seemed thicker, brighter, stronger despite its close military cut. Yet there was something else, something that the picture had entirely failed to convey, though Saltwood was damned if he could figure out what. Strong as a physical impact, he had a sense of evil, of wrongness – of darkness masquerading as triumphant light.

Oh, come on! he chided himself, disgusted. *I thought you got over that Good Guys/Bad Guys stuff in Spain!*

But when von Rath's frost-silver gaze touched him he shivered, and came at the Major's beckoning with an unwillingness that went to the bone.

'Short in the wiring someplace,' Tom explained, his ingratiating grin feeling like a badly-made denture. 'Buggered up half the lines around here. We need to check whether it was in a phone here, either one that's still in use or an outlet that was taken out, see.' Von Rath made no response, and he felt the sweat start under his cheap billed cap.

Tom had talked strike in mines and on factory-floors, never knowing which of those scared and angry men were the management bulls, but he'd never in his life had this sense of irrational terror of another man. As he spoke he noticed small details: the almost metallic quality of the pale gaze, the short sabre-scar on the cheek and the white slimness of the hands. Of course with a 'von' hanging off the front of his name he'd never done a day's manual work in his life. Like Marvello the Magnificent and every other carney magician Tom had ever met, von Rath wore hoodoo amulets around his neck – twenty or more circles made of jewels and glass and what looked like animal-bone on one necklace, and on another a single uneven ring of woven silver, crystal, and iron. This medicine-show fooferaw should have been funny, like Hitler wearing *lederhosen*, but it wasn't. Tom couldn't tell why.

'There is a telephone in my study,' said von Rath at last, 'and another upstairs in my room. A third is in the guards' lodge out back. Those are all that have ever been in this house. Take him around, Weber, and see that I am not disturbed again.'

While Saltwood opened up the bottom of the study telephone and poked around inside von Rath returned to his bulbous Beidermeyer desk and his book, but Tom was nerve-rackingly conscious of the man's presence in the room. *Get a hold of yourself,* he thought irritably, trying not to run out of the room when he was done; but by the gleam of sweat on Trooper Weber's upper lip when that young man met him in the hall again, he saw that von Rath had that effect on others as well.

And why not? he thought, disgusted with himself as he followed Weber upstairs. *He looks like a dangerous hombre to cross even if he does wear Woolworth's Finest strung around his neck. HE's the one I ought to kill.*

But ten years of bar-fights, of tangles with management stooges on picket-lines and occasional pop-skulled crazies in hobo-jungles made him think uneasily, *I'd sure hate to try.*

'Chilly bugger,' he volunteered, pulling apart the phone in von Rath's Spartan bedroom and giving it, and the skirting-boards, a cursory once-over. Trooper Weber, his arrogance still cowed by the encounter with von Rath, nodded. Von Rath's chamber was by no means the original master bedroom of the house – either Sligo had that one or they were using it as a workroom. 'Any chance of getting a quick look at the other rooms in case there's a dead lead? It'll take just a glance around the skirting and save me a trip back here if we *still* can't find the short. That way we won't have to disturb His Nibs again.'

Weber hesitated, then nodded, and gave Tom a tour of three other bedrooms on the upper floor during which Tom was able to mentally orient himself and establish entries and possible escape-routes. Only at the far end of the passage, where the two major bedrooms stood opposite one another, did Weber demur. 'It is forbidden to go into either of those.'

'What's in there? Secret plans?' The locks on both were new.

Trooper Weber gave him a fishy stare. 'There is nothing in there.' He was a lousy liar.

Tom shrugged. 'No old phone-leads? It'd be a wire about so long sticking out of the skirting . . .'

'There is nothing like that.'

'Thank Christ for that.' He turned, and limped back down the hall, deliberately slowing his pace to irritate his guard, who had to keep stride with him. To the right of the stairs as he emerged on the ground floor was a sliding door of polished mahogany, also recently decorated with a brand new lock, but as he limped over to investigate the door was shoved open from within and a young man poked his head out.

'Who are you? What do you want? What is this man doing here, Trooper?' The boy was short, fat, and coked stupid – past him Tom had an impression of black tapestries and some sort of altar, candles, chalked circles on the bare floorboards, and a stink like a San Francisco joss-house.

Trooper Weber saluted smartly. 'A man from the Fernsprechamt, Herr Twisselpeck. He wants to know if there was at any time a telephone in that room which might be causing a short in the lines in the neighbourhood.'

Herr Twisselpeck – the boy couldn't have been over eighteen – swivelled weak tea-coloured eyes up to Saltwood, and beneath thick glasses and enough dope to raise the dead Tom could see the jealousy in them at his height and the breadth of his shoulders. 'So they're hiring c-cripples these days, are they?' he demanded nastily. 'No, there isn't a telephone in here. There never was a telephone in that room. You should know we'd never have ch-chosen it for the Temple, the Holy Place of Power, if there had been any kind of electrical wiring in its walls.' He jerked back into the darkness of the Temple and tried to slam the doors – the heavy, sliding mahogany slipped out of his jittering hand on the first try and he heaved and fussed at it for a moment to coax it closed. A moment later the lock clicked.

Tom shook his head. 'Takes all kinds.'

As he was limping after his escort towards the guards' station – once the old carriage-house – and taking more accurate note of the wilderness of overgrown shrubbery which should conceal very nicely his appearance over the wall, he espied an old man, clothed in nothing but a loincloth despite the autumn chill of the day, standing rigidly on a little terrace at one corner of the house, his left arm held to his side, his right crooked out before him, elbow bent so that his fingers pointed back at his abdomen, right knee bent up to rest his foot on his left knee, for all the world as if he endeavoured to mould his body into an approximation of the letter B. As they passed the old man began to yodel, a long, undulating, full-throated howl in which the drawn-out sounds 'Booo-o-o-o-e-r-r-r-ccccc . . .' could be barely distinguished.

Tom had seen weirder things in California.

He came back later that night.

He'd repaired the junction-box, lest the inconvenience drive von Rath to contact the real Fernsprechamt. It was an easy matter to disconnect the entire box again at two A.M. With luck no one would know of Sligo's death until morning, but if there were a slip-up and the alarm was raised, they would be that much later getting the dogs after him. With even a few hours' start he'd be well on his way back to Hamburg.

He approached the house from behind, sliding under the wire and crawling through the scrubby sedges of the enclosed field, his black SS uniform hidden under a ragged grey blanket. The field, unlike much of the wasteland of the Jungfern Heide, had been recently mowed; in places the bare ground showed signs of fire. The moon was a few days past full, bright as a beacon in an almost cloudless mid-heaven. A bomber's moon, they were already calling such conditions in London.

At Commando headquarters in Lochailort they'd given him a collapsible ladder, a lightweight steel alpenstock with rungs folded into it on either side. The wall was higher than the ladder's six-foot length, but not by more than a yard. He'd picked his spot carefully that afternoon, where the bulk of the old coach-house would screen him from the sentry who would in all probability be stationed by the kitchen door. Once he was over his uniform would almost guarantee anonymity – he'd thankfully disposed of the eyepatch, boot, and four-day beard that had constituted his disguise – and he made the jump down, taking the stock with him and stowing it out of sight in the bushes, without a sound.

The house was dark. There was a tiny chink of light around a blackout curtain in the front hall, where a guard would probably be dozing; another guard stood by the back door. Like a spectre Saltwood glided through the dark laurels, forced open a dining-room window, and stood listening for a moment to the silence of the house. A chair creaked in the front hall. Looking through the dining-room door he saw a Storm Trooper sitting in a hard-backed chair beside a lamp in the front hall, reading a lurid-covered paperback novel and moving his lips slightly with the effort. Tom slipped the garrotte from his pocket, disposed of the man without trouble, took his keys and manhandled the limp body into the bottom cabinet of a built-in china-hutch where nobody was likely to look. Folding the wire garrotte back around its wooden handles he stepped quickly over to the 'Temple' doors, and with his pocket flashlight shielded behind his hand had a quick look around to make sure it was no more than it seemed.

It wasn't. A black-draped Inner Sanctum straight out of the Benevolent Protective Association of the Rhinoceros

Lodge, a Rosicrucian's lobster-supper dream complete with a closetful of white, black, and scarlet robes and a louring stench of old blood and charred meat that even the whorehouse incense couldn't conceal. He wondered what they'd sacrificed. Jemal Nightshade, a slow-spoken Negro who'd worked beside him in the West Virginia mines, had confessed one night over a couple of drinks to offering chickens to the *loa* back in Port au Prince – a goat, if the family could afford it.

Did they really believe this stuff?

Saltwood remembered those bone amulets and shrivelled little skin bags hanging around von Rath's neck, and shivered unaccountably. Evidently twelve years of being force-fed the Opium of the Masses in Lutheran Sunday-School hadn't been completely eradicated by the big doses of Voltaire, Marx, and Hobbes he'd had since, he thought, hugging the wall as he climbed the stairs to keep his weight from creaking the risers. The lab, at a guess, would be in one of those two locked bedrooms upstairs, or in one of the attics . . .

In the darkness the sense of the infernal in the place was stronger, revolting him as none of Jemal Nightshade's talk of *veves* and *legba* ever had – when it came right down to it, Nightshade's voodoo had never struck him as being that different from old Tommy Wu's ginseng Buddhism or the sight of those old Spanish women in Saragosa, crawling over cobblestones with bleeding knees to kiss a pillar in a church. *Come on!* he told himself. *All this is just to make people think they're crazy . . . And anyway, let's not talk about evil after you've just added that Storm Trooper – not to mention that Merced County 'special deputy' the orange-growers hired to bash the migrants – to your body-count in Spain.*

You're here to do a job.

A wavery thread of candlelight marked the bottom of one of the locked upstairs doors; the other room was dark.

Tom entered that one first, gingerly trying key after key in hair-prickling silence, then stepping cautiously inside and flashing the light quickly around. It was a laboratory, all right – an absurd wizard's-kitchen straight out of L. Frank Baum, stocked with everything from mandrake roots (in a wooden box labelled with Teutonic thoroughness) to a collection of revolting mummy-fragments undoubtedly looted from every museum from Paris to Warsaw. Not a shred of wire, not a radio-tube, not a soldering-iron to be seen, even in the drawers and cabinets.

Saltwood smiled inwardly. *What a collection! Old Marvello would swap his first-born child for a crystal ball that size!*

That means the real lab must be across the hall, or in one of the attics upstairs. But the lab itself was of only secondary importance.

He looked back at the thread of light under the door. *Not strong enough for a working-light . . .*

A bedroom, then. And since he'd seen von Rath and Twisselpeck, and the old geezer on the terrace that afternoon fit the description Mayfair had given him of the third member of this particular cell of the Occult Bureau, Jacobus Gall . . .

At a guess, this room would be Sligo's.

Of the three new keys on the ring, he'd already eliminated one as belonging to the lab door; the first of the remaining two he tried fit. He had a story ready which his uniform would have backed up, but when he stepped silently through the door he found he didn't need it. The man sitting perched on a laboratory-stool at the table had his back to the door, and was far too absorbed in what he was doing to look around or even, evidently, notice that someone had entered. Even in the dim glow of a single candle, which was all the illumination the room could boast, Saltwood recognized him: Professor Rhion Sligo, self-styled wizard and pet mad scientist of the SS, a broad-shouldered, bearded little man clothed in a hand-me-down Wehrmacht sweatshirt and patched fatigue-pants, bent over a weird construction of braided metal wires, small glass spheres, and the biggest hunk of rock-crystal Saltwood had ever seen.

Both Sligo's chubby hands rested on the twisted wire base of the thing – crude and lumpy iron wound around with something that looked like gold but was probably brass. His head was bowed, his eyes shut and his breathing slow, as if in sleep or deep meditation. Saltwood took the garrotte from his pocket and silently unwound it, wrapping the handles tight in his hands.

He really does believe it . . .

His face still turned away from Saltwood, the Professor straightened up a little on his backless stool and raised his head, but the candlelight showed his open eyes focussed inward, devoid of any awareness of his surroundings. It seemed to Tom, standing behind him, that a faint secondary glow seemed to be coming from the crystalline gizmo on the table, shining faint bluish-white, like distant stars, in the lenses of Sligo's glasses.

Sligo stretched out one hand, keeping the other on the gizmo's base.

It has to be a reflection. An optical illusion . . . But it seemed to Tom that in Sligo's cupped hand a seed of blue-white light blossomed, cold St Elmo's Fire that threw a ghostly radiance on every line and ridge of his fingers without appearing to burn the flesh. *But if it's a reflection of the candleflame, shouldn't it be orange . . .?*

Tom stepped nearer. Sligo stretched out his hand, and the ball of light drifted upwards like an ascending balloon. He raised his head to follow it with his eyes, and fascinated as Saltwood was by the trick, the trained assassin in him said, *Now.*

Tom stepped soundlessly forward and crossed his arms; Sligo never knew what hit him until the garrotte pulled tight. With the dancer's grace that an Italian thug had taught them all at Lochailort Tom turned his body, hooked his shoulder under the taut wires, and dragged the little man off his stool and up onto his back. He felt the futile twist of Sligo's body, the slapping, desperate grope of his hands as he tried frantically to find something to grab or strike. But in this position there was nothing, no purchase possible, no way to make contact with anything but the strangler's back and sides. Thirty, forty seconds at most . . .

But with a final convulsion Professor Sligo hooked one foot in the stool on which he'd been sitting and kicked it as hard as he could against the wall. In the dead silence of the night it made a noise like the house falling down, and von Rath's room, Saltwood knew, was immediately next door.

Cursing, he threw Sligo's limp body to the floor and whipped out the dagger that was a part of the SS uniform, jerked his victim's head back by the hair and slashed at the exposed throat. For one split-second he found himself looking into Sligo's wide, terrified blue eyes . . .

And the next instant light exploded, blinding as the glare of a welder's torch, inches in front of his nose. Taken totally by surprise Tom flinched back from it and felt the body pinned beneath him twist free. Blinded by the aftermath of the glare he made one flailing cut at where he thought Sligo would be as he tried to get to his feet, and, a split-second too late, thought, *That stool* . . .

Somewhere behind him Tom heard the sobbing gasp of Sligo's breath – then the lab-stool connected full-force with his head and shoulders.

Saltwood couldn't have been unconscious for more than a few seconds. Electric light flooded the room as he came to; yells, curses drifted into his awareness, and a black ring of shapes swimming like sharks through his returning vision. He curled instinctively as a boot crashed into his belly; a second one exploded against the back of his head . . .

And then silence.

Swamped in pain and half-stunned, still he knew what that silence meant.

'Stand up,' said the voice like the whisper of silk over the point of a knife.

It wasn't easy to do so without retching. Groping at the table for support Saltwood noticed the lumpy gizmo of iron and crystal was gone. Professor Sligo stood next to the door, green with shock except for the livid red bruise of the garrotte across his throat.

'Lay him on the bed,' instructed von Rath quietly, not moving from the doorway where he stood. 'Get him brandy.' Over the dark red silk of his dressing-gown the double chain of amulets gleamed faintly, the small circles of bone clinking against one another and against the twisted ring of silver and iron. His face was calm, impersonal, but Saltwood knew that with him in charge of it, whatever would happen next was going to be bad.

'Who sent you?'

'He's one of ours!' gasped Baldur Twisselpeck, stumbling belatedly through the door and shoving his smudged glasses onto his face as one of the half-dozen Storm Troopers pulled the forged SS ID from Saltwood's pocket.

'Don't be stupider than you are.' Von Rath barely glanced at the young man. 'Papers can be faked – as can a patched eye, a limp, and a telephone repair kit.'

'You mean that was him today . . . ?' gaped Baldur, blinking. He was shouldered out of the doorway by Jacobus Gall, barefooted and, like von Rath, evidently naked under his dressing-gown, and like von Rath also seemingly indifferent to cold. Gall went to where Sligo lay, eyes shut now under a tangle of hair that was almost black against his waxy skin, on the bed that occupied most of the narrow room's western wall. Looking around him, Saltwood saw in the better light that the room was, in fact, Sligo's bedroom. Its windows were boarded up; the door had no handle on the inside.

Tom realized that Sligo was a prisoner, and not a free agent as Mayfair had believed.

'He should have a doctor,' stated Gall, examining the bruises left by the garrotte. 'If he is to assist in the demonstration Monday . . .'

'The phones are dead again, Major,' reported an SS sergeant, entering from the lights of the hall. 'We could send Reinholt to the Lebensborn in the Grunewald – that's the nearest doctor – and from there he could phone the Gestapo . . .'

'I expect you put the telephone out again before entering this house.' Von Rath's ice-grey eyes returned to Saltwood's face. 'Didn't you?'

Saltwood said nothing.

Without looking back at them, von Rath added, 'As for the Gestapo, I think not.' Head tilted a little to one side, he continued to study Saltwood with disquietingly impersonal interest. 'He is of a higher type, isn't he, than the Jew and Slavic swine they've been sending us from the camps?' he went on softly. 'A finer body, certainly, and therefore a stronger and fitter mind.'

Saltwood felt his stomach curl with dread. *Oh, Christ . . .*

'Shameful, isn't it?' said Baldur Twisselpeck sententiously, crowding back to von Rath's side. 'The orphans of the race, betraying the heritage of their Fatherland to breed with the corrupt ape-men of Jewish-dominated countries like . . .'

'Oh, I think not,' purred von Rath, with a dreaminess in his level voice that was almost pleasure, though his eyes remained chill, almost blank, as if whatever dwelled inside were wholly occupied with itself and itself alone. 'If that is the case – if his blood is corrupt – he is certainly a throwback to the original root-race, and that's all we need. It is all the best of the British will be. Gall, be sure to take his cranial index and other physical data tomorrow. Himmler will want to see them.' He signed with his finger to the sergeant, and two Storm Troopers closed in on Tom from either side, handcuffing his wrists behind him and shoving him before them out of the room. Behind him, he heard von Rath say 'Take him to the house on Teglerstrasse for tonight and tomorrow. We'll need him there for the demonstration in any case. See that he comes to no harm.'

Looking back over his shoulder, Saltwood saw von Rath step through the door of the bedroom, switching off the lights so that only the candle's feeble gleam illuminated the boarded-up chamber. Taking a key from his dressing-gown pocket, he locked Sligo in. As Saltwood's guards pushed him down the stair the murmur of von Rath's voice drifted behind him, with Gall's crisp Viennese tones and Baldur's adolescent adenoidal whine.

'Should we send for a doctor?'

'I don't think it will be necessary. I've mastered all he can teach me.'

'Then after the demonstration Himmler can have him? I'm sure Himmler's right – I'm sure there's some k-kind of physical difference that gives him his powers. Mengele should be able to make something of it . . .'

'Nonsense! Proper purification of the body, proper nutrition and mental attitude is all that is needed for the working of magic . . .'

'Scarcely,' purred von Rath. 'Nevertheless, I don't think we need share with Herr Himmler what can be learned from – ah – experimentation. And after Monday's demonstration we may not need to deal with Himmler again. For you see, Providence has been kind. We needed a higher type of subject for our final demonstration, the type of trained warrior with whom our invading forces will actually have to contend. And now we have him.'

19

The solar at Erralswan was a small room, situated in the stumpy tower at the southwest corner of the rambling sandstone manor-house, the windows which on three sides overlooked the walled-in orchards and gardens making it, on these cold autumn afternoons, the warmest and sunniest place in the house. Even so, fires had been kindled in the braziers of beaten copper; the sun which strewed an intricate lacework of bare tree-shadows through the latticed window-panes had lost its power to warm.

Tallisett of Erralswan stood for a long time in that bright, chilly drench of light, looking down at the locked doors of the cupboard-desk which stood between the windows, her arms folded, almost literally shivering, not with cold, but with a gust of irrational rage.

The cupboard-desk was of the old-fashioned, simple kind frequently found in the seats of country lords like this one, made of pickled pearwood, simply and cleanly carved. The pale wood showed up admirably the half-dozen small, oval splotches of indigo that dotted the edges of the tall, narrow, enclosing doors – when Tally took the desk's small key from her belt and opened those doors, she had to do so carefully, so exactly did those telltale smudges coincide with where it was easiest to place her hands.

She already knew what she'd see when she opened the desk, but at the sight of her letters, in their neat pigeonholes, all daubed and thumbed with more spots of indigo, renewed anger swept her, so that for a moment she felt she could scarcely breathe. The top sheet of the little pile of half-written stationery on the minuscule writing-surface was smeared, not only with those grubby blue thumb-prints, but with a very fine white powder that in places had begun, itself, to turn a faint blue. This sheet she lifted carefully, holding it by the very tips of her fingernails, and carried it to the brazier in the corner; the two silky red bird-dogs sleeping in front of it in the scattered glory of the autumn sunlight raised sleepy, hopeful heads as her skirt-hem brushed their fur, but for once she had no greeting for them. She placed the sheet on the blaze, and waited until it caught.

After it had completely burned she turned away, to descend the stone stairway to the gardens, and seek her husband.

'It's Neela, it has to be,' she said.

Marc frowned irritably, though whether it was because she'd interrupted him while he was working one of his new horses, or because he resented an accusation against the pretty black-haired housemaid whom Tally knew he was planning to bed – if he hadn't done so already – she wasn't sure. From this, the largest of the paddock yards, one could look down the length of the narrow, upland vale nestled between the shouldering walls of the Lady Range and the granite cliff of the main mass of the Mountains of the Sun: sheep-country, green and empty of trees, with low stone fences and crystal-cold despite the deceitful brilliance of the sun. Tally pulled the long feather-work shawl more closely about her shoulders and shivered.

She went on, 'I've thought before this that my desk was being searched, my letters read. Last week when I went into Yekkan I bought a powder from a Hand-Pricker, that will cling to a human hand and leave purple stains on whatever it touches, stains that appear only hours later. I found such stains not only on the papers of my desk, but on the sheets of my bed, and around the fireplace, and on brooms and rags in the servants' hall . . .'

'You went to a *Hand-Pricker*?' Marc caught her by the

arm in a crushing grip, and she saw, not anger, but fear in his dark eyes. Then he cast a swift look behind him, at his stablemaster who was training another of his dark, thick-necked two-year-old colts in the first of the elaborate carousel-figures which would be required in the mounted fetes of the capital that winter, and drew Tally closer to the yellow sandstone wall that flanked the paddock on that side, so that his horse stood between them and any possibility of being seen from the yard. 'My lady . . .' he said warningly.

She shook her head, baffled by how much he was making of it. 'Everyone goes to Hand-Prickers . . .'

'*Not* everyone,' he whispered hoarsely. 'In fact it's far fewer than most people believe.'

'That's nonsense,' she said, still puzzled at the look in his eyes. 'If nobody goes how do they make the kind of living they do – and what does it matter anyway? What matters is that one of my servants is searching my rooms . . .'

'Hand-Prickers make their living as poisoners, as abortionists, as everyone knows – by transmuting base metals into gold . . .'

'*Marc* . . .' Tally pulled a little away from him, shocked at hearing this kind of thing from him. From Damson, last June, it was to have been expected – she was close to the inner circles of Agon's cult and would promulgate their oversimplifications whether she believed them or not. But with all the years Marc had been at her father's court he had to have known better. 'You know as well as I do that they can't make base metals into gold without expending more energy than it's possibly worth . . .'

Marc shook his head. 'They only say that.' He placed his big hands on her shoulders and looked gravely down into her eyes. Out of court costume, in the plain green tunic and close-fitting sleeves of a country squire and with his hair braided back, he seemed both older and more approachable than he did in Bragenmere, where the ceremonial of her father's household gave them the ability to distance themselves from one another. Here at Erralswan, though the summer had not been an easy one, she had remembered why she had always liked the big, easy-going young man who she had part-bullied, part-bribed, part-begged to marry her seven years ago.

'It's only a story they put around,' said Marc, in a still lower whisper, as if he feared that some wizard would overhear, 'to keep the secret of their wealth to themselves – so they can buy the influence of powerful nobles. My lady, these days it doesn't pay to be seen having anything to do with people like that, particularly for you.'

Behind them the horse, bored, tossed its head. Past the low sandstone wall of the paddock Kir's voice could be heard, raised in a joyous shout as he led a pack of the half-dozen pages of the household in a charge down one of the long arboured walks which connected the main house with its several attendant pavilions. Tally caught a glimpse of them through the latticework of the vines, now nearly bare of their summer leaves, and felt a cold little dart of fear.

Carefully she said, 'Why, "particularly", for me?'

'My lady,' said her husband quietly, using the honorific in which he had always addressed her, 'the days are past when you, or anyone, could be seen associating with . . . well, with just anyone. They're finding out things about wizards, and how they work . . .'

'*Who* is finding out "things"?' insisted Tally warily. 'What kind of "things"?'

'About what they do to people who come within their power.' Marc glanced around him again, though there was no one in the yard but the stablemaster and he was fussing lovingly over the colt's feet. 'Now, I know you – and in fact anyone who knows you can attest that you haven't had your soul stolen, or your will taken over, by wizards . . .'

'That's ridicu . . .'

He put a finger to her lips. 'They do it, my lady,' he said softly. 'They do it. We're only just finding out how frequently. And they turn such people into their servants, to get them still other slaves.'

For a moment she could only stand, open-mouthed with shock at the enormity of this lie. The sheer scope of it took her breath away almost as much as the fact that it was coming to her from Marc, Marc who had always been cheerfully friendly to the wizards at her father's court, who had bought Mhorvianne only knew how many love-philtres from Jaldis and Rhion over the years . . . 'That's the most absurd thing I've ever heard!'

He bit his lip, hesitating for a long moment – Tally felt almost that he was waiting for the groom to get out of earshot before he spoke again. 'I see I'm going to have to tell you,' he said softly. 'I didn't want to, because I know you liked old Jaldis and Rhion, and I swear to you I've never heard a thing against either one of them, even if they did . . . Well, everyone says their disappearance was opportune.'

He lifted his hand to silence her as she opened her mouth again, but the gesture was needless – Tally was outraged beyond speech.

He went on, 'They arrested a conspiracy of wizards the night you left Bragenmere, in your father's very palace, in Jaldis' rooms. I'd like to assume that with his disappearance they were trying to take your father's library for whatever knowledge it contained, and not that Jaldis himself had summoned them . . .'

Tally closed her mouth, stood for a time looking up into the handsome, healthy tanned face bent so gravely above her own. All these endless summer months she had suspected something had happened after her departure, though out here in the deeps of Marc's countrified fief there had been no way of knowing for certain, and she had feared to write to anyone she knew at court. Damson's words to her before she had left had frightened her; she knew how easily letters could be intercepted and read. So she had waited, knowing that if Rhion had indeed been brought back with the turning of the Summer-tide she would eventually hear of it . . . someone would get word to her . . .

And so she had waited, through the nerve-racking weeks.

Marc went on in almost a whisper, 'So you see, they have this information from the wizards themselves. From their confessions.'

'Under torture.' Her heart was beating heavily, hurtingly in her chest. *Shavus* . . . she thought. The old man was vain, arrogant, maddening, but never did he deserve that. *The Serpentlady, Harospix . . . Dear Goddess, did the Gray Lady get away safely? Did Gyzan?*

Marc nodded. 'Of course. The things they've confessed to aren't anything you would learn of without torture. But that doesn't mean they aren't true.'

Of course, she thought bitterly. *I chose Marc for my husband partly because he was easily led – because he'd believe what I told him and not ask questions . . . Why be surprised that I'm not the only one he'll believe?*

'And Father let them?' Her mouth felt dry. She remembered her father and the gruff old Archmage duelling with the salt-spoons.

'Your father's been very ill,' said Marc. 'You know that, Damson's been writing all his letters for him, with only his signature . . . but yes, his signature was on the orders. He must protect his realm – and not only his own realm, but humankind.'

Tally was silent. A part of her felt very still and cool, detachedly contemplating pieces of a puzzle fitting together. She didn't even feel anger – at Damson, or at Marc – only a sort of clarity, as if she were seeing them for the first time in decent lighting. For no reason she remembered the tiny, crystalline clinking of her sister's lace-spindles, and the breath of incense that moved about the shrine of the Veiled God. A cold mountain wind breathed down across the stable-yard, stirring her heavy skirts and making the feathers of her shawl ripple in the light like a meadow of iridescent, red-bronze grass.

But part of her remembered Gyzan, and Shavus, and the other mages who'd been in Jaldis' tower that night, remembered Jaldis' sunken, empty eyepits and limping step, and she felt her breath thicken and heard the dizzying roar of blood sounding in her ears. It seemed to take her forever to collect her thoughts. 'Do you know . . . who was among those arrested?'

'The Archmage,' said Marc quietly. 'The Harospix Harsprodin, who had been one of the Queen's advisors. The Queen was deeply shocked at his betrayal, and by his confession that it was he who'd been causing her little boy's seizures, and even more shocked when it became obvious that your father's illness was almost certainly the result of the Archmage's spells.'

'Shavus wouldn't . . .'

Marc shook his head. 'According to his own confession, he cast the illness upon your father when your father began to suspect him of trying to steal his soul, of trying to rule the country through him. Tally . . .' he insisted, as she shook her head, refusing to believe, 'it was written in his confession! It was what he told Mijac – the doctors sent to your father's bedside by the priests of Agon can't make head nor tail of his illness! He betrayed your father. The wizards he has sheltered for so long, befriended for so long, were only using him! Don't you understand?'

With a feverish shiver Tally remembered the letters she'd had all summer from her father, written in Damson's neat, secretarial hand – the wording had been frequently reminiscent of Damson as well. She wondered if the signature on the orders for arrest had been the same as on her letters:

unsteady, mechanical, like a man gravely ill – or a man deeply drugged.

'Do you know,' she faltered, 'what time that night the wizards were arrested? Whether it was before or after midnight?'

And Marc shook his head.

They will have destroyed the Dark Well, thought Tally, crossing the paddock quietly and turning towards the villa, almost shocked at her own ability to appear calm. Her heart pounded sickeningly in her breast, and her belly turned cold every time she thought about how confession was extracted – about what Rhion had told her of his own brush with the priests of Agon.

Was he one of the ones they took? She thought about it for a moment and found it unlikely. *Even if he had . . .* Her mind shied from the thought of what Esrex would have done to force a confession from Rhion as to the paternity of her sons. *Even if he had withstood it, and died, Esrex wouldn't have passed up the chance to let me know.*

But if he didn't make the crossing before the arrest – if he didn't come stumbling out of the Dark Well right into the arms of Esrex and the masked servants of the Hidden God – that means he's still stranded wherever he is, with Jaldis dead, without magic, in trouble, he said . . .

And there was no one of sufficient power to bring him home.

She paused at the rear door of the house, hating the thought of returning to her rooms. The purple handprints would be fading by this time, as they did after a few hours, though the Hand-Pricker in the village had assured her that at a word from him they would return. *For all the good that would do,* she thought bitterly. *Marc would never consent to bringing him here – and as things are, if he has any sense of self-preservation he won't come . . .*

And in any case, disposing of one spy would only mean

there'd soon be another one that she didn't know about. *His devotees are everywhere,* Damson had said . . .

With sudden resolution, Tally turned her steps left, crossing behind the rustic sandstone of the stable's east wall and thence around to the long, sloppy succession of sheds and huts that housed the kennels and the mews. At this time of the day the dog-boy was in the rough brick kitchen, preparing the mulch of chopped mutton and grain the dogs were fed on those days when they weren't hunting; the pack bounded happily to the low fence to greet her, swarming around her skirts, tails lashing furiously as she climbed over the stile and hopped down among them. Despite her fears, despite her dread, she had to laugh at the earnest joy in those furry unhuman faces, and clucked to them, calling them the love-names that always made Marc roll up his eyes: 'My rosy peaches, my angelmuffins, my little wuzzlepoufkins . . .' The big staghounds and mastiffs, the rangy wolf-killers whose shoulders came up to her waist, rolled ecstatically on the ground, long legs waving in the air, for her to scratch their bellies.

In time she made her way into the first of the half-dozen huts where the dogs slept, raised a little off the ground for ventilation, low-roofed and smelling of the old blankets on which they slept and the herbs hung from the rafters to freshen the air. Tucking up her skirts, Tally knelt in the sun-splintered shade at the back, surrounded by a sniffing congregation of interested wolfhounds, pulled aside the mass of blankets and lifted the floorboard beneath.

Barely visible in the gloom below the floor, she could make out the shape of a large square bundle, wrapped in waxed leather: under the leather, she knew, for she was the one who had wrapped it and the four others like it hidden in other holes and corners of the kennel – was oiled silk, and then the spell-woven cloth they'd been swathed in when she'd first smuggled them out of her father's strongroom. All summer she had been waiting for a question from someone – her father, Shavus, *someone* – about where they were.

Now she knew the question wouldn't come.

No one but her father knew where Jaldis' books had been bestowed – her father, and the wizards. And she.

I feared that the knowledge would be lost, the Gray Lady had said. And, speaking of the wizards, *Without them it would become a contest of strongmen.*

And very calmly, she wondered where it would be best to hide her children, when she fled from Erralswan and made her way to the Ladies of the Moon.

20

The room was small, smaller than the attic cell in which Saltwood had spent last night and the long, nerve-racking day before, and empty save for the wooden chair in which he sat and the mirror on the wall. Its windows, like the ones of the cell, were boarded over, the boards not hastily nailed but screwed down with proper Teutonic thoroughness and the screw-heads countersunk. Since the Storm Troopers who'd searched him – none too gently – had taken his watch he could only estimate the passage of time but in the locked attic room with its iron military cot he'd been fed three times, and by the raw cold – what? twelve hours ago? Anyway between Meal #2 and Meal #3 – he'd assumed it was night. At least the bed had had blankets.

And that made today Monday, the 22nd of September.

The day of von Rath's 'demonstration'.

Restless, he rose from the hard-backed chair and prowled the room again, as if he hadn't done so immediately upon being locked in. It told him nothing he didn't already know with dreary intimacy – that the room was ten feet by ten, that the bare walls had been papered once and later thickly painted in yellowish white, that the naked floorboards were stained and dirty and that at one point whoever had owned the house had possessed a small dog, imperfectly trained. A wire screen protected the mirror, clearly a one-way window. *Spying bastards.*

He'd been here nearly an hour already, to the best of his estimation, and wondered how long it would be before anyone came. Boredom and tension had long ago erased most of his fear of the Nazis, even some of his dread of von Rath, and he would have welcomed almost anything as an alternative to this hideous combination of inaction and surmise.

Yesterday, as von Rath had instructed, the magician Gall and a grey-haired female SS doctor with a face like the sole of a boot had come to his cell, backed up by four Storm Troopers. They'd ordered him to strip at gunpoint, and conducted a physical examination in eerie silence, never asking him a question, never even giving him a verbal order after the first, as if he were a beast whose docility was assured. And with four automatics pointed at him, he reflected wryly, it sure as hell was. In the event it hadn't been nearly as bad as being gone over by Franco's boys.

The really unpleasant part of all this, he figured, was only a matter of time.

A sharp, whining buzz made his head jerk up, while his hackles prickled with loathing at the unmistakable quality of the sound. *Hornet!* There'd been nests of them in the tangled creek-bottoms where cows habitually got themselves hung up, and over the years he'd been stung enough to give him a healthy loathing of all insects which flew with their feet hanging down.

Black and ill-tempered, it was banging against the ceiling over his head, wings roaring in a fashion reminiscent of the Heinkels over London.

They should be nesting in September, dammit, he thought, and then, *How the hell did it get in here?* Then it buzzed him with a strafing run like a Messerschmitt's and he backed away, ducking and swatting with his hand. There had to be a nest in the rafters above the ceiling panels, though how it had got into the room was a mystery.

The hornet, fully aroused now, dived at his face, and he swatted at it again, cursing the Nazis for taking away his belt, his cap, and anything which might be used to protect his hand. He crowded into a corner as the insect whirred up against the ceiling again, where it droned in furious, thwarted circles, banging against the plaster in its rage.

Finally it lit, crawling discontentedly around like a huge, obscene fly.

Saltwood didn't budge. It buzzed and circled a time or two more, then lighted on the wall.

Cautiously, Tom edged forward, flattening and stiffening the muscles of his hand. The hornet remained where it was. A quick glance around the room revealed no way it could have got in, no crack or chink, but the concern was academic at the moment. He moved out of his corner, more slowly, more carefully than he had stalked the guard he'd killed last night, more delicately than he had entered that poor wretch Sligo's little cell. He needed all the experience he'd picked up in Spain and all the training Hillyard had beaten and cursed into him at the Commando base at Lochailort – if he missed now he was in for a hell of a stinging.

The insect heard him and was in flight when he struck it. It made a satisfying crunch and splat on the wall.

Great, he thought, wiping his ichored palm on his thigh. *You're looking at torture by the Gestapo and what really scares you? Two inches of black bug.*

But at least he could fight back against the bug.

Slowly, he walked around the room again. *Dammit, the bastard has to have got in somehow. If there was access to a crawlspace . . .* The thought of wriggling out through a crawlspace filled with hornets wasn't particularly appealing, but neither was the alternative. And in any case he'd *been* over the place . . .

He stopped, staring up at the ceiling. How he'd missed it before he couldn't imagine, but there it was – the faint, unmistakable outline of a trap-door. It fit flush. Nailholes marked where a moulding had been pulled off and painted over . . . *Painted over? So how had the hornet got into the room?*

He couldn't imagine, but didn't particularly care. The ceiling was high, higher than he could reach even at nearly six feet with long arms. He cast a wary glance at the mirror – Who knew when they'd come into that side of it to watch him get the third degree? – and fetched the chair. It wouldn't buy him much time, but anything would help . . .

With a roar like a thunderclap the chair burst into flames.

He flung it from him, flattening back against the wall in shock. The chair bounced against the opposite wall near the door, the fire spreading across the dry wood of the floor in greedy amber trails. *Diversion?* he thought, ripping off his clay-coloured uniform shirt to wad over his mouth and nose against the smoke. *Maybe. It'll weaken the door, if the smoke doesn't get me first* . . . A firefighter in Tulsa had told him once that most victims of fire weren't burned but smothered. The flames were spreading fast, but he pushed back his panic at being locked in with the blaze, and crouched low to the floor where the air would be better. The fire was around the door, but it was eating its way across the planks towards him as well. In the midst of it the chair was beginning to fall apart, smoke-streaks crawling up to blacken the walls. He shrank back as the fire's heat seared his bare arms and chest. The blaze was all around the door – if he miscalculated his timing, flung himself at the door and it *didn't* give, he'd burn . . .

Then, abruptly as it had begun, the fire began to sink. Before Saltwood's startled eyes the flames ceased their advance, flickering down into fingerlets and then tiny tongues no bigger than two-penny nails which guttered out one by one. Within minutes the only things left of the blaze were a huge patch of charred floor, the still-guttering chair, the suffocating heat and the upside-down waterfall of smokestains around the door.

What the HELL . . . ?!?

He crossed swiftly to the door, pulling his shirt hastily on without bothering to button it, and tried body-slamming the door. It didn't give, though it was roasting-hot to the touch. He kicked it, hoping the wood had weakened. It hadn't.

Puzzled, shaken, he turned back to stare at the flame still flickering over what was left of the chair. He'd seen a dozen fires in his year in the Tulsa oil-fields, but *nothing* like that. Doubtfully, he took a step towards it.

What happened then took him so completely by surprise that his mind barely registered the impossibility of it, only reacted in terror and shock. *Something* came at him, from out of where he couldn't imagine – *something* round and small and bristling with dripping scales, something with huge jaws and tiny black hands like a monkey's, something that whizzed through the air like a thrown baseball straight at his face.

With a yell of horror he struck at it, dodging back. It zig-zagged crazily after him, chisel teeth snapping in a spray of sulphur-smelling slime. He retreated across the room, slapping at it in growing panic, his mind stalled with fear; his back hit the wall and the thing dove in under his block, the claws of its little hands ripping and digging in the flesh of his arm. He yelled again as it began to climb towards his shoulder, smashed it against the wall – it bounced squishily and continued fighting its way up, its round mouth tearing tablespoon-sized chunks of his flesh, its slobber and the ooze that dripped from its smashed head burning the ripped muscle like lye. He beat it again and again on the wall, shoulder numb from the impact, and still it came on. It was making for his face, his eyes . . .

In panic he dove for the burning chair, and shoved his arm, the thing still clinging greedily, into the centre of the sinking blaze.

His shirt caught immediately, but the creature fell off, wriggling and twisting like a lizard with a broken back. Saltwood stripped off his shirt, flung it away to burn itself out in a corner, arm seared and blistered and throbbing with pain, flesh hanging in gory flaps and blood dripping from his fingers. Staggering, he fell back against the rear wall of the room, watching the creature's death-agonies in the fire until it was still. A stench like burning rubber filled the room, with the hideous smell of his own charred flesh.

The secret weapon, he thought, gripping his burned arm tight against him, fighting the nauseating wash of shock and pain. *Damn Sligo, damn that crazy little bastard . . .* His breath came in ragged sobs, sweat burning his eyes, the agony in his arm making him dizzy. He had no idea how the Nazis would use this secret, these hideous things, but whatever he had experienced here he wouldn't wish on Hitler.

Well, he thought, *maybe . . .*

And then he blinked. The pain in his arm was gone.

The burned patches on the floor were gone.

The chair was whole, lying on its side near the door where he'd thrown it.

There was no dead creature, no ashes, no little trap-door in the ceiling . . . not even the smashed remains of a hornet on the wall.

The room was precisely as it had been when he'd been brought here. His shirt, unburned, lay crumpled on the floor. He looked at his left arm, and saw the skin whole with its dusting of sunburn over the thick core of muscle and bone.

He went and got his shirt, because even the heat of the fire had died out of the room and it was unpleasantly chilly, but as he put it on he wedged himself in the far corner, and waited without moving until an hour later, when the door opened and von Rath came in.

'You were apprehended in the uniform of a Storm Trooper, bearing Schutzstaffel identification papers.' Von Rath folded his arms and tipped his head a little to one side. 'It makes no difference to me, or to our experiment, whether you are English or German, but as Reichsführer-SS

Himmler will point out, the penalties attached to espionage are far less exacting than those for treason to the Black Order, and to the Reich.' As he spoke von Rath nodded towards the two men who had entered the room in the wake of his little knot of guards. One was a golden giant of a man, like an overweight Norse god with the left breast of his white uniform jacket plastered in medals – Saltwood knew his face from the newspaper photograph he and other members of the Brigade had thrown darts at in their quarters in Madrid. It was Hermann Goering. Had it not been for the military gingerbread decorating the other man's black SS uniform Saltwood would have taken him for somebody's clerk: small, mild, bespectacled and self-effacing, clutching his clipboard with a slightly apologetic air and completely overshadowed by the splendid commander of the Luftwaffe. With a shock Saltwood realized that it was Heinrich Himmler, head of the SS and the Gestapo.

After a moment he said quietly, 'Captain Thomas Saltwood, Eleventh Independent Battalion.' He'd been promoted after the big raid on Boulogne.

'The Commandos,' said von Rath, and nodded as if pleased. 'Not only the highest racial type, but trained.'

The air of smugness clung to him, radiated from him; Saltwood could see by the slight dampening of his ivory-fair hair he had gone through some exertion, but there was no sign of it in the glowing pinkness of his face. Over his black uniform jacket he still wore his hoodoo-beads, and looking at them more closely – for they were almost on level with his eyes where he sat handcuffed to the same chair that had appeared to burst into flames an hour ago – Saltwood realized with a shock of revulsion that several of the discs were made of human skin stretched over what must have been human bone. They were wrapped and trimmed in gold, and written over with the kind of weird magic-signs Marvello had decorated his blue stage-robe and pointed hat with, a horrible juxtaposition of the gruesome and the absurd.

Oddly enough even those didn't trouble him as much as the iron circle, hanging alone upon its silver chain. There was some kind of disturbing optical effect connected with it, a sort of blurring, as if it was impossible to see it directly. And yet, when he looked again, he could see the buttons of the man's uniform clearly through its ring, the texture of the jacket wool and the links of the chain beneath.

'And yet he is an American,' said Goering thoughtfully.

Saltwood looked across at him. 'Some of us don't need an Anschluss to tell us who our brothers are.'

The big man's eyes gleamed approvingly at this show of defiance, but von Rath said, 'It makes no difference. Our purpose is not to gather intelligence, but to conduct a psychological test. If you do not give us accurate answers about what you experienced we have thiopental available, but we would prefer an undrugged subject, as much as you, I am sure, would prefer to avoid being drugged.'

Saltwood glanced up at him. 'You realize using prisoners of war for tests of any kind is against the Geneva accord?'

The cold face twitched in a smile that looked strangely automatic. 'You are not a prisoner of war,' he pointed out gently. 'You are a spy. If you prefer, we will turn you over to the Gestapo, whose methods, as you will learn, are also against the Geneva accords.'

No way out, thought Saltwood. He might as well find out what the hell had been going on here. If Himmler and Goering – the second and third honchos of the Reich – had shown up to watch, this device of Sligo's, whatever it was or did, was big stuff. He shivered, remembering the slashing, clawing thing chewing its way up his arm, and looked again down at the uncharred shirtsleeve, the uninjured flesh beneath, the unburned wood of the chair in which he sat. His arm still hurt like hell. Impossible to believe it hadn't been real.

'Fair enough.'

The door opened quietly, and the fat boy Baldur Twisselpeck entered, followed by white-bearded Jacobus Gall, both carrying clipboards similar to those held by the two Nazi bigwigs. Von Rath gave them an inquiring glance; Gall nodded and said, 'You may question her after you are done with him.'

Von Rath turned back to Saltwood. He, too, held a clipboard, but didn't bother to look at it; he spoke as if he knew it all by heart. 'At 10:45 today you looked up at the ceiling of this room, started striking at something in the air. What was it?'

'A – A hornet,' said Saltwood, after a moment of fishing the German word – *eine Hornisse* – from the disused memories of the high plains. 'It struck at my face. I don't know how it got into the room. I waited till it lighted, then crushed it.'

'Have you been stung by a hornet before, Captain Saltwood?'

'Yes.'

'And you suffered no extraordinary adverse effects?'

'I puff up and hurt like hell; I don't know if you Aryans do it differently.'

'You are obviously of Aryan stock yourself, Captain,' said Himmler in his soft voice, looking up from his clipboard and blinking behind his round spectacles. 'It grieves me to hear such treason to your birthright.'

'I'll tell that to my Sioux grandmother,' retorted Saltwood. 'She'll be flattered.'

Very calmly von Rath struck him, an open-handed blow across the face that wrenched his head on his neck and brought blood from his lip. Saltwood jerked angrily against the handcuffs that held him to the chair, and heard the guards behind him move, ready for trouble, but nothing came of it. He settled back, blue eyes glittering dangerously, and after a moment's silence von Rath went on, 'Then at 10:52 you started looking around the room. What did you seek?'

'The place where the hornet got in. I can't swear to the exact time because your little cherubs lifted my watch . . . I wanted to know if there were going to be more of them, or if it might lead to some way out.'

'And did you find the place?'

'There was . . .' He paused, glancing up at the corner of the ceiling where the trap-door had been – *It really had, dammit!* – and wondering how stupid this was going to sound. 'I thought I saw a kind of trap-door up there, the kind that gives access to . . .' He didn't know the German for crawlspace, so finished with, '. . . attics.'

Goering and Himmler looked quickly at one another. Himmler asked, 'What part of the ceiling? What corner of the room?'

'Left-hand rear corner as you come in the door. It was about two feet square, painted over white. I know I didn't see it when I came in.'

'And when did you first see it?' asked Himmler, leaning forward, fascinated.

'Only when I killed the hornet. In fact I was looking at the ceiling when the damn bug was flying around up there, wondering how it had got in. I'm sure – I'm *almost* sure – there was no trap-door then.'

Von Rath went on, 'And you brought the chair over directly underneath the trap-door as soon as you noticed it, presumably to attempt an escape.'

'To see if I could get out that way, yes.'

'This chair you're sitting on now?'

'Yes.'

Goering was staring at von Rath with unbelieving awe; Himmler's attention was fastened on Saltwood, his moist little lips parted with eagerness, his dark eyes bright.

'And what happened?'

Saltwood took a deep breath. 'I – The chair caught fire.'

If von Rath had been a cat he would have purred, and washed himself the way cats do when they know they're being admired.

'Did it?'

Hell, thought Saltwood, *dammit, it did!* 'Yeah. I don't understand . . . I felt the heat. I threw it away – it hit the wall over by the door. The fire spread . . .' Once in Tulsa Saltwood had had his boss's car stolen from him by a troop of Cherokee teenagers on bicycles. He recited his story as he'd recited his explanation then, keeping his eyes straight forward and simply recounting the events, ridiculous and unbelievable as they sounded, as they'd happened, but he was conscious of the two Reichsministers whispering together, comparing notes on their clipboards, gesturing with covert amazement.

'It is incredible,' whispered Goering, when Saltwood had finished. He was looking stunned. Himmler, throughout the narrative, had been gradually puffing himself up with the same kind of gratified smugness that characterized von Rath, and now looked so pleased Saltwood wished the bigger man would swat him. 'Absolutely unbelievable. And the other subject . . .'

'I have no doubt,' purred Himmler, 'that the results will be exactly the same.'

'Bring her in,' said von Rath, and Gall and Baldur, who had been standing listening, turned and left. To the SS guards von Rath said, 'Take this man into the other room.' And, as Saltwood's hands were unmanacled and he stood up, von Rath continued to his two distinguished visitors, 'Other experiments can be devised, of course, using more subjects simultaneously, but I'm sure this proves . . .'

The closing of the door shut out the sound of his voice – the room was soundproofed.

Like the house out in the Jungfern Heide this place – the house on Teglerstrasse, von Rath had called it – was a modestly isolated villa set in its own wide grounds, which were also walled, though, as far as Saltwood could tell from the glimpse he'd got by the combined moonlight and headlamps when they'd brought him here, without the fortresslike quality of the house where they were keeping Sligo. The district, where middle-class suburban villas had begun to encroach on country cottages, lay well to the northeast of Berlin's sea of industrial slums, but it was more heavily built up than the Jungfern Heide. During the day, listening against the slant of the attic ceiling, he'd been able to make out occasional sounds of traffic on Teglerstrasse itself. He wondered why von Rath had wanted two separate establishments. As part of this 'demonstration' of theirs?

The place was smaller than von Rath's headquarters, having, Saltwood guessed, four rooms downstairs and four, maybe six, up. His guards now escorted him to what had been an upstairs parlour, rugless, cold, and containing a plain wooden table and three more hard kitchen chairs of the pattern already familiar to him. Evidently all the better pieces of furniture had found their way into some Party official's residence. Its window wasn't covered, but it *was* barred; as soon as the guards had re-cuffed his hands in front of him and locked the door, leaving him alone, he strode over and looked out. Treetops were visible over a buff sandstone wall more decorative than functional, and the roofs of neighbouring 'villas'. On the gravel drive below were parked two large Mercedes staff-cars, a three-ton Benz LG.-3000 transport with a tie-down canvas cover, and a number of motorcycles. Storm Troopers and two minor officers in the uniforms of the Luftwaffe stood by them, smoking. Beyond he could see iron gates, backed with sheet-metal as were those of the house in the Jungfern Heide on the other side of town. It was broad daylight, by the angle of the cloud-filtered sun shortly after noon.

Escaping over the wall with six-guns blazing didn't look like a real promising bet.

Nevertheless Tom began a meticulous examination of the room.

There were two doors – one into the hallway, the other, presumably, into another room. Both were locked – new locks, as in the Jungfern Heide house, set in the old oak of the doors. At a guess, he thought, looking at the scratches on the bare floorboards beneath the three chairs and the way they were grouped around the table, prisoners were interviewed here. A Gestapo safe-house? God knew how many of those there were around the outskirts of Berlin. Easy enough for the Gestapo, or the SS, to acquire from those 'enemies of the Reich' who disappeared into concentration camps. *Real nice property,* his mind framed an advertisement, *comfortable detached suburban villa; privacy, security, all the modern conveniences and a place to put the kiddies when they're bad . . .*

He thought, as he had many times during last night's interminable incarceration in the attic cell, about poor Professor Sligo, locked in his windowless room and completely at the mercy of a fruitcake like von Rath. No improvement over whatever insane asylum they'd got him from . . .

But he'd sure as hell come up with something. Possibly not of his own free will, but *something*.

He shivered again, and rubbed his arm. Hallucinogenic gas? *Never spend your hard-earned cash on liquor again, folks – skip all that time-consuming drinking and go straight to the D.T.s!* As he never had before, he pitied old Charlie the wino who'd hung around the West Virginia mines, screaming as he tore imaginary snakes from his clothing. *Christ, if that's what it's like I'm going teetotal.*

And he grinned mirthlessly. *Right – you'll turn down the glass of brandy von Rath's going to offer you before he shoots you as a spy.*

He had to get out. If he'd been shocked enough, panicked enough, to shove his own arm into what he thought was a fire to get rid of that thing eating its way up it towards his face, God knew what havoc Sligo's invention would work in the forces defending the roads up from the English beaches against the first Panzer divisions, the RAF boys going against the Luftwaffe in the Sussex skies.

No wonder Mayfair wanted Sligo destroyed – and no wonder Intelligence wouldn't believe the rumours they'd heard.

Having made a circuit of the room, he went back to the second, inner door. Hinges on the other side, dammit – in any case he didn't have so much as a belt-buckle to pry them out with. He didn't have a cigarette, either, and was feeling the need of one badly. As he knelt to examine the lock he became aware of voices in the other room, the faint creak of footsteps, and the dim, protesting groan of an overburdened chair.

'Damn it, Captain, it's unbelievable!' came a booming voice he recognized as Goering's. 'I wrote out those instructions myself! Even Himmler didn't know what they were going to be until I made them up! And you on the other side of Berlin, miles away . . . For him to see them in that kind of detail . . .'

'It is . . . quite commonplace,' said von Rath's soft voice.

'I only wish you'd had this perfected a month ago! Because of the damned British air-cover Hitler's been vacillating on the invasion plans for weeks! We're down to the last possible days – and if he puts them off again we might as well forget it until next spring! Dammit, I keep telling him I only need four clear days . . .'

'You shall have them, now.' Von Rath's voice was clearer, then softer as if he were pacing; Saltwood bent his head, listening, knowing if he could only get this information back to Mayfair somehow . . . 'And as you see, you will no longer be troubled by the RAF. I am sorry about the delay – it was a question of accumulating – ah – sufficient strength. We came to Berlin as soon as we could. If the invasion itself can be launched on the twenty-fourth –'

'The day after tomorrow?'

Holy Christ! He wondered if he could make it to Hamburg, get in touch with the radio-man there – to hell with getting himself taken off, if he could just warn them . . .

'Is it possible? Is that time enough?'

There was a long pause. 'Just,' said Goering at last. 'The forces are assembled, the landing-barges are ready . . . We've been on stand-by, then stand-down, then stand-by again since July. All we need is to convince our Leader that such an enterprise will, in fact, succeed.'

'After the demonstration you will have this afternoon, believe me, you need have no fear.'

'Damn it, Captain . . .' The chair creaked again, and Goering's voice got louder. Saltwood could almost see them standing together, overweight Thor and darkly shining Loki.

'You will have your four days of clear weather,' promised von Rath again, his voice sinking low, 'and the wherewithal to blast the RAF from the sky. And in return . . .'

Boots thudded in the hall. Saltwood was on his feet and over to the window in one swift move as a key rattled in the lock. He had a brief glimpse of three Storm Troopers, guns pointed, in the hall as the door was opened and a woman shoved unceremoniously in. Then the door banged, and the lock snapped again.

Not a woman, he thought, taking another look. *A girl.*

She looked about twenty-two, her pointy white face framed in hair that was frizzed electric red from ears to her slender shoulders, and above that, along the part, dark and luxurious brown-black with highlights of mahogany. Her eyes, taking in the black uniform pants and boots he wore, the clay-coloured regulation shirt with its Death's-Head emblems, were soot-dark and filled with spit-cat hate.

‘Don’t jump to conclusions,’ said Saltwood. ‘I’m an American – a Captain in the MO9.’

In English she said, ‘Oh, yeah?’

‘Yeah,’ he replied in the same language with as flat a Midwestern accent as he could still conjure to his tongue. With a shock he realized she was American, too.

‘So who pitched for Cincinnati in ’38?’

Saltwood stared at her, appalled. ‘I don’t know, I always thought baseball was a Christly dumb game! I mean, Jesus, paying two bits to watch a bunch of guys in knickers stand around in the sun all day and scratch and spit?’

She perched one slim haunch on the corner of the table, and shook back her parti-coloured hair. ‘Some American!’ But the hate was gone from her eyes.

She dug in her pocket for cigarettes and a lighter – she wore some kind of ill-fitting uniform, short-sleeved white blouse and grey skirt and sensible shoes wildly at odds with the voluptuous figure beneath. As he took the smoke she offered him he saw her nails were bitten to the quick.

‘You have any idea what’s going on around here?’ he asked, raising his manacled hands to take a thankful drag. ‘Those hallucinations . . . That – that hornet, and the fire . . . that thing that flew at me through the air . . .’

‘What?’ She blew a line of smoke. ‘You missed the trap-door?’

21

'You gotta remember I grew up with this stuff.' Sara crossed one knee over the other – she had beautiful legs, shapely, strong, and slim-ankled, and to hell with the black stubble that sprinkled them and the white ankle socks of the League of German Maidens – and drew on her cigarette while Saltwood prowled, for the fifth time, from the window to the inner door to the outer door, checking, testing, trying to put something together before it was too late. The guards were always there outside.

'I don't know *how* many reincarnated ancient Egyptian priests I met when I was a little girl, or travellers from other dimensions or other astral planes, and they were *all* wizards, or used to be but they couldn't practice in this dimension for one reason or another. You might as well sit down and take a break, cowboy – I've been over this room half a dozen times in the past week or so. You could fill it up with water and it wouldn't leak.'

'That's how long you've been here?' After one final glance out the windows at the guards standing around the vehicles he came back to her, but remained on his feet beside the table where she sat, unable to conquer his restlessness.

She nodded, setting her cigarette to burn itself out on the table's edge. 'Eleven days – I kept count, scratching marks on the inside of the dresser-drawer in my cell.'

Tom had seen the marks when he'd gone over the room where he'd been kept. 'Why inside the drawer?'

She shrugged, long black lashes veiling her eyes as if embarrassed at the childishness of her impulse. 'If they knew I was keeping track they'd erase them or add to them or change them when they searched the room, just to make me crazy. To make me – I don't know, feel helpless. Feel off-guard, like nothing was my own. Papa says they did that a lot in the camp.'

'Hell,' said Tom, feeling the old anger heat in him. 'And I thought the special deputies were bad, that the fruit-growers hired to chouse the migrants from camp to camp.' He settled on the edge of the table, his handcuffed hands folded on his thigh. 'Your father's here too?'

'Yeah. I bunked in his room last night, sleeping on the floor.' She glanced up at him, and he saw, in spite of the cynical toughness in her eyes, how close she was to tears of sheer exhaustion, worn down by the bitter grindstone of being always watched, always helpless, of never knowing what would happen next. Her brows, heavy and unplucked, grew together in a dark down over the bridge of her nose; there was a fine little pen-scratch line on either side of her mobile red mouth that emphasized each wry twist, each smile.

She shrugged again, and made her voice off-hand. 'One more strike against that momzer von Rath. They kept us in the solitary cells at Kegenwald when Rhion was still at Schloss Torweg. They'd bring him in once a week to talk to us, once he was on his feet again. They – hurt him pretty bad after they caught him,' she added slowly. 'There was a limit to what they could do if they wanted him to go on working for them, but I don't think he ever really got over it. But he insisted on seeing us, talking to us, to make sure we were all right, and hadn't been taken away.' Her gaze returned to her lap, where her small, hard fingers traced over and over again a seam of her skirt.

Great, thought Saltwood. *And after all that I come along and try to assassinate the poor stiff for being a Nazi. And I may have to yet,* he reflected. 'So what is it he's doing?' he asked gently. 'What is it he's made?'

Her mouth twisted, and the old gleam of ironic humour

came back to her eyes. 'Like I said,' she grinned up at him, 'I've met *dozens* of wizards in my life, and they were *all* working on some kind of *shmegegeleh* that let them do magic, or would once they got it perfected. Usually out of the damnedest stuff – cardboard pyramids, "sympathetic vibrating generators" made out of old colanders and copper wire, hoodoo amulets with stuff I didn't want to know about wadded up and stinking to high heaven inside. But none of them gave me the creeps the way that Spiracle does. Old Pauli'll stand there fingering it, either on the chain around his neck with all his other damn filthy *tchotchkes*, or fixed on the head of a wooden staff, and the look in his eyes is the same as I'd see in the eyes of the real crazy ones, the ones who claimed to hear God or the Devil whispering at them . . .'

She shook her head again, her dark brows pinching together; then she dismissed the fear with a dry chuckle. 'Rhion – and Papa, who's just as bad – claim it gives von Rath magic powers.'

'Great!' He made a gesture of disgust with his manacled hands. 'That gets us exactly nowhere.'

'You got to remember Rhion believes it himself . . .' She swung around at the sudden throb of engines in the driveway below. Tom was already halfway to the window to look – she scrambled leggily down and followed. Shoulder to shoulder they watched through the bars as Storm Troopers and Luftwaffe bodyguards clambered into cars and truck, and mounted the phalanx of motorcycles. Foreshortened almost directly below them von Rath exchanged crisp Heil Hitlers with Goering and Himmler on the gravel of the drive.

'You heard about the new system of National Socialist weights and measurements?' asked Sara absently. 'A "goering" is the maximum amount of tin a man can pin to his chest without falling over on his face. God knows what's really going on.' She turned her head to look up at

Saltwood, pale noon sunlight glinting in her coffee-black eyes. 'What happened to us could have been nothing more than post-hypnotic suggestion . . .'

'I was never hypnotized!'

'The hell you weren't.' She stepped back a pace from the glass and regarded him, hands on hips. 'They could have hypnotized you and told you not to remember it – that's one of the oldest ones in the book.'

Tom was silent a moment, considering that. He could remember everything clearly, except for a certain patchiness in his recollections immediately preceding Rhion smashing him over the head with the lab-stool. At least he *thought* he could remember everything. 'Maybe,' he said slowly. 'If von Rath was supposedly sending those – those halucinations – from his HQ on the other side of town, I suppose Goering's instructions could have been transmitted here by some kind of code-words over the phone, like the carney magicians do. But what would be the point, if they couldn't repeat it in a combat situation? And that invasion starts Wednesday – the day after tomorrow . . .'

Sara swore in Polish. 'You sure?'

'I heard Goering talking about it in the next room. He and von Rath are cutting a deal of some kind. Von Rath claims he can give Goering four days' clear weather, which is a hell of a promise over the English Channel this time of year, plus this hallucination thing and God knows what else. You don't . . .' He paused, uncertain. 'This is going to sound stupid, but you don't think there's some kind of – of thought-amplification device involved, do you?'

'What the hell do you think magic is supposed to be, if not the action of thought-waves on the material world? But I'm here to tell you, cowboy, in four years of analytical chemistry I have yet to see anybody circumvent the law of conservation of energy, or make two things like hydrogen and ethylene combine without throwing in some platinum as a catalyst. It just doesn't work that way.' She frowned.

'What scares me is there obviously *is* something going on. It doesn't hook up with any of the stuff Heisenberg and Einstein have been doing – or at least not with anything they've published – but once you get unpicking atomic structure, who knows? But there's got to be instrumentality of some kind. Anything else is like trying to change gears without a differential. And whatever the hell Rhion *did* come up with – whatever he *thought* he was doing – von Rath's going to be able to use it.'

'I was with the Eleventh Commandos when they hit Boulogne in July,' said Saltwood quietly. 'I saw the landing barges the Germans have ready. And whatever's going on, I have to get the hell out of here and let London know the balloon's about to go up.'

Sara started to reply, but before she could, boots thudded outside the door. Another woman might have edged closer to him, for the illusion of protection if for nothing else – she only set her fragile jaw, but he saw the fear in her eyes.

The door banged open. Von Rath stood framed against a black wall of Storm Troopers, gun-muzzles bristling around him. A moment later guards entered the room, keeping the two prisoners covered. As Sara had said, the German was fingering the Spiracle on its silver chain, absently and yet lovingly, his head tilted a little as if listening for sounds no human should hear. 'It is time,' he said, 'for the second part of our – ah – psychological tests.'

Sara folded her arms. 'Does that mean I get my room back?'

The opal glance touched her without a shred of humanity. 'You are welcome to it for the remainder of the day,' he said in his soft, well-bred voice. 'But by tonight the question will be academic.'

Saltwood saw the impact of that widen her eyes as he was pushed through the door.

* * *

Soldiers were everywhere in the wide wire-fenced enclosure that encircled the house in the Jungfern Heide when von Rath's little cavalcade rumbled carefully through the opened wire gate and off the drive. Sitting with half a dozen Storm Troopers in the back of the covered transport, Saltwood got a glimpse through its canvas curtains of the men who closed the gate behind them. They turned to look at him with stony hatred in their blue eyes. *Must have found the body of their pal in the downstairs hall.* A bad look-out when von Rath was done with him – always provided he survived this round of 'psychological tests'.

As the truck pulled around he could see Goering, with his mob of Luftwaffe bodyguards, walking slowly back and forth across the flat, weedy ground of the field, pausing now and then to stamp the hard-packed earth. 'Absolutely no hidden wires, ladies and gentlemen,' said Saltwood wryly to no one in particular in the voice of W.C. Fields. 'You will observe that there is nothing up my sleeve but my arm.' Closer to, Himmler was making a much more cursory examination, which he broke off when von Rath's car braked to a halt and came hurrying to its side.

'It was astounding, Captain,' Saltwood heard the little Reichsfuhrer-SS say. 'You have completely vindicated the Occult Bureau! Completely vindicated the true purposes of the SS as the spearhead of our Race's destiny. And if you have, as you say, found a method to release the *vril*, the sacred power bequeathed to the Aryan race from the root-race of Atlantis, we will indeed have nothing further to fear from those who oppose us. I have already put you in for promotion to full Colonel, and a position as First Assistant to the head of the Occult Bureau . . .'

'I am honoured.' Von Rath inclined his head respectfully to the nervous, bespectacled bureaucrat before him. But by the steely edge of his soft reply Saltwood guessed that Sara had been right. *Completely vindicated Himmler's pet bureau and all he gets out of it is full Colonel? First Assistant?*

He'd heard Himmler was stingy, and jealous of his influence and power. How long would it be, he wondered, before the Reichsfuhrer-SS went diving out a window for fear of something he thought he saw in the middle of the night, leaving the power of the SS like a honed dagger in von Rath's patrician hands?

Did von Rath believe it was magic? Or were the chain of faintly-clinking amulets, and the concealment of the control-mechanism of Sligo's hellish device as an iron circle which, sure enough, he now carried on the head of a bona fide wizard's staff, merely cover, a ruse to approach that clever, sneaky, powerful little man on his credulous blind side?

Sara was right about the Spiracle, too. It *did* give him a faint creeping sensation. Not when he looked at it straight, but a moment ago, glimpsing it from the corner of his eye, he'd seen – he didn't know what he'd seen. A darkness that wasn't really darkness radiating around it; a sense of spider-strands of something too fine to see floating in all directions, webbing the air . . .

A fragmented picture flashed through Saltwood's mind, something driven from his memory by the blow which had knocked him out – maybe only a hallucination itself . . . Rhion Sligo, perched in the darkness on his tall-legged stool, watching raptly as a ball of bluish light drifted slowly up from his hand . . .

But before he could think about it he was being shoved over the lowered tailgate, and walked between four guards to where Paul von Rath, accompanied now by Himmler and Goering as well as the inevitable swarm of bodyguards, stood beside a slightly smaller – maybe two-ton – covered flatbed transport truck.

A man in the clay-coloured uniform of the motor pool was holding the hood propped open, a Luftwaffe captain reverently held Goering's white gloves as the big Reichsmarshal poked around the engine.

'It hasn't been out of my sight all day, Herr Reichsmarshal,' the driver was saying. 'You can see yourself there's nothing in the engine . . .'

The huge man grunted and straightened up, chest-ribbons flashing like an unimaginative rainbow in the pale sunlight. Saltwood remembered Sara's joke and grinned. 'I'm more familiar with a plane's engine than a car's,' Goering said, as the driver shut and latched the hood, 'but I'll swear he's right. Very well, then.' He slapped the fender. 'Let him drive this.'

Himmler said nothing, but his dark eyes blazed with suppressed excitement, like a child about to see a show. Saltwood felt his flesh crawl.

Von Rath turned to him, his voice soft and polite, as if he barely remembered striking him – barely remembered, except in a cursory way, who he was. 'You will drive the truck around the course marked by those orange flags.' They were only scraps of cloth tied to weeds and brambles, and here and there to a stake where the ground was bare. 'You may drive inside or outside of them, but if you attempt to crash the fence I can assure you that you will be killed instantly.'

There were no guards on the perimeter of the field. Looking back at von Rath's calm smile Saltwood knew that their absence was not an oversight.

'May I walk the course?'

The Captain – *oops, sorry, Colonel now, thank you Mr Himmler* – considered it a moment, one hand idly fingering the pale staff of stripped, close-grained greenish wood on which the iron Spiracle was mounted. Then he shook his head. 'I assure you it has been examined for hidden devices by men at least as sceptical as yourself.'

Saltwood almost asked, *Who, for instance?* – Himmler and Goering both seemed to have swallowed the whole malarkey hook, line, and sinker – but knew that particular piece of smart-assery would only get him another smack in the mouth. So he shrugged, and said in English, 'It's your ballgame,' and turned to the cab of the truck.

The blood pounded in his ears as they handcuffed his left wrist to the steering wheel, leaving his right hand free to work the ignition and gears. Were they counting on him to make a run for it? It would be child's play to crash the fence, a jolting dash to the driveway or, if necessary, cross-country to the Alt-Moabitstrasse – he was pretty sure of his way back to the house on Teglerstrasse where Sara and her father were . . .

The house on Teglerstrasse?!? he demanded, aghast at himself. *What the hell are you thinking? You'd be GUARANTEEING your capture to go back there. Your first duty is to get your arse to Hamburg and get London word of the invasion . . . Sara knows that if anyone does . . .*

And what makes you think you're coming out of this alive anyway?

Dammit, he thought, studying those beautifully smiling lips, those weirdly empty eyes, *what the hell has he got? Does he believe this crap himself?*

'Drive three times around the course,' said von Rath, as Tom turned the key in the ignition, 'and then return here.'

And disregard any fire-breathing monsters that get in your way. He pressed the accelerator, let out the clutch, jolted towards the first of the orange flags.

On the first half of the circuit he was taken up with getting the feel of the truck over the bumpy, unpaved ground, with scanning the earth all around him, particularly around the stakes and flags for signs that it had been dug up, tampered with. Though of course Goering had had a much better view . . . At the far end of the field he had a panicky impulse to crash the fence, head like hell towards the Spandau canal, but a second later cold feet overcame him. There was something wrong with the setup. He knew it, smelled it, as he had smelled thunderstorms when he was a kid riding herd, as he had smelled ambush in the dry canyons of the Meseta. He had no doubt that if he tried it, somehow, von Rath would kill him. Or were they counting on that fear?

Rounding the far turn he saw them standing like an official photograph in *Das Reich*: Goering in white and Himmler in black, with von Rath holding his iron-headed staff like some strange, glittering angel between them. Around the cars and back towards the house a shifting mill of men formed an obscuring backdrop from which an occasional face emerged – he thought he saw the pale flutter of Gall's long beard, the glint of glasses that had to be Baldur's. But he sensed all eyes on him, all attention on the grey truck as it moved and jerked over the rutted ground.

Then Himmler, his glasses gleaming in the wan light, leaned over and said something to von Rath, and the SS Captain lifted his hand, the crystals in the staff-head flashing . . .

The explosion of light nearly blinded Saltwood, the roaring blast deafening and for one second he thought, *That's it* . . . But with almost comic simultaneity he realized he was still alive, that the only jarring came from the truck bouncing over the field – *No blast effect* . . . Only light that turned his vision to a whirling mass of purple spots and a noise like the German ammo dumps at Boulogne going up . . .

The next second the shooting started, and yelling like everyone from Goering on down had simultaneously discovered that their hair was on fire. As his vision cleared a little he saw Storm Troopers dashing from all corners of the field towards the place where the two *Reichshonchos* were staggering about, half-doubled over and holding their eyes. Lights ripped the afternoon brightness like flashbulbs at a Hollywood premiere and someone was running towards the truck, desperately waving the iron-circled magic staff and yelling for him to stop.

He recognized Rhion Sligo.

The truck fishtailed in a cloud of thrown dirt as he hit the brake. Bullets had begun to spatter but because of the lights still popping with gut-tearing intensity all around them nobody could aim. Rhion flung himself up on the off-side running-board and hooked one arm in a death-grip through the frame of the open window – the other hand still firmly hanging onto the staff – and yelled 'Get us out of here *fast*!'

Saltwood was already in gear and heading for the fence.

'You know the city?' panted the little professor, as bullets ripsawed the ground a dozen feet away and a few strays pinged off the hood of the truck. 'Seven twenty-three Teglerstrasse – it's out past the Weisensee – don't pay any attention to anything you see or hear . . .'

Seven twenty-three Teglerstrasse was the Gestapo safe-house where Sara and her father were kept.

Wire whipped and sang around the radiator, then ground lumpily under the tyres. Saltwood pointed to the right, 'Blow the top off that pole.'

Rhion shook his head, too out of breath to explain.

'Catch it on fire, then – it's the phone junction . . .' *What the hell am I saying? This isn't even REAL . . .*

The pole was in flames as Rhion scrambled through the door and dragged it shut after him, awkwardly because he would not release his hold on von Rath's infernal stick. Things were not helped by the fact that Saltwood had begun to veer and swerve to avoid the hail of bullets now spattering all around them.

'And get down on the floor. I'm Tom Saltwood, American volunteer – British Special Forces.'

'Rhion Sligo.' He raised his hand in an unsteady Nazi salute and added politely, 'Heil Roosevelt.'

And at that moment, far off, barely to be heard above the chaos of submachine-guns, shouting, revving engines, rose the long, undulating wail of air-raid sirens. Tom twisted in his seat, scanning the colourless sky. Through the window of the cab he saw them, the black silhouettes of the escorting Hurricanes, the heavier, blunter lines of a phalanx of Wellingtons and Whitleys, swinging in from the northwest.

'It's a raid!' He let out a long Rebel yell of delight. 'It's a . . .'

There had been sporadic raids on Berlin for nearly a month, but if Mayfair had known one was due to coincide with his own project, he hadn't said anything about it. Though the main bomber group was still far off there must have been one overhead he hadn't seen – hadn't heard, either, when he thought of it – for as the first of the swastika-marked cars swung onto the drive to pursue the escaping truck there was a groundshaking roar and every vehicle in the field behind them went up in flames.

'Fast,' whispered Rhion, slumped grey-faced and sweating against the grimy cloth of the seat. 'For Chrissake, get out of here fast . . .'

Like a cow climbing free of a mudhole the truck heaved itself onto the Alt-Moabitstrasse, and ran before the bombers like a stampede before summer lightning.

The first bombs started falling as Saltwood and Sligo hit the outskirts of Berlin. As their truck cut on to See Strasse to avoid the thicker traffic of the city centre a half-dozen yellow-white flares sprang up, dazzling in the waning afternoon light, ahead of them and to their right. 'They're going for the railroads,' guessed Saltwood, veering sharply around a panicked flock of women dragging children across the road to a shelter. 'That'll be the Settiner Station. Those off to the far right will be the Anhalter goods yards . . . Dammit, lady, look where you're going!' he yelled as a young blonde woman, eyes blank with terror, came pelting out of an apartment-house with her arms full of something lumpy wrapped in a blanket and dashed almost under his wheels. He missed her with a screeching of tyres, and in the rear-view mirror saw two gold-rimmed Meissen teacups fall out of the blanket and shatter on the tarmac of the road.

Another explosion went off close enough to make the ground shudder. 'For Chrissake they're not anywhere *near* you yet . . .' he muttered, slamming on the horn, then the brakes, and swerving around a panic-stricken elderly couple in the road. 'Worse than the goddam Londoners . . .'

The Berliners, of course, were not nearly as used to air-raids – *Yet*, he thought grimly – as Londoners. And it was obviously the first time for Sligo, though locked up in the Jungfern Heide he might have heard the sound of far-off bombs. The little professor's face was pale with shock, appalled horror in his blue eyes behind their rimless specs as he looked around him at the panic and the rising flames.

'This is . . . how you people fight wars . . .'

'You oughta see London if you think this is good,' muttered Tom savagely, slewing through the intersection of Turm Strasse, the steely waters of the Landwehr Canal winking bleakly through brown and yellow trees. 'Or Rotterdam – what the Luftwaffe left of it. Or Guernica and Madrid, for that matter.' An explosion to their left jerked the vehicle almost off its wheels – Saltwood flinched at the roar of the blast, the shattering storm of fragments of brick, window-glass, and filth that came spitting from the mouth of one of those narrow working-class streets that surrounded the canal-locks. For a moment the cloud of plaster-dust and dirt was a yellow-grey fog through which nothing was visible, and Tom slowed as much as he dared, knowing by the droning buzz that the Wellies were directly overhead now. 'I'm just hoping to hell the bridge across the locks is still standing when we get there – it'll be one of their main targets.'

'It will be,' said Rhion softly. His hands, chubby yet curiously skilled-looking, moved along the rune-scratched wood of the staff. His eyes were shut.

'Right,' Saltwood muttered, gunning again through the clearing fog of debris, the wheels jerking and bumping over the edge of a vast talus-slope of loose bricks, broken lathe, twisted pipe and shattered glass that lay half across the road.

And by some miracle the bridge over the Landwehr Canal still stood, though the locks themselves were a shambles of burning weirs and floating debris. Looking across that vast span of unguarded concrete Saltwood felt his stomach curl in on itself. Buildings were burning on all sides here, the heavy grey nineteenth-century warehouses and the massive, six-storey tenement warrens of the working-class districts all around. He slowed, feeling safer in the shadows of the buildings.

'There's got to be a toolkit in this thing,' he said, twisting his body to grope with his free hand behind the seat. 'I want you to hunt for a hacksaw, get me out of this damn handcuff . . .'

'Later!' said Rhion urgently. 'After we get across the bridge!'

'Yeah? You're not the one who's gonna be handcuffed to four thousand pounds of internal combustion engine if that bridge takes a hit when we're in the middle of it.'

'It won't,' insisted Rhion, fixing Tom with a desperate blue stare. 'Believe me, it won't! We have to get across, now – it could be destroyed while we're trying to get the cuffs off . . .'

'So we just backtrack to the Turm Strasse and go around. Christ knows the streets are clear.' Another blast, very close this time, and both men ducked involuntarily as brick and glass spattered on the side of the cab like a shotgun blast.

'No! Please believe me, I know what I'm talking about, we've got to get across it, put as much distance between ourselves and that house as soon as possible . . .'

Through the clearing dust Saltwood saw the bridge still stood. Would it ten minutes from now? Always supposing they could *find* the goddam hacksaw and the blade didn't break . . . ?

He let out the clutch. 'If we go down I'm taking you with me, pal.'

He hit the bridge at fifty and accelerating. Concrete abutments flashed past, a glimpse of fires roaring up out of oil spilled on roiled brown water, of metal snags and cables floating like water-weeds. Once clear of the buildings he saw how many bombers were overhead – the whole sky was crossed with the smoke of rising fires. Like a bird laying eggs on the wing he saw a Wellington directly above them drop its load, black teardrop shapes drifting leisurely down.

Though Tom would have taken oath the bombs were dead on target the nearest hit the water thirty yards away. The blast nearly swept the truck off the bridge – he felt the tooth-jarring clatter of the speeding vehicle's door bouncing on the railings and veered, blinded, into the tidal wave of brown water hurled up by the blast. He cut in the windscreen wipers, through a grimy blur glimpsed – impossibly – the concrete span still arrowing before them, and hit the gas as hard as he could. At the same time he screamed 'You crazy Jew . . . !'

A second stick of bombs took out the bridge as the truck slewed on to See Strasse and away through the burning town.

'Right,' whispered Tom, braking to a halt. They had passed the big intersection of Muller Chausse, and the main force of the bombing lay behind them now, though the streets were still empty as if in a city of the dead. 'Now you dig out that toolkit and cut me the hell out of this!'

'How far have we come?' asked Rhion, not moving, though he cast a panicked glance at the streets behind them.

'Six or seven miles, and what the hell difference . . .'

'More than you think.' He fumblingly unfixed the Spiracle from the head of the staff – it was held on with a wrapped iron wire – his hands shaking so he could barely manage it, and shoved the iron circlet into his shirt-pocket before he'd set the staff aside and get out of the cab. Bombs were still falling as close as a half-mile away in the cramped, sprawling labyrinths of the nineteenth-century factory-districts around the canals, and though Rhion flinched at the sound he moved swiftly, decisively, as he came around the cab and dug behind the seat for the grey-painted tin box. 'I don't know how far the Talismanic Resonator's field extends, for one thing. For another, von Rath's bound to search the house . . .'

'How the hell did you get out of your cell anyway?' Saltwood looked up from pawing, one-handed, through the toolkit. 'I thought they locked you in.'

'They did.' Rhion grinned shakily. 'But you left the key in the lock when you – ah –'

'Uh – yeah,' finished Tom. In brief silence they regarded one another. There was a shiny patch of red scar-tissue on the inside of the bridge of Rhion's nose, close to his left eye: circular, almost half an inch across, the size of the end of a cigarette. The burn was only a few months old; Saltwood could see another one in the pit of Rhion's throat through the open collar of his shirt. *They hurt him pretty bad*, Sara had said. The bruise of the garrotte was still purple-red and angry under the clipped line of his beard.

'Look,' said Rhion awkwardly, starting to saw inexpertly at the handcuff-chain. 'I'm sorry I knocked you out. I didn't know . . . I hope they didn't . . .'

'Nah. They needed me in one piece to blow me up. Here, be careful – there's no replacement blade in that kit. You ever used one of these things before? Put your strength in the pull, and keep it straight . . .'

'I could have used the power of the Resonator itself to open the lock,' went on Rhion matter-of-factly, bending over his work, 'but even that little – comparatively little – might not have left me enough power of my own to put on the light-show that blinded von Rath and his guards long enough to let me grab the Spiracle itself, and Baldur or Gall might have sensed something. Frankly, I don't know whether they could nor not. So the keys helped. Surprise was the only edge I had . . . I was hoping you'd figure out what was going on and pick me up, since I'm not sure I could drive one of these things and I had to get enough distance between the Spiracle and the Resonator to break up the field before von Rath figured out what I'd done.'

'Uh-huh,' said Tom soothingly, as Rhion glanced behind him again – Tom had seen him look in the truck's side- and rear-mirrors a dozen times on the hellish dash along See Strasse. Not surprisingly, of course. Bombs were still falling to the south and west of them, close enough for the ground to shudder under the nearer blasts. It was typical of the way things were done, thought Saltwood dourly, that it would be these sprawling slums, where two and three families shared windowless and crowded flats, to get the pulping, and the millionaires' houses over in the Grunewald to go untouched. In that way it was London all over again.

'The problem is,' went on Rhion, 'I don't know how far the field extends, or how far away I have to be to be safe . . .'

'Hunh?' said Tom. 'What field?'

The Professor raised his head again, and behind the rimless glasses his blue eyes were filled with a growing fear. 'Magic field.'

Oh, Christ, Sara warned me . . . 'Well,' said Tom, 'I think we're probably pretty safe . . .'

'The hell we are.' For a moment their eyes met, and there was something in the older man's that made Saltwood pause. When he spoke again his voice was low and deadly earnest. 'I had to set up a Talismanic Resonator in the Temple in that house, it was the only place where there was any kind of stored power at all. It drew on the Void-energies coming through the Spiracle. At the level of power available in the Temple, you'll get a field if they're within, oh, maybe a mile, two miles of each other . . .'

Oh, Hillyard's gonna love this. That the crazy little coot had something there Tom didn't doubt – enough to startle and blind von Rath and his minions sufficiently for Rhion to seize the control-mechanism concealed in the Spiracle, at any rate. And it was abundantly clear to him by the Professor's taut voice and desperate eyes that he wholeheartedly believed everything he said.

'But they're not,' he pointed out, latching onto the one element of Professor Sligo's discourse he felt he could answer intelligently. 'We've got to be five, six miles from the house by this time . . .' The chain was cut almost through. Saltwood took the hacksaw from Rhion, who had begun to shiver with shock and reaction, and worked and twisted at the half-sawn link with a screwdriver from the kit until the chain broke with a loud snap. 'Besides, even if von Rath has got some kind of transport by this time the raid's still going on, and the bridge is out.' And by the sound of it, he thought uneasily, the second wave of Wellies was on the way.

'We can't risk it.' Rhion hurried around the other side of the cab again, scrambled in as the boom of explosions resumed over the long, shuddering siren-wails. 'Don't you understand? If von Rath gets within two miles of us – of the Spiracle . . .' He touched his pocket, where the thing's lumpy outline stood out against the cloth '. . . or if he manages to find some kind of power-source to increase the potential of the Talismanic Resonator – he's going to be able to use magic.'

22

Whew, thought Saltwood, as he dropped the truck into gear again and jerked into motion, *for a minute there he had me worried.*

In the empty streets – the panic-stricken populace not yet having acquired the casual attitude the Madrilenos had eventually achieved about bombing not in their immediate neighbourhood – and away from the danger of any but stray drops, Saltwood was able to make good speed. They left the sea of crowded grey monoliths of the working-class districts gradually behind them, the heavy developments giving place first to two-storey shops and shabby, semi-detached houses, then to trees, free-standing *Biergartens*, petty-bourgeoise villas, open fields. Here an occasional car passed them, driving fast without headlights in the slow-gathering twilight; an occasional family could be seen, crowding near a garden wall, staring southwestward towards the burning centre of Berlin with horrified eyes. *Get used to it,* thought Tom savagely, remembering the motionless red-blanketed lumps carried away by the Air Raid Wardens from collapsed piles of London tenements, the overcrowded school-buildings filled with homeless people and the stench of fear and excrement, the middle-aged men and women picking through the piles of smoking brick for something salvageable from the only homes they'd ever known. *It's going to be bad,* Hillyard had said, back in the pub before this had ever started, little knowing how bad it would get. *Here's a little greeting from your brothers and sisters in London.*

It was clear the guards at 723 Teglerstrasse weren't going to be conveniently crouched in the cellar.

'When they bring me here they hoot one long, two short,' said Rhion quietly, as the dented and mud-covered truck pulled up before the iron-sheeted gate. He'd replaced the Spiracle on von Rath's magic staff, and was again clutching it like a child hanging onto a favourite toy.

'Be ready,' muttered Saltwood, hooting out the code. He slipped the truck into first again and prepared himself for a frenzy of strong-arm. 'With luck they won't see half those dents are bullet-holes till it's too late.'

Only one Storm Trooper opened the gate. He stepped back to let the truck pull in, then stepped casually close, his Schmeisser dangling at his back.

Saltwood slammed the door open into the man's face, threw himself out before the guard had regained either his balance or his wits, pulled the Schmeisser from him with one hand and slugged him hard and clean across the chin with the other. The Storm Trooper staggered and Saltwood shot him with a fast burst of shells, ripped the sidearm from the bloody corpse's holster as Rhion was springing down from the cab on the other side. He grabbed the Professor's arm and the two of them pelted up the gravel drive at a weaving run.

Bullets spattered from the open door. Saltwood returned fire and the guard there fell out forward, sprawling at the top of the steps with blood trickling down the worn marble in the dove-grey evening light. Without letting go of his staff Rhion bent and pulled the man's weapons free: automatic, submachine-gun, the silver-mounted dagger of the SS.

'Search him,' yelled Saltwood, ducking into the door and covering the downstairs hall. 'Get his identity papers, any money you can . . .'

A head appeared around a door and Saltwood fired at it with the automatic, ducked back at a returning shot and flung himself down with a long, low roll to catch the guard as he leaned around the door for a second try. Weaving from side to side Rhion darted into the shadows of the hall and stopped to relieve Saltwood's newest victim of his weapons as well.

'You ever fired one of those things?'

The Professor shook his head as he followed Saltwood up the stairs at a run.

'Stand guard here. Tuck it into your arm like this, arm *tight* to the body, pull the trigger – it'll fire a burst as long as you hold the trigger down. Aim *low*. The kick'll pull the gun up. And put down that goddam stick . . .'

Rhion's hand tightened stubbornly around the smooth wood as Tom yanked on it, his eyes suddenly blazing. There was no time to argue so Tom let the matter drop, muttering 'Crazy bastard . . .' to himself as he dashed up the attic stairs to the room where he himself had been kept.

The doors up there were bolted, not locked with keys. He slammed the bolts back and threw the door open, and only a residual burst of caution, like a sixth sense, stopped him on the threshold when he saw the room empty. The next second a chair swooshed down hard enough to have broken his shoulder – Sara had been hiding next to the door.

'Christ almighty . . .'

She saw who it was – she already had the chair coming up for another swipe – and her pointed pale face burst into a smile that stopped Saltwood dead in his tracks, as if he'd seen a striking snake unfurl butterfly wings. 'Tom!' And, a second later, the child-nymph turned lynx again, 'There's five, six guards in the house . . . I heard shooting . . .'

On the other side of a narrow hall was another locked door. Throwing it open he saw a mirror image of the room where he'd been kept two nights and a day – like a cheap hotel with cot, chair, a few books and magazines and a copy of *Mein Kampf* instead of a Gideon Society Bible. For a moment he saw no one. Then Sara yelled 'Papa!' and a tall, gangly, bearded old man emerged from crouching behind the door of the tiny washroom.

'So is this the cavalry or the Indians?' he demanded in German with a thick Yiddish accent, cocking one wise dark eye at Saltwood.

'Cavalry,' said Sara briefly, already helping herself to the spare pistol and SS dagger Saltwood had stuck through his belt. 'There's a shed out back, I didn't hear them take out the staff car today . . .'

A shot rang out somewhere below as they were racing down the attic stairs. Rhion was flattened behind the corner at the top of the next flight, the Schmeisser in one hand and his magic wand tucked awkwardly under his arm. Keeping his grip on the staff he stepped quickly around the corner and let fly a burst from the submachine-gun that knocked him staggering and ripped holes in every direction in the wall-panels and ceiling before the gun juddered itself completely out of his hands.

Sara scooped it from the floor with a blistering oath in Polish and fired down the stairwell, ducked a returning burst, then fired again, her grip steady as if on a range. There was the sound of something falling at the bottom. Then silence, and the stench of cordite. She started to move, and Rhion shook his head violently, waving her back. Distantly, over the long, continuous ululation of the air-raid sirens, another siren could be heard, the grating two-note see-saw of the police.

Rhion made a gesture with his fingers.

There was a clattering below and Saltwood saw, past Sara's shoulder and down the stairs, a Storm Trooper leap out of hiding behind a door in the hall, spinning to point his gun away from them, towards the front door, as if startled by something there. Sara fired. The man flung out his arms as the bullets smashed through his ribcage, and went sprawling. The four of them barrelled down the stairs. Oddly enough, Saltwood could see nothing in the downstairs hall that might have startled that last trooper into exposing himself to Sara's fire.

'Check the shed out back for a car,' he ordered, and Sara vanished through the rear door under the stairs while Saltwood methodically stripped every body he could find of weapons, spare clips, money, and papers. The police sirens were getting closer. Von Rath must have got to a phone. Rhion and Sara appeared at the back door again at the same moment Sara's father emerged from another door, carrying the sort of string shopping-bag German housewives took to market, bulging with bread, cheese, bottled water and beer.

'Car out back,' yelled Sara. 'We threw two spare petrol-cans in the boot . . .'

Tyres crunched in the gravel out front. Saltwood made a dash for the back, hoping against hope they'd make it out of the alley before the inevitable flanking-parties blocked both ends. Rhion paused in the doorway and made a gesture of some kind with his staff. From the front drive there was a shattering explosion, yellow and white light stabbing through the gathering twilight.

So there was some kind of radio-controlled bomb in the truck after all, thought Saltwood, as the Professor dashed to join them, the crystals in the staff-head winking sharply in the reflected light of the fires. *So much for Goering's expertise.*

The car was an open staff Mercedes, sleek and well cared-for. Despite the fact there were no keys in the fascia-board it was running. Somehow it was no surprise to Saltwood to learn that Sara could hot-wire cars. The fugitives piled in over the doors with their gear, guns, magic wand and picnic-lunch and then Tom had it in motion, roaring out into the narrow, moss-cobbled alley in time to see two motorcyclists and half a dozen running Storm Troopers appear around the corner to their left, and a carfull of machine-gun brandishing Luftwaffe to their right.

'Right!' yelled Rhion, half-standing in the front seat and raising the gleaming Spiracle against the evening light.

'We'll have a better chance . . .' began Saltwood, jamming into first.

'*Right*, Goddammit!'

Not quite knowing why but figuring the odds were really pretty much the same Saltwood swung the wheel right and floored it.

For a second Tom thought the bang he heard was a bullet – single-shot auto – but then realized it had been the sound of the oncoming Luftwaffemobile's right front tyre blowing out. The big car jumped, swerved frenziedly, then slewed sidelong into the brick wall of the alley. Saltwood scraped paint from his own right-hand door on the stone alley wall as he barely avoided the still-bounding vehicle and gunned on up the alleyway while the other car caromed into the foremost of the motorcycle brigade, coming to a stop with one bumper against the alley wall and the other braced on the corner of the shed, effectively blocking all further pursuit from that direction.

'Well I'll go to hell,' said Tom, his eyes on the rear-view mirror.

The flames rising from the front courtyard seemed awfully comprehensive for just one car, and there was no pursuit from that direction, either. If the pursuit cars were parked close around the truck a spark could have jumped . . .

'We've got to switch cars.' Sara leaned forward over the back of the seat. 'They'll know we've got a staff Mercedes. Turn that way, down that alley . . .'

'You know Berlin?' demanded Tom, obeying.

'Don't you?'

'Just the main streets, from the maps.'

In the gathering twilight it was growing hard to see, for every house was blacked out, every street-lamp in this quiet suburb unlit, and Tom kept the Mercedes' lights off. No sense getting stopped for violating blackout regulations. Overhead the droning of the bombers still filled the sky, the far-off thunder of explosions and glare of fire to the southwest marked where the RAF was still taking its revenge.

'I don't need a map to tell me this is a neighbourhood where people can afford cars,' returned Sara, gesturing to the monotonous brick villas, the occasional cottages and countrified houses whose rooflines loomed against the flame-lit sky. 'Most people put their cars up on blocks because of the petrol-rationing . . . We've got ten gallons in back and whatever I can siphon out of the tank and I hope to hell you got ration-cards . . .'

'Do I look like an idiot?' retorted Tom.

She poked him in the back. 'You're wearing an SS uniform, cowboy – what do you think?'

Then she leaned over to Rhion, put her arms around his neck, and kissed him a little awkwardly on his untidy brown curls. 'God, am I glad to see you safe.' She turned back to Tom. 'Thank you.' The gruff uncertainty in her voice was odd, considering her earlier sophisticated calm. 'I – I don't know how the hell you managed to escape and get Rhion out of there, but thank you.'

'It was an allied effort,' replied Tom with a grin. 'The Prof managed to break up their demo and after that they were too busy dodging the bombs to follow us too hard. Once we switch cars we can head for Hamburg. There's enough farm-tracks and country-roads that run parallel to the autobahn that we shouldn't get too lost . . .'

'As long as we don't get too found we'll be fine. Down that alley there . . .' She nodded towards a dark gap between two grey-stuccoed walls – a line of sheds and garages loomed dimly out of the darkness as they turned, and beyond them the roofs of a line of semi-detached houses, eloquent of the hopes of real-estate developers and the pretentions of well-to-do shopowners and the managers of banks. 'That looks promising.'

Several of the doors stood agape, revealing an assortment

of garden-tools and broken furniture – one or two were locked.

'My daughter the car-thief,' sighed Rebbe Leibnitz, as Sara crowbarred the padlock hasp free of the nearest door's brittle wood with a screwdriver from the Mercedes' toolkit, and a moment later pushed it back to reveal a massive green American Packard saloon.

'Better your daughter the car-thief than your daughter the deceased former hostage of the Reich,' she muttered, opening the car door and perching on the seat with one graceful white leg dangling out the door for Saltwood to admire. 'This heap still got its batteries or are we gonna have to jump it?' A moment later the engine coughed into life. The leg retreated into the car, and the Packard itself grumbled out into the narrow lane, shuddering with the effort of its long-silenced motor to stay awake. 'Got a piece of tubing? Some hose?' She leaned out the door again. 'What is this, the minor leagues?' she added, getting out and leaving the car to idle as she darted back into the utter blackness of the garage.

She emerged a moment later with her stolen SS dagger in one hand and a piece of rubber garden-hose in the other, with which she siphoned most of the gasoline from the grey car's tank to the green's. 'Which way are we heading?' she asked as she worked. 'I'll drive ahead and you follow me for a couple miles, so they won't connect finding this buggy . . .' She kicked the Mercedes' tyre '. . . with the report of a stolen car and know what to start looking for.'

'You used to do this for a living or something?' inquired Saltwood, closing the door once more and manoeuvring the lock back into semblance of its former appearance while Rhion and Rebbe Leibnitz transferred their belongings from one vehicle to the other.

'Just brains, cowboy.'

'And dating every gangster on the East Side,' added her father glumly. '"A tree shall be known by the fruit it bears . . ." And what's the date of your birth, by the way, Captain Saltwood . . . ?'

'Down this alley,' Saltwood replied to Sara's earlier question, 'two rights should get us back onto See Strasse. We can cut back to the Alt-Moabitstrasse and head for Hamburg that way . . .'

'No!' said Rhion sharply.

The others looked at him, baffled.

'We can't go back the way we came! I left the Resonator in the Temple at von Rath's headquarters. If we get too close we risk it picking up the Void-energies of the Spiracle and re-establishing the field . . .'

'Dammit,' snapped Saltwood, 'I'm not taking a fifteen-mile detour around the other side of Berlin because you don't want to step on the cracks of the sidewalk! They're gonna have the dogs on us fast enough! Now get in the car!'

Rhion balked. 'You don't understand . . .'

'I understand we haven't got the time or the gas to waste. We've only got a couple hours' lead, if that, before they figure out where we're headed and get the whole SS on our butts, and I for one would rather risk all the wicked wizards in the world than half a squad of sore-assed Death's-Heads, so get in the car and quit arguing!'

Rhion opened his mouth to protest further, but Sara reached out, grabbed the Professor by the arm, and dragged him into the Packard with her and set off down the lane. Muttering to himself, Saltwood slammed into the Mercedes and followed, hoping they wouldn't encounter any unscheduled pedestrians in the utter darkness to complicate matters still further. As they neared Berlin again the red light of fires illuminated their way, burning out of control among the endless blocks of workers' flats. Smoke stung Saltwood's eyes as he drove.

'Friggin' crazy – loony,' he muttered to Leibnitz, who sat in the back seat of the open Mercedes like a king en route to his coronation. 'When I tried to get him to let go of that silly stick I thought he was going to tear into me! He may be some kind of genius, but . . .'

'He surrendered it once three months ago,' said the old scholar softly, 'and has regretted it since. I think he would die rather than let von Rath have it again.' The wind flicked back his silky white hair and the ragged strands of his grizzled beard. In spite of the plain grey Labour Service uniform he wore – like Sara's and Rhion's, stripped of all its emblems – he reminded Tom strongly of the old Jewish men who'd argue *pilpul* and politics on the stoops of Yorkville, thrashing the easy theories of Communism and Socialism and the Industrial Workers of the World into their component atoms and examining them one by one, as is the fashion of Talmudic scholars everywhere. 'So what did he mean, field? What Resonator was he talking about?'

'Christ knows.' Saltwood frowned, concentrating on keeping the Packard in sight. Its taillights had been removed to comply with blackout regulations, and in blocks where intact buildings shielded them from the glare of the fires it was difficult to see anything at all. The night was getting cold, too. In spite of having stripped a uniform jacket from one of the less gory corpses Saltwood felt chilled driving in the open car. 'He made this widget out of wire and glass and claims it lets him do magic if it gets within a couple miles of that – that Spiracle of von Rath's.'

He heard Leibnitz gasp. The old man leaned forward sharply, white hair fluttering back over his shoulders. 'Did he say how?'

The desperate earnestness in his voice made Tom remember Sara had described her father as being as crazy as Sligo. *Just what I need – TWO of them!* 'I don't know. Some *boruyo* about drawing energy through the Spiracle and setting up a resonating field.'

'*Kayn aynhora,*' whispered Leibnitz in horror. '*Chas vesholem,* he can't have . . .'

'He sure as hell thinks he has.' And yet, unbidden, there rose again to his mind that half-obliterated fragment of memory, Rhion Sligo with one hand on that tangle of wire and crystal in the dim candlelight of his prison-room, and the bluish drift of ball-lightning floating upwards from his other – empty – palm.

Hallucination, he thought, made uncomfortable at some deep level by the thought, as if, back in his Socialist days, he'd stumbled across conclusive evidence that it was not economics, but women's fashions – or sunspots – or maybe even God – which ruled History. *Maybe some kind of electrical by-product of the device, whatever it is, like the St Elmo's Fire that burned on the horns of the cattle on the nights of thunderstorms, when they were thinking about stampeding . . .*

'Stop them,' ordered Leibnitz. His long, blue-veined hands, resting on the seat-back beside Tom's head, were shaking. 'He's right, we'll have to detour through the centre of the city . . .'

'Down Prinzalbertstrasse past SS headquarters? Don't you start!'

'You don't understand! We can't risk . . .'

They rounded a corner, and Saltwood jammed on the brakes just in time to prevent a collision with the Packard in front of him. They were in among the narrow streets of tenement warrens now, pitch dark save where they were lit by the yellow glare of fires. A bombed building had disgorged a vast talus-spill of debris across the road before them. Beyond, the street was a chaos of flames, of firemen and tangled hoses, of brown water trickling down the broken asphalt glittering hotly in the reflections of the blaze. Men and women crowded around them, dazed and quiet. A little boy in the brown uniform of the Hitler Youth stood alone, sobbing in helpless pain and terror with blood running down the side of his face from a huge cut in his scalp. Above them loomed what was left of the tenement, the rooms ripped open as if by a giant knife, shabby wallpaper, dirty old furniture and cramped, tiny chambers laid bare to the glaring orange inferno.

Saltwood set the brake and got out of the car. Rhion and Sara had already debarked. For a few moments the four of them stood together on the fringe of the ruin, unnoticed by the people coming dazedly from the shelter across the road or stumbling, bleeding and covered with filth and a hundred years' worth of coal- and plaster-dust, from the cellars of the buildings all around.

Aside from the boy, who couldn't have been more than seven – God knew where his parents were, or if they'd survived – there wasn't a Nazi uniform in sight but Saltwood's own.

Rhion whispered, 'And I wondered why magic had been taken from this world.'

Around them there was a mutter of voices: 'The English . . . The English . . .' 'Everything we saved . . .' 'Maybe we can sleep at Aunt Berthe's . . . But she was down in Templehof, they were hit, too . . .' 'Has anyone seen a little girl? Six years old – her name is Anna, she has brown hair . . .' 'He won't let this go unavenged. Our Fuhrer won't let them get away with this . . .'

Rhion's hands closed tight over the staff he held, the crystals of its iron head glinting softly, as if with a light of their own, in the leap and jitter of the shadows. 'Christ, what would they do if they had it?'

Over the city, the sirens were sounding the all-clear.

As they drove south again through the Moabit district, avoiding the fires and ruins and tangled traffic of the industrial targets, Rhion was silent, sitting beside Saltwood with closed eyes, head bowed and hands folded tight around the smooth, rune-scrawled wood of the staff. Leibnitz, leaning forward from the back seat of the Packard, was speaking to him in low, passionate German which lapsed frequently into Yiddish: '. . . Already you have endangered all the world in making the Spiracle . . . given them a chance to use magic, to call up the forces of the Universe . . . open the windows to let through the energies of the Void into this world, where only the Most High knows what they will do . . .'

'I had to do something,' whispered Rhion. 'I had to get it back . . .'

'At the cost of bringing to life again the magic they seek? And if he takes the Spiracle from you this time . . .'

'He won't.' The little man did not open his eyes, but Saltwood could feel him shiver as if, beneath that quiet, the tension of fear, of dread, of grief were nearly unbearable. 'He won't . . .'

'And you grew up with this going on?' Tom threw a glance back to the seat behind him, where Sara was half turned-around, watching through the small oval of the rear window for signs of pursuit.

She half laughed. 'This and worse. We'd always have somebody staying with us: Kabbalists arguing until four in the morning whether the path between the Cosmic Spheres of Yesod and Netzach was represented by the Star or the Emperor; White Witches cussing like fishwives at the Adepts of the Golden Dawn; Pyramidiots and menhir-hunters pulling each other's hair about how many inches are in a megalithic foot and whether Easter Island lies on a ley . . . *oy gevalt*! And Papa making his little number-squares and adding up the letters of everybody's names and birth-planets while Mama hunted through all the pockets of all the coats in the house for enough kopecks to buy bread for the next day. And then like as not Papa would give whatever was in the cupboards to some crazy Rosicrucian who needed it to get to France where he'd been "directed in meditation" he'd find the clues that would lead to the rediscovery of Atlantis . . . not that there was ever very much,' she added, her voice turning small. 'In the cupboard, I mean.'

Tom was silent, remembering the pinched grey look on his own mother's face those nights after an oatmeal supper when she'd sit working on the bills. Though there'd always been food of some kind on the table he'd always been hungry – especially in the spring, when they simply couldn't afford to lose what one steer would bring them towards the mortgage and the costs. Towards the end it had been the worst. 'What happened to her?' he asked quietly. 'Your mother?'

'She died.' The words were like the chop of a kindling-axe. In the dark of the back seat she turned her face away, a delicate shadow profiled against the blackness of the city, the occasional flare where a far-off blaze burned near a warehouse or factory. There were few of those here in the Charlottenburg district, amid the blocks of expensive flats with their pseudo-Assyrian cornices, their Hollywood-gothic turrets and pillars – every window blacked out, but the very air around those eyeless monoliths seeming to seethe with suppressed life.

After a moment Sara added quietly, 'While I was in America. Of influenza. I should have gone back to Warsaw then, tried to make Papa come with me, but there just wasn't the money. I could barely make my school expenses, much less get passage for one over and two back. And anyhow the immigration quotas for Jews were jammed, and nobody was gonna let an extra one through.'

He wondered how she'd got the passage-money when she'd heard her father had been interned – much less the dough it would cost for the black-market identity-cards she'd mentioned – but didn't ask. The lines around her mouth and in the corners of those coal-black eyes said things about where she'd been and what she'd passed through on her way, and he knew better than to touch those open wounds. He found her beautiful, with her dark hard eyes and her crazy parti-coloured hair, in the way he'd found the Spanish girls beautiful, who'd fought beside him in the hills, a beauty of voice and inflection, a beauty of toughness, like cats who fend for themselves and can only occasionally be coaxed to curl purring on a man's knee.

Beside him, Rhion seemed to have revived a little, eating bread and cheese out of Leibnitz's little string shopping-bag and gesturing with it as he said, '. . . And in any case I had no choice. I could never have got the edge over him, even for the second I did, without magic of some kind, and by myself I didn't have the power to keep the field going. Everything here requires such a *hell* of a lot of power. The Temple there was the only place to get it. There any fruit in there? Or chocolate?'

'Chocolate, ha! They all trade it for cigarettes, the Nazi *chozzers* . . . You still shouldn't have left it.'

'As long as we stay away from that house we're safe. Outside the range of a couple of miles from the Spiracle the Resonator's inert. The way it draws power it should be even less than that, by this time. We should be far enough away to be safe. By the way . . .' He turned to Saltwood, glasses flashing dimly in the darkness. 'Where are we headed?'

But even as he spoke Tom was hitting the brakes, cursing, his stomach sinking within him. 'Gestapo headquarters, it looks like,' he said grimly, shifting gears and starting up again slowly, knowing there was no escape, no evasion. 'Or Hell. So hang onto your hats.'

Ahead of them, in a line of flashing red lights, dark forms, and bobbing electric torches, stretched an SS roadblock.

23

In the throat of the Pass of God's Ax Tally drew rein and rose in her stirrups, for the tenth time that day, turning her head and listening. The wind keened thinly along the high stone faces of the cliffs that lined the way, whined among the boulders that strewed their feet and roared with a soughing like the sea in the pines that formed a spiky black rampart along their brows, a hundred and twenty feet above. But when it eased for a moment the sound came again, unmistakable, and then Tally knew.

She was being followed.

Wind caught at her hair and whipped it in her eyes as she scanned the pass behind her. The Earthquake which had twisted the foundations of the world six hundred years ago had changed the shape of this pass; steep and jagged now, it ran straight for barely a hundred yards at any one time, winding back and forth through the fractured bones of the Mountains of the Sun; only in the thirty years of her father's rule in Mere had it been possible for a lone rider to pass through without fear of being robbed, not once, but several times.

Worriedly she reached inside her grimy sheepskin jacket, to touch the amulet she wore.

This is the only road down to the Drowned Lands, she told herself firmly. *It's logical I'd be taking it; logical they'd guess where I'd be going. The fact that they're coming doesn't mean I was betrayed.*

Her horse jittered uneasily, and the spare mount, burdened with food and the leather-wrapped bundles of Jaldis' books, flicked its ears and snuffed at the wind. Tally gauged the length of this particular reach of the pass, calculated in her mind how many more miles of narrow canyon, hemmed in by unscalable cliffs, lay between her and the wet, cloud-scarved woods of the downward slopes beyond.

A burst of speed . . .

But no burst of speed would take her beyond the sight of the riders in the pass behind her, and the clatter of her horses' hooves would carry. Then they'd know she was there, and the amulet she wore would not hide her from their eyes.

But if that old Hand-Pricker told them to look twice at any sloppy-looking man in an old sheepskin coat, she thought, panic rising in her chest, *it won't hide me anyway . . .*

Whatever happened, she knew she must not let herself be caught. Not in flight from Erralswan. Not with Jaldis' books.

In a scattered few seconds the whole scene in the Hand-Pricker's hut returned to her, and with it the memory of the smell of the place, the reek of filth, old blood, dirty bedding, and cats. The Hand-Pricker himself had shrunk blinking from her, an emaciated man of middle age whose light-brown hair and beard had both been crusted stiff at the ends with the blood of sacrifices made years ago; bloodstains had shown up even on the faded black of his robe. He'd stammered, 'The woman who wanted the powder,' and in his watery yellow eyes was the fear that more trouble was coming to him.

'I need an amulet,' Tally had said, setting down a small bag of money among the litter of herbs and sticks and crumbling fragments of half-mummified toads on the table. She'd already cropped her hair short like an urchin boy's, and wore a boy's breeches and shirt and dirty sheepskin jacket. 'An amulet that will turn aside men's eyes, make them believe that they see a man in these clothes, fat and harmless and bearded; and I need it quickly.'

'Who – Whom do you flee?'

In his eyes she saw that he'd already half-guessed. *The eyes of Agon are everywhere . . .*

'Isn't it enough to know,' she had asked softly, 'that I fear for my life, and the lives of those I love?'

Fumblingly, he had made the amulet, pulling at the cords that passed through his fingers and palms and ear-lobes until the blood came, rocking and whispering above the flat rock in the corner of his hut, stretching forth his bleeding hands to murmur the name of the familiar spirit that gave him – so the Hand-Prickers believed – his power. And Tally, sitting at the table with the Hand-Pricker's cats purring around her boots and sleeping on her lap, had strained her ears for sounds in the village back-lane outside, praying that no one had yet marked her lateness in returning to her husband's house.

She had already left Kir and Brenat, in the charge of their nurse, with the local physician. That worthy had been sufficiently puzzled by Kir's symptoms – hallucinations, convulsions and pains in the joints unaccompanied by any fever or inflammation (Kir was an enthusiastic actor but Tally had drawn the line at drugs that might do him real harm) – to recommend sending him immediately to a more skilled practitioner in Brottin, far down the mountain and, she hoped, out of harm's way. But there was always a chance that their nurse was one of Agon's spies. Or one of the grooms. Or . . .

Or anyone.

That was the worst, the nightmare of all this. Not knowing whom to trust.

Those who did not serve Agon through hate, like Mijac, or cynicism, like Esrex, might just as easily do the Veiled God's bidding through fear.

'I'm sorry to have brought this upon you,' she said, reaching out to take the dirty little bolus of wax, blood, sticks and feathers that the wizard held out to her in his sticky hands. 'But truly, even if I hadn't come here, trouble would come upon you. The men who hate magic are moving – the men who seek to remove magic from the world, so that no one may challenge their power, or see their doings and expose them for the lies they are.'

'But I – I'm not one of the great ones, you know,' the mage had whispered. 'I stay out of the way – I don't make trouble – the Lord of Erralswan has never . . .'

'The Lord of Erralswan has never thought of you one way or the other,' Tally said sadly. 'And now people are making him think. If you can use a scrying-crystal, to see the movements of armies – if you can cast a spell of darkness, or confusion, or illness, against an enemy's troops – if you have the slightest ability to read the winds or the signs of the bones that would tell of treachery and ambush – people will make the Lord of Erralswan think that you are his enemy, you are a traitor, you are not deserving of even a hearing because you are who and what you are. It needs no magic to cast an illusion like that.'

The man had only looked at her, holding his big grey cat in his arms, his eyes stupid with fear and the hope that she wasn't right.

Tally looped the amulet's cord about her neck, and slipped the blob of gritty wax into her jacket. 'Flee, if you can,' she said, her voice quiet and her eyes holding his. 'The Lady of the Drowned Lands is gathering mages on her islands; you will be safe there. She needs the help of everyone who can do magic, everyone who was born with that seed in his blood . . .'

'Is that where you are going?'

She hesitated, but knew the man would guess it; then nodded.

He'd swallowed hard, his thin fingers, pierced through with bits of twine and string for the small blood-sacrifices of his system of power, stroking the soft, thick fur of his cat's head while the animal rubbed its cheek against the tattered black sleeve. 'I – I've lived here all my life,' he'd said uncertainly. 'The people here know me . . .'

But as Tally turned to go he'd stepped quickly forward, to touch her sleeve.

'That amulet . . .' he said. 'It won't . . . My power, the power of my blood, of my familiar spirits, isn't – isn't great. The amulet will keep you cloaked from the eyes of your foes, only as long as you don't draw attention to yourself. If they know you're there, if they've noticed you, or are looking for you, it won't help you. You must keep still.'

You must keep still.

Rhion had said something of the kind to her also, when he'd given her similar talismans to keep the neighbours from seeing her, all that long summer she'd first known him, when he and Jaldis had been living in the Lower Town. But listening to the jingle of harness, the strike of hooves, clear and sharp now in the stony pass behind her, she knew that if these riders had visited the Hand-Pricker in Yekkan and had forced from him that the woman they sought was going disguised as a man, the amulet would do her no good.

Even as the scene had returned to her – whole and complete in seconds – she had been scanning the pass, seeking cover in the rocks, looking for anything, a stand of trees, a boulder large enough to conceal a woman and two horses . . .

But there was nothing. A few scrubby knots of mountain laurel halfway up the grey-yellow shale of the cliffs, a low-growing tangle of heather among the rocks . . .

Her gloved hands, aching from the unaccustomed work of making and striking camp, of caring for the horses and loading the packs, felt cold on the reins. She must either sit in full sight of the riders when they came into view, and pray that the Hand-Pricker hadn't told them who to look for . . . or flee.

If she fled they would certainly see her. And she wasn't

at all sure she could outrun riders in the rocky tangle of the pass.

Panic pounded at her, flapping like a bird against the cage of her ribs . . . Every second lost made it increasingly unlikely she could escape if she bolted . . .

It would be a long way down the damp grey forests of the north side of the mountains, misty country among the clouds and then the rainy lower slopes leading down to the Drowned Lands below. She could never do it with the riders of Esrex' household, the riders of the White Bragenmeres, on her heels. Not travelling alone.

What it came to, she thought, was trust. Trust in that scabby, frightened man in Yekkan; trust in his not-very-strong amulet; trust in the strength of his heart against the fear of the Veiled God. She drew her horse a little out of the main road and bowed her head, feeling as if she were drawing in upon herself, making herself invisible in spirit and hoping that Shilmarglinda, Goddess of Beasts and Fruit and Birth, would keep the horses from snorting or neighing.

And waited.

From the misty shadows of the pass the masked riders of Agon appeared, anonymous, dark-clothed, empty-eyed and at least thirty strong, and swept down the road beside which she sat, their hoof-beats ringing in the narrow way.

24

'Right,' said Tom grimly, slowing and downshifting. 'Rabbi, Sara, down on the floor. Rhion, get one of those guns and get ready. We're going to crash it.'

'No!' said Rhion sharply.

At the same moment Sara added 'If you give Rhion a gun we're *all* gonna be killed,' a judgment call with which Saltwood had to agree, though he wanted to point out that the chances that they would all be killed in the next five minutes were astronomically high as things stood.

While the car slowed Rhion busily unwrapped the iron wire which held the circlet to the staff, and, concentrating on the barricade, Saltwood was conscious again of a strange and disturbing optical effect whose nature he couldn't quite define connected with the Spiracle. In the dim flare of the approaching flashlights he had an evanescent sense once more of seeing something floating around the twined iron loop, something that wasn't precisely a webby cloud of spider-strands, but which made him think of one for reasons he couldn't guess.

Yet when he turned his head he saw nothing strange and in fact wondered why he had thought he had. It was only a ring of twisted iron and silver, scratched with odd little marks and holding five crystals in a pattern not symmetrical, but certainly definite, a pattern governed by what he dimly guessed to be the proportions of some non-Euclidean geometry. He noticed how gingerly the Professor cupped the Spiracle in his hand, framing it with thumb and middle finger and never allowing his fingers to pass through its rim.

Rhion's voice was very calm. 'Lie on the floor over the

guns and gear,' he instructed, handing the decapitated staff back over the seat. He glanced at Tom. 'You have a pass . . . ?'

'Yeah, but they're looking into the cars with flashlights, in case you didn't notice.' Slowing down he had to talk fast – in another few seconds he'd have to decide whether to hit the gas or the brake. 'If we stop long enough for that . . .'

'Don't worry about it.' Rhion settled himself back into the seat, folded his arms with the circlet concealed in his hand, and bowed his head, his eyes slipping shut.

'*Don't worry about it?!?* Are you out of your frigging mind? You think they're not going to notice two people crouching down on the floor . . . Not to mention you sitting there looking like a picture on a wanted-poster . . .'

'I said don't worry about it! Tell them you're transporting the car through to somebody important at Ostend! Don't mention us at all.'

'You're nuts!'

'Do it, Tom!' Rhion's head came up, his eyes blazing behind the glasses that flashed redly in the lights of the barrier. 'There are about forty soldiers on the other side of that barrier with guns. You crash it and we're Swiss cheese!'

Saltwood wasn't sure how he'd deduced that, for beyond the lights of the barrier he himself could see only darkness. 'Dead is one thing! Trying out the electrical-fittings at Gestapo headquarters is another!'

'Don't you think I know that?' demanded Rhion, his voice shaking, the burn-scars on his face and throat catching shiny in the moving glare. 'Do it. They won't see us.'

The barrier was twenty feet away – yellow-and-black striped sawbucks stretched between a couple of trucks parked across the road, around which hooded lights threw a feeble blur of illumination. Beyond that the blackout made anything further impossible to determine. At least a dozen Storm Troopers were in evidence, plus one or two civilians – Gestapo. He threw a fast glance at Rhion, who had subsided again into his attitude of meditative stillness. Did he only guess there were more men waiting in the darkness, or could the man really somehow see without light?

Muffled from the floor behind him, Sara's voice said, 'Trust him, cowboy. He got Papa out of the camp at Kegenwald in the weirdest cockamamie way I've ever seen.'

After one last agonizing waver Tom eased on the brake. 'If this goes wrong I'll kill you.'

'You do that,' mumbled Rhion. He sounded half asleep.

A flashlight slammed its beam into Saltwood's eyes and he squinted against it and wondered if they noticed the sweat that prickled his hair and every inch of his backbone. 'Name?' demanded a voice from behind the light.

'Deitmarr, and get that bloody light out of my eyes!' snapped Saltwood furiously.

The light moved aside as he thrust the late Corporal Deitmarr's identity-card up at the SS lieutenant in charge of the barrier. 'I'm taking this heap through to Kesselring at Ostend,' he added, jerking his hand to indicate the shiny length of the Packard. 'And a damned cow it is, too, but he says he wants it.'

The flashlight beam flicked over Rhion's still, dozing form, swished the back seat mechanically while the lieutenant was still studying Saltwood's pass. 'You seen any sign of a grey open Mercedes, four passengers, bearded man, red-haired girl, blonde man in part of an SS uniform . . .' He rattled the words off mechanically, as if his mind were on something else.

'Crucifix, no! I've spent all afternoon in the damn garage trying to get this expletive deleted bastard of a car to bloody start.' *Aren't you going to ask me about those people crouched down in the back seat? Or this handcuff manacle on my left wrist?*

'You taking it all the way to Ostend?'

'If the thing doesn't effing die on me on the way.' It was impossible that the man didn't hear the slamming of Saltwood's heart.

'Good luck, then.'

He thumped the roof of the car. Saltwood drove on, wondering if he'd somehow been shot without noticing it and this was delirium. He forced himself not to pat the dried blood on his uniform jacket, the bullet-holes that had finished off its last occupant. *Dammit, they HAVE to have shown up that close, the guard HAS to have seen them . . . !* The headlights flashed across lines of armed shadows, massed in the darkness behind the trucks. Tom wondered how Rhion had known that.

'Nobody get up,' mumbled Rhion into his beard, the iron circlet still cradled between thumb and middle finger, almost out of sight against his side. 'There'll be more. Tell me when the next one's coming up, please, Tom.'

Saltwood swore, quietly but with considerable feeling, through the next three miles of street, pausing only long enough to repeat the entire performance at the next roadblock. When he glanced beside him he could see in the gleam of the receding flashlights the sweat that trickled down the sides of the Professor's forehead and matted the long strings of his hair. As they drove on into the blackness of the countryside, Saltwood was quiet for a long time.

'He did that getting Papa out of the camp.' Sara fished in the pocket of the SS field-jacket she wore over her somewhat grubby BDM uniform and produced a couple of cigarettes which she must have looted from the dead guards on Teglerstrasse. Crouched by the dim glow of the hooded headlight with a local map, Saltwood grinned – he hadn't thought of looking for cigarettes himself, but the woman didn't miss a trick.

Behind them, above the dark blur of half-naked trees, Berlin was a smear of smoke, lit from beneath by the fevered glare of fires still burning out of control in every industrial district in the city, and from above by ice-hard diamond stars. Sara's breath puffed in the deepening cold as she went on, 'He told me to go up and cut my way through the wire in full sight of two guard-towers, with every floodlight in the place on . . . He'd told Papa to just walk out the door and over to the fence to meet me. And all the time he just sat there at the edge of the woods, like he did in the car tonight, with his eyes shut, meditating.' She pulled a lighter out of another pocket, steel with the wreathed death's-head of the SS embossed upon it. The bright leaf of flame called reddish echoes from even the dusky hair that framed her face, picked sharp little shadows from the corners of her eyes. In the car behind her the Professor and Rebbe Leibnitz were conferring quietly, heads together. She glanced back at the two shadowy forms and her dark brows pulled down over her nose. 'Sometimes it's like he's just another of Papa's harmless lunatics,' she said softly. 'Other times . . .'

She held out the lighter. When Saltwood touched her hand to steady it, she flinched very slightly, but consciousness of her fingers' touch went through him like a swig of brandy, warming even when he took his hand away.

It seemed impossible to him that when he'd woken up that morning he hadn't known her. In a way he had, he thought . . . He'd seen the scratches she'd made on the inside of the dresser-drawer, marking off days in defiance of captivity, in defiance of helplessness. And he grinned to himself. *Now there's a step better than those heroes of legend who fall in love with a lady's portrait . . .*

And now it was like he'd known her for years.

'You figured out where we are?' she asked, her scratchy

Brooklyn accent breaking into reveries he knew he had no business having until they were safely back in England – or at least safe on the submarine.

'Uh – I think so.' There had been half a dozen maps in the glove-box, but only this one had shown the countryside around Berlin in any kind of detail. 'That T-fork we just passed must be this one here . . .' He pointed on the map. Around them the thin woods of birch and elm were silent, save where, not too far in the distance – probably at the end of this twisting, weed-choked lane – a wireless chattered in some farmhouse in the cold stillness of the night. 'Which means that has to be the road to Rathenow. Even if we keep to the side-roads we can make Hamburg easy by midnight. The people I know can get in touch with the patrol-boat . . .'

'That's in the wrong direction.'

Saltwood looked up, startled. Rhion and Rebbe Leibnitz had got quietly out of the car and were standing behind him in the deep, dew-soaked grass that clogged the lane. Rhion wore the black greatcoat of an SS officer which reached nearly to his ankles, starshine glimmering faintly in the round lenses of his glasses and in the irregular pentangle of crystals on the head of his staff. Leibnitz, still in shirtsleeves, was hugging himself and shivering with cold.

'Papa, for Chrissake put on a jacket . . .' began Sara, exasperated, and Leibnitz shook his head stubbornly.

'I wear what they give me because I will not go naked like Noah before the eyes of the Lord, but before I put on their damn *Todtenkopf* uniform I will freeze.'

'What do you mean,' asked Saltwood wearily, 'the wrong direction?' He stood up out of the dingy pool of headlight-glow, a powerful bulk towering over the smaller Professor. Weariness and hunger and the exertions of the day were catching up with him – his left arm still hurt damnably, as if the monster-head that had ripped his flesh, the fire that had seared it, had been real, and the manacle of the sawed-off handcuff chafed painfully at the wristbones. The last thing he needed, he reflected irritably, was another of Rhion's meaningless quibbles about where they should and shouldn't go. 'It's the only direction there is, pal, if we want to get to England.'

'But I don't,' said Rhion. 'Where the hell *is* England, anyway?'

He really IS nuts, thought Saltwood, exhaling a thin trail of cigarette-smoke that shimmered white in the icy dark. *Not that I had any question about it before* . . . 'You want to stay in Germany, maybe? I guarantee you won't like it.'

The Professor shook his head. Starlight caught the silver bevel of his spectacle-edge, the cold double-Seig-rune on the collar of his coat. He gestured with the staff he held, and the Spiracle's crystals winked frostily, an all-seeing, faceted eye. 'I didn't take this back from von Rath – I didn't risk what's going to happen to me if he catches me this time – to go to work for the people who were dropping those bombs this afternoon.' He nodded back towards the glowing red stain in the sky.

Saltwood began, outraged, 'Do you know what the Nazi bombers have been doing to London . . .'

'And what would *you* people do if you had magic?' asked Rhion quietly. 'If you could use the powers channelled through the Spiracle? Pulp Berlin, maybe, to convince Hitler to withdraw from the war?'

Saltwood hesitated. Later he supposed he shouldn't have. But he remembered Spain – that war of freedom against fascism in which the 'free' countries of the world had declined to participate – and he knew full well how the military mind worked. He should, he supposed, have denied the possibility utterly. Maybe if he'd been a real soldier he would have.

'I don't know.'

'Nor do I.' A skiff of wind moved the skirts of Rhion's

greatcoat like a dark wing. 'And I don't want to find out. Or what you'd do with it after that. I never wanted to come to your world, or to have anything to do with your *verkakte* war. In any case my only way out of Germany – my only way out of your world – lies at the Dancing Stones near Schloss Torweg. That's the only place the wizards in my world will know where to look for me, and tomorrow night, the night of the Autumn Equinox, is the only time when I'll be able to raise enough power to reach out to them and make the crossing. And that's where I'm going.'

'The hell you are,' said Tom, his voice now equally soft.

'Rhion,' said Sara quietly, 'you did that at the Summer Solstice. Nothing happened. Except that you got caught.'

The Professor flinched at her words, averting his face; his pudgy hands tightened around the pale wood of the witch-staff. 'I don't know why it didn't work last time,' he said, keeping his voice level with audible effort. 'Anything could have gone wrong. The political situation there was unstable when I left . . .' He shook his head, as if trying to clear some cloudy image there, some half-remembered dream. 'But I do know it's my only chance. My last chance. I have to believe they'll try again, at least this once. I have to be there.'

Kindness, pity, compassion deepened Sara's voice. 'And if it doesn't work?'

There was long silence, broken only by the distant hooting of an owl in the frost-thick silence of the starlight. Then Rhion whispered, 'I can't think about that.'

She moved towards him, hand outstretched, but he stepped back abruptly, dark against the starry darkness, the light catching in his glasses and the crystals of the ring. Looking at him, Saltwood had the curious impression that the night sky seen through the Spiracle was different. Perhaps it was only the way the crystals caught the light . . . but it seemed to him for a split-second that half a galaxy of brightness, of tiny pinlights infinitely far away, seemed caught within that loop, an alternate firmament that had nothing to do with the one overhead.

'Tom,' came the soft voice from that compact silhouette, 'if you could get Sara and her father to England I'd appreciate it. Von Rath planned to use the magic of the Spiracle to take out the RAF. Without it they've got no illusion, they've got no weather-witching – they've got no more than they had in June. By the time they can reformulate a plan – any plan – it'll be winter. Tomorrow, and the next few days, are really their last chance this year. Just by escaping, just by taking this, I've put a hole in their plans, and von Rath knows it . . .'

'That doesn't mean they couldn't make another one, or use that Resonator thing . . .'

'If they made one they couldn't charge it,' argued Rhion in the self-evident tone of a medium explaining why the lights have to be turned down before George Washington's spirit will tip tables. 'The Resonator's useless away from the Spiracle. Believe me, once the Spiracle is gone there'll be no way they can convert psychic energy to magic.'

'Not so fast.' Saltwood dropped his cigarette-end and stepped clear of Sara, his automatic now in his hand, levelled at Sligo's chest. 'I don't want to take you to England at gunpoint, Professor, but I'll do it. We need you and we need that widget of yours, whatever the hell it really is and whatever it really does. And don't think I won't pull the trigger,' he added quietly, as Rhion made a move to step past him, 'because I will.'

Behind him he heard the whisper of Sara's indrawn breath, but after all she said nothing. She understood.

'Now, I was sent here to kill you. I'd rather take you back alive – I'd rather you *came* back with me willingly – but I'll kill you rather than let you fall into Nazi hands again, which is exactly what you'll do if you pull this dumb Prisoner's Base routine because you think the fairies are gonna come take you away if you stand in the right place. So sit down

. . . Sara, there's a couple pairs of handcuffs in the gear we took from Teglerstrasse. Get me one.'

Sara stepped towards the car.

Saltwood remembered her doing that. She was still standing a few feet from him, her hand on the car door, moments – *but how many moments?* – later, when he realized that Rhion Sligo was gone.

Stunned – more than stunned – he shook his head. He hadn't – he *couldn't* have – fallen asleep on his feet . . .

He looked down at his hands. He still held the gun, but the map of the area he'd shoved into his pants pocket was gone.

Sara whispered, '*Mah nishtanna* . . .' and staggered, and Saltwood sprang to steady her – she pushed him away in swift revulsion. 'All right already, I'm fine . . .' In the reflected glare of the headlights she was white. 'What the *hell* did he do? He was just standing there one second . . .'

In the long weeds of the road-bank Rhion's track was starkly clear where he'd waded through the powder of glittering dew.

'He has the Spiracle,' said Leibnitz's voice, deep and quiet, out of the darkness. 'He can do pretty much whatever he can conjure up the strength within him to do – whatever he dares do.' In the starlight his white hair and beard glittered as if they, like the grass, were touched with frost, his eyes pits of shadow under the long jut of brows. 'I only hope – and you should hope too, Captain Saltwood – that he makes it back to those stones okay, and that his friends really do pick him up at midnight tomorrow night.' His breath was steam as he spoke, his long hands, wrapped around his arms, colourless as a mummy's against the grey cloth.

'Because if he doesn't – if Paul von Rath gets his hands on that Spiracle again – I'm telling you now the Nazis invading England are going to be the least of everybody's problems.'

'*Goddam* crazy little bastard.' Saltwood eased the car through the long weeds, overgrown branches of elder and hawthorn slapping wetly against the windscreen, wishing to hell he dared uncover the headlights enough to get a good view of the potholes of the farm-track which led back to the main road. But the risk of being stopped was great enough without tampering with blackout regulations, and without Rhion and the Spiracle – whatever it really was – there was little chance a questioner wouldn't notice the bullet-holes in Saltwood's uniform jacket, the pile of gear in the back seat, his lack of true resemblance to any of the various ID papers he carried or the startling similarity of all the car's passengers to the descriptions of fugitives undoubtedly being circulated by this time to every corner of the Third Reich.

In addition to the map it rapidly became clear that Rhion seemed to have taken a third of their money and food, and assorted ration-books and identity papers as well. Those last had been stowed in the car, and thinking about that made the hair creep on Saltwood's scalp. How the hell long had he been standing there, gun pointing at nothing, unaware of anything taking place around him?

'Where the *hell* did they dig him out of?'

'I been trying to figure that out for months.' Sara pulled her knees up under a second field-jacket she'd put over them like a blanket, and huddled tighter into the one over her shoulders. Her father, on her other side, still sat ramrod-straight and shivering in his shirtsleeves, his dark gaze turned worriedly out into the frost and blackness of the night.

'My *guess*,' she went on slowly, 'is that who he thinks he is is based on some kind of distorted reality, though it's hard to tell what that originally was. And he believes in it 100 percent himself.'

Saltwood glanced curiously sidelong at her as the car emerged onto the Rathenow road. Instead of turning left, which would have taken them eventually to the Elbe and thence to the Hamburg autobahn, he turned right, eyes straining in the darkness for the crossroad where he'd turn off towards Brandenburg and thence swing south of Berlin and head east. *Thank God the Germans can't stand anything that isn't neatly labelled.* He recalled only too clearly trying to get around in London after its inhabitants – expecting an invasion any hour – had taken down every street- and road-sign in the city, not that London was ever oversupplied with such things.

'So he told you?'

She nodded, and brushed back a tendril of the dark hair which framed her face. 'Three, four days after they took us prisoner last June that bodyguard of his, Horst Eisler, showed up at Kegenwald one night and drove me back to the Schloss. Rhion was still laid up – I don't think he'd have told me some of the things he did if he hadn't been doped up and hurting and scared. He . . .' She paused, and Saltwood felt, rather than saw, the change in the way she sat, the lessening of the reflex tension of her muscles as she forgot where she was, remembering only the darkened room, the pudgy hand desperately gripping her own.

Then she shrugged, rearranging the first thoughts to cut less close to her own heart. 'He talked to me then about his woman and his kids back in Oz or wherever the hell he thinks he comes from. About his old master who was supposed to come here with him but died or disappeared on the way through this Void thing he talks about, and how his parents wrote down in the family Bible that he'd died the day he told them he was going to be a wizard. The whole set-up – he claims his woman's father is a Duke or something – makes me think he might be a Hungarian or Austrian Jew from one of the old University towns, except that when I met him he claimed he didn't even know what a Jew was. A Freudian would say that's significant in itself.

'But you know,' she went on softly, 'he didn't have to do what he did. He didn't *have* to give von Rath that Spiracle in the first place, or let them make him teach them how to use the device it's a control to, if there is one. I mean, Papa and I had no claim on him. He'd only met me about three weeks before, only broke Papa out of the camp because of some magic ceremony he claimed he needed to work down in the cellars under Schloss Torweg.'

'Then he isn't . . .' began Tom, with elaborate casualness, swinging the car to the right and heading down the two-lane strip of asphalt through the dark, tree-sprinkled fields that would eventually lead to the old Prussian capital. 'You and he aren't . . .'

He hadn't thought so, watching them together – the physical stiffness, so at odds with the sensuality of her face, was noticeable with him as well. But though the affection between them seemed casual it clearly ran very deep. His impression was that she regarded the Professor as an uncle or an older brother . . . only not quite. And in the panic confusion of flight from Berlin, of the bombing and getting through the blockades and out into the open darkness of the countryside, there had been no time for unnecessary words, no way to tell for sure. He felt more relief than he'd have cared to admit when she laughed, startled and tickled, and said 'Rhion? Oh, Christ . . .' and laughed again.

Good, he thought.

'But you know,' she added more quietly, switching to English with a quick glance at her father, who was deep in trying to calculate, with a pencil-stub on the back of a ration-book, some elaborate *kamea* regarding the superimposition of the number-keys of all of their names over the Seal of Mars, 'if I ever *do* get interested in a man again, it'll be because . . .' Then she shied away from that train of thought, too. 'Well . . . Rhion was the first man I've met in – oh, years – who wasn't a bastard.' She spoke a little defensively, seeming to retreat in on herself again, and Tom felt a flash of anger at them, whoever they were: the man or men who had put that wariness in this dark-haired girl's eyes.

She'd been a hostage, a prisoner of the SS – the way she watched him, the way she'd pulled away from the touch of his hand, the grim set to her mouth as she'd got back in the car, might, he had thought, have stemmed from that. But now he wasn't so sure. Very carefully, he said, 'Be that as it may – whatever happens, I promise you I'm not a bastard.'

Their eyes met, and held; then Tom flicked his gaze back to the dark road unwinding before them. The sinking glow of the fires in Berlin was to their left now, and farther off in the darkness. Overhead the gypsy-moon did a fan-dance with the clouds.

'Thank you,' said Sara softly, and after that was silent for some time.

It was a hundred and sixty miles to Kegenwald, eastwards towards the Polish border. Beyond that, according to Sara, another fifteen or twenty to Schloss Torweg itself. 'These stones he's heading for are in a kind of overgrown meadow the other side of the hills from the Schloss – which is just an old hunting-lodge from back in Bismarck's time. There's a farm-track through the hills . . . Let me borrow the pencil, Papa . . .'

The old man sniffed, and relinquished it. He'd outgrown the back of the ration-book and was currently filling up both sides of an envelope he'd unearthed from beneath the seat with abstruse numerical calculations, magical squares, and jotted transliterations between Hebrew and Greek. 'Those stones probably started life as an observatory of some kind,' he remarked, angling the envelope to what little moonlight filtered through the window. 'They're a hundred and fifty kilometres east of the easternmost examples of chambered barrows, let alone stone circle or alignments. I'll have to write my friend Dr Etheridge in Florida about this . . . We've been corresponding now fifteen years . . .'

'I don't think there was anybody who published anything in an anthropology or linguistics or archaeology journal in the last thirty years Papa *didn't* correspond with,' explained Sara. 'Not that he ever got them before they were at least six and usually ten years out of date . . .'

'If it was real knowledge it never goes out of date.'

'Tell that to all those Newtonian physicists . . .'

'So Newton wasn't wrong. Gravity still works, nu?'

'Here.' Sara held up the map she'd drawn – Tom risked a glance at it, then went back to concentrating on the road. 'That noise better be the tappets knocking,' she added after a moment, cocking an ear at the dry rattle the engine had developed.

'Doesn't sound like a valve,' replied Tom. 'Though God knows how long this baby was driven after grease and oil got scarce . . . Thanks,' he added. 'If it wasn't for you coming with me I'd have hell's own time catching up with our Professor. It looks like he could have picked up a train in any of three places that would get him to Kegenwald by tomorrow afternoon. At least I'll know where to intercept him.'

Sara didn't answer, and he felt her silence, as surely as he felt the vibration of the road through the tyres, the engine's choking clink. Her father had gone back to making sigils and demon-keys on the back of the envelope.

Hesitantly, Saltwood asked, 'You do understand that's my first duty, don't you? To find him. To bring him back with me, if I can, but . . . to make sure the Nazis don't get him or his device again, one way or the other.'

She sighed deeply, as if giving up something she knew she never could have. 'I understand. It's what you came here to do – I know that. But I think after midnight tomorrow he'll come. He'll have noplace else to go. You think I'm riding along just to act as your guide?'

'I hoped it was because you'd fallen desperately in love with me,' he said, and she flashed him a wicked grin. 'But I still think we should have found a hiding-place to leave your father . . .'

'If you think I'm going to let my daughter go hotzeplotzing around the countryside with some shaygets Amerikanischer goy, you got another think coming,' said Leibnitz resignedly. 'And besides, according to these calculations . . .'

'By the way,' Tom asked Sara, anxious to avert another spate of numerological abracadabra, 'have you ever heard Rhion speak anything other than German?'

'N-No,' said Sara. 'That is . . .' She hesitated, and a glance sideways in the muted lights of a passing military convoy showed him a look of bafflement, as if she had suddenly been faced with a memory that did not fit. He eyebrowed for amplification, but after a moment she shook her head, dismissing something for which she could find no words. 'No.'

They met no opposition, as they drove on eastward in the cold Prussian pines. All the roadblocks, Saltwood guessed, had been set with the assumption that they'd take the westward road: *To England, home and glory*, as Hillyard would have said. Obviously no one was counting on the fact that their mad professor was even madder than they'd thought.

They stopped at eleven in Custrin, the little town sunk in darkness and sleep. While Sara 'laid chick', as they said on the East Side, watching out for the local bulls, Saltwood broke the lock on the gas-pump in front of the general store, filled the Packard's tank and the jerry-cans, then raided the store itself for several quarts of oil and as much bread, cheese, mineral water, and bottled beer as he could cram into his pockets. He left the late Corporal Deitmarr's money in a pile on the counter, and, as an afterthought, helped himself to a cheap cloth labourer's cap which he presented to Rebbe Leibnitz on his return to the car. There was nothing resembling a blanket or jacket in the ranks of tinned food, cheap galoshes, and clothes-pins, or he would have taken that, too, but the old man greeted the gift of the cap with startled joy, and with thanks and a murmured benediction immediately put it on.

There were, of course, a number of SS uniform caps in the back of the car – Saltwood had needed one, as well as a tie and a belt and various odds and ends to complete his disguise – but he'd guessed the old Jew would rather go bareheaded and disrespectful in the eyes of the Lord than wear one, and no wonder. 'I didn't think you cowboys knew about things like that,' said Sara softly, in English, as they pulled away from the darkened store and once more into the sandy pine-barrens.

'What's not to know?' shrugged Tom. 'Half the agitators in the Union were Jewish. We had this Trotskyite Chassidic rabbi who used to come in to play chess with me and argue politics with old Stegler every Saturday as soon as it got dark enough so you couldn't tell a black thread from a white one. He told me that a man of your people would no more walk around without his head covered than he'd walk around without pants.' And, seeing how she still looked at him, half unbelieving, like men he'd seen when a woman turned out to know what a manifold was, he added with a grin, 'You been hanging around with Nazis too long.'

She smiled back slowly. 'I guess I have.'

'*Chas vesholem*.'

Even asleep – if the restless doze in which he drifted could be so termed – Saltwood heard the shock in the old man's voice, and felt him startle through the worn leather of the Packard's lumpy seats. He came awake at once. Dark pines still flashed past the car's windows, as they had when he'd given the wheel to Sara and tried to get some rest. The rattle in the engine was worse – *Just what we need. A ring-job in the middle of Germany . . .* The windows were fogged with the outer cold, save for long smears on the front where Sara had wiped them with her sleeve. It was too dark to see his watch – or, more accurately, the late Corporal Deitmarr's watch.

'What's up?'

Leibnitz shook his head. He, too, had clearly been asleep, blinking and startled, like a man waked by an evil dream. 'I don't know.' He took off his cap, smoothed his rumpled hair and replaced it, looking around him, disoriented, shaken. 'Something – Some feel in the air. Can't you feel?'

Saltwood shook his head, but said softly, 'Pull over, Sara, and cut the lights.'

She obeyed. They all had far too much respect for instinct to quibble over the delay. Without asking she got out, and Tom behind her. For a moment they stood listening, the air like bitter steel on their faces, their breath a steam of diamonds in the moonlight filtering down through the black pine-branches above. The weeds on the banks above the road were stiff with frost like a white salt-rime which would show the smallest track. On such a night noise would carry. But Saltwood heard nothing: no rustle of bracken in the woods all around, no crunch of tyres on the ill-tended asphalt. He checked his watch by the moonlight: quarter past two.

Uneasily he got back into the car, taking the wheel once more. Irritated as he had once been by the hooded headlights which kept their speed down in the flat stretches, now they made him feel safer.

'Where are we?' he asked quietly.

'About twenty miles from Kegenwald.'

'We pass anyone?'

'Not since that motorcyclist an hour ago . . . What's

that?' He felt the jerk of her body as she slewed around in the seat. At the same moment light flicked in the corner of his vision, and, a second later, gleamed in his rear-view mirror. Leibnitz and Sara were both pressed to the side window, their breath misting it again, peering tensely into the dark. 'Cut the lights,' ordered Sara hoarsely, and Tom obeyed. With the strength of the moonlight there wasn't much difference, except where the pines overgrew the road in pockets of inky shadow. 'There,' she breathed. 'See?'

Blue lights were moving among the pines along the side of the road. Saltwood felt the hair lift on his neck.

They were not lanterns. They were moving too fast, for one thing; for another, some of them floated far too high for a man to be holding. By the eerie glow in the bracken, others were rolling along the ground, though the undergrowth, stiff and brittle with frost, did not rustle, only shone with that skeletal light. It was hard to tell how many of them there were, weaving in and out among the trees, but they were definitely following the course of the car.

Saltwood turned on the headlamps and pressed the accelerator, thankful that these Prussian roads ran straight and flat as a Kansas highway and to hell with the ruts and potholes and teeth rattling jolts of the chewed and broken paving. Whatever was happening, he wanted no part of it.

In the rear-vision mirror he saw the lights swirl down the bank onto the road, then pour after the car like bubbles on a river. He pressed the pedal harder, and the lights followed in a bobbing swarm; Saltwood thought they were growing brighter. The car bucked and pitched over the broken road, and he veered, trying to avoid the worst of it. But his eyes kept returning to the mirrors as he sped faster and faster, fear growing within him at what he saw – or thought he saw – or almost saw – behind the lights. Something dark and large, something that ran silent, vibrationless, with a faint glint of metal. Something which moved with level and deadly speed.

He pushed the car for more jolting speed, Sara and her father clinging to the interior straps for all they were worth, knowing to the marrow of his bones that whatever was back there, its black shiny smoothness catching the blue gleams of the lights, he must not let it overtake them. Peripherally he was aware of other lights, a bluish glow powdering the frost-stiff bracken and thin blue discharges like tiny lightning sparking down the trunks of the pines. The granite faces of the old glacial boulders by the road glittered as if laced with diamonds. He barely saw them, his eyes glued now to the mirror.

Why did he have the impression that whatever moved behind those blue lights, metallic, shining, mechanical though it seemed, was alive? More speed, the Packard's old motor clanking hideously . . .

'*Tom*!'

His eyes flashed back to the road in time to take in a blurred impression of the road's sudden curve, the black masses of boulders looming directly ahead. He hit clutch and brake, the heavy car fishtailing wildly – they should have ploughed straight into those boulders but somehow didn't, and he felt the wheels leave the road.

The car rolled at least once – Tom wasn't sure – and struck something glancing before it came to a rocking halt on its side. Sara twisted on top of him, her flat-heeled shoes digging into his thigh as she wrenched her door open like a hatch. Tom remembered the three five-gallon cans of petrol in the trunk and was halfway out of the door after Sara before it occurred to him to wonder if the pain in his legs was because one of them might have been broken. Together they dragged open the rear door, in crammed black panic during which his mind registered nothing but the seconds ticking by until the car would go up like a bomb, and dragged the stunned Leibnitz out of the tangled welter of guns, groceries, and papers in the back. Dragging the old man between them, they ran.

The Packard blew up in a fireball of red light, Tom and Sara falling flat with Leibnitz between them, while fragments of metal and stray bullets from all the spare clips exploded like shrapnel and hissed on the frosted ground. Frozen pine-needles jabbed Saltwood's stubbled cheeks like splintered glass as he buried his face in his arms. *Maybe it'll think we died in the crash.*

It?

The blackness moving behind the blue lights, implacable and deadly and . . . real?

As real as the flying demon-head that had ripped his arm?

He sat up slowly, his legs stabbing with pain. Now that the fluid in his veins was turning from adrenalin back to blood again the pain was starting, in his legs, in his back, in his thigh where Sara had stepped on him getting out of the car and in a dozen other places where he'd hit the framis in the crash, or flying clips of ammo or miscellaneous junk had hit him . . .

Sara, too, was sitting up, shuddering with cold and shock, pine-needles sticking in her hair.

The blue lights were gone. Beyond the glare of the burning car, which lay on its side with its front end twisted where it had struck a tree, the road ran straight as an arrow out of sight in both directions under pine-shrouded blackness. Tom could see the black tyre-lines where he'd hit the brakes, the swerve and jag marking the skid where he'd tried to turn to avoid rocks that weren't there.

Around them in the dark, boots crunched shrilly on the frost.

Tom scrambled to his knees, gun in hand, as metal glinted in the dark of the trees all around. *Dozens of them, Jesus . . .*

The flames on the car leaped suddenly higher, outlining

a single shape before him, thick ivory hair and the face of a scarred angel.

With a dozen guns levelled on him Saltwood pulled the trigger. The gun clicked harmlessly.

Automatics *did* jam, of course.

'Throw it down.' Von Rath's voice was still that same soft level, as calm as if he had known all along that it would misfire. They might have been back at the house in the Jungfern Heide – Jesus, had it just been that morning? – getting ready for another 'psychological test'. Yet there was a difference. The cold angel face almost glowed, coruscating with a kaleidoscope of emotion, fever and hate and triumph like the crack of lightning that bursts planets asunder; in the red reflection of the flames the amulets of bone and jewel seemed to bleed glowing blood.

More Storm Troopers materialized from the woods, fire glinting on the muzzles of their guns. To fight would be hopeless, suicidal . . . Tom wondered how they'd known where the car would go off the road.

'Throw it down,' repeated von Rath. 'I'm going to give you a demonstration and you might not wish to lose your hand just yet.'

'Throw it down already!' breathed Leibnitz, using his daughter's shoulder to haul himself painfully to his feet.

Though it went violently against the grain to do so Saltwood obeyed, tossing the weapon onto the frozen pine-straw between them and standing up carefully, keeping his hands raised and in view. Von Rath looked down at the gun for a moment, and moved his fingers.

With a rending bark, the clip blew up.

Von Rath smiled, and one fine, slender hand came up to stroke the talismans that rattled and whispered around his neck. 'So,' he said softly. 'I was correct in my guess. Rhion Sligo has come east, bringing the Spiracle with him. The invasion will not have to be postponed after all. I should hate to disappoint Reichsmarshal Goering, after all of this.' The cold grey eyes, no more human now than a snake's, passed over Tom and touched Sara briefly, then came to rest upon her father.

'Very good,' he murmured. Two men came up behind him, the bearded wizard Gall and a tall fair Storm Trooper of unbelievable beauty whom Saltwood had the dim impression he'd seen before but knew he never had. 'Just in time for the sacrifice of power, to raise the forces of the Equinox to help the invasion of England. There will be, of course, another sacrifice later . . .' His lips stretched a little, as if part of him still remembered about smiling without remembering why, and he spoke to the beautiful youth who came crowding close to his side. 'And that, my Baldur, though a little late for the Equinox, will I'm sure give us no less of a yield of talismanic power – and no less gratification in the making of it. Take them away.'

25

'You brought the Resonator here, didn't you?' Rebbe Leibnitz spoke so calmly, so conversationally, that for a moment Saltwood thought von Rath was going to be surprised into answering him man to man. The SS wizard paused on the threshold of the great, grim old stone lodge on its flattened hill, startled, and looked back at the elderly Jew in the glow of the hall lights as they passed inside; he even opened his mouth to reply. Then he seemed to settle back a little – Tom had seen the same effect when an Alabama bigot was addressed from behind by an educated black man – and cold superiority returned to his eyes. He had, after all, been addressed not by a real man, but by only whatever an 'only' was in these parts.

His smile was that same flat stretching of the lips. 'He was a fool to have left it,' he said softly. 'Did he think I would bow meekly to that imbecile Himmler's insistence that you were headed west to England? That I couldn't come up with enough of my own men to follow him to the ends of the earth to recover the Spiracle and avenge its theft?'

'I thought he'd made it to begin with,' said Tom, and the frosted quicksilver gaze turned upon him.

'The Spiracle is the property of the Reich's destiny, the tool of its ultimate triumph. As I am its tool.' Saltwood wasn't fooled by the well-bred calm of his voice: it was the voice of a man insane with jealousy quietly citing every rational reason why his woman had no right to leave him – to leave HIM. He could see the man almost visibly trembling with hate.

'We are all its tools,' said that shiningly beautiful youth –

whose name was apparently Baldur, too – who dogged at his elbow in the same fashion Baldur Twisselpeck had back in Berlin. And where was Twisselpeck, anyway? wondered Saltwood obliquely.

The young man sniffled, and put a hand on von Rath's elbow, and went on in a curiously familiar whining voice, 'And he'll pay for it, P-Pauli. Don't worry. Let me do it this time instead of Gall – I'll see to it . . .'

'Indeed.' This time von Rath's smile was genuine. 'And the Resonator can run for years, I expect, on the power we will raise from that – payment. The soul of a wizard, trained and empowered . . .'

Madre de Dios! thought Saltwood, shaken by what he saw in that dreamy smile. *He really BELIEVES it*!

'A pity we won't be able to take him until nearly midnight,' said Gall, coming up to join the other two, like a demented patriarch with his flowing locks and silver beard. 'Between the old Jew and the forces of the Equinox itself I should be able to raise the energies to make quite a tolerable talisman of power – although not as much as if you yourself were to be officiating – but it does seem a waste.'

But if von Rath believes it's magic, thought Saltwood, groping in confusion for some thread of rationality in all this, *and Rhion believes it, and evidently Gall and Twisselpeck and this other Baldur, whoever HE is . . . Then who IS the scientific brains behind this – this device whatever it is? How can they make it work if they're ALL nuts*?

Von Rath turned and studied them by the dreary glow of the hallway lamps. The fading of the smile he'd worn when contemplating Rhion's death under the knife – and Sara had told Saltwood during the drive of how these self-styled mages 'raised power' – left his face completely inhuman again, as if the only emotion of which he was capable were inseparably connected to the Spiracle. As if to him, only the Spiracle and the powers it gave him were real.

He reached out, and cupped Sara's chin with his hand. 'Where will he be?'

She pulled back angrily and the gloved black grip tightened, the guard who held her handcuffed wrists behind her shoving her forward again. Saltwood was aware that any struggle on his part would be useless, for there were two guards holding his arms, besides the dozen or so ranged around the wood-panelled hallway with guns. But he was aware of an overwhelming desire to smash in that scarred, godlike face.

Sara said, 'I don't know, goy.'

As calmly as he had struck Saltwood for mouthing off at Himmler, von Rath slapped her, keeping hold of her chin with his other hand to prevent her head from giving with the blow. Tom gritted his teeth and looked away, knowing a struggle wouldn't help Sara and might get him hurt badly enough to prevent later escape. When he looked back he saw the red welt puffing up on the girl's cheekbone, the involuntary tears of pain in her eyes.

'I know he's in the neighbourhood by the fact that the Resonator has come to life,' went on von Rath softly. 'Ironic, isn't it? Had he not been approaching – though to be sure, with the power from the Temple *here* the field of magic is nearly eighty kilometres wide – I would not have been able to use my powers to capture you with such ease. I shall have to tell him that, as he watches you die. And having captured you, I think taking him will be an easy matter. Surely he isn't fool enough to come here with any kind of foolish notion of reopening the Dark Well – I'm sure he knows as well as I do that it cannot be done. Will it be the Dancing Stones again? Or that barn Poincelles used? I never was certain how much power that French *untermensch* was able to raise with those degenerate rites he practiced, and our little friend may know some way to utilize it . . . Was that why he wanted you?'

Her voice shook slightly. 'He never laid a hand on me.'

The golden Baldur giggled like a schoolboy. 'Didn't want a dose of the clap, I expect.'

'Be still.' The inflection was as a man will order a dog to sit, and Baldur's square, noble mouth puckered in a pout. 'Where will he be?'

'He didn't say.'

Von Rath shrugged, and nodded to his men. 'Take her into the dining-room. Gall, get the tools . . .'

'This is stupid!' raged Saltwood, yanking against the grip of the men who held him, and at the same moment Leibnitz spoke quickly.

'Don't tell him anything.'

'For Chrissake . . . !'

All trace of the old man's slightly comic air of resignation was gone. His dark eyes flashed with calm authority. 'Better she should die than the Spiracle fall into their hands again,' he said quietly. 'She knows it.' He turned back to his daughter. 'Don't you, Saraleh?'

Sara hesitated, mouth taut and eyes darting, suddenly huge in a face white as chalk. *She doesn't know THAT*, thought Tom, *but she sure as hell knows what von Rath will do to Rhion when he catches him.*

'To hell with that,' he said sharply, his eyes going to von Rath. 'He's heading for the standing stones.'

Von Rath's cold glance went immediately to Leibnitz, who had turned his face away, then to Sara's tear-brimming eyes and the relaxed slump of her shoulders. 'So,' he said quietly. 'Baldur, see them locked up. Jacobus, come with me. If the two of you are going to be performing the sacrifice without me tomorrow night . . .' His voice faded as he climbed the stairs, the white-haired crackpot and two stone-faced guards in his wake.

Baldur signalled the other guards with a jerk of his hand, a weirdly schoolboyish gesture for an officer of the SS, and started after his master towards the stairs. Leibnitz turned to the young man as if they had been alone in the dingy hallway, and said quietly, 'He's mageborn, Baldur. You think he doesn't see you as you are?'

The young man stopped, his ridiculously crestfallen expression wildly inappropriate on that beautiful face. 'I –' he stammered, halting, and the guards, too, stopped. He sniffled, and wiped his nose on his sleeve. 'Of – of c-course he sees everything. But one has one's p-pride, and – and there are the others . . . And after all these years . . .'

What the HELL are they talking about?

The beautiful youth shuffled his feet, sniffled again, and ran a nervous hand through the tawny splendour of his hair. 'It – it came to me tonight, when Paul's power . . . That is – I realized I c-could be however I chose, look however I willed. With the field of the Resonator I have power! For the first time in my life, it is as I have always dreamed it would be! Would you like to see it?' There was suddenly an ugly glitter in his eyes. 'You'll see it tomorrow night anyway, Jew . . .'

'Yes,' said Leibnitz gently. 'Yes, I would.'

Baldur snapped his fingers at the guards like the Crown Prince of Ruritania in an MGM musical. 'Bring them.'

To do him credit the sergeant hesitated, but apparently thought better of any remark containing the words *ought not*. In any case, thought Saltwood, there were enough and more than enough guards to subdue the three of them, and more yet visible through the door of the watchroom which led off the hall. Led by Baldur the squad escorted them down a short corridor to a locked door, Saltwood wondering how much more insane things would get. There had to be reality *somewhere* under this increasingly baffling layer-cake of fantasy, reality that could be used to escape, to at least get word to England . . .

As he unlocked the double mahogany doors Baldur said, quite seriously, to the sergeant, 'Kill them if they attempt to cross the threshold. Beyond it is holy ground.'

Oh, boy!

For the first moment Saltwood had a vague impression of darkness, of black walls on which silver hoodoo-signs gleamed softly in the reflection of the dim corridor light, of a faint smell that must have been much worse closer up, for the old rabbi drew back with an expression of revulsion and horror, as if the door had been opened to a charnel-house.

And with Leibnitz out of the doorway, Saltwood could peer inside.

There still wasn't much to see. Marvello the Magnificent had put up a better front in a canvas tent. By comparison with the Meditation Chamber of the Swami of the Celestial Realms the place was stark and the decorations amateurish. There wasn't even the inevitable portrait of Hitler on the wall – only a crimson swastika, seeming to burn sombrely against the darkness. And yet . . . and yet . . .

The place raised the hackles on Tom's neck.

On the black altar in the centre stood the widget he'd last seen by candlelight in the locked bedroom in Berlin, the device he hadn't paid much attention to, being in the process of getting ready to strangle its inventor. The grimy light from the hall must have caught odd reflections in those spheres of glass wound like bubbles in kelp among the strips of iron, for they had an odd glow that seemed to be answered from one portion of the heart of that fist-sized lump of raw crystal. Even the rough iron and the other metal – brass or gold, though surely it couldn't be gold – had a glitter which, through a trick of the shadows – maybe one of the guards behind him was moving – seemed to pulse like the beat of a heart.

Whatever was going on, thought Saltwood uneasily, backing away, it might not be magic but it was pretty damn weird. Just what *had* he seen in his rear-vision mirror? How *had* von Rath been so sure his gun would jam?

Magnetic field? he wondered, trying to separate what little he knew of actual science from Einstein's speculations and Flash Gordon serials. *Something under the altar, maybe? It's one for Mayfair's boffins, if I can even get word of it back to them . . . Christ, they're starting the invasion the day after tomorrow . . . !*

Leibnitz' deep voice interrupted his thoughts. 'I wonder how long it's going to take Himmler – and Hitler, for that matter – to realize they're playing Frankenstein to von Rath's Adam.'

'And why not?' retorted Baldur hotly, his voice scaling up nearly an octave with excitement, his eyes glittering as if drugged. 'Not the Adam of that stupid fable, not a monster against nature, but the culmination of nature, the New Adam of the Reich's destiny. Why shouldn't it be P-P-Paul? He can raise power! He can store it in talismans! And when he achieves the Spiracle Rhion stole from him he'll be able to use it against his enemies, outside the Reich and within it. The SS has always known the virtue of magic, so what better glory can they ask than magic itself . . .'

The boy was working himself into a frenzy. Saltwood, feverishly calculating ways and means of escaping at least long enough to get hold of a radio and warn England, barely listened. But as Baldur turned to close and lock the 'Temple' doors and the guards led their prisoners away, he cast one glance back, and wondered why he had the impression, even as the shadows fell across it, that Rhion's Resonator glowed more brightly in the dark.

'Now would you mind telling me,' asked Saltwood, crossing the bedroom to make sure the window-bars were as firmly embedded in the concrete of the sill as they looked, 'what the *hell* that was all about? You sounded like you knew that kid.' The bars were solid. They were lucky, he supposed, that the window wasn't boarded over, as it had been quite recently by the look of the woodwork around it. It would have been nice had the heat in the rest of the house penetrated to this room, but one couldn't expect everything.

The salt-white glare of the arclights in the yard – they were far out of range of even the most stray British bomber – turned Leibnitz' long hair to silver as he sat wearily down on the bare mattress of the bed. 'Oh, I do. Baldur Twisselpeck, one of von Rath's tame wizards . . .'

'Baldur Twisselpeck?'

At the same time Sara, halting in her examination of the wooden walls, the floorboards, the ceiling for possible means of egress, turned to stare at her father. 'That's crazy! Baldur was that poor greasy *shmendrik* who followed von Rath everyplace . . .'

'That was him.' And, when Sara stared at him in the dense pewter-coloured gloom, 'Wasn't that his voice?'

She hesitated, thinking back. Then she shook her head, the tangle of her red-and-black hair swirling. 'Papa, that's insane! Baldur was a geek, a *nuchshlepper*! It couldn't be a disguise, that kid's six inches taller, the eyes weren't the same colour, the face . . .' She hesitated again.

'It is illusion.' Leibnitz drew up his long legs to sit tailor-fashion on the end of the iron-framed cot. 'Like the illusions of the lights which pursued us on the road, the illusions you both saw in their little tests . . . Like half those guards downstairs were illusions. Von Rath hasn't got twenty guys in this house. How could he have got more than that away when Himmler wanted them all on the westward roads?'

'Thanks for not telling me that downstairs,' grumbled Saltwood, prowling back to the door to verify that the hinges were, in fact, on the outside. 'I'd have had a nervous breakdown trying to figure out which ones to watch out for.' What *would* he have done, he wondered, if Leibnitz had said down there, *Hey, pal, half those guys aren't real.* Like Rhion, the old man could be weirdly authoritative. *If I stay here much longer I'm going to be as crazy as the rest of them.*

But from what von Rath had said a long association didn't look at all likely.

'Don't you understand?' The old man leaned forward, his brown-spotted hands curiously graceful in the bars of bitter light. 'The Resonator that didn't work two miles from the Spiracle back at that little *pishke* Temple in Berlin has all the power, everything, they raised here all summer. It's pulling the energies of the Void through it and feeding them back into one hell of a field, and in that field von Rath, and Gall, and that poor *doppess* Baldur can do as they please . . . What you got there, Saraleh?'

While he'd been speaking Sara had been testing the floorboards under the bed, and had found a loose one. But when she crawled out of the leaden bar of shadow Saltwood saw only a few bits of chalk in her hand, and the glinting flash of a piece of broken mirror. She shook her head, her shoulders slumped under the baggy and bullet-holed black jacket she still wore. 'Nothing, Papa. Just chalk.'

'Nothing is nothing,' said Leibnitz, and rose stiffly. Saltwood, his own bruises seizing up, hated to think how a sixty-five-year-old man's brittle bones and unworked muscles were handling that kind of maltreatment.

He was sore enough to be sarcastic, however. 'There's a piece of wisdom for you.'

'Good,' approved Leibnitz, nodding. 'Your *shaygets* does recognize wisdom when it comes up and bites his ankle. There's hope for the *goyim* yet.' He took the odd collection of fragments from Sara's hand and carried them back to the wan stripes of the window-light.

'Some kid's collection, it looks like . . .'

'No,' corrected her father, stirring them with his fingers. It really was only a few pieces of odd trash. His breath made a smoke against the sharp chiaroscuro of the floodlights, for it was icy cold in the room. Outside, frost glimmered silver upon the ground, the guards' tracks leaving a ragged streak of black along the perimeter fence. 'This was the room where they kept Rhion after they caught him, wasn't it? I think they were his things.'

While the old man muttered and poked at the bits of glass and chalk Sara walked back to where Saltwood stood next to the rump-sprung plush easy-chair which, with the bed and a broken-down dresser, was all the furniture that the room contained. Her arms were folded as if for protection across her breasts, her face drawn and waxy with strain and tiredness. It was close to dawn. Half-hidden by that weirdly parti-coloured hair the bruise on her cheek from von Rath's slap was darkening, and by the way she walked the wreck had left a couple of doozies on her shoulder and hip.

'Thank you,' she said softly, not looking up at Tom for a moment, speaking English so her father would not hear. 'I – I didn't know what to say. To von Rath, I mean. I didn't want to tell them – I know what they'll do to him – but . . .'

'Did your father really mean that?' he asked, still more softly, as if speaking English were not sufficient to exclude the old man from their conversation. 'That he'd expect you to die – to let them torture you – before you'd let them get hold of that stupid magic wand Rhion's so crazy over?'

She sighed, still hugging herself, a small, compact dark figure, save for those splendid white legs, that pointed little face. 'Papa . . . Yes, he meant it. And he would die, over those crazy magic games he plays. I used to think I was tough enough to die before I'd rat on a friend, on someone I cared as much about as I care about poor old Rhion. And I'd like to think I am that tough. But still . . .' She looked up at him through the tangles of her black hair, and there was a tiny gleam of self-deprecating humour in her eyes. 'Does it sound as awful to you as it does to me to say I'm glad you told him?'

'Yep,' he said, and reaching out, gently took her hand, drawing her down into the chair with him. It was almost big enough for them both to sit comfortably – he felt her shy from the touch of his arm around her, his shoulder against hers. Then she relaxed, a wordless *Oh, what the hell* that went from her body to his like a sigh of relief; he'd been afraid she'd pull away, and lie the night in uncompromising loneliness and pain. After forty-eight hours of physical and mental strain, of which the last twenty-four had been without sleep, culminating in violent physical exertion, a drive halfway across Germany, and an automobile accident, he couldn't get interested in much more, even if she'd let him.

But though he felt her uncertainty still, her hesitance and reflex caution, it was a start – the start of something he wanted more, and differently, than anything he could remember wanting since he'd gone back to Detroit from a year in the oilfields to discover his mother and sisters were gone, no one knew where.

Things took time. He sensed that time was what he would need with this woman, this girl. To gain her trust, her (*Go on, say it, Tom*!) love, he was willing to put in all the time he had.

Which was, at a rough guess, about twenty hours. But they drifted to sleep together in the armchair as if world enough and time lay before them like a warm English summer, back in the days before the sun-cross was anything more than a good-luck symbol superstitious women stitched into baby-quilts.

In the hard electric glare of a corner of the Kegenwald train-station, Rhion of Sligo, wizard, mad professor, exile from another universe and fugitive-at-large, sat huddled in a black SS greatcoat with his staff propped at his side, staring down at the broken fragment of mirror in his hand. He couldn't see clearly, for even the little effort involved in scrying tired him and he was exhausted already from the thin cloak of look-over-there and who-me? that he'd held about him for the past eight hours – the spells that had let ticket-sellers be distracted as they glanced not-quite-at the identity-cards of men seven inches taller than he with blond hair, the spells that had caused pretty girls to walk past or minor fights to break out as the police or the SS came near him in train-stations, the spells that had given people the impression he was a smelly old derelict like Johann at The Woodsman's Horn, a presence to be noted very briefly and then resolutely ignored.

But he was very tired now. He was freezing cold, for the night ticket-seller and the single police guard on duty at the station were sitting next to the electric stove at the far end of the bare little room – men who had not seen him get off the train and would not see him leave. He was worn out physically with the sustained effort of magic-working in a world where the energy-levels of air and earth were so low, despite the coming Equinox, his body hurting for sleep that he knew would be far too dangerous a luxury. Food helped, though it was difficult to get the sweets he chiefly craved – he'd scored some black-market chocolate on the train but that hadn't lasted long – and what passed for coffee in stations along the route didn't have nearly the kick of the rations the SS got.

So his vision in the fragment of mirror was at first only shapes against darkness. He had, of course, used a shard of mirror to keep tabs on Sara and her father while they were at Kegenwald, to make sure von Rath didn't move them elsewhere, or hurt them . . . though there was nothing he could have done if von Rath had.

Then the vision cleared a little, and he felt a pang go through him as he realized what he saw.

Sara and Saltwood.

Well, that was logical, he thought, seeing how dark the girl's hair was, pressed to Saltwood's shoulder, only flaming into its old crazy, frizzed red down at the level of her ears. There was the peace of friendship in the way they held one another – the way he'd never dared touch her, had always been too cautious to touch her, too careful of those old wounds, old hurts.

He ought simply to be glad she was on her way to healing.

And there was Tallisett.

The hurt inside him crushed tighter at the thought of her, the slowly growing knowledge that he would never see her, or his sons, again. The loneliness he had endured for six endless months in hell.

He realized that what he grudged was the easing of that loneliness. In his hornier moments he had considered going to bed with Sara, but only with part of his heart. What he had really wanted was to be held, to be loved, to know he wasn't so goddam alone.

He was very tired of being alone.

Or just very tired. He shook his head. It was nearly dawn outside. It was an all-day walk to Witches Hill if he was going to reach the standing stones well before midnight tonight, and he'd have to find food and, hopefully, someplace to rest between here and there.

The worst of it was wondering whether he was, in fact, insane. It had occurred to him before this, jostling in the crowded trains, shoulder-to-shoulder with old women, fretful children, unshaven men nervous with the nervousness of the unemployed in a land where unemployment was a crime – it had occurred to him again and again in his months of captivity, when the only faces he had seen, the only voices he had heard, had been von Rath, and Baldur, and Gall, and the guards.

It was a very real possibility that he was a lunatic, who had dreamed all the complexities of his former life – dreamed of Tally, and his children, and the calm peace of the Drowned Lands – while incarcerated in a madhouse somewhere. That Tom and Sara were right. That he was only imagining that he could see his friends in this fragment of glass he'd picked up in a corner of the washroom in the Frankfurt-am-Oder station, and that he only believed he was in control of the actions of others when they did not pay attention to him.

It certainly made more sense than his own version of events.

Yet try as he would, he could conjure no picture of a former life, no 'rational explanation' for his escape save cause and effect . . . no reason why von Rath and the SS would be so interested in the madness of one patently Jewish lunatic. But if he were mad, perhaps the pursuit was as illusory as the rest of it?

He shook his head, exhausted and eroded and cold to the marrow of his bones.

If he was mad, he was left with nothing – only this bleak train-station, with its clean-painted white walls and its posters of noble Aryan manhood in uniform performing feats of heroism under the dingy electric glare.

If he was sane, he was left with only the standing-stones, and the hope that Shavus had somehow heard his cry three months ago – the hope that it had only been some unforeseen hitch which had prevented the Archmage from gathering the requisite congregation of wizards to reach across the Void and bring him back. The hope that, in the precarious moments of the Universe's balance at midnight of the Equinox, he could somehow raise enough power to open a gate in the fabric of Being.

And beyond the standing-stones there was nothing. Exile from Germany – exile from his own world forever – at the rosiest stretch of hysterical optimism. Or death. He'd been around the SS long enough – he knew von Rath well enough – to know that a bullet in the back of the neck was another exercise in rosy optimism.

He closed his eyes, not wanting to think about the endless walk from Kegenwald to Torweg, while the sun-tides gathered, and he waited for the night.

Twenty-four hours, he thought. In twenty-four hours it would all be over, one way or the other. He would be at the stones at midnight . . . It was his final chance.

Outside the church-clock struck four. By the electric

stove at the far end of the room the guard rustled a newspaper, the station-attendant asked whether it looked like there'd be war with Russia.

Rhion opened his eyes, and looked again at the glass.

And realized where Tom and Sara were.

The dark bulk behind them was the bed where he himself had slept during those almost three months. The white glow of the floodlights lay in cross-barred patches over the beaky dark shape of Rebbe Leibnitz's forehead and nose. The chair where Saltwood and Sara curled together in a tight knot of trust was the one where he'd sat endless hours, peering at his broken piece of scrying-glass alone.

They were at Schloss Torweg.

Rhion lowered his forehead to his hand and thought, *No. PLEASE, no.*

They must have come after him.

And somehow stumbled into Nazi hands. Evidently von Rath hadn't completely shut up the Schloss when they'd come to Berlin for the demonstration.

If they were there the place would be guarded. He thought about what it would take, the strength it would need to work the requisite spells, the drain on the last thin reserve he was keeping to catch the momentum of the Universe, to fling across the Void in the hopes of reaching the furthest extent of Shavus' power . . .

He couldn't do it.

His power was exhausted.

In any case he doubted he could do it before midnight. And if he wasn't at the stones at midnight . . .

Sitting slumped on the bench, shivering in his long black coat, Rhion cursed for several minutes in German, in Polish, in Yiddish and in his own rich, half-forgotten tongue. Then he got to his feet, stiff and aching and leaning on his crystal-headed staff, and wondered where in Kegenwald it would be possible to buy black-market chocolate.

26

It was afternoon when Saltwood woke up, feeling worse than he'd felt since his teen-aged bar-fighting days in Tulsa. There were other similarities to those days, too, besides the general sensation of having gone to sleep wadded up in the bottom of a clothes hamper after having been thoroughly beaten with a chair: the gluey stickiness in his mouth, the feeling that his eyeballs had been deep-fried, and the sleeping presence in his arms of a woman whose existence he hadn't even suspected forty-eight hours ago.

The differences were that he was starving hungry instead of nauseated by the mere mention of food, that he felt awe and admiration as well as tenderness for the woman curled up against his chest, and that her father was sitting on the floor six feet away, rocking back and forth whispering Hebrew magic to himself.

It was the day of the autumn equinox. The twenty-third of September. Tomorrow – unless by some miracle Rhion Sligo could avoid capture – the invasion of England was going to start, spearheaded by Paul von Rath and whatever infernal device was controlled by the iron Spiracle. That the device in some fashion caused the most believable hallucinations this side of the soft room was beyond question. Whether it could or couldn't affect the weather or blow things up at a distance was undecided, but that first effect would be enough to give the Luftwaffe the edge they needed over the RAF. Hell, he thought, they might be able to use it to fox that secret early-warning system the Brits were said to be using – who knew?

He knew already that with von Rath and his men waiting for Sligo on Witches Hill tonight both rescue and assassination were out of the question. There were simply too many of them – in the face of those odds his own recapture would be a foregone conclusion. Everything within him might revolt at the thought of leaving the device and its hapless inventor in the hands of the Nazis, but at the moment the thing of paramount importance was to get word back to England somehow, and warn them at least what to expect.

And here he was, the only man who might possibly be able to save England, locked up in a Gothic mansion in Prussia with a woman he suspected he was falling in love with and a lunatic rabbi.

Cautiously so as not to wake Sara he wormed his way out of the worn plush chair, gritting his teeth at the thought of what straightening his back was going to be like. Bar-fights with the oil company goons, he decided, had nothing on explosions and car-crashes. Clutching at furniture and cursing all the way, he stumbled into the little wash-room – barred and secured as tight as the main bedroom – that adjoined it.

After dashing cold water on his face – which didn't help – he studied himself for a moment in the mirror. No wonder Sara'd had second thoughts about sitting on his knee. There was a cut on his forehead and a blackening bruise on his cheek he hadn't even noticed from the crash last night, as well as an itchy pyrite glitter of stubble. No razor, of course. Considering the amount of time the Professor must have spent in places where they wouldn't give him a razor it was no wonder he wore a beard.

When he came out, finger-combing his short fair hair back from his face, Sara was awake, and her smile when she saw him reduced Hitler, the war, von Rath, the invasion of England, the fact that he was surrounded by candidates for the funny farm and stood in immediate danger of being killed to inconsequential sidelights.

'You look awful,' he said conversationally, and Sara

grinned back, shoving the red-streaked raven tangle of hair back from her bruised face.

'Well, your resemblance to Clark Gable at the moment isn't strong enough to knock me down. I feel like I fell down a flight of stairs.'

He nodded towards her father. 'What's he up to?'

'About the eighth Sephiroth.' The old man had chalked a giant diagram on the floor before him, three interlocked lines of circles connected by trails of Hebrew letters and surrounded by a cloud of jotted notes in the same writing. 'It's the Tree of Life, supposedly the diagram of the way the Universe works. Meditating on it and calling on the names of the angels of each Sephiroth – each of those little circles – you're supposed to be able to summon sparks of holy fire down from the Outer Aether to help you out with your spells.'

He leaned his shoulders against the wall, hands hooked in his pockets, and studied the complicated maze of abracadabra scribbled across the grey floorboards. 'He know any?'

'Sure.' She got to her feet and began gingerly twisting her back and shoulders, her black brows pulled together in pain. 'Call up fabulous wealth, yes; fame and fortune, yes; the wisdom of Solomon, yes; avert an Evil Eye the size of Ebbets Field, yes; but unlock the door? Nah!' She winced at an incautious movement of her neck, and added, 'Ow! Aunt Tayta always told me never to go driving with American boys and by damn she was right. Those *chozzers* took my cigarettes, too.'

She padded over to him in her stockinged feet, the SS jacket still wrapped stole-wise around her shoulders, the sunlight from the window calling electric gleams of copper and cinnabar from the red portion of her hair as she looked out at the men moving in the yard below. By the light Tom calculated it was just past one o'clock, and more or less warm.

'They all look pretty real to me,' he commented, and Sara gave a wry chuckle.

'He must have called in reinforcements from Kegenwald,' she said after a moment. 'The ones in the grey field-dress are Waffen from the camp – I recognize a couple of them. The ones in black must be those Pauli brought with him from Berlin.'

Tom frowned. There were, in fact, not very many of those, not nearly as many as he'd seen when they were taken last night.

'Look,' he said quietly, still keeping to English. 'They were serious about your father, weren't they?'

She nodded.

'When will they come for him?'

'A little before sundown. They have to – to make certain preparations in the Temple.'

'They'll probably take you away then, too, if they're going to use you as a hostage when they wait for Rhion up on Witches Hill. Since they haven't tried to feed us so far we'd better not count on anyone coming in before that.' He took a deep breath, knowing what he had to say next and hating the expediency of it, hating those dry odds of life and death. 'You know if we do manage to get out of here we can't stick around to save him.'

Her mouth compressed hard, but she said nothing.

'The only place we know where to find him, they'll be there, too. And right now the thing that has to be done is to get word back to England. With luck we might – just – make it to Danzig by morning. That's the bottom line, Sara. I'm sorry.'

For a moment he was afraid she'd suggest that she remain and attempt the rescue, but she didn't. Her square, thin shoulders relaxed; her breath blew in a soft sigh of defeat. 'I know. I probably couldn't make it through to Danzig by myself and anyhow I wouldn't know who to get in contact with – I could be Gestapo for all your contacts know . . .'

And if you were killed I don't think I could stand it. He bit his tongue on the words, a little surprised even at himself. But there was something inside him that had lost one too many things, one too many people, in the course of his life. The thought of losing her before they'd even properly begun was a darkness he couldn't bear to face.

'. . . and anyhow,' she finished, her face still turned away, 'I couldn't leave Papa. No.' Then she shrugged, and chuckled grimly, looking up at him with bitter amusement in her eyes. 'What the hell are we talking about anyway? We're never gonna get out of here.'

His voice was very quiet. 'I'll be fast.' Their eyes met, and he saw the fear in hers.

'You'll still be . . .'

'Rhion?'

Leibnitz' whisper brought both their heads around sharply. The old man was bent over the fragment of mirror-glass he held cupped in his palm, his open eyes fixed upon it with an odd, glazed expression. In German he said 'Rhion, is this you, can you hear me?' And he leaned down towards the glass, a listening expression on his face.

Saltwood tiptoed soundlessly up behind him, Sara close at his side. Looking down over the old man's shoulder he could see only a broken triangle of Leibnitz's lined face reflected in the glass.

'Rhion,' breathed the old man, 'a door-unlocker spell I need, fast, and whatever you do to make them not see you.'

They traded glances. Sara's expression was one of deep concern and pity, but Saltwood felt the hairs creep on the back of his neck as Leibnitz added querulously, 'No, I don't know what kind locks they are!' His exasperated tone was exactly that of a man having an argument on the telephone. 'They're the locks on your room at the Schloss!'

There was a long silence. Baffled, Saltwood stepped

around in front of him to watch his eyes. At the move the old man's head jerked up. 'Don't step on the . . .'

Saltwood looked down at the lines of chalk under his feet.

Leibnitz relaxed in disgust, straightening his bowed back, and finished, '. . . Tree. And now we have lost him.' He held out his other hand to Sara, and she had to almost lift him to his feet.

'Papa . . .' she began worriedly.

'Come,' he cut her off, staggering as he turned towards the door so that she had to catch him again. Saltwood realized the old scholar had been sitting in meditation all night. The room had been far from warm, and his injuries had stiffened; he was lucky he could stand. It didn't seem to have affected the calm serenity of his madness. 'We got no time to lose.'

'Papa, for crying out loud . . .'

'You got a better way to spend the afternoon waiting for them to come kill us?'

Pretty inarguable. Saltwood hid a grin and turned back to the window, rubbing absently where the manacle of the cut-off handcuff still chafed his left wrist and studying the yard once more. Electrified fence, though that wouldn't be on during the day when the main gate was open. The Schloss stood on high ground, sloping down on three sides outside the perimeter of the fence. All the land around the bottom of its little rise was clear. Only on the side towards the hills did the pines crowd in close on the fence, though there was still a gap of thirty feet. He couldn't see any vehicles from here, though the guards last night had had an LG-3000 and the Waffen Troopers had to have got here somehow from Kegenwald. Stealing something from Kegenwald village looked more promising, though it would be a hell of a hike. They could get food there, too, and be on the main road east to Danzig.

But, as Sara had said, what the hell was he talking about? They still had to get out of the room.

He turned around to study the layout of the place once more just in time to see Leibnitz open the door.

'We've got to destroy the Resonator!' whispered Leibnitz urgently. 'At the cost of our own lives the thing has got to be destroyed!'

'The hell it has,' muttered Saltwood back, keeping a firm grip on the old man's skinny arm. There was no guard in the upstairs hall, but he could hear them below, lots of them, as they slipped into the little dressing-room next door and down the old backstairs. 'If they're getting ready for some kind of fandango at sunset that Temple's gonna be crawling. What we've got to do is get the hell out of here.'

In broad daylight? demanded the part of his mind that still didn't believe Leibnitz had picked the lock on the door. It had to have been jammed, or not caught in the first place – Jesus, what an idiot he'd been for testing all the window-bars six times and not thinking to check whether the lock on the door had really caught! But he was positive he *had* checked. Anyway, they could have been in Danzig by this time.

Across – what? – thirty feet of open ground and under the wire?

The insanity around here must be contagious. Rebbe Leibnitz certainly seemed to believe he'd received instructions for invisibility through a two-by-three-inch chunk of broken mirror, but Saltwood was still wondering how he'd been talked into making a break for it under those circumstances.

Perhaps, he thought, as Sara opened the door to the lightless and mildew-stinking pit of the backstairs, because they had no choice. If they stuck around they were dead meat anyway, and being the only three people in the history of Nazism who actually *were* shot while trying to escape beat hell out of getting asked questions by the Gestapo. So in the long run it probably didn't matter.

And just as they reached the end door of the old service-wing, a fight broke out on the other side of the Schloss.

The noise was unmistakable – from the Tulsa oil-fields to the West Virginia mines, in the migrant camps of California and every dockside bar from New York to San Francisco, it was the same – the way every Storm Trooper, whether von Rath's black-uniformed goons or the grey-clothed stooges from Kegenwald, dropped whatever they were doing and ran around the corner of the building. God knew what it was about, thought Saltwood – *Cigarettes, at a guess, since there're no women around.*

It's damn convenient, he reflected, as the three of them walked rapidly across to the wire and Tom held it up for Sara and her father to slip under, then rolled through the little gully himself. *But it ain't magic.*

They crossed the open ground, and disappeared into the woods beyond.

'There's a big farm about three miles this side of Kegenwald where they've got a Hillman Minx up on blocks,' panted Sara, striding as rapidly as she could under the added burden of helping her father. 'The owner's one of the local Party bosses. He used to see me when I was – ah – tending bar in town . . .'

'*Kayn ayhora*,' groaned Leibnitz. 'You lay on top of the piano and sang songs too?'

'Don't gripe, Papa, it's how I found you. Anyhow,' she went on hastily, 'once they find out we're gone they'll sure as hell guard the camp and may be able to spare a patrol or two in town, but they can't cover all the farms . . .'

'A Minx is a trashcan!'

'It's the newest car in the neighbourhood – besides, the Nazi *chozzer*'s got a tractor too we can steal the battery out of, and there'll be petrol. He wangles the rationing.'

'Let's hope he wangles oil and grease as well,' grumbled Tom, wading ahead through a waist-deep pocket of soft autumn bracken. 'Minxes *eat* grease – if we can't get some we're gonna be walking to Danzig.'

'Danzig, shmanzig,' muttered Leibnitz, balking as his daughter tried to hurry him over the uneven ground. 'If we don't go back and destroy that Resonator this whole thing is pointless.'

'When we radio for a pickup in Danzig I'll ask for an airstrike, how's that?' said Saltwood, more to pacify him than because he had any intention of demanding bombers which would, he suspected, be desperately needed on the southern beaches by morning.

'And what makes you think they'll be able to find it?' demanded the rabbi, limping heavily, his dark eyes grim in the shadow of his billed cap. 'What makes you think they won't crash on the way, the same way they're going to crash when they come against the Luftwaffe over the Channel?'

'Oh, hell, Papa, if they've got the device out at the Channel they can't use it to guard the Resonator here, can they?' added Sara.

'You don't understand! The Resonator . . .'

'Don't worry about it,' snapped Saltwood, feeling like he was in an argument with a six-year-old about where the Lone Ranger gets his silver bullets from. 'Let's take first things first.'

'The car,' said Sara.

'No – food.'

'Destroying the Resonator should be the first thing . . .'

Saltwood sighed. It was going to be a long, long way to Tiperary.

It had been a number of years since Saltwood had had occasion to live entirely off the countryside. In Spain he and his mates had usually been able to scrounge a meal out of republican partisans, even if it had only been bread and goat-cheese. But the memories of his hobo days, of riding the rails in search of work or travelling to organize for the union, stood him in good stead now.

Sara, a denizen of the streets first of Warsaw, then of New York, looked askance at the berries he gathered from the hedges and stared at him in disbelief when he offered her a handful of rose-hips. 'You sure they're not poison?'

At the far end of a pasture he cut a milk-cow out of a small herd – 'This was easier when I had a horse,' – and improvised a pail from a tin can found in a ditch and washed out in one of the ponds which dotted the countryside. 'For somebody who looks like a big dumb farmboy you know a lot . . .'

'For a Yankees fan,' he replied with a grin, 'you're not too bad yourself.'

She stuck out her tongue at him and handed the improvised cup on to her father. It was good to be in the open air again. Purely aside from the swarms of SS goons, lunatics, and self-proclaimed wizards that had thronged it, there was something Tom had definitely not liked about that house. The rough country of sandy pine hills and isolated farmsteads through which they travelled, swinging wide to avoid the roads whenever they could, slowed them down but kept them out of sight of whatever authorities might be around; it also impressed on Saltwood the impossibility of intercepting Rhion before the Professor walked into von Rath's trap.

'Poor little bastard,' he remarked, keeping a weather eye down the farm-track beside whose weed-grown ditch they had paused to rest. The sun was touching the tips of the pine-cloaked hills to the west, gilding the throw-pillow clouds heaped around it and covering all the eastwards lands in a pall of cold blue shadow. 'I wish there was something we could do for him. I wouldn't leave a dog to the SS, but he's the one who ducked out on us.'

And if it wasn't for him and his stubbornness about returning to those damn stones we wouldn't even BE in this mess.

As if she read his mind Sara sighed, and shook her head. She'd grown quieter during the day's long hike, exhaustion and hunger slowing her down more than she'd counted on, though up until an hour or so ago she'd still frothed every time Saltwood had insisted they take a rest. 'I felt terrible, you know, watching him standing there on that stupid stone with his hands upraised, waiting. Like watching – I don't know. Some poor *goyische* kid on Christmas Eve waiting for Santa Claus.' Sitting on a felled and rotting fence-post she pitched a pebble across the narrow road into the thickets of brown sedge and fireweed. She glanced up at Tom. 'You ever have Santa not show up, cowboy?'

He shook his head, remembering paper-chains and popcorn strings, and the line of shabby stockings pinned to the wall near the belly-stove – Tom-John-Kathy-Helen-Shanna-Ma'n'Pa. He still rattled off the family names as they all had, as a single word, and smiled a little at the memory. He'd spent a year searching for Ma and the girls, and still wondered what had become of them, and if there was something else he should have done.

'Nope. Sometimes he didn't bring a whole lot, but he always showed.' He glanced at the sky. 'It'll be dark in an hour,' he said quietly. 'We've got to stick closer to the roads if we're not going to get lost.'

'They'll know we're gone now.' She pulled the scuffed jacket closer around her and rubbed her hands. The evening was cold already, and from the feel of the air, by morning there would be hard frost. 'They'll be hunting.'

'They'll be sore as wet cats,' said Tom, 'but as bad as they want Sligo and that patented whizzbang of his, most of their men will be up at the hill. There's just too much territory for them to cover to find us.' He held a hand down, and helped Sara and her father, who had sat silent, numbed with exhaustion, to their feet. If they didn't get a vehicle soon the old man wouldn't be able to go on, and Saltwood didn't like to think about what might happen in that event. Sara might realize the impossibility of risking England's defeat to go back for Rhion, but she'd never leave her father. And in that case . . .

He pushed the thought of that decision away. *First things first.* He shrugged his shoulders deeper into his scarred and bullet-holed jacket, and revised his estimate of times again to allow for a slower pace.

It was an hour after full dark, and icily cold, when they saw the first of the lights.

A bluish ghost-flicker of ball-lightning far to their right in the trees; catching a glimpse from the corner of his eye Tom halted in his tracks, but when he scanned the rustling darkness it was gone. 'What is it?' asked Sara quickly, looking up at him in the gloom, and her father, taking advantage of the halt, leaned against a pine-trunk, his hand pressed, as it had been more and more frequently, to his chest.

Saltwood shivered, wondering just what kind of powers the Resonator – whatever it did – gave to von Rath, and at how great a distance. '*Nada*,' he breathed. 'Let's get moving.'

The second light flickered a hundred yards ahead of them ten minutes later, and this time they saw it clear. Over head-high – ten, twelve feet above the tips of the bracken and weeds – it bathed the delicate fans of dry foliage around it with cold dim light for a few seconds, then vanished as inexplicably as it had come. Distantly Saltwood thought he heard a truck pass on the road which their course had paralleled since dark. It was hardly unusual for a rural district on a clear autumn evening, but something inside him prickled a warning. 'Move back into the woods.'

The third light flickered into being closer still and to their left a few minutes later, and after a short time appeared again, near enough to shine on their upturned faces. It was small, the size of a child's hand, a round blue-white bubble like the glow around some innermost seed of brightness. The chilly light reminded Saltwood of something . . . candlelit darkness . . . the phosphor reflection in upturned glasses . . . They pressed on, both of them supporting Leibnitz now, deeper into the blackness between the trees. Increasing cold made their breath steam and stung the inside of his nostrils. The old man, who still adamantly refused to wear any part of the SS uniform, had begun to shiver.

Then that glowworm brightness glimmered into being directly over their heads, and somewhere not too far behind them he heard the muffled confusion of men's voices.

'Christ, they're trackers!'

'Can you kill it?' whispered Saltwood, turning to Leibnitz and not even thinking about what that question implied. 'Or send it someplace else?'

'I . . . I think . . .' The old scholar frowned, his high forehead corrugating into thick lines of concentration as he held onto the younger man's broad shoulder. Above their heads the light faded, wavered a little where it hung, then slowly began to drift away.

Mental powers, decided Saltwood. *A brain-wave amplification device and to hell with your ethylene and platinum, Saraleh.* Unless it was sheer coincidence . . . He tightened his grip around the old man's ribcage and headed up the rising ground. Glancing back he saw the light bobble uncertainly and go out.

'I – Rhion said . . .' The old man spoke with difficulty, his eyes shut, still concentrating hard. 'He said a wizard . . . cannot scry the presence of another wizard . . . The Resonator field . . .'

They were right at the feet of a line of low moraine hills, nearly invisible above them in a vast looming bulk of pine-trees, and the countryside here was littered with granite boulders half-buried in weeds and sedge. Saltwood left father and daughter in the dark blot of one such outcrop's shadow, moved softly back towards the oncoming swish of boots in bracken, flexing his hands. In the shadows of the trees it was almost impossible to see, save where the starlight caught on silver and on the blued gleam of a rifle-barrel. A nervous guttural voice whispered something about '*Die Hexenlichte* . . .'

Tom rose out of the bracken almost under the Trooper's feet. It was very fast – grab, strangle, twist, and then the man's body was sinking down into the deep pocket of brown fern, and Tom was moving off, dagger, sidearm, rifle in his hands. He supposed he should have stopped to strip the coat but it would have occupied dangerous seconds – the man's companions weren't fifty feet away among the pitchy shadows of the trees – and Leibnitz would have put up a fight about wearing it anyway.

The old man was shuddering, his eyes pressed shut, his breathing the rasp of a saw, when Saltwood reached their hiding-place again. Without looking up Leibnitz whispered 'I can't . . . He is stronger than I. I feel his will pressing on me . . . his strength . . . The talismans he has made . . . Ach, that strength . . .'

Dimly, blue lights began to flicker and weave among the black pine-needles overhead.

Saltwood handed Sara the rifle and dragged Leibnitz to his feet. 'Move!'

Behind them someone yelled.

Lights were bobbing everywhere now, the yellow lances of flashlight beams springing on, zagging wildly among the trees. Tiny balls of witchlight, purplish flecks of St Elmo's Fire, swirled like fireflies overhead, and against him Saltwood could feel Leibnitz sobbing for breath as they ran. The lights broke and scattered, but it was like trying to elude a swarm of softly shining hornets – they re-formed, drifted, darting here and there in a numinous cloud. Had Sara been Saltwood's only companion he would have told her to head in another direction to split the pursuit, but knew she was as exhausted as he, and unable to manage her father's unwieldy bulk alone.

Leave her. He could just hear Hillyard saying it. *It's your duty to warn England, your duty not to be taken no matter what the cost . . .*

Stick my bloody duty. He shoved aside the image of the RAF Spitfires crashing on the Sussex beaches in flames. Rhion had said, *I didn't risk what's going to happen to me to work for the people who were dropping those bombs . . .*

The words echoed in his mind. *What the hell's the point of defeating the Nazis if you become one inside?* 'There anyplace to go?' he gasped, as they thrashed their way up the high ground, dodging trees and flashlights, stumbling over rocks half-buried in the pine-mast and ferns. 'Cover, anything?'

'Not with those frigging lights overhead there's not!' In the blue glow the sweat made points of her dark hair around that pale triangular face, moisture gleaming on her cheeks in spite of the cold that turned their breath to steam.

Creepers, wild ivy and morning-glory, snagged at their feet, branches slashed their faces as they stumbled on. Leibnitz gasped '. . . strength is growing . . . talismans . . . all those deaths . . . He can use it . . . Equinox . . . midnight . . .'

Midnight. It must be close to that. Rhion would walk slap into the ring of SS troopers on Witches Hill . . . von Rath would head for Ostend in the morning with the Spiracle to take part in the invasion . . . The Brits wouldn't get so much as a warning as to what was coming up the beaches, out of the skies . . . until their pilots bailed out because of imaginary cockpit-fires or imaginary monsters chewing on the wings. The lights poured around them in a bluish cloud. Stumbling under Leibnitz's weight Saltwood couldn't imagine why they hadn't been shot yet . . .

The ground fell out from under them so abruptly it was only Saltwood's hair-trigger reflexes that kept them from going over. He felt the gravelly clay crumble under his boots before he actually saw anything but darkness ahead, and flung himself back, catching Sara and her father. Beyond the last overhanging thickets of dead and dying undergrowth the road lay at the bottom of a twelve-foot bank where it cut through the saddle of land between the hills. Blue light flooded them as they skidded to a halt on its brink, searchlight-bright, only it blazed from over their heads: the glow of witchfire, of magelight . . . of magic.

There were two covered trucks and an open Mercedes down on the road below, with half a dozen Storm Troopers grouped around them. Baldur – the godlike golden SS Baldur, not the podgy, bespectacled Baldur Twisselpeck from Berlin – was at the wheel of the car, and as the guards levelled their submachine-guns on the fugitives, Paul von Rath stood up in the back seat, Lucifer ascendant in fire and shadow and rage.

27

'Bring them down.'

Saltwood had already heard the men come up behind him, crowding out of the shadows of the trees. With a bitter oath Sara turned, bringing up her rifle, but the range was already too close. A trooper tore it out of her hand and shoved her backwards over the edge of the bank. Saltwood, hampered by Leibnitz's full weight, was only starting to turn when three rifle-barrels thrust into his back, and then he was falling, too, rolling down a slide of desiccated ivy and fern in a tangle of arms and legs.

He landed hard in a cold puddle of water, started to rise, and was struck over the back of the head by somebody's gun-butt, driving him to his hands and knees. Gun and dagger were ripped from his belt before he recovered enough to think about committing suicide by putting up a fight.

'Put the Jew in the truck,' went on that calm, soft voice, shaking now with an inner core of blinding rage. 'Bind him, gag him, blindfold him. Baldur, remain with him, as he seems to be able to twist the powers we have released to his own corrupt and dirty spells.'

Raising his head Tom could see the golden youth and three or four Storm Troopers cross to where Leibnitz lay face-down in the wet yellow leaves of the roadside ditch. They picked the old man up, a broken scarecrow with his patched grey clothing and emaciated limbs. Only when they were halfway to one of the covered trucks did Leibnitz show by the feeble, disoriented movements of returning consciousness that he was still alive. Baldur struck him.

'*You goddam Nazi coward . . . !*' Sara flung herself

towards them but was caught, easily, by two Storm Troopers – Saltwood lunged to his feet more to protect her than to go after Baldur the Beautiful, and the men behind him had been waiting for that. The struggle wasn't long.

'Bind the whore and put her in the other truck,' said von Rath calmly, still standing in the back seat of the open Mercedes, Satan in uniform, the thick chain of talismans lying like a hellish emblem of office over shoulders and breast. Those that had been made of jewels seemed to burn in the shadowless blue magelight that flickered all around him, and even those wrought of bone and skin and twisted hair pulsed, in that strange radiance, with something that might have been a kind of light but was more probably, Saltwood thought distractedly, a reflection sparked from the jewels, or the silver on his uniform, or something . . . some rational explanation . . . In some odd way those dead and mounted mementos of past sacrifices seemed more living than von Rath's eyes.

The wizard went on, 'We have just time to reach Witches Hill, if we drive fast. Gall is waiting there already but with our hostage guaranteed now we should have no trouble. So the night will not be totally lost. But you . . .' He turned to Saltwood, and a spiteful vindictiveness crept into his voice. 'By leading this escape you have cost me the power I could have raised through an Equinox sacrifice. You have almost cost me what I could have had from a second sacrifice, the sacrifice of a wizard, for without his Jewish whore as hostage he would not have let himself be taken alive. You will pay for that.'

Saltwood felt something twist inside of him, a sharp stab of pain in his entrails, like the appendicitis he'd had as a kid. He bit his lip, gasping, trying not to cry out, but the pain grew, turning his knees to water. For a moment the men who were holding him took his weight; then they dropped him to the icy and broken pavement of the road.

Christ, he thought, *what is this . . . ?* all the while curling tighter over himself, tighter, retching as red claws ripped at him inside, like taking a bayonet in the gut, worse . . . He heard Sara cursing, was dimly aware of her fighting like a wildcat against the men who held her, men who were staring from him to von Rath's cool face and back with growing uneasy horror. He tasted blood and bile in his mouth, blood trickling from his nose, and his teeth shut on a scream, fighting to keep himself from screaming *Stop it! STOP IT! PLEASE!!* and thinking *Bastard, I won't give that to you . . .* Powder-trails of pain and fire ignited along every nerve, burning up his flesh, it was all he could do not to scream and he could feel that, too, coming . . .

Then the pain was over and he was lying on the wet gravel, weak and shaking and scared as he had never been scared before. Cloudily he was aware of a man swearing, 'Bite me, you Jew bitch . . . !' and von Rath's voice, querulous and peremptory, commanding, 'No!'

Looking up, Tom saw one of the guards who'd been holding Sara shaking his bloodied hand, the other still gripping her, his fist frozen in mid-draw.

Von Rath shook his head, his brows pulling slightly together, the expression of a man puzzled by something he has done flickering, very briefly, to life in his inhuman eyes. His soft voice had a halting note. 'We – We have no time for this.' He passed his hand across his eyes and then the expression was gone, but for a moment Tom had the impression the SS wizard had been too involved in his own display of power to remember even the necessity of capturing Sligo alive. As if, for the moment of the exercise of his power, he had forgotten, literally, everything.

Then he looked back at Saltwood, the inhuman calm returning to his eyes. 'I must . . .' A last fragment of uncertainty flawed his voice, then was gone. 'I must try this again with someone of equal strength.' His glance shifted to the guards. 'Kill him.'

Saltwood felt the barrel of an automatic press the back of his neck and heard the trigger pull.

Only the silence after Sara's scream 'TOM!' made it possible to hear the flat click of the hammer coming down.

As if he didn't quite believe that nothing had happened the guard pulled the trigger twice more, the clicks very loud now in the growing silence that spread among the men gathered beneath the cold umbrella of phosphor light, and all heads turned, not to von Rath, but to the dark of the road beyond.

Beyond the range of the corpse-candle glow, feral starlight caught in the lenses of glasses, in the five crystals of the Spiracle at the head of a staff. Then darkness fell, blinding and total, and Saltwood whipped one leg behind him and jerked down the guard with the gun, smashing the man's head on the pavement and ripping the dagger from his belt while noise erupted all around him, a chaos of shouts, curses, the crunch of boots and the slap of bodies running head-foremost into the sides of trucks.

Then the darkness split, lightning tearing down in splattering flame as the bolts hit the road where Rhion had stood. In the white-purple glare Tom saw Sara standing still a foot or so away and grabbed her wrist as darkness slammed down on them again, some instinct telling him to pull her away from the truck behind her. An instant later the vehicle burst into flames that illuminated a milling chaos of black- and grey-uniformed men surging all around them.

'Papa . . . !' yelled Sara as the bushes on both sides of the road went up, and lunged for the second truck. For the first time Saltwood noticed she, too, had acquired a dagger, and at the same moment almost tripped over the body of the Storm Trooper whom von Rath had stopped in the act of striking her. Baldur the Beautiful met her in the dark arch of the truck's canvas cover, his own dagger held point-down for the overhead stab favoured by Hollywood directors – Saltwood hurled him easily aside into the path of another advancing Trooper. Sara was already dragging her stunned father from the back of the truck; Tom kicked another attacker in the groin, grabbed the old man's arm, and as the second truck burst into flames bolted for the dark of the road cut where Rhion had last been seen.

Underfoot the potholed pavement heaved and split, hurling the three of them to their knees. Its centre buckled upward, pulling apart to spew forth what seemed, for a hideous second in the holocaust of shadows, to be black things, shining, living, glittering and crawling among a sticky ooze of glowing greenish slime. The next instant fire swept across it and the things were still – pebbles, Saltwood thought dimly, scrambling back into the shelter of a granite boulder which projected from the tall road-bank – only pebbles and water after all, but burning, burning in impossible flame . . .

Lightning struck the bracken of the opposite bank, the dry brush roaring up in a screen of incandescent gold. A dark figure broke from it a second before it flared, darting across the lowering flames that still flickered on the pavement as if every crack and pothole were filled with gasoline. Another levin-bolt cracked, tearing the road to pieces behind them, and then Rhion rolled into the shelter of the boulder, face streaming sweat as if he'd plunged it into a sink.

'They took that Resonator you made to the Schloss,' gasped Saltwood. 'Whatever the hell it does . . .'

'He still thinks it's a Flash Gordon death-ray,' chipped in Leibnitz, as were-light exploded around them and Rhion flinched and gasped.

'Yeah, I figured that out.' He was holding himself upright on the staff, his face drawn with pain – Saltwood remembered as if from a nightmare the gut-rending agony von Rath had . . . *willed on him? But that was impossible* . . . Then Rhion drew a deep breath, and the pain seemed to ease. But in his blue eyes the haunted look of darkness remained, of grief and hopeless loss.

It was, Saltwood realized, only minutes short of midnight. Quite quietly, he said, 'Sorry we made you miss your bus.'

'Not your fault.' Lightning flashed again, striking at the boulder behind which they crouched and seeming to shatter off it, splattering in all directions and running down the stone in lapis rivulets of fire.

'Gall's waiting for you up there, you know – or at least he was. He's probably hot-footing it back here as fast as he can to cut us off.'

Rhion nodded. Beneath the brown tangle of his beard his face was ashy and taut with pain, his breathing a ragged gasp.

'We couldn't warn you . . .'

'This flat-footed goyischer *shlemeil* stepped on the Tree of Life before I could tell you . . .'

'It's all right. I'd hoped . . .' He gasped, averting his face for a moment, his whole body shuddering under the renewed onslaught of pain. Leibnitz reached quickly up, his bony, age-spotted hands folding over the smooth pudgy ones where they clung to the wood of the staff. For an instant Saltwood felt a burn of heat on his back, smelled scorching wool – then with a cry he saw spots of flame spring up on the back of Sara's jacket. He struck them out, panicked and disoriented, feeling heat breathe on his face, his hair . . .

Then it was gone, and Rhion was straightening up again, shaking, as if his strength had gone with it. 'I can't . . .' he whispered. 'He has the talismans . . . all their power, drawn into himself . . . Poincelles, and the strength of the Summer Solstice. All the sacrifices they did . . .' He shook his head. In a small voice he added, 'And he was stronger than me from the start.'

Slowly, between the surface of the rock and Sara's shoulder, Leibnitz levered himself to his feet. 'It will be midnight soon,' he said softly, and Rhion nodded. Under the scratched spectacles and the sweaty points of his hair his eyes were shut. Sara's image sprang to Saltwood's mind again, of the mad Professor standing on his magic stones, arms outspread, waiting to be taken away by wizards and enchantments that never came.

Dimly, from down the road beyond them, the growl of truck motors could be heard. A moment later hooded headlights flashed into view, and standing up in the lead truck's open cab Saltwood made out the long white mane and silvery beard of the wizard Gall, cutting them off from any hope of flight.

On their other side von Rath had stepped forth into the roadway. The blazes that still flickered, impossibly, on the riven asphalt sank; the ranks of Storm Troopers formed up behind him like a wing of darkness and steel. A nimbus of shadow seemed to surround the Nazi wizard himself, that queer, eldritch, spider-shot aura that Saltwood had once or twice thought he'd seen from the corner of his eye floating near the Spiracle. But this darkness was growing, spreading, lifting like a column of smoke around a core of lightless flame.

'Can you run for it?' asked Rhion quietly.

'Are you kidding? With Gall and his stooges behind us and von Rath able to zap us the minute we . . .'

Rhion shook his head, and for an instant, from the corner of his eye, Saltwood had the same strange sense he'd had before about the Spiracle – that the shadow-twin of the darkness which surrounded von Rath gathered there like a veil of impossibly fine black silk, shot through with invisible silver. Its crystals seemed to have caught the cold glitter of the stars, but no stars at all could be seen, now, through the centre of its iron ring. Saltwood wasn't sure what it was that he *did* see there, in that terrible, shining abyss.

'No.' Rhion's voice was barely audible, his eyes, not on Saltwood, but on von Rath's advancing form. 'No. It will be all right. It was my fault – my doing . . . But it will be all right.'

His face like chalk, Rhion stepped from cover and walked to the centre of the charred and rutted ruin of the road. Gall called out something and men sprang down from the truck and started to run forward, but something about that solitary brown figure made them hesitate and stumble to a halt.

In the silence of midnight, Rhion held up the staff in both his hands.

It seemed to Saltwood that the lightning came down from five separate points of the heavens – heavens deep and star-powdered and impossibly clear. They hit the head of the staff and for one second he thought the darkness – the veil – the whatever-it-was that had always seemed to hang there invisibly – was illuminated with a horrible electric limmerance that speared out in all directions along those silver spider-strands.

Von Rath shouted 'NO!' in a voice of rage and disbelief and inhuman despair.

And the very air seemed to explode.

Von Rath screamed.

It was like twenty men screaming, a hundred – dunked into acid, eaten by rats, rolled in fire that wouldn't die. The chain of amulets around his neck burst simultaneously into – not flame, but something else, something worse, something Saltwood had never seen before – something that sheathed the Nazi wizard in searing brightness even as it sank into his flesh, eating into him as fire streamed back out of every orifice of his body, as if he had been ignited by that lightning from within. The screaming seemed to go on for minutes but couldn't have lasted for more than twenty seconds or so, while Rhion stood braced, the glare of the lightning that never ceased to pour like water down into the head of the staff blazing off his glasses, and von Rath screaming, screaming like the damned in their long plunge to hell.

Then silence, and the dying crackle of flame. The Spiracle at the head of the staff was gone, the staff itself burned down to within inches of Rhion's hands. The troops on both sides stood back in frozen horror, staring at the crumbling, burning thing in the SS uniform slowly folding itself down to the blackened ground.

A voice shrieked '*Pauli, NO!*' There was the flat crack of an automatic, and Rhion twisted, his body buckling over, and fell without a cry.

Baldur Twisselpeck – short and fat *And where the hell did he come from*? – stood in front of von Rath's Mercedes, clothed in a straining SS uniform to which he couldn't possibly have had any right and clutching an automatic, tears pouring down his pimply cheeks.

Ashen-faced, the men started to move forward in the sinking illumination that came from the fires along the roadbed and the two burning trucks, towards Rhion's body and what was left of Paul von Rath. None of them seemed to notice Baldur, who had fallen to his knees, sobbing hysterically, clutching his gun to him and groaning 'Paul . . . Paul . . .'

'Let's go,' breathed Saltwood, turning to Sara – and found her gone.

The first spattering burst of machine-gun fire from the abandoned Mercedes cut Baldur nearly in half. The second sustained volley took out both Gall and the gas-tank of the truck in which he stood, and as men scattered in all directions the Mercedes jumped forward, bounding like a stallion over the chewed-up pavement to screech to a stop a few feet from the boulder where Saltwood and Rebbe Leibnitz still crouched.

Sara yelled, 'Get in, goddammit!' from behind the wheel.

Saltwood heaved Leibnitz into the back seat, which contained all the guns Sara could collect, grabbed a Schmeisser and sent raking bursts in both directions at the men who were already starting to run towards them. Bullets panged noisily off the fenders and hood and Saltwood felt one of them sting the back of his calf as he bent down to haul Rhion's body out of the way of the wheels.

How much of that HAD been real? he wondered, looking down at the slack face, the broken glasses, the black bruise of the garrotte across the throat. If they got out of this alive there'd be time to mourn. But he was acutely aware that Rhion had done what he himself had refused, for expediency's sake, to do: he'd come back for them, and to hell with what it cost.

Then he saw Rhion's eyelids flinch. One of those chubby hands tried to close around his wrist, then loosened again, but by that time Saltwood was hauling him into the back seat of the Mercedes, heedless of the rifle-bullets whining like angry flies around him. 'Drive like hell!' he yelled as Sara hit the gas. 'He's still with us!'

'How bad?' she yelled back, as Storm Troopers scattered before the big car's radiator like leaves in a gutter. The burning truck with Gall's half-roasted body still hanging out of it flashed past; a last bullet sang off the fender and Sara swore. Then darkness, and the remote white light of the cold half-moon.

There was an entry-wound between the two middle ribs, the exit-wound, gaping and messy with splintered bone, just under the shoulder-blade, which hissed faintly with every gasping breath. Behind the rimless glasses Rhion's eyes were open now, staring with a curious, terrible bitterness into the midnight sky. 'Bad.'

With a small sigh that broke off sharply in a wince of pain Rhion turned his head, beard and eyebrows standing out blackly with shock in the moonlight. 'Can you get me to the stones?' His voice sounded normal but very quiet.

'Oh, for Chrissake . . . !' groaned Sara, exasperated. 'We've got enough of a head start to make it to Danzig . . .'

'Please.'

'It's too goddam late! You said midnight, and midnight is over! Do we need to keep on with this . . . ?'

'Saraleh,' said Leibnitz gently, 'the reason it's too late is because he came back to help us.'

The fires had vanished into the darkness behind them. On the other side of the hills another glare of orange flame and rising smoke marked where Schloss Torweg would be, and Saltwood was so numbed, so exhausted, so shaken that he didn't bother trying to think up a reasonable explanation for that.

The big car rocked and jolted over the sorry road and, beyond the spiky black of the pines, the wheel of the stars moved calmly past its point of balance, down the long road to the next solstice at the dead heart of winter, three months away. The cinnamon tips of her hair flicking back under the fingers of the night wind Sara continued to expostulate, 'We're gonna get frigging caught! This is our chance, our last chance . . . There'll be search-parties all over the goddam countryside . . .'

Rhion, teeth shut hard now, said nothing, but Saltwood said, 'Get us there, Sara, okay?' and felt Rhion's hand tighten on his own.

'He's not gonna make it,' said Sara softly, 'is he?'

Around them, the countryside was deeply silent. They had found the stones deserted, though ringed with plentiful evidence of Gall's earlier ambuscade – cigarette butts, tramplings in the wet grass, an occasional puddle of urine behind a tree. That no one had been there since they'd departed shortly before midnight was obvious: dew had formed already on the grass, and would hold the slightest mark. In the deepening cold it was already turning to frost.

Saltwood looked back at the form lying on the fallen stone in the cold starlight, which picked out in chilly relief the lenses of his glasses, the silver swastikas and buttons of the SS greatcoat they'd put over him. 'Not the way we'd have to be travelling.'

Like a bent, grey stork in the wavery shadows, Rebbe Leibnitz sat on the edge of the stone at Rhion's side, sketching the arcane circles of the Sephiroth and writing all the Angelic Names he knew in the last crumbling fragments of the chalk he'd had in his pockets. The Hebrew letters formed a pale shroud of spiderweb, draped over the ancient stone of sacrifice and trailing away into shadow. In its centre Rhion lay without moving, his breathing agonizing to hear.

Hesitantly, Sara said, 'The Nazis would probably patch him up if they found him. With von Rath gone they're going to need him . . .'

'No!' Rhion half-raised himself from where he lay on the stone, then sank back with a gasp, his hand pressed to the makeshift bandages on his side. As they strode back to him Saltwood could see the track of blood glittering in his beard, and the dark seep dripping through his fingers. 'Don't let them . . .' Then his eyes met Saltwood's, and he managed a faint grin. 'Oh, hell, it's your job not to let them, isn't it?'

''Fraid so.' His voice was gentle.

Rhion coughed, fighting hard not to. When he was twelve, Saltwood remembered, he'd been chousing cows out of the edges of the badlands twenty miles from the ranch when his horse Mickey had broken a leg. He'd known that to leave the animal alive would be to condemn it to being brought down and torn to pieces by coyotes. The hurt had lasted in him till he'd left the ranch completely . . . and enough of it remained even now to make him remember as he unholstered his gun.

Glancing up, he could see the echo of his thoughts in Sara's eyes. It was after three in the morning of the first day of the long slide of autumn to winter. It would be a cold drive to Danzig.

Hesitantly, Sara said, 'We – We don't need to travel that fast. I mean, with von Rath dead and the Spiracle gone that puts the kibosh on whatever secret plan they had for the invasion of England. Like Rhion said, even a week's delay to figure out something else is going to put them into winter. We could keep ahead of them . . .'

'It wouldn't do us any good,' said Saltwood gently. 'He needs a doctor, and he needs care, and long before we could get him either of those he'd be dead in a lot of pain and we'd have put ourselves in a concentration-camp for nothing.'

He looked back at the stone, where Leibnitz, draped like a Roman patriarch in the carriage-rug that had been in the back of the Mercedes, was inscribing the pyramids of power over the numerological squares of the planets, scribbling the names of the 1,746 Angels in charge of the Cosmos and all its myriad doings. Saltwood still wasn't entirely certain what had gone on back there on the road. Whatever the device had been – radio-controlled explosives or clairvoyant hallucinogens or whatever – Rhion had somehow caused it to backfire on itself badly, that was clear. That he'd done so under the impression that he was destroying his only means of returning to his fantasy home lent a quixotic heroism to the little madman that dragged on some corner of Tom's heart he thought he'd left in a Spanish prison.

And he had saved their lives – and bought England and the world time – at the cost of his own.

Sara walked back to the altar-stone, her Schmeisser tucked under one arm. Her breath was a ghostly cloud in the moonlight as she said, 'Papa, you should be back in the car.' The open vehicle wouldn't be much warmer, but Leibnitz was clearly at the end of his strength. 'You can't do anything further here.'

Saltwood half-expected the old man to protest, but he didn't. He stepped back, holding the blanket around his skinny shoulders with one hand.

'No,' said the old scholar softly, and the moonlight glimmered on the steam of his breath, the silky stiffness of his ragged beard, like quicksilver frost. 'I have summoned it back, all the power that went forth from their meeting; summoned it back from the energy-tracks along which it dispersed to all the corners of this sorry earth.'

He turned his head to look down at the still, dark shape lying upon the altar, and in the emaciated wrinkles of his face Saltwood could see the glint of tears. 'It is sacrifice which gives power, you see, Saraleh,' the old man whispered. 'Not death, but the willingness to give up everything, to burn the future to ashes, and all that it could have been, and to let it go. That is what they did not and could not understand, wanting power only for what it could give to them. That is what raises the great power from the earth and the air and the leys beneath the ground, that thunderclap of power that went forth; that is why he conquered.'

His hand sketched a magic sign in the air; then, bending, he kissed the tangled hair that lay over Rhion's forehead. 'The Lord go with you, my friend – to wherever it is that you will go.'

Rhion made no response. Sara stepped forward, and kissed him in her turn. Then she turned quickly away, hitching the machine-gun under her arm. Taking her father's elbow she walked slowly back towards the car, the tracks of their footprints dark and broken in the first glitter of the frost.

Saltwood walked over to the stone. In the moonlight the chalked Kabbalistic symbols seemed to glimmer on the close-grained dolomite of the ancient altar. The night was still, but with the passage of shadows across their ice-powdered faces the other two stones did, in fact, seem ready to begin dancing, as soon as no one remained to see.

His automatic felt like lead in his hand.

Rhion raised his head a little, propping himself on one elbow. His hand, pressed to his side, was black with blood. 'I know you have to get moving if you're going to make it to Danzig ahead of the pursuit,' he said, his breath a blur of whiteness in the freezing air, slow and ragged as if he fought for every lift of his ribs. His eyes were sunk back into hollows of shadow behind the broken spectacles, his forehead creased with pain. 'But can you give me till dawn?'

For what? Saltwood thought. *For your magic friends to get their act together and show up with the fiery chariot after all?*

But something told him Rhion didn't really expect that to happen anymore. A rime of frost glittered already on the coarse wool of the greatcoat draped over him – its hems and sleeves, even, scribbled with the seals of Solomon, the Tetragrammaton and the Angelic names – and turned the weeds around the stone to a frail lace of ice, and the night promised colder yet.

With any luck, thought Saltwood, cold as it was, by dawn Rhion would be dead.

He put the automatic back in its holster. 'Hell,' he said softly, 'you gave us till spring.'

Rhion shook his head, his strength leaving him as he sank back down onto the bloody stone. 'When I came here,' he said quietly, 'it was because I couldn't imagine anything worse than a world where magic no longer existed. But I've seen . . .' He coughed again, pressing his hand to his side. 'I've seen what is worse – a world where even the concept that other human beings are as human as you are is disappearing . . . and I see now too that this – this kind of lie – is what was starting in my own world. Was being used like a weapon for whoever cared to wield it. That is how it starts . . .' He was silent for a moment, his face tense with the struggle against agony, and Tom saw the dark threads of blood creep from beneath him to mingle with the pale signs of the chalk.

Then he whispered, 'I couldn't let them have it. But when I went back . . . it wasn't for that.'

'I know,' said Saltwood.

'Take care of her.'

He grinned wryly. 'You think she'll let me?'

A sharp spatter of gunfire crackled on the edge of the woods. Saltwood ducked instinctively, turned and ran back along the black track of footprints in the palely shining grass towards the red flash of Sara's gun-barrel. It was a party of Storm Troopers from Kegenwald. The whole countryside was probably alive with them, either seeking vengeance for the somewhat confused events of the night or still hunting for Rhion, unaware of what had gone on down in the road-cut. It really didn't matter. The results would be the same.

The skirmish was sharp but protracted, a cat-and-mouse game of quick firefights and long waiting in the deepening cold, of slipping and stalking painstakingly through the absolute darkness of the pine-woods, of waiting for a whisper, a breath, the movement of a shape against the slightly paler gleam of the frozen pine-mast. Saltwood had done it a hundred times over the last few years, in the mountains of Spain and in training in the hills of Scotland, and upon occasion, more recently, in the wet fields of France. He had fought colder, fought hungrier, fought in worse physical shape, but when he came back to the car with the thin dawnlight streaking the sky above the trees he didn't remember ever being this tired, this bone-weary of fighting, this fed-up with the expediency of killing men to make the world a better place.

Since he'd got into the unions in his early twenties, it seemed to him that he'd always been fighting *somebody* to make the world a better place to live in. One day, he thought, if he survived the war, it would be good simply to live in it for a change.

Like Rhion, he wanted to go home.

Sara came out of the woods, an officer's greatcoat slung over one arm and three more submachine-guns hanging by their straps from her other shoulder. With characteristic practicality she had been looting the bodies of the slain. In the frame of her dark hair her face was grey with strain and exhaustion, and blood smeared her hands, her knees, and tipped the ends of her hair. She stood for a long moment in the deep, frozen grass looking at Tom, and in her face, in the tired stoop of her body, he saw the sickness of utter weariness, of nausea with everything she had done from the day she had set out for Germany to rescue her father. She did not move towards him, but when he crossed to her, his feet crunching in the brittle weeds, she held out her arms, and they stood pressed together, locked in one another's warmth, for a long time while she wept.

'I'm sorry,' she whispered finally, scrubbing at her eyes with the back of her sleeve, a schoolgirl gesture that touched his heart. 'I don't . . . I'm not usually this stupid . . .' Her arms tightened around his waist, and he felt her shivering. 'I'm really not – not like you've seen me at all. It's just . . .'

'I hope you're not too different when things are quiet,' said Tom, and kissed her gently on the lips.

She shook her head, holding him closer, her face pressed to the old, dry bullet-holes and bloodstains of his jacket. 'I don't know what I'm like anymore. Like I've been torn apart and haven't been put back together yet. That's – That's the worst of this.'

'Well,' he said softly, 'I'll be there, if you want me to stick around, while you're figuring it out. There's no hurry. Warm up the car.' From the tail of his eye he could see her father crawling stiffly out from under the Mercedes where he'd taken refuge during the shooting, picking frozen weed-stems out of his car-rug and beard. 'I'll be back,' Tom promised gently. 'And then I'll take you home.'

He climbed the sloping meadow in the pewter twilight of dawn, the frost-thick grass crunching under his boots, his automatic in his hand. He'd been afraid the Storm Troopers had got to Rhion, but a glance at the stiffened carpet of the grass told him otherwise – it would have held the mark of a butterfly's foot. It shimmered eerily, like powdered silver, in the light of the moon which hung like a baroque pearl above the hill where the old holy place had been. The frost there was thicker, all but covering the tracks he, Sara, and her father had left a few hours ago. It furred the ancient altar of sacrifice, half obscuring the crooked abracadabra that Leibnitz had written there in the hopeless hope of attracting the attention of some mythical convocation of wizards gathered in the Emerald City of Rhion's deranged dreams.

But the odd thing was that it seemed to have worked.

The black greatcoat lay flung back, stiff with rime and patched with blood, and blood lay in congealing puddles on the age-pitted surface of the enchanted stone itself, mixing with the Kabbalistic nonsense of signs. But of Rhion himself there was no trace, nor did any track but Saltwood's own cut the frost that glittered in a carpet of fragile ice in every direction.

28

'D'you think he made it?'

The drone of the DC-3's engines steadied as they reached cruising speed; Tom Saltwood turned away from the icy window-glass through which could be seen a fumy, tossing ocean of cloud, ink and pewter meringued with the icy white of the late-rising moon. Pillars and columns of vapour loomed around them, solid-seeming as the mountains of some fantastic landscape – Tom hoped the gangly Yorkshireman in the cockpit knew what the hell he was doing, because at black and freezing three A.M. he wasn't even sure he himself could have said which way England lay under all that cloud-cover, much less how to get there without crashing. He also hoped the Freedom Fighters in Danzig had got their radio-message through to England and they weren't going to be met by a squad of Spitfires, after all the long, exhausting journey to Danzig and two days of hiding out in the radio-man's cellar living on canned beans.

But at the moment, he scarcely cared. They were airborne. The Luftwaffe, being largely occupied elsewhere, hadn't sent a plane after them beyond one or two cursory shots as they'd passed over Danzig.

It was over.

He felt as he had felt jammed in a corner of the destroyer *Codrington*'s gun-deck, grimy, exhausted, amid stinks of oil and cordite, sweat and vomit, and feeling glad to be there with all of his soul still awake enough to feel anything . . .

It was over. He was heading home.

The DC-3 had been stripped for conversion to a cargo-carrier, and rattled like an empty boxcar. Curled on the cleated wood decking at his side, Sara lay wrapped in a couple of grey Army blankets, her crazy red-and-black hair glinting every now and then when the jogging gleams of the dim cockpit lights struck it. Other than that the narrow hold was in darkness, Rebbe Leibnitz's hawklike face no more than a pale blur and a liquid gleam of eyes.

'Made it?' the old man asked, the lift of his eyebrow audible as a note in his voice.

Shadow blotted the dim glow of the cockpit lights; a voice with a soft Somersetshire burr said, 'We're levelled off – will you have a cigarette, Captain?'

'Yeah – thanks,' said Tom, and the co-pilot leaned in to extend a pack. 'Mind if I take another for Miss Leibnitz when she wakes up? She'll kill me if I don't ask.'

The man laughed, 'By all means. By the way, we got word just before we left England, a message for you from a Mr Mayfair. He said he'd put through special immigration papers for Mr Leibnitz – as a former prisoner of the SS there'll be no problem.'

'When I was just somebody Hitler wanted to have starved and beaten to death it was, "Well, everybody's got their troubles,"' muttered Leibnitz under his breath as the co-pilot's dark form vanished once more behind the cockpit curtain. 'But let them think I can be of some use to them, and they're baking me a cake. Made it where?'

Tom glanced down at Sara's sleeping form, tucked one cigarette behind his ear and busied himself with lighting the other. The gold glow of the match outlined his cupped hands in light, sparkled in the coarse white stubble of Leibnitz's beard. He lowered his voice, as if fearful that even in her sleep, Sara would sigh and roll her eyes in disgust. 'Made it back to where he came from.'

The smell of burnt sulphur whiffed a little in the cold air of the cabin, then a draught dispersed the thin ribbon of smoke to nothing again.

Leibnitz' voice spoke out of the dark. 'There was a

lot of power released that night – in the battle, in the destruction of the Spiracle, in the implosion of the field and the rising-up in rage of all those talismans von Rath had made for himself . . . All that power channelled to magic, picked up by the net of the leys, spread out to the corners of the world and brought back again. Power far beyond the power of the Equinoxes, the power of the Heavens . . . power such as this world has not known in a long time.'

By daylight, Tom thought – when they stumbled off this flying sardine-can onto the tarmac of Coventry Field in the grey fog of an English morning – he wouldn't believe this anymore, either. He knew he'd start to wonder if he'd looked closely enough at the frost around the standing-stones, or if Rhion had been less badly wounded than he'd seemed. But now he remembered only the glint of the five jewels in that last pouring stream of lightning, and the way Rhion's upturned glasses had picked up the glare of it; the dark blood mingling with the scribbled spiderweb of chalk upon the stone, and no body in the centre where a body had lain before.

And months later, long after it had become obvious that the cross-Channel invasion had, in fact, been cancelled for that year, on one of his trips down to London he was to stop in at the Red Cow again and encounter Alec Mayfair, grizzled and slow and cautious as ever . . .

And because of their conversation on that occasion Mayfair lent him a copy of a dossier, a folder filled with copies of Intelligence reports not considered secret enough or important enough to rate special classification. The reports spoke of a massive series of escapes from concentration camps and labour camps throughout Germany: during an outbreak of inexplicable fires at Dachau which kept the guards too busy to notice the departure of eighty-seven Jews led by three of von Rath's 'specially designated' Kabbalists; unexplained quarrels among the guards at Buchenwald which amounted to a camp-wide riot during which fifty-four Polish, Jewish, and gypsy children vanished from the camp along with a 'specially designated' gypsy witch; the execution of three guards at Gross Rosen for neglect of duty in allowing twelve Jewish and Polish occultists apparently to cut the wires literally under their noses and walk out, and others, many others . . . all, apparently, at or about midnight on the night of September 23rd.

There were other matters in the file, too: notes of a British coven raising a visible cone of white light that was seen by a number of witnesses to stretch eastward through the black overcast of the skies towards Germany; a copy of a Gestapo report of the collapse of scaffolding supporting landing-barges destined for the invasion at Brest pinned to a local newspaper-clipping from the village of Carnac on the Quiburon Peninsula forty miles to the south telling of 'lights' seen among the long rows of standing-stones at the very hour of the scaffolding's collapse – midnight of the 23rd – and of the strange things found in the morning among cold ashes at the foot of a menhir known as Le Manio. An article from the Indian Hill, Massachusetts *Intelligencer* describing the on-stage heart-attack of a vaudeville magician during the six P.M. show on the 23rd, when, as he later said, he'd looked out over the audience and actually seen around each patron a halo of colours, filled with pictures of their pasts, their hopes, their dreams . . . An article from the *Sentinel* of Rattlesnake Mound, Mississippi, about a sixteen-year-old Negro girl who'd found $8000 worth of long-buried Indian artifacts by placing three pieces of brass in her hand and walking along the ridge where pirate-treasure was said to be buried, late in the afternoon of that same day. There was an account of a near-riot at the *San Francisco Chronicle* when representatives of eight prominent Chinatown families came demanding information on an alleged Japanese dawn offensive against Chinese nationalist forces around the Sczechwan village of Weihsien in Western China, about which they had heard from a geomancer making feng-shui calculations on Mt. Diablo in Berkeley . . . and an intelligence report, dated two weeks later, regarding such an offensive at dawn of the 24th – or two in the afternoon on the 23rd in Berkeley – or midnight in Germany . . .

There were other reports – the death of a planter in Haiti when he inexplicably swerved his car into one of his own gateposts while going down his drive; rumours of werewolves among the Navajo and rumours of shamanic activity in Siberia against the marching Japanese; an unexplained fire in the barracks of occupying German forces in Denmark, and the discovery the following morning of a horse's skull, inscribed with runes of hatred and defiance, close by. And annotated in a woman's hand, calculations backwards and forwards through time-zones: all of these incidents had taken place at, or about, the 23rd of September, at the hour when it was midnight on the sunken back-road in Germany that led to Witches Hill.

There was no explanation appended to any of them. Nor did Mayfair offer any, when he took the folder back.

But that lay in the future. Now Tom only sat, weary in all his bones with Sara's head pillowed against his thigh, tasting the welcome bitterness of nicotine and watching the unsteady movement of the chill edge of starlight on Leibnitz's face as he spoke.

'Oh, he made it, all right,' said Leibnitz softly. 'But as to what his stay in this world made of him – as to what power will cling to him from the magic of sacrifice – it is hard to say. And those wizards who brought him back – I don't think they quite know what they have.'

It will be all right, Rhion had said. *It will be all right.*

Tom blew a stream of smoke, and reached down with his free hand to touch Sara's hair. It was far from over yet . . .

Due to Mayfair's good offices he knew Sara would be

staying in London with her father, while he himself would be going back to the Commandos at Lochailort . . . But London wasn't so far.

He glanced back up at the old man, already feeling that he'd known him and his daughter half his life and rather looking forward to knowing them for the other half. 'We'll never know.'

And in the faint gleam of the cockpit light he saw the old scholar smile as he folded bony hands about his knee. 'And what makes you think one day we won't?'

'Will he live?'

Rhion heard the words from deep in darkness – a darkness that flashed with pain at every breath he drew despite the cloudy blur of what he dimly recognized as poppy-syrup and spells; a darkness safe and warm after the soul-fraying chaotic night of the Void. A darkness that beckoned deeper, and to which he wanted, more than anything, to retreat forever.

The Gray Lady's voice said, 'I don't know.'

No, thought Rhion, drawing further back into that darkness. He didn't know.

Soul and body he felt empty and broken, as he had when von Rath's men had finished with him. The sweetness of the Lady's voice-spells, like the scent of roses carried over water in the night, had drawn his spirit back to his shattered flesh, had given him something to hold to . . . if he chose to hold.

But he had had enough. And the voices he heard around him in that darkness, drifting nearer and then away again, were not encouraging.

'The cult of Agon has to have wizards of its own in its employ,' said someone at one point, a young man's voice that Rhion dimly recognized as belonging to one of the Ebiatic novices he'd occasionally met at the Duke's court. 'Powerful wizards . . .'

'It would explain how the Town Council of Imber was able to enter our House to make its arrests,' agreed someone else, and in a half-forgotten chamber of Rhion's mind the ghost of a former self smiled, for it was Chelfrednig of Imber, who'd once had him and Jaldis run out of town for practicing magic in the territory of the Selarnist wizards. 'I was only fortunate that I was gathering herbs that evening . . .'

'It explains the arrests of Mernac and Agacinthos in Nerriok, and the Blood-Mages in the In Islands last week . . .' added Cuffy Rifkin, an Earth-witch from up the Marshes whom Rhion knew well.

'And it *certainly* makes clear how they managed to get the better of Shavus and the other Morkensiks at the turning of summer.'

So that's what happened . . .

But it was still apart from him, still distant. More near, more important, were the smells of peat-smoke and herbs and water, the smells of the Drowned Lands; wet fern, mossed stone, and bread. The grey curtain of sound that rustled like silk in a darkened room was the stirring of rain on the ivy of the walls of his own house, and in the long cattail-beds below the terrace.

He was home.

Something would have stirred within him at that, he thought, only it had not the strength.

'What I'm saying,' went on the witch Cuffy's voice, 'is that though he's the only Morkensik we've got, he's not what you'd call a powerful mage.'

'I don't know,' said the Gray Lady softly. 'The magic that carried him across the Void – the strength I felt out there on the Holy Isle – was not the magic of sun-tide or star-tide or anything else I have felt. I don't know what he is now, what he has become.'

Lying in darkness, Rhion knew. Beneath the drugs, beneath the drained exhaustion left by the traversing of the Void, beneath the agony of splintered ribs and torn flesh, he knew. Power lay in him like a fist of light, sleeping in the core of pain that lay at the centre of his being. He could open that fist, and the power would radiate forth from his hands.

If he were willing to do it. But he knew what it would mean.

It would mean taking responsibility for this ragtag of mages who had gathered here. It would mean pitting himself against the might of the cult of the Veiled God, and against the men who found it increasingly convenient to use its lies. It would mean enduring what that responsibility, that leadership, would cost.

The power was in him, willed to him by those murdered Kabbalists, by the gypsy-woman whose body he'd seen, by the old runemasters and young psychics and even by the darkly grinning Poincelles: fragments of power that could never have been power in the world to which it had been born, fused now in darkness and in light.

But to use that power . . .

Dying would be easier. And no one could say he hadn't earned that right.

A hand brushed his hair, touched his beard, and his hands. Someone whispered, 'Rhion?'

And it wasn't any thought of power, or responsibility, of sacrificial shoulds or future ifs, that made him open his eyes. Only that hearing her voice, he couldn't do otherwise – couldn't imagine doing otherwise, though he knew that the choice was between that sweet, dark peace and going through all that he had gone through again . . .

But this time he would go through it with her beside him.

Tally had cut her hair. Without the sugar-brown silk cloak of it her head looked small and delicate, like a bird's.

He wondered how he could ever possibly have considered dying.

'The boys?' he asked, after their mouths parted again.

His voice was inaudible and the two words left him as breathless as if he'd lifted them, like huge rocks. She had to bend close to hear.

'They're safe. The Lady's keeping an eye on them through her Mirror – we're bringing them here as soon as we can figure out how to do it safely.'

The mages gathered round – the Lady, with her long hair greying where it hung over the lilies embroidered on her dress; Gyzan, touching his forehead with spells of healing and ease in his mutilated hand. Cuffy Rifkin in rags and necklaces of spellbones, Chelfrednig and his Selarnist companion Niane, their white robes stained and patched; a couple of Ebiatics in black and a scrawny, chinless Hand-Pricker with a big grey cat in his arms . . .

And others. Rhion thought if there'd been a concerted round-up of wizards, it had clearly gone after the powerful ones – aside from the Lady and Gyzan there was no one here of any great strength. It was the first time he'd seen mages of so many different orders working together, something which probably wouldn't have happened, he thought, if any of them had been very powerful alone.

He whispered, 'Thank you,' and the effort of it took all he had. He closed his eyes and for a time heard nothing but the voice of the rain.

'Rhion, I'm sorry.'

He looked up again. The room was empty, but for Tally, still sitting on the low stool at the side of his bed. The single candle made a halo of her short-cropped hair. He moved his hand a little to touch it, then whispered in mock severity, 'I won't beat you this time, but you'd better grow it back,' and it surprised her into laughing, as he'd hoped it would.

'No,' she said, her grey eyes growing sombre again. 'I'm sorry that after all you've been through to come home, home isn't . . . isn't . . .'

'Isn't what I left?' He looked around him, at the age-bleached stone of the walls, dyed amber where the candle-flame touched, at the half-opened shutters and the glisten of green-black ivy in the rain beyond. Her fingers over his were cool, as they always had been; he knew that his own hands had lost the chill of death.

'But it is, you know,' he said. 'I just didn't know it at the time. What did Jaldis say? *We can afford to think neither of the future, nor of the past we leave behind . . .* He was wrong.' He sighed. 'He was wrong.'

'Tally?' The door-curtain at the far end of the room moved aside; framed in the darkness were two dark blurs of shadow, one his own height, the other tall. 'Vyla of Wellhaven says she has seen in her crystal the armies of Bragenmere moving down the passes towards Fell,' said Gyzan's voice. 'They will be besieging that city in the morning.'

The Gray Lady added, 'If the worshipers of Agon don't open the gates to them, under the impression that doing so would please the Veiled God.'

'So,' said Rhion, as Tally's fingers closed involuntarily tighter over his. 'It's started here.' As if at a great distance he thought he saw peace and darkness beckon to him, like a tiny figure at the crown of a far-off hill. But he turned from it, as he had turned from the Dancing Stones, and said softly, 'There's work to do.'

'Now?' Tally looked down at him worriedly, as the dark figures melted back into the shadow of the door, leaving the whispering, rainy stillness of the night to close them round.

Rhion smiled and drew her down to him. 'In the morning.' And he fell asleep with his head on her arm.

AUTHOR'S NOTE

This was an extremely difficult book to write for a number of reasons, chief among them being the number of books which *could* have been written. But I did *not* want to write a book about the Holocaust, I did *not* want to write a history of the SS, or an examination of the Occult Bureau, or an account of occultism in general, or the Blitz, or Operation Sea Lion. All of those books have been written, by people more qualified than I.

What I *did* want to do, was to do justice to those topics where they touched upon my own piece of magical fantasy, without being led too far astray. This I hope I have accomplished – I certainly did the best I could. World War II is an area awkwardly placed historically as far as I am concerned. It lies beyond the scope of my own memories, but it is close enough in time to the present to be massively documented, and I frequently found myself swimming in a morass of details, trying to decide which to include and which would only bog down the storyline in endless sidetracks.

I know that I got many things wrong. To the best of what I could learn, there was a distinction between the smaller labour-camps and concentration-camps per se, and everything I have read indicates that the systematic construction of death-camps for the stated purpose of exterminating Jews, Poles, gypsies, and other 'undesirable races' did not begin until early in 1941, though the intention and the plans predated that time. I have tried to be accurate about vehicles, weaponry, and technology, and about the major events of the war insofar as occasionally-conflicting accounts would let me. I have stuck to the attitudes expressed in Nazi literature as closely as I could – certainly no modern parallels of events, personalities, or groups are intended, either in the historical or the fantasy components of my tale.

To those who lost family and loved ones in the disasters of those years, who might feel that I have violated the importance of their deaths by turning the whole thing into a background for what is, basically, entertainment, I apologize sincerely. I lost no one – my mother's family left Poland years before, and it could be justly argued that I operate from a position of ignorance.

My intention is, as it has always been, strictly to entertain – but in doing so, at least I have tried not to gloss over facts, or do violence to the truth as I could learn it. I hope that I have succeeded on both counts.